DOVER · THRIFT · EDITIONS

The Hound of the Baskervilles

SIR ARTHUR CONAN DOYLE

DOVER PUBLICATIONS, INC.
New York

DOVER THRIFT EDITIONS

GENERAL EDITOR: STANLEY APPELBAUM
EDITOR OF THIS VOLUME: ALAN WEISSMAN

AUTHOR'S DEDICATION

My Dear Robinson:

It was your account of a west country legend which first suggested the idea of this little tale to my mind. For this, and for the help which you gave me in its evolution, all thanks.

Yours most truly,
A. CONAN DOYLE.

Bibliographical Note

This Dover edition, first published in 1994, is an unabridged republication of the work first published in installments in *The Strand Magazine* from August 1901 through April 1902, and in book form by George Newnes, Limited, London, 1902. Both versions were subtitled "Another Adventure of Sherlock Holmes." A new Note has been written for the present volume.

Library of Congress Cataloging-in-Publication Data

Doyle, Arthur Conan, Sir, 1859–1930.
    The hound of the Baskervilles / Sir Arthur Conan Doyle.
        p.   cm. — (Dover thrift editions)
    ISBN 0-486-28214-7
    1. Holmes, Sherlock (Fictitious character)—Fiction.   2. Private investigators—England—Fiction.   I. Title.   II. Series.
    PR4622.H6   1994b
    823'.8—dc20
                                                                        94-26077
                                                                        CIP

Manufactured in the United States of America
Dover Publications, Inc., 31 East 2nd Street, Mineola, N.Y. 11501

Note

In 1901, Arthur Conan Doyle (1859–1930), already famous as the creator of Sherlock Holmes and soon to be Sir Arthur for his patriotic services in the Boer War, was recuperating from his exertions in that conflict when he heard a curious legend about a fearsome, ghostly hound supposed to haunt the lonely wastes of Dartmoor. Inspired, he visited the place, soaked up the atmosphere and began a new story. When the first installment appeared in *The Strand Magazine* for August 1901, readers were delighted and surprised to find "Another Adventure of Sherlock Holmes." Surprised, because the author had meant to be finished with his famous detective in 1893 when "The Final Problem" had really been intended as final.

When the memorable sleuth was brought back in *The Hound of the Baskervilles* (not the last and, in fact, not really the first Holmes revival), all lovers of mystery and detection rejoiced, and with good reason. For time has stamped it as one of the finest mysteries of them all, with or without Sherlock Holmes.

All the features we expect in a Sherlock Holmes story are there, including a procession of colorful characters, Holmes's marvelous feats of deduction as recounted by an astonished Dr. Watson, and an abundance of strange incidents.

Conan Doyle was always superior at mining the suggestiveness of bizarre occurrences that disturb the serenity of civilized English life; here, there are many such incidents, each following quickly upon the last and deepening our sense of the mysterious. In addition, the tale is well punctuated by surprises and culminates in an exciting climax.

The Hound of the Baskervilles is especially notable for what is loosely termed "atmosphere." There is of course the atmosphere of 221B Baker Street and its environs, enough of it to please all but the most fanatical of Sherlockians. Most of the story, however, is set in the country. Elsewhere, in one of his many memorable pronouncements, Holmes had maintained that "the lowest and vilest alleys in London do not present a more dreadful record of sin than does the smiling and beautiful countryside." With the present book, Doyle went a step further: he demonstrated what criminal possibilities there are in the rugged and forbidding countryside — and frightful they are!

Little wonder, then, the high regard in which *The Hound of the Baskervilles* has been held for nearly a century.

Contents

1   MR. SHERLOCK HOLMES

Mr. Sherlock Holmes, who was usually very late in the mornings, save upon those not infrequent occasions when he was up all night, was seated at the breakfast table. I stood upon the hearth-rug and picked up the stick which our visitor had left behind him the night before. It was a fine, thick piece of wood, bulbous-headed, of the sort which is known as a "Penang lawyer." Just under the head was a broad silver band, nearly an inch across. "To James Mortimer, M. R. C. S., from his friends of the C. C. H.," was engraved upon it, with the date "1884." It was just such a stick as the old-fashioned family practitioner used to carry—dignified, solid, and reassuring.

"Well, Watson, what do you make of it?"

Holmes was sitting with his back to me, and I had given him no sign of my occupation.

"How did you know what I was doing? I believe you have eyes in the back of your head."

"I have, at least, a well-polished, silver-plated coffee-pot in front of me," said he. "But, tell me, Watson, what do you make of our visitor's stick? Since we have been so unfortunate as to miss him and have no notion of his errand, this accidental souvenir becomes of importance. Let me hear you reconstruct the man by an examination of it."

"I think," said I, following as far as I could the methods of my companion, "that Dr. Mortimer is a successful, elderly medical man, well-esteemed, since those who know him give him this mark of their appreciation."

"Good!" said Holmes. "Excellent!"

"I think also that the probability is in favour of his being a country practitioner who does a great deal of his visiting on foot."

"Why so?"

"Because this stick, though originally a very handsome one, has been so knocked about that I can hardly imagine a town practitioner carrying it. The thick iron ferrule is worn down, so it is evident that he has done a great amount of walking with it."

"Perfectly sound!" said Holmes.

"And then again, there is the 'friends of the C. C. H.' I should guess that to be the Something Hunt, the local hunt to whose members he has possibly given some surgical assistance, and which has made him a small presentation in return."

"Really, Watson, you excel yourself," said Holmes, pushing back his chair and lighting a cigarette. "I am bound to say that in all the accounts which you have been so good as to give of my own small achievements you have habitually underrated your own abilities. It may be that you are not yourself luminous, but you are a conductor of light. Some people without possessing genius have a remarkable power of stimulating it. I confess, my dear fellow, that I am very much in your debt."

He had never said as much before, and I must admit that his words gave me keen pleasure, for I had often been piqued by his indifference to my admiration and to the attempts which I had made to give publicity to his methods. I was proud, too, to think that I had so far mastered his system as to apply it in a way which earned his approval. He now took the stick from my hands and examined it for a few minutes with his naked eyes. Then with an expression of interest he laid down his cigarette, and, carrying the cane to the window, he looked over it again with a convex lens.

"Interesting, though elementary," said he as he returned to his favourite corner of the settee. "There are certainly one or two indications upon the stick. It gives us the basis for several deductions."

"Has anything escaped me?" I asked with some self-importance. "I trust that there is nothing of consequence which I have overlooked?"

"I am afraid, my dear Watson, that most of your conclusions were erroneous. When I said that you stimulated me I meant, to be frank, that in noting your fallacies I was occasionally guided towards the truth. Not that you are entirely wrong in this instance. The man is certainly a country practitioner. And he walks a good deal."

"Then I was right."

"To that extent."

"But that was all."

"No, no, my dear Watson, not all—by no means all. I would suggest, for example, that a presentation to a doctor is more likely to come from a hospital than from a hunt, and that when the initials 'C. C.' are placed before that hospital the words 'Charing Cross' very naturally suggest themselves."

"You may be right."

"The probability lies in that direction. And if we take this as a working hypothesis we have a fresh basis from which to start our construction of this unknown visitor."

"Well, then, supposing that 'C. C. H.' does stand for 'Charing Cross Hospital,' what further inferences may we draw?"

"Do none suggest themselves? You know my methods. Apply them!"

"I can only think of the obvious conclusion that the man has practised in town before going to the country."

"I think that we might venture a little farther than this. Look at it in this light. On what occasion would it be most probable that such a presentation would be made? When would his friends unite to give him a pledge of their good will? Obviously at the moment when Dr. Mortimer withdrew from the service of the hospital in order to start in practice for himself. We know there has been a presentation. We believe there has been a change from a town hospital to a country practice. Is it, then, stretching our inference too far to say that the presentation was on the occasion of the change?"

"It certainly seems probable."

"Now, you will observe that he could not have been on the staff of the hospital, since only a man well-established in a London practice could hold such a position, and such a one would not drift into the country. What was he, then? If he was in the hospital and yet not on the staff he could only have been a house-surgeon or a house-physician—little more than a senior student. And he left five years ago—the date is on the stick. So your grave, middle-aged family practitioner vanishes into thin air, my dear Watson, and there emerges a young fellow under thirty, amiable, unambitious, absent-minded, and the possessor of a favourite dog, which I should describe roughly as being larger than a terrier and smaller than a mastiff."

I laughed incredulously as Sherlock Holmes leaned back in his settee and blew little wavering rings of smoke up to the ceiling.

"As to the latter part, I have no means of checking you," said I, "but at least it is not difficult to find out a few particulars about the man's age and professional career." From my small medical shelf I took down the Medical Directory and turned up the name. There were several Mortimers, but only one who could be our visitor. I read his record aloud.

"Mortimer, James, M. R. C. S., 1882, Grimpen, Dartmoor, Devon. House surgeon, from 1882 to 1884, at Charing Cross Hospital. Winner of the Jackson prize for Comparative Pathology, with essay entitled 'Is Disease a Reversion?' Corresponding member of the Swedish Pathological Society. Author of 'Some Freaks of Atavism' (*Lancet*, 1882). 'Do We Progress?'

(*Journal of Psychology*, March, 1883). Medical Officer for the parishes of Grimpen, Thorsley, and High Barrow."

"No mention of that local hunt, Watson," said Holmes with a mischievous smile, "but a country doctor, as you very astutely observed. I think that I am fairly justified in my inferences. As to the adjectives, I said, if I remember right, amiable, unambitious, and absent-minded. It is my experience that it is only an amiable man in this world who receives testimonials, only an unambitious one who abandons a London career for the country, and only an absent-minded one who leaves his stick and not his visiting-card after waiting an hour in your room."

"And the dog?"

"Has been in the habit of carrying this stick behind his master. Being a heavy stick the dog has held it tightly by the middle, and the marks of his teeth are very plainly visible. The dog's jaw, as shown in the space between these marks, is too broad in my opinion for a terrier and not broad enough for a mastiff. It may have been—yes, by Jove, it *is* a curly-haired spaniel."

He had risen and paced the room as he spoke. Now he halted in the recess of the window. There was such a ring of conviction in his voice that I glanced up in surprise.

"My dear fellow, how can you possibly be so sure of that?"

"For the very simple reason that I see the dog himself on our very doorstep, and there is the ring of its owner. Don't move, I beg you, Watson. He is a professional brother of yours, and your presence may be of assistance to me. Now is the dramatic moment of fate, Watson, when you hear a step upon the stair which is walking into your life, and you know not whether for good or ill. What does Dr. James Mortimer, the man of science, ask of Sherlock Holmes, the specialist in crime? Come in!"

The appearance of our visitor was a surprise to me, since I had expected a typical country practitioner. He was a very tall, thin man, with a long nose like a beak, which jutted out between two keen, gray eyes, set closely together and sparkling brightly from behind a pair of gold-rimmed glasses. He was clad in a professional but rather slovenly fashion, for his frock-coat was dingy and his trousers frayed. Though young, his long back was already bowed, and he walked with a forward thrust of his head and a general air of peering benevolence. As he entered his eyes fell upon the stick in Holmes's hand, and he ran towards it with an exclamation of joy. "I am so very glad," said he. "I was not sure whether I had left it here or in the Shipping Office. I would not lose that stick for the world."

"A presentation, I see," said Holmes.

"Yes, sir."

"From Charing Cross Hospital?"

"From one or two friends there on the occasion of my marriage."

"Dear, dear, that's bad!" said Holmes, shaking his head.

Dr. Mortimer blinked through his glasses in mild astonishment.

"Why was it bad?"

"Only that you have disarranged our little deductions. Your marriage, you say?"

"Yes, sir. I married, and so left the hospital, and with it all hopes of a consulting practice. It was necessary to make a home of my own."

"Come, come, we are not so far wrong, after all," said Holmes. "And now, Dr. James Mortimer——"

"Mister, sir, Mister—a humble M. R. C. S."

"And a man of precise mind, evidently."

"A dabbler in science, Mr. Holmes, a picker up of shells on the shores of the great unknown ocean. I presume that it is Mr. Sherlock Holmes whom I am addressing and not——"

"No, this is my friend Dr. Watson."

"Glad to meet you, sir. I have heard your name mentioned in connection with that of your friend. You interest me very much, Mr. Holmes. I had hardly expected so dolichocephalic a skull or such well-marked supraorbital development. Would you have any objection to my running my finger along your parietal fissure? A cast of your skull, sir, until the original is available, would be an ornament to any anthropological museum. It is not my intention to be fulsome, but I confess that I covet your skull."

Sherlock Holmes waved our strange visitor into a chair. "You are an enthusiast in your line of thought, I perceive, sir, as I am in mine," said he. "I observe from your forefinger that you make your own cigarettes. Have no hesitation in lighting one."

The man drew out paper and tobacco and twirled the one up in the other with surprising dexterity. He had long, quivering fingers as agile and restless as the antennæ of an insect.

Holmes was silent, but his little darting glances showed me the interest which he took in our curious companion.

"I presume, sir," said he at last, "that it was not merely for the purpose of examining my skull that you have done me the honour to call here last night and again to-day?"

"No, sir, no; though I am happy to have had the opportunity of doing that as well. I came to you, Mr. Holmes, because I recognized that I am myself an unpractical man and because I am suddenly confronted with a most serious and extraordinary problem. Recognizing, as I do, that you are the second highest expert in Europe——"

"Indeed, sir! May I inquire who has the honour to be the first?" asked Holmes with some asperity.

"To the man of precisely scientific mind the work of Monsieur Bertillon must always appeal strongly."

"Then had you not better consult him?"

"I said, sir, to the precisely scientific mind. But as a practical man of affairs it is acknowledged that you stand alone. I trust, sir, that I have not inadvertently——"

"Just a little," said Holmes. "I think, Dr. Mortimer, you would do wisely if without more ado you would kindly tell me plainly what the exact nature of the problem is in which you demand my assistance."

---

2 THE CURSE OF THE BASKERVILLES

"I have in my pocket a manuscript," said Dr. James Mortimer.

"I observed it as you entered the room," said Holmes.

"It is an old manuscript."

"Early eighteenth century, unless it is a forgery."

"How can you say that, sir?"

"You have presented an inch or two of it to my examination all the time that you have been talking. It would be a poor expert who could not give the date of a document within a decade or so. You may possibly have read my little monograph upon the subject. I put that at 1730."

"The exact date is 1742." Dr. Mortimer drew it from his breast-pocket. "This family paper was committed to my care by Sir Charles Baskerville, whose sudden and tragic death some three months ago created so much excitement in Devonshire. I may say that I was his personal friend as well as his medical attendant. He was a strong-minded man, sir, shrewd, practical, and as unimaginative as I am myself. Yet he took this document very seriously, and his mind was prepared for just such an end as did eventually overtake him."

Holmes stretched out his hand for the manuscript and flattened it upon his knee.

"You will observe, Watson, the alternative use of the long *s* and the short. It is one of several indications which enabled me to fix the date."

I looked over his shoulder at the yellow paper and the faded script.

At the head was written: "Baskerville Hall," and below, in large, scrawling figures: "1742."

"It appears to be a statement of some sort."

"Yes, it is a statement of a certain legend which runs in the Baskerville family."

"But I understand that it is something more modern and practical upon which you wish to consult me?"

"Most modern. A most practical, pressing matter, which must be decided within twenty-four hours. But the manuscript is short and is intimately connected with the affair. With your permission I will read it to you."

Holmes leaned back in his chair, placed his finger-tips together, and closed his eyes, with an air of resignation. Dr. Mortimer turned the manuscript to the light and read in a high, cracking voice the following curious, old-world narrative:

"Of the origin of the Hound of the Baskervilles there have been many statements, yet as I come in a direct line from Hugo Baskerville, and as I had the story from my father, who also had it from his, I have set it down with all belief that it occurred even as is here set forth. And I would have you believe, my sons, that the same Justice which punishes sin may also most graciously forgive it, and that no ban is so heavy but that by prayer and repentance it may be removed. Learn then from this story not to fear the fruits of the past, but rather to be circumspect in the future, that those foul passions whereby our family has suffered so grievously may not again be loosed to our undoing.

"Know then that in the time of the Great Rebellion (the history of which by the learned Lord Clarendon I most earnestly commend to your attention) this Manor of Baskerville was held by Hugo of that name, nor can it be gainsaid that he was a most wild, profane, and godless man. This, in truth, his neighbours might have pardoned, seeing that saints have never flourished in those parts, but there was in him a certain wanton and cruel humour which made his name a byword through the West. It chanced that this Hugo came to love (if, indeed, so dark a passion may be known under so bright a name) the daughter of a yeoman who held lands near the Baskerville estate. But the young maiden, being discreet and of good repute, would ever avoid him, for she feared his evil name. So it came to pass that one Michaelmas this Hugo, with five or six of his idle and wicked companions, stole down upon the farm and carried off the maiden, her father and brothers being from home, as he well knew. When they had brought her to the Hall the maiden was placed in an upper chamber, while Hugo and his friends sat down to a long carouse, as was their nightly custom. Now, the poor lass upstairs was like to have her wits turned at the singing and shouting and terrible oaths which came up to her from below, for they say that the words used by Hugo Baskerville, when he was in wine, were such as might blast the man who said them. At last in the stress of her fear she did that which might have daunted the bravest or most active man, for by the

e growth of ivy which covered (and still covers) the south wall she
wn from under the eaves, and so homeward across the moor, there
being three leagues betwixt the Hall and her father's farm.

"It chanced that some little time later Hugo left his guests to carry food
and drink—with other worse things, perchance—to his captive, and so found
the cage empty and the bird escaped. Then, as it would seem, he became
as one that hath a devil, for, rushing down the stairs into the dining-hall,
he sprang upon the great table, flagons and trenchers flying before him, and
he cried aloud before all the company that he would that very night render
his body and soul to the Powers of Evil if he might but overtake the wench.
And while the revellers stood aghast at the fury of the man, one more wicked
or, it may be, more drunken than the rest, cried out that they should put
the hounds upon her. Whereat Hugo ran from the house, crying to his grooms
that they should saddle his mare and unkennel the pack, and giving the
hounds a kerchief of the maid's, he swung them to the line, and so off full
cry in the moonlight over the moor.

"Now, for some space the revellers stood agape, unable to understand all
that had been done in such haste. But anon their bemused wits awoke to the
nature of the deed which was like to be done upon the moorlands. Everything was now in an uproar, some calling for their pistols, some for their
horses, and some for another flask of wine. But at length some sense came
back to their crazed minds, and the whole of them, thirteen in number, took
horse and started in pursuit. The moon shone clear above them, and they
rode swiftly abreast, taking that course which the maid must needs have
taken if she were to reach her own home.

"They had gone a mile or two when they passed one of the night shepherds
upon the moorlands, and they cried to him to know if he had seen the hunt.
And the man, as the story goes, was so crazed with fear that he could scarce
speak, but at last he said that he had indeed seen the unhappy maiden,
with the hounds upon her track. 'But I have seen more than that,' said he,
'for Hugo Baskerville passed me upon his black mare, and there ran mute behind him such a hound of hell as God forbid should ever be at my heels.'
So the drunken squires cursed the shepherd and rode onward. But soon
their skins turned cold, for there came a galloping across the moor, and the
black mare, dabbled with white froth, went past with trailing bridle and
empty saddle. Then the revellers rode close together, for a great fear was on
them, but they still followed over the moor, though each, had he been alone,
would have been right glad to have turned his horse's head. Riding slowly
in this fashion they came at last upon the hounds. These, though known for
their valour and their breed, were whimpering in a cluster at the head of a
deep dip or goyal, as we call it, upon the moor, some slinking away and some,
with starting hackles and staring eyes, gazing down the narrow valley before
them.

"The company had come to a halt, more sober men, as you may guess,
than when they started. The most of them would by no means advance,
but three of them, the boldest, or it may be the most drunken, rode forward
down the goyal. Now, it opened into a broad space in which stood two of
those great stones, still to be seen there, which were set by certain forgotten
peoples in the days of old. The moon was shining bright upon the clearing,

and there in the centre lay the unhappy maid where she had fallen, dead of fear and of fatigue. But it was not the sight of her body, nor yet was it that of the body of Hugo Baskerville lying near her, which raised the hair upon the heads of these three dare-devil roysterers, but it was that, standing over Hugo, and plucking at his throat, there stood a foul thing, a great, black beast, shaped like a hound, yet larger than any hound that ever mortal eye has rested upon. And even as they looked the thing tore the throat out of Hugo Baskerville, on which, as it turned its blazing eyes and dripping jaws upon them, the three shrieked with fear and rode for dear life, still screaming, across the moor. One, it is said, died that very night of what he had seen, and the other twain were but broken men for the rest of their days.

"Such is the tale, my sons, of the coming of the hound which is said to have plagued the family so sorely ever since. If I have set it down it is because that which is clearly known hath less terror than that which is but hinted at and guessed. Nor can it be denied that many of the family have been unhappy in their deaths, which have been sudden, bloody, and mysterious. Yet may we shelter ourselves in the infinite goodness of Providence, which would not forever punish the innocent beyond that third or fourth generation which is threatened in Holy Writ. To that Providence, my sons, I hereby commend you, and I counsel you by way of caution to forbear from crossing the moor in those dark hours when the powers of evil are exalted.

"[This from Hugo Baskerville to his sons Rodger and John, with instructions that they say nothing thereof to their sister Elizabeth.]"

When Dr. Mortimer had finished reading this singular narrative he pushed his spectacles up on his forehead and stared across at Mr. Sherlock Holmes. The latter yawned and tossed the end of his cigarette into the fire.

"Well?" said he.

"Do you not find it interesting?"

"To a collector of fairy tales."

Dr. Mortimer drew a folded newspaper out of his pocket.

"Now, Mr. Holmes, we will give you something a little more recent. This is the *Devon County Chronicle* of May 14th of this year. It is a short account of the facts elicited at the death of Sir Charles Baskerville which occurred a few days before that date."

My friend leaned a little forward and his expression became intent. Our visitor readjusted his glasses and began:

"The recent sudden death of Sir Charles Baskerville, whose name has been mentioned as the probable Liberal candidate for Mid-Devon at the next election, has cast a gloom over the county. Though Sir Charles had resided at Baskerville Hall for a comparatively short period his amiability of character and extreme generosity had won the affection and respect of all who had been brought into contact with him. In these days of *nouveaux riches* it is refreshing to find a case where the scion of an old county family which has fallen upon evil days is able to make his own fortune and to bring it back with him to restore the fallen grandeur of his line. Sir Charles, as is well known, made large sums of money in South African speculation. More wise than those who go on until the wheel turns against them, he realized his gains and returned to England with them. It is only two years since he took up his residence at Baskerville Hall, and it is common talk how large were those schemes of reconstruction and improvement which have been interrupted by his death. Being himself childless, it was his openly expressed desire that the whole countryside should, within his own lifetime, profit by his good fortune, and many will have personal reasons for bewailing his untimely end. His generous donations to local and county charities have been frequently chronicled in these columns.

"The circumstances connected with the death of Sir Charles cannot be said to have been entirely cleared up by the inquest, but at least enough has been done to dispose of those rumours to which local superstition has given rise. There is no reason whatever to suspect foul play, or to imagine that death could be from any but natural causes. Sir Charles was a widower, and a man who may be said to have been in some ways of an eccentric habit of mind. In spite of his considerable wealth he was simple in his personal tastes, and his indoor servants at Baskerville Hall consisted of a married couple named Barrymore, the husband acting as butler and the wife as housekeeper. Their evidence, corroborated by that of several friends, tends to show that Sir Charles's health has for some time been impaired, and points especially to some affection of the heart, manifesting itself in changes of colour, breathlessness, and acute attacks of nervous depression. Dr. James Mortimer, the friend and medical attendant of the deceased, has given evidence to the same effect.

"The facts of the case are simple. Sir Charles Baskerville was in the habit every night before going to bed of walking down the famous yew alley of Baskerville Hall. The evidence of the Barrymores shows that this had been his custom. On the fourth of May Sir Charles had declared his intention of starting next day for London, and had ordered Barrymore to prepare his luggage. That night he went out as usual for his nocturnal walk, in the course of which he was in the habit of smoking a cigar. He never returned. At twelve o'clock Barrymore, finding the hall door still open, became alarmed, and, lighting a lantern, went in search of his master. The day had been wet, and Sir Charles's footmarks were easily traced down the alley. Halfway down this walk there is a gate which leads out on to the moor. There were indications that Sir Charles had stood for some little time here. He then proceeded down the alley, and it was at the far end of it that his body was discovered. One fact which has not been explained is the statement of Barrymore that his master's footprints altered their character from the time that he passed the moor-gate, and that he appeared from thence onward to have been walking upon his toes. One Murphy, a gipsy horse-dealer, was on the moor at no great distance at the time, but he appears by his own confession to have been the worse for drink. He declares that he heard cries but is unable to state from what direction they came. No signs of violence were to be discovered upon Sir Charles's person, and though the doctor's evidence pointed to an almost incredible facial distortion—so great that Dr. Mortimer refused at first to believe that it was indeed his friend and patient who lay before him—it was explained that that is a symptom which is not unusual in cases of dyspnœa and death from cardiac exhaustion. This explanation was borne out by the post-mortem examination, which showed long-standing organic disease, and the coroner's jury returned a verdict in accordance with the medical evidence. It is well that this is so, for it is obviously of the utmost importance that Sir Charles's heir should settle at the Hall and continue the good work which has been so sadly interrupted. Had the prosaic finding of the coroner not finally put an end to the romantic stories which have been whispered in connection with the affair, it might have been difficult to find a tenant for Baskerville Hall. It is understood that the next of kin is Mr. Henry Baskerville, if he be still alive, the son of Sir Charles Baskerville's younger brother. The young man when last heard of was in America, and inquiries are being instituted with a view to informing him of his good fortune."

Dr. Mortimer refolded his paper and replaced it in his pocket.

"Those are the public facts, Mr. Holmes, in connection with the death of Sir Charles Baskerville."

"I must thank you," said Sherlock Holmes, "for calling my attention to a case which certainly presents some features of interest. I had observed some newspaper comment at the time, but I was exceedingly preoccupied by that little affair of the Vatican cameos, and in my anxiety to oblige the Pope I lost touch with several interesting English cases. This article, you say, contains all the public facts?"

"It does."

"Then let me have the private ones." He leaned back, put his fingertips together, and assumed his most impassive and judicial expression.

"In doing so," said Dr. Mortimer, who had begun to show signs of some strong emotion, "I am telling that which I have not confided to anyone. My motive for withholding it from the coroner's inquiry is that a man of science shrinks from placing himself in the public position of seeming to indorse a popular superstition. I had the further motive that Baskerville Hall, as the paper says, would certainly remain untenanted if anything were done to increase its already rather grim reputation. For both these reasons I thought that I was justified in telling rather less than I knew, since no practical good could result from it, but with you there is no reason why I should not be perfectly frank.

"The moor is very sparsely inhabited, and those who live near each other are thrown very much together. For this reason I saw a good deal of Sir Charles Baskerville. With the exception of Mr. Frankland, of Lafter Hall, and Mr. Stapleton, the naturalist, there are no other men of education within many miles. Sir Charles was a retiring man, but the chance of his illness brought us together, and a community of interests in science kept us so. He had brought back much scientific information from South Africa, and many a charming evening we have spent together discussing the comparative anatomy of the Bushman and the Hottentot.

"Within the last few months it became increasingly plain to me that

Sir Charles's nervous system was strained to the breaking point. He had taken this legend which I have read you exceedingly to heart—so much so that, although he would walk in his own grounds, nothing would induce him to go out upon the moor at night. Incredible as it may appear to you, Mr. Holmes, he was honestly convinced that a dreadful fate overhung his family, and certainly the records which he was able to give of his ancestors were not encouraging. The idea of some ghastly presence constantly haunted him, and on more than one occasion he has asked me whether I had on my medical journeys at night ever seen any strange creature or heard the baying of a hound. The latter question he put to me several times, and always with a voice which vibrated with excitement.

"I can well remember driving up to his house in the evening, some three weeks before the fatal event. He chanced to be at his hall door. I had descended from my gig and was standing in front of him, when I saw his eyes fix themselves over my shoulder and stare past me with an expression of the most dreadful horror. I whisked round and had just time to catch a glimpse of something which I took to be a large black calf passing at the head of the drive. So excited and alarmed was he that I was compelled to go down to the spot where the animal had been and look around for it. It was gone, however, and the incident appeared to make the worst impression upon his mind. I stayed with him all the evening, and it was on that occasion, to explain the emotion which he had shown, that he confided to my keeping that narrative which I read to you when first I came. I mention this small episode because it assumes some importance in view of the tragedy which followed, but I was convinced at the time that the matter was entirely trivial and that his excitement had no justification.

"It was at my advice that Sir Charles was about to go to London. His heart was, I knew, affected, and the constant anxiety in which he lived, however chimerical the cause of it might be, was evidently having a serious effect upon his health. I thought that a few months among the distractions of town would send him back a new man. Mr. Stapleton, a mutual friend who was much concerned at his state of health, was of the same opinion. At the last instant came this terrible catastrophe.

"On the night of Sir Charles's death Barrymore the butler, who made the discovery, sent Perkins the groom on horseback to me, and as I was sitting up late I was able to reach Baskerville Hall within an hour of the event. I checked and corroborated all the facts which were mentioned at the inquest. I followed the footsteps down the yew alley, I saw the spot at the moor-gate where he seemed to have waited, I remarked the change in the shape of the prints after that point, I noted that there were no other footsteps save those of Barrymore on the soft gravel, and finally I carefully examined the body, which had not been touched until my arrival. Sir Charles lay on his face, his arms out, his fingers dug into the ground, and his features convulsed with some strong emotion to such an extent that I could hardly have sworn to his identity. There was certainly no physical injury of any kind. But one false statement was made by Barrymore at the inquest. He said that there were no traces upon the ground round the body. He did not observe any. But I did—some little distance off, but fresh and clear."

"Footprints?"

"Footprints."

"A man's or a woman's?"

Dr. Mortimer looked strangely at us for an instant, and his voice sank almost to a whisper as he answered:

"Mr. Holmes, they were the footprints of a gigantic hound!"

---

3 THE PROBLEM

I confess that at these words a shudder passed through me. There was a thrill in the doctor's voice which showed that he was himself deeply moved by that which he told us. Holmes leaned forward in his excitement and his eyes had the hard, dry glitter which shot from them when he was keenly interested.

"You saw this?"

"As clearly as I see you."

"And you said nothing?"

"What was the use?"

"How was it that no one else saw it?"

"The marks were some twenty yards from the body and no one gave them a thought. I don't suppose I should have done so had I not known this legend."

"There are many sheep-dogs on the moor?"

"No doubt, but this was no sheep-dog."

"You say it was large?"

"Enormous."

"But it had not approached the body?"

"No."

"What sort of night was it?"

"Damp and raw."

"But not actually raining?"

"No."

"What is the alley like?"

"There are two lines of old yew hedge, twelve feet high and impenetrable. The walk in the centre is about eight feet across."

"Is there anything between the hedges and the walk?"

"Yes, there is a strip of grass about six feet broad on either side."

"I understand that the yew hedge is penetrated at one point by a gate?"

"Yes, the wicket-gate which leads on to the moor."

"Is there any other opening?"

"None."

"So that to reach the yew alley one either has to come down it from the house or else to enter it by the moor-gate?"

"There is an exit through a summer-house at the far end."

"Had Sir Charles reached this?"

"No; he lay about fifty yards from it."

"Now, tell me, Dr. Mortimer—and this is important—the marks which you saw were on the path and not on the grass?"

"No marks could show on the grass."

"Were they on the same side of the path as the moor-gate?"

"Yes; they were on the edge of the path on the same side as the moor-gate."

"You interest me exceedingly. Another point. Was the wicket-gate closed?"

"Closed and padlocked."

"How high was it?"

"About four feet high."

"Then anyone could have got over it?"

"Yes."

"And what marks did you see by the wicket-gate?"

"None in particular."

"Good heaven! Did no one examine?"

"Yes, I examined, myself."

"And found nothing?"

"It was all very confused. Sir Charles had evidently stood there for five or ten minutes."

"How do you know that?"

"Because the ash had twice dropped from his cigar."

"Excellent! This is a colleague, Watson, after our own heart. But the marks?"

"He had left his own marks all over that small patch of gravel. I could discern no others."

Sherlock Holmes struck his hand against his knee with an impatient gesture.

"If I had only been there!" he cried. "It is evidently a case of extraordinary interest, and one which presented immense opportunities to the scientific expert. That gravel page upon which I might have read so much has been long ere this smudged by the rain and defaced by the clogs of curious peasants. Oh, Dr. Mortimer, Dr. Mortimer, to think that you should not have called me in! You have indeed much to answer for."

"I could not call you in, Mr. Holmes, without disclosing these facts to the world, and I have already given my reasons for not wishing to do so. Besides, besides——"

"Why do you hesitate?"

"There is a realm in which the most acute and most experienced of detectives is helpless."

"You mean that the thing is supernatural?"

"I did not positively say so."

"No, but you evidently think it."

"Since the tragedy, Mr. Holmes, there have come to my ears several incidents which are hard to reconcile with the settled order of Nature."

"For example?"

"I find that before the terrible event occurred several people had seen a creature upon the moor which corresponds with this Baskerville demon, and which could not possibly be any animal known to science. They all agreed that it was a huge creature, luminous, ghastly, and spectral. I have cross-examined these men, one of them a hard-headed countryman, one a farrier, and one a moorland farmer, who all tell the same story of this dreadful apparition, exactly corresponding to the hell-hound of the legend. I assure you that there is a reign of terror in the district, and that it is a hardy man who will cross the moor at night."

"And you, a trained man of science, believe it to be supernatural?"

"I do not know what to believe."

Holmes shrugged his shoulders.

"I have hitherto confined my investigations to this world," said he. "In a modest way I have combated evil, but to take on the Father of Evil himself would, perhaps, be too ambitious a task. Yet you must admit that the footmark is material."

"The original hound was material enough to tug a man's throat out, and yet he was diabolical as well."

"I see that you have quite gone over to the supernaturalists. But now, Dr. Mortimer, tell me this. If you hold these views, why have you come to consult me at all? You tell me in the same breath that it is useless to investigate Sir Charles's death, and that you desire me to do it."

"I did not say that I desired you to do it."

"Then, how can I assist you?"

"By advising me as to what I should do with Sir Henry Baskerville, who arrives at Waterloo Station"—Dr. Mortimer looked at his watch—"in exactly one hour and a quarter."

"He being the heir?"

"Yes. On the death of Sir Charles we inquired for this young gentleman and found that he had been farming in Canada. From the accounts which have reached us he is an excellent fellow in every way. I speak now not as a medical man but as a trustee and executor of Sir Charles's will."

"There is no other claimant, I presume?"

"None. The only other kinsman whom we have been able to trace was Rodger Baskerville, the youngest of three brothers of whom poor Sir Charles was the elder. The second brother, who died young, is the father of this lad Henry. The third, Rodger, was the black sheep of the family. He came of the old masterful Baskerville strain and was the very image, they tell me, of the family picture of old Hugo. He made England too hot to hold him, fled to Central America, and died there in 1876 of yellow fever. Henry is the last of the Baskervilles. In one hour and five minutes I meet him at Waterloo Station. I have had a wire that he arrived at Southampton this morning. Now, Mr. Holmes, what would you advise me to do with him?"

"Why should he not go to the home of his fathers?"

"It seems natural, does it not? And yet, consider that every Baskerville who goes there meets with an evil fate. I feel sure that if Sir Charles could have spoken with me before his death he would have warned me against bringing this, the last of the old race, and the heir to great wealth, to that deadly place. And yet it cannot be denied that the prosperity of the whole poor, bleak countryside depends upon his presence. All the good work which has been done by Sir Charles will crash to the ground if there is no tenant of the Hall. I fear lest I should be swayed too much by my own obvious interest in the matter, and that is why I bring the case before you and ask for your advice."

Holmes considered for a little time.

"Put into plain words, the matter is this," said he. "In your opinion there is a diabolical agency which makes Dartmoor an unsafe abode for a Baskerville—that is your opinion?"

"At least I might go the length of saying that there is some evidence that this may be so."

"Exactly. But surely, if your supernatural theory be correct, it could work the young man evil in London as easily as in Devonshire. A devil with merely local powers like a parish vestry would be too inconceivable a thing."

"You put the matter more flippantly, Mr. Holmes, than you would probably do if you were brought into personal contact with these things. Your advice, then, as I understand it, is that the young man will be as safe in Devonshire as in London. He comes in fifty minutes. What would you recommend?"

"I recommend, sir, that you take a cab, call off your spaniel who is scratching at my front door, and proceed to Waterloo to meet Sir Henry Baskerville."

"And then?"

"And then you will say nothing to him at all until I have made up my mind about the matter."

"How long will it take you to make up your mind?"

"Twenty-four hours. At ten o'clock to-morrow, Dr. Mortimer, I will be much obliged to you if you will call upon me here, and it will be of help to me in my plans for the future if you will bring Sir Henry Baskerville with you."

"I will do so, Mr. Holmes." He scribbled the appointment on his shirt-cuff and hurried off in his strange, peering, absent-minded fashion. Holmes stopped him at the head of the stair.

"Only one more question, Dr. Mortimer. You say that before Sir Charles Baskerville's death several people saw this apparition upon the moor?"

"Three people did."

"Did any see it after?"

"I have not heard of any."

"Thank you. Good-morning."

Holmes returned to his seat with that quiet look of inward satisfaction which meant that he had a congenial task before him.

"Going out, Watson?"

"Unless I can help you."

"No, my dear fellow, it is at the hour of action that I turn to you for aid. But this is splendid, really unique from some points of view. When you pass Bradley's, would you ask him to send up a pound of the strongest shag tobacco? Thank you. It would be as well if you could make it convenient not to return before evening. Then I should be very glad to compare impressions as to this most interesting problem which has been submitted to us this morning."

I knew that seclusion and solitude were very necessary for my friend in those hours of intense mental concentration during which he weighed every particle of evidence, constructed alternative theories, balanced one against the other, and made up his mind as to which points were essential and which immaterial. I therefore spent the day at my club and did not return to Baker Street until evening. It was nearly nine o'clock when I found myself in the sitting-room once more.

My first impression as I opened the door was that a fire had broken out, for the room was so filled with smoke that the light of the lamp upon the table was blurred by it. As I entered, however, my fears were set at rest, for it was the acrid fumes of strong coarse tobacco which took me by the throat and set me coughing. Through the haze I had a vague vision of Holmes in his dressing-gown coiled up in an armchair with his black clay pipe between his lips. Several rolls of paper lay around him.

"Caught cold, Watson?" said he.

"No, it's this poisonous atmosphere."

"I suppose it *is* pretty thick, now that you mention it."

"Thick! It is intolerable."

"Open the window, then! You have been at your club all day, I perceive."

"My dear Holmes!"

"Am I right?"

"Certainly, but how——?"

He laughed at my bewildered expression.

"There is a delightful freshness about you, Watson, which makes it a pleasure to exercise any small powers which I possess at your expense. A gentleman goes forth on a showery and miry day. He returns immaculate in the evening with the gloss still on his hat and his boots. He has been a fixture therefore all day. He is not a man with intimate friends. Where, then, could he have been? Is it not obvious?"

"Well, it is rather obvious."

"The world is full of obvious things which nobody by any chance ever observes. Where do you think that I have been?"

"A fixture also."

"On the contrary, I have been to Devonshire."

"In spirit?"

"Exactly. My body has remained in this armchair and has, I regret to observe, consumed in my absence two large pots of coffee and an incredible amount of tobacco. After you left I sent down to Stamford's for the Ordnance map of this portion of the moor, and my spirit has hovered over it all day. I flatter myself that I could find my way about."

"A large-scale map, I presume?"

"Very large." He unrolled one section and held it over his knee. "Here you have the particular district which concerns us. That is Baskerville Hall in the middle."

"With a wood round it?"

"Exactly. I fancy the yew alley, though not marked under that name, must stretch along this line, with the moor, as you perceive, upon the right of it. This small clump of buildings here is the hamlet of Grimpen, where our friend Dr. Mortimer has his headquarters. Within a radius of five miles there are, as you see, only a very few scattered dwellings. Here is Lafter Hall, which was mentioned in the narrative. There is a house indicated here which may be the residence of the naturalist—Stapleton, if I remember right, was his name. Here are two moorland farmhouses, High Tor and Foulmire. Then fourteen miles away the great convict prison of Princetown. Between and around these scattered points extends the desolate, lifeless moor. This, then, is the stage upon which tragedy has been played, and upon which we may help to play it again."

"It must be a wild place."

"Yes, the setting is a worthy one. If the devil did desire to have a hand in the affairs of men——"

"Then you are yourself inclining to the supernatural explanation."

"The devil's agents may be of flesh and blood, may they not? There are two questions waiting for us at the outset. The one is whether any crime has been comitted at all; the second is, what is the crime and how was it committed? Of course, if Dr. Mortimer's surmise should be correct, and we are dealing with forces outside the ordinary laws of Nature, there is an end of our investigation. But we are bound to exhaust all other hypotheses before falling back upon this one. I think we'll shut that window again, if you don't mind. It is a singular thing, but I find that a concentrated atmosphere helps a concentration of thought. I have not pushed it to the length of getting into a box to think, but that is the logical outcome of my convictions. Have you turned the case over in your mind?"

"Yes, I have thought a good deal of it in the course of the day."

"What do you make of it?"

"It is very bewildering."

"It has certainly a character of its own. There are points of distinction about it. That change in the footprints, for example. What do you make of that?"

"Mortimer said that the man had walked on tiptoe down that portion of the alley."

"He only repeated what some fool had said at the inquest. Why should a man walk on tiptoe down the alley?"

"What then?"

"He was running, Watson—running desperately, running for his life, running until he burst his heart and fell dead upon his face."

"Running from what?"

"There lies our problem. There are indications that the man was crazed with fear before ever he began to run."

"How can you say that?"

"I am presuming that the cause of his fears came to him across the moor. If that were so, and it seems most probable, only a man who had lost his wits would have run *from* the house instead of towards it. If the gipsy's evidence may be taken as true, he ran with cries for help in the direction where help was least likely to be. Then, again, whom was he waiting for that night, and why was he waiting for him in the yew alley rather than in his own house?"

"You think that he was waiting for someone?"

"The man was elderly and infirm. We can understand his taking an evening stroll, but the ground was damp and the night inclement. Is it natural that he should stand for five or ten minutes, as Dr. Mortimer, with more practical sense than I should have given him credit for, deduced from the cigar ash?"

"But he went out every evening."

"I think it unlikely that he waited at the moor-gate every evening. On the contrary, the evidence is that he avoided the moor. That night he waited there. It was the night before he made his departure for London. The thing takes shape, Watson. It becomes coherent. Might I ask you to hand me my violin, and we will postpone all further thought upon this business until we have had the advantage of meeting Dr. Mortimer and Sir Henry Baskerville in the morning."

4   SIR HENRY BASKERVILLE

Our breakfast table was cleared early, and Holmes waited in his dressing-gown for the promised interview. Our clients were punctual to their appointment, for the clock had just struck ten when Dr. Mortimer was shown up, followed by the young baronet. The latter was a small, alert, dark-eyed man about thirty years of age, very sturdily built, with thick black eyebrows and a strong, pugnacious face. He wore a ruddy-tinted tweed suit and had the weather-beaten appearance of one who has spent most of his time in the open air, and yet there was something in his steady eye and the quiet assurance of his bearing which indicated the gentleman.

"This is Sir Henry Baskerville," said Dr. Mortimer.

"Why, yes," said he, "and the strange thing is, Mr. Sherlock Holmes, that if my friend here had not proposed coming round to you this morning I should have come on my own account. I understand that you think out little puzzles, and I've had one this morning which wants more thinking out than I am able to give it."

"Pray take a seat, Sir Henry. Do I understand you to say that you have yourself had some remarkable experience since you arrived in London?"

"Nothing of much importance, Mr. Holmes. Only a joke, as like as not. It was this letter, if you can call it a letter, which reached me this morning."

He laid an envelope upon the table, and we all bent over it. It was of common quality, grayish in colour. The address, "Sir Henry Baskerville, Northumberland Hotel," was printed in rough characters; the postmark "Charing Cross," and the date of posting the preceding evening.

"Who knew that you were going to the Northumberland Hotel?" asked Holmes glancing keenly across at our visitor.

"No one could have known. We only decided after I met Dr. Mortimer."

"But Dr. Mortimer was no doubt already stopping there?"

"No, I had been staying with a friend," said the doctor. "There was no possible indication that we intended to go to this hotel."

"Hum! Someone seems to be very deeply interested in your movements." Out of the envelope he took a half-sheet of foolscap paper folded into four. This he opened and spread flat upon the table. Across the middle of it a single sentence had been formed by the expedient of pasting printed words upon it. It ran:

As you value your life or your reason keep away from the moor.

The word "moor" only was printed in ink.

"Now," said Sir Henry Baskerville, "perhaps you will tell me. Mr. Holmes, what in thunder is the meaning of that, and who it is that takes so much interest in my affairs?"

"What do you make of it, Dr. Mortimer? You must allow that there is nothing supernatural about this, at any rate?"

"No, sir, but it might very well come from someone who was convinced that the business is supernatural."

"What business?" asked Sir Henry sharply. "It seems to me that all you gentlemen know a great deal more than I do about my own affairs."

"You shall share our knowledge before you leave this room, Sir Henry. I promise you that," said Sherlock Holmes. "We will confine ourselves for the present with your permission to this very interesting document, which must have been put together and posted yesterday evening. Have you yesterday's *Times*, Watson?"

"It is here in the corner."

"Might I trouble you for it—the inside page, please, with the leading articles?" He glanced swiftly over it, running his eyes up and down the columns. "Capital article this on free trade. Permit me to give you an extract from it.

"You may be cajoled into imagining that your own special trade or your own industry will be encouraged by a protective tariff, but it stands to reason that such legislation must in the long run keep away wealth from the country, diminish the value of our imports, and lower the general conditions of life in this island.

What do you think of that, Watson?" cried Holmes in high glee, rubbing his hands together with satisfaction. "Don't you think that is an admirable sentiment?"

Dr. Mortimer looked at Holmes with an air of professional interest, and Sir Henry Baskerville turned a pair of puzzled dark eyes upon me.

"I don't know much about the tariff and things of that kind," said he, "but it seems to me we've got a bit off the trail so far as that note is concerned."

"On the contrary, I think we are particularly hot upon the trail, Sir Henry. Watson here knows more about my methods than you do, but I fear that even he has not quite grasped the significance of this sentence."

"No, I confess that I see no connection."

"And yet, my dear Watson, there is so very close a connection that the one is extracted out of the other. 'You,' 'your,' 'your,' 'life,' 'reason,' 'value,' 'keep away,' 'from the.' Don't you see now whence these words have been taken?"

"By thunder, you're right! Well, if that isn't smart!" cried Sir Henry.

"If any possible doubt remained it is settled by the fact that 'keep away' and 'from the' are cut out in one piece."

"Well, now—so it is!"

"Really, Mr. Holmes, this exceeds anything which I could have imagined," said Dr. Mortimer, gazing at my friend in amazement. "I could understand anyone saying that the words were from a newspaper; but that you should name which, and add that it came from the leading article, is really one of the most remarkable things which I have ever known. How did you do it?"

"I presume, Doctor, that you could tell the skull of a negro from that of an Esquimau?"

"Most certainly."

"But how?"

"Because that is my special hobby. The differences are obvious. The supraorbital crest, the facial angle, the maxillary curve, the——"

"But this is my special hobby, and the differences are equally obvious. There is as much difference to my eyes between the leaded bourgeois type of a *Times* article and the slovenly print of an evening half-penny paper as there could be between your negro and your Esquimau. The detection of types is one of the most elementary branches of knowledge to the special expert in crime, though I confess that once when I was very young I confused the *Leeds Mercury* with the *Western Morning News*. But a *Times* leader is entirely distinctive, and these words could have been taken from nothing else. As it was done yesterday the strong probability was that we should find the words in yesterday's issue."

"So far as I can follow you, then, Mr. Holmes," said Sir Henry Baskerville, "someone cut out this message with a scissors——"

"Nail-scissors," said Holmes. "You can see that it was a very short-bladed scissors, since the cutter had to take two snips over 'keep away.'"

"That is so. Someone, then, cut out the message with a pair of short-bladed scissors, pasted it with paste——"

"Gum," said Holmes.

"With gum on to the paper. But I want to know why the woord 'moor' should have been written?"

"Because he could not find it in print. The other words were all simple and might be found in any issue, but 'moor' would be less common."

"Why, of course, that would explain it. Have you read anything else in this message, Mr. Holmes?"

"There are one or two indications, and yet the utmost pains have been taken to remove all clues. The address, you observe, is printed in rough characters. But the *Times* is a paper which is seldom found in any hands but those of the highly educated. We may take it, therefore, that the letter was composed by an educated man who wished to pose as an uneducated one, and his effort to conceal his own writing suggests that that writing might be known, or come to be known, by you. Again, you will observe that the words are not gummed on in an accurate line, but that some are much higher than others. 'Life,' for example, is quite out of its proper place. That may point to carelessness or it may point to agitation and hurry upon the part of the cutter. On the whole I incline to the latter view, since the matter was evidently important, and it is unlikely that the composer of such a letter would be careless. If he were in a hurry it opens up the interesting question why he should be in a hurry, since any letter posted up to early morning would reach Sir Henry before he would leave his hotel. Did the composer fear an interruption—and from whom?"

"We are coming now rather into the region of guesswork," said Dr. Mortimer.

"Say, rather, into the region where we balance probabilities and choose the most likely. It is the scientific use of the imagination, but we have always some material basis on which to start our speculation. Now, you would call it a guess, no doubt, but I am almost certain that this address has been written in a hotel."

"How in the world can you say that?"

"If you examine it carefully you will see that both the pen and the ink have given the writer trouble. The pen has spluttered twice in a single word and has run dry three times in a short address, showing that there was very little ink in the bottle. Now, a private pen or ink-bottle is seldom allowed to be in such a state, and the combination of the two must be quite rare. But you know the hotel ink and the hotel pen, where it is rare to get anything else. Yes, I have very little hesitation in saying that could we examine the waste-paper baskets of the hotels around Charing Cross until we found the remains of the mutilated *Times* leader we could lay our hands straight upon the person who sent this singular message. Halloa! Halloa! What's this?"

He was carefully examining the foolscap, upon which the words were pasted, holding it only an inch or two from his eyes.

"Well?"

"Nothing," said he, throwing it down. "It is a blank half-sheet of paper, without even a water-mark upon it. I think we have drawn as much as we can from this curious letter; and now, Sir Henry, has anything else of interest happened to you since you have been in London?"

"Why, no, Mr. Holmes. I think not."

"You have not observed anyone follow or watch you?"

"I seem to have walked right into the thick of a dime novel," said our visitor. "Why in thunder should anyone follow or watch me?"

"We are coming to that. You have nothing else to report to us before we go into this matter?"

"Well, it depends upon what you think worth reporting."

"I think anything out of the ordinary routine of life well worth reporting."

Sir Henry smiled.

"I don't know much of British life yet, for I have spent nearly all my time in the States and in Canada. But I hope that to lose one of your boots is not part of the ordinary routine of life over here."

"You have lost one of your boots?"

"My dear sir," cried Dr. Mortimer, "it is only mislaid. You will find it when you return to the hotel. What is the use of troubling Mr. Holmes with trifles of this kind?"

"Well, he asked me for anything outside the ordinary routine."

"Exactly," said Holmes, "however foolish the incident may seem. You have lost one of your boots, you say?"

"Well, mislaid it, anyhow. I put them both outside my door last night, and there was only one in the morning. I could get no sense out of the chap who cleans them. The worst of it is that I only bought the pair last night in the Strand, and I have never had them on."

"If you have never worn them, why did you put them out to be cleaned?"

"They were tan boots and had never been varnished. That was why I put them out."

"Then I understand that on your arrival in London yesterday you went out at once and bought a pair of boots?"

"I did a good deal of shopping. Dr. Mortimer here went round with me. You see, if I am to be squire down there I must dress the part, and it may be that I have got a little careless in my ways out West. Among other things I bought these brown boots—gave six dollars for them—and had one stolen before ever I had them on my feet."

"It seems a singularly useless thing to steal," said Sherlock Holmes. "I confess that I share Dr. Mortimer's belief that it will not be long before the missing boot is found."

"And, now, gentlemen," said the baronet with decision, "it seems to me that I have spoken quite enough about the little that I know. It is time that you kept your promise and gave me a full account of what we are all driving at."

"Your request is a very reasonable one," Holmes answered. "Dr. Mortimer, I think you could not do better than to tell your story as you told it to us."

Thus encouraged, our scientific friend drew his papers from his pocket and presented the whole case as he had done upon the morning before. Sir Henry Baskerville listened with the deepest attention and with an occasional exclamation of surprise.

"Well, I seem to have come into an inheritance with a vengeance," said he when the long narrative was finished. "Of course, I've heard of the hound ever since I was in the nursery. It's the pet story of the family, though I never thought of taking it seriously before. But as to my uncle's death—well, it all seems boiling up in my head, and I can't get it clear yet. You don't seem quite to have made up your mind whether it's a case for a policeman or a clergyman."

"Precisely."

"And now there's this affair of the letter to me at the hotel. I suppose that fits into its place."

"It seems to show that someone knows more than we do about what goes on upon the moor," said Dr. Mortimer.

"And also," said Holmes, "that someone is not ill-disposed towards you, since they warn you of danger."

"Or it may be that they wish, for their own purposes, to scare me away."

"Well, of course, that is possible also. I am very much indebted to you, Dr. Mortimer, for introducing me to a problem which presents several interesting alternatives. But the practical point which we now have to decide, Sir Henry, is whether it is or is not advisable for you to go to Baskerville Hall."

"Why should I not go?"

"There seems to be danger."

"Do you mean danger from this family fiend or do you mean danger from human beings?"

"Well, that is what we have to find out."

"Whichever it is, my answer is fixed. There is no devil in hell, Mr. Holmes, and there is no man upon earth who can prevent me from going to the home of my own people, and you may take that to be my final answer." His dark brows knitted and his face flushed to a dusky red as he spoke. It was evident that the fiery temper of the Baskervilles was not extinct in this their last representative. "Meanwhile," said he, "I have hardly had time to think over all that you have told me. It's a big thing for a man to have to understand and to decide at one sitting. I should like to have a quiet hour by myself to make up my mind. Now, look here, Mr. Holmes, it's half-past eleven now and I am going back right away to my hotel. Suppose you and your friend, Dr. Watson, come round and lunch with us at two. I'll be able to tell you more clearly then how this thing strikes me."

"Is that convenient to you, Watson?"

"Perfectly."

"Then you may expect us. Shall I have a cab called?"

"I'd prefer to walk, for this affair has flurried me rather."

"I'll join you in a walk, with pleasure," said his companion.

"Then we meet again at two o'clock. Au revoir, and good-morning!"

We heard the steps of our visitors descend the stair and the bang of the front door. In an instant Holmes had changed from the languid dreamer to the man of action.

"Your hat and boots, Watson, quick! Not a moment to lose!" He rushed into his room in his dressing-gown and was back again in a few seconds in a frock-coat. We hurried together down the stairs and into the street. Dr. Mortimer and Baskerville were still visible about two hundred yards ahead of us in the direction of Oxford Street.

"Shall I run on and stop them?"

"Not for the world, my dear Watson. I am perfectly satisfied with your company if you will tolerate mine. Our friends are wise, for it is certainly a very fine morning for a walk."

He quickened his pace until we had decreased the distance which divided us by about half. Then, still keeping a hundred yards behind, we followed into Oxford Street and so down Regent Street. Once our friends stopped and stared into a shop window, upon which Holmes did the same. An instant afterwards he gave a little cry of satisfaction, and, following the direction of his eager eyes, I saw that a hansom cab with a man inside which had halted on the other side of the street was now proceeding slowly onward again.

"There's our man, Watson! Come along! We'll have a good look at him, if we can do no more."

At that instant I was aware of a bushy black beard and a pair of piercing eyes turned upon us through the side window of the cab. Instantly the trapdoor at the top flew up, something was screamed to the driver, and the cab flew madly off down Regent Street. Holmes looked eagerly round for another, but no empty one was in sight. Then he dashed in wild pursuit amid the stream of the traffic, but the start was too great, and already the cab was out of sight.

"There now!" said Holmes bitterly as he emerged panting and white with vexation from the tide of vehicles. "Was ever such bad luck and such bad management, too? Watson, Watson, if you are an honest man you will record this also and set it against my successes!"

"Who was the man?"

"I have not an idea."

"A spy?"

"Well, it was evident from what we have heard that Baskerville has been very closely shadowed by someone since he has been in town. How else could it be known so quickly that it was the Northumberland Hotel which he had chosen? If they had followed him the first day I argued that they would follow him also the second. You may have observed that I twice strolled over to the window while Dr. Mortimer was reading his legend."

"Yes, I remember."

"I was looking out for loiterers in the street, but I saw none. We are dealing with a clever man, Watson. This matter cuts very deep, and though I have not finally made up my mind whether it is a benevolent or a malevolent agency which is in touch with us, I am conscious always of power and design. When our friends left I at once followed them in the hopes of marking down their invisible attendant. So wily was he that he had not trusted himself upon foot, but he had availed himself of a cab so that he could loiter behind or dash past them and so escape their notice. His method had the additional advantage that if they were to take a cab he was all ready to follow them. It has, however, one obvious disadvantage."

"It puts him in the power of the cabman."

"Exactly."

"What a pity we did not get the number!"

"My dear Watson, clumsy as I have been, you surely do not seriously imagine that I neglected to get the number? No. 2704 is our man. But that is no use to us for the moment."

"I fail to see how you could have done more."

"On observing the cab I should have instantly turned and walked in the other direction. I should then at my leisure have hired a second cab and followed the first at a respectful distance, or, better still, have driven to the Northumberland Hotel and waited there. When our unknown had followed Baskerville home we should have had the opportunity of playing his own game upon himself and seeing where he made for. As it is, by an indiscreet eagerness, which was taken advantage of with extraordinary quickness and energy by our opponent, we have betrayed ourselves and lost our man."

We had been sauntering slowly down Regent Street during this conversation, and Dr. Mortimer, with his companion, had long vanished in front of us.

"There is no object in our following them," said Holmes. "The shadow has departed and will not return. We must see what further cards we have in our hands and play them with decision. Could you swear to that man's face within the cab?"

"I could swear only to the beard."

"And so could I—from which I gather that in all probability it was a false one. A clever man upon so delicate an errand has no use for a beard save to conceal his features. Come in here, Watson!"

He turned into one of the district messenger offices, where he was warmly greeted by the manager.

"Ah, Wilson, I see you have not forgotten the little case in which I had the good fortune to help you?"

"No, sir, indeed I have not. You saved my good name, and perhaps my life."

"My dear fellow, you exaggerate. I have some recollection, Wilson, that you had among your boys a lad named Cartwright, who showed some ability during the investigation."

"Yes, sir, he is still with us."

"Could you ring him up?—thank you! And I should be glad to have change of this five-pound note."

A lad of fourteen, with a bright, keen face, had obeyed the summons of the manager. He stood now gazing with great reverence at the famous detective.

"Let me have the Hotel Directory," said Holmes. "Thank you! Now, Cartwright, there are the names of twenty-three hotels here, all in the immediate neighbourhood of Charing Cross. Do you see?"

"Yes, sir."

"You will visit each of these in turn."

"Yes, sir."

"You will begin in each case by giving the outside porter one shilling. Here are twenty-three shillings."

"Yes, sir."

"You will tell him that you want to see the waste-paper of yesterday.

You will say that an important telegram has miscarried and that you are looking for it. You understand?"

"Yes, sir."

"But what you are really looking for is the centre page of the *Times* with some holes cut in it with scissors. Here is a copy of the *Times*. It is this page. You could easily recognize it, could you not?"

"Yes, sir."

"In each case the outside porter will send for the hall porter, to whom also you will give a shilling. Here are twenty-three shillings. You will then learn in possibly twenty cases out of the twenty-three that the waste of the day before has been burned or removed. In the three other cases you will be shown a heap of paper and you will look for this page of the *Times* among it. The odds are enormously against your finding it. There are ten shillings over in case of emergencies. Let me have a report by wire at Baker Street before evening. And now, Watson, it only remains for us to find out by wire the identity of the cabman, No. 2704, and then we will drop into one of the Bond Street picture galleries and fill in the time until we are due at the hotel."

5   THREE BROKEN THREADS

Sherlock Holmes had, in a very remarkable degree, the power of detaching his mind at will. For two hours the strange business in which we had been involved appeared to be forgotten, and he was entirely absorbed in the pictures of the modern Belgian masters. He would talk of nothing but art, of which he had the crudest ideas, from our leaving the gallery until we found ourselves at the Northumberland Hotel.

"Sir Henry Baskerville is upstairs expecting you," said the clerk. "He asked me to show you up at once when you came."

"Have you any objection to my looking at your register?" said Holmes. "Not in the least."

The book showed that two names had been added after that of Baskerville. One was Theophilus Johnson and family, of Newcastle; the other Mrs. Oldmore and maid, of High Lodge, Alton.

"Surely that must be the same Johnson whom I used to know," said Holmes to the porter. "A lawyer, is he not, gray-headed, and walks with a limp?"

"No, sir, this is Mr. Johnson, the coal-owner, a very active gentleman, not older than yourself."

"Surely you are mistaken about his trade?"

"No, sir! he has used this hotel for many years, and he is very well known to us."

"Ah, that settles it. Mrs. Oldmore, too; I seem to remember the name. Excuse my curiosity, but often in calling upon one friend one finds another."

"She is an invalid lady, sir. Her husband was once mayor of Gloucester. She always comes to us when she is in town."

"Thank you; I am afraid I cannot claim her acquaintance. We have established a most important fact by these questions, Watson," he continued in a low voice as we went upstairs together. "We know now that the people who are so interested in our friend have not settled down in his own hotel. That means that while they are, as we have seen, very anxious to watch him, they are equally anxious that he should not see them. Now, this is a most suggestive fact."

"What does it suggest?"

"It suggests—halloa, my dear fellow, what on earth is the matter?"

As we came round the top of the stairs we had run up against Sir Henry Baskerville himself. His face was flushed with anger, and he held an old and dusty boot in one of his hands. So furious was he that he was hardly articulate, and when he did speak it was in a much broader and more Western dialect than any which we had heard from him in the morning.

"Seems to me they are playing me for a sucker in this hotel," he cried. "They'll find they've started in to monkey with the wrong man unless they are careful. By thunder, if that chap can't find my missing boot there will be trouble. I can take a joke with the best, Mr. Holmes, but they've got a bit over the mark this time."

"Still looking for your boot?"

"Yes, sir, and mean to find it."

"But, surely, you said that it was a new brown boot?"

"So it was, sir. And now it's an old black one."

"What! you don't mean to say——?"

"That's just what I do mean to say. I only had three pairs in the world —the new brown, the old black, and the patent leathers, which I am wearing. Last night they took one of my brown ones, and to-day they have sneaked one of the black. Well, have you got it? Speak out, man, and don't stand staring!"

An agitated German waiter had appeared upon the scene.

"No, sir; I have made inquiry all over the hotel, but I can hear no word of it."

"Well, either that boot comes back before sundown or I'll see the manager and tell him that I go right straight out of this hotel."

"It shall be found, sir—I promise you that if you will have a little patience it will be found."

"Mind it is, for it's the last thing of mine that I'll lose in this den of thieves. Well, well, Mr. Holmes, you'll excuse my troubling you about such a trifle——"

"I think it's well worth troubling about."

"Why, you look very serious over it."

"How do you explain it?"

"I just don't attempt to explain it. It seems the very maddest, queerest thing that ever happened to me."

"The queerest perhaps——" said Holmes thoughtfully.

"What do you make of it yourself?"

"Well, I don't profess to understand it yet. This case of yours is very complex, Sir Henry. When taken in conjunction with your uncle's death I am not sure that of all the five hundred cases of capital importance which I have handled there is one which cuts so deep. But we hold several threads in our hands, and the odds are that one or other of them guides us to the truth. We may waste time in following the wrong one, but sooner or later we must come upon the right."

We had a pleasant luncheon in which little was said of the business which had brought us together. It was in the private sitting-room to which we afterwards repaired that Holmes asked Baskerville what were his intentions.

"To go to Baskerville Hall."

"And when?"

"At the end of the week."

"On the whole," said Holmes, "I think that your decision is a wise one. I have ample evidence that you are being dogged in London, and amid the millions of this great city it is difficult to discover who these people are or what their object can be. If their intentions are evil they might do you a mischief, and we should be powerless to prevent it. You did not know, Dr. Mortimer, that you were followed this morning from my house?"

Dr. Mortimer started violently.

"Followed! By whom?"

"That, unfortunately, is what I cannot tell you. Have you among your neighbours or acquaintances on Dartmoor any man with a black, full beard?"

"No—or, let me see—why, yes. Barrymore, Sir Charles's butler, is a man with a full, black beard."

"Ha! Where is Barrymore?"

"He is in charge of the Hall."

"We had best ascertain if he is really there, or if by any possibility he might be in London."

"How can you do that?"

"Give me a telegraph form. 'Is all ready for Sir Henry?' That will do. Address to Mr. Barrymore, Baskerville Hall. What is the nearest telegraph-office? Grimpen. Very good, we will send a second wire to the post-master, Grimpen: 'Telegram to Mr. Barrymore to be delivered into his own hand. If absent, please return wire to Sir Henry Baskerville, North-umberland Hotel.' That should let us know before evening whether Barrymore is at his post in Devonshire or not."

"That's so," said Baskerville. "By the way, Dr. Mortimer, who is this Barrymore, anyhow?"

"He is the son of the old caretaker, who is dead. They have looked after the Hall for four generations now. So far as I know, he and his wife are as respectable a couple as any in the county."

"At the same time," said Baskerville, "it's clear enough that so long as there are none of the family at the Hall these people have a mighty fine home and nothing to do."

"That is true."

"Did Barrymore profit at all by Sir Charles's will?" asked Holmes.

"He and his wife had five hundred pounds each."

"Ha! Did they know that they would receive this?"

"Yes; Sir Charles was very fond of talking about the provisions of his will."

"That is very interesting."

"I hope," said Dr. Mortimer, "that you do not look with suspicious eyes upon everyone who received a legacy from Sir Charles, for I also had a thousand pounds left to me."

"Indeed! And anyone else?"

"There were many insignificant sums to individuals, and a large number of public charities. The residue all went to Sir Henry."

"And how much was the residue?"

"Seven hundred and forty thousand pounds."

Holmes raised his eyebrows in surprise. "I had no idea that so gigantic a sum was involved," said he.

"Sir Charles had the reputation of being rich, but we did not know how very rich he was until we came to examine his securities. The total value of the estate was close on to a million."

"Dear me! It is a stake for which a man might well play a desperate game. And one more question, Dr. Mortimer. Supposing that anything happened to our young friend here—you will forgive the unpleasant hy-pothesis!—who would inherit the estate?"

"Since Rodger Baskerville, Sir Charles's younger brother, died unmarried, the estate would descend to the Desmonds, who are distant cousins. James Desmond is an elderly clergyman in Westmoreland."

"Thank you. These details are all of great interest. Have you met Mr. James Desmond?"

"Yes; he once came down to visit Sir Charles. He is a man of venerable appearance and of saintly life. I remember that he refused to accept any settlement from Sir Charles, though he pressed it upon him."

"And this man of simple tastes would be the heir to Sir Charles's thousands."

"He would be the heir to the estate because that is entailed. He would also be the heir to the money unless it were willed otherwise by the present owner, who can, of course, do what he likes with it."

"And have you made your will, Sir Henry?"

"No, Mr. Holmes, I have not. I've had no time, for it was only yesterday that I learned how matters stood. But in any case I feel that the money should go with the title and estate. That was my poor uncle's idea. How is the owner going to restore the glories of the Baskervilles if he has not money enough to keep up the property? House, land, and dollars must go together."

"Quite so. Well, Sir Henry, I am of one mind with you as to the advisability of your going down to Devonshire without delay. There is only one provision which I must make. You certainly must not go alone."

"Dr. Mortimer returns with me."

"But Dr. Mortimer has his practice to attend to, and his house is miles away from yours. With all the goodwill in the world he may be unable to help you. No, Sir Henry, you must take with you someone, a trusty man, who will be always by your side."

"Is it possible that you could come yourself, Mr. Holmes?"

"If matters came to a crisis I should endeavour to be present in person; but you can understand that, with my extensive consulting practice and with the constant appeals which reach me from many quarters, it is impossible for me to be absent from London for an indefinite time. At the present instant one of the most revered names in England is being besmirched by a blackmailer, and only I can stop a disastrous scandal. You will see how impossible it is for me to go to Dartmoor."

"Whom would you recommend, then?"

Holmes laid his hand upon my arm.

"If my friend would undertake it there is no man who is better worth having at your side when you are in a tight place. No one can say so more confidently than I."

The proposition took me completely by surprise, but before I had time to answer, Baskerville seized me by the hand and wrung it heartily.

"Well, now, that is real kind of you, Dr. Watson," said he. "You see how it is with me, and you know just as much about the matter as I do. If you will come down to Baskerville Hall and see me through I'll never forget it."

The promise of adventure had always a fascination for me, and I was complimented by the words of Holmes and by the eagerness with which the baronet hailed me as a companion.

"I will come, with pleasure," said I. "I do not know how I could employ my time better."

"And you will report very carefully to me," said Holmes. "When a crisis comes, as it will do, I will direct how you shall act. I suppose that by Saturday all might be ready?"

"Would that suit Dr. Watson?"

"Perfectly."

"Then on Saturday, unless you hear to the contrary, we shall meet at the ten-thirty train from Paddington."

We had risen to depart when Baskerville gave a cry of triumph, and diving into one of the corners of the room he drew a brown boot from under a cabinet.

"My missing boot!" he cried.

"May all our difficulties vanish as easily!" said Sherlock Holmes.

"But it is a very singular thing," Dr. Mortimer remarked. "I searched this room carefully before lunch."

"And so did I," said Baskerville. "Every inch of it."

"There was certainly no boot in it then."

"In that case the waiter must have placed it there while we were lunching."

The German was sent for but professed to know nothing of the matter, nor could any inquiry clear it up. Another item had been added to that constant and apparently purposeless series of small mysteries which had succeeded each other so rapidly. Setting aside the whole grim story of Sir Charles's death, we had a line of inexplicable incidents all within the limits of two days, which included the receipt of the printed letter, the black-bearded spy in the hansom, the loss of the new brown boot, the loss of the old black boot, and now the return of the new brown boot. Holmes sat in silence in the cab as we drove back to Baker Street, and I knew from his drawn brows and keen face that his mind, like my own, was busy in endeavouring to frame some scheme into which all these strange and apparently disconnected episodes could be fitted. All afternoon and late into the evening he sat lost in tobacco and thought.

Just before dinner two telegrams were handed in. The first ran:

Have just heard that Barrymore is at the Hall.

BASKERVILLE.

The second:

Visited twenty-three hotels as directed, but sorry to report unable to trace cut sheet of Times.

CARTWRIGHT.

"There go two of my threads, Watson. There is nothing more stimulating than a case where everything goes against you. We must cast round for another scent."

"We have still the cabman who drove the spy."

"Exactly. I have wired to get his name and address from the Official Registry. I should not be surprised if this were an answer to my question."

The ring at the bell proved to be something even more satisfactory than an answer, however, for the door opened and a rough-looking fellow entered who was evidently the man himself.

"I got a message from the head office that a gent at this address had been inquiring for No. 2704," said he. "I've driven my cab this seven years and never a word of complaint. I came here straight from the Yard to ask you to your face what you had against me."

"I have nothing in the world against you, my good man," said Holmes. "On the contrary, I have half a sovereign for you if you will give me a clear answer to my questions."

"Well, I've had a good day and no mistake," said the cabman with a grin. "What was it you wanted to ask, sir?"

"First of all your name and address, in case I want you again."

"John Clayton, 3 Turpey Street, the Borough. My cab is out of Shipley's Yard, near Waterloo Station."

Sherlock Holmes made a note of it.

"Now, Clayton, tell me all about the fare who came and watched this house at ten o'clock this morning and afterwards followed the two gentlemen down Regent Street."

The man looked surprised and a little embarrassed. "Why, there's no good my telling you things, for you seem to know as much as I do already," said he. "The truth is that the gentleman told me that he was a detective and that I was to say nothing about him to anyone."

"My good fellow, this is a very serious business, and you may find yourself in a pretty bad position if you try to hide anything from me. You say that your fare told you that he was a detective?"

"Yes, he did."

"When did he say this?"

"When he left me."

"Did he say anything more?"

"He mentioned his name."

Holmes cast a swift glance of triumph at me. "Oh, he mentioned his name, did he? That was imprudent. What was the name that he mentioned?"

"His name," said the cabman, "was Mr. Sherlock Holmes."

Never have I seen my friend more completely taken aback than by the cabman's reply. For an instant he sat in silent amazement. Then he burst into a hearty laugh.

"A touch, Watson—an undeniable touch!" said he. "I feel a foil as quick and supple as my own. He got home upon me very prettily that time. So his name was Sherlock Holmes, was it?"

"Yes, sir, that was the gentleman's name."

"Excellent! Tell me where you picked him up and all that occurred."

"He hailed me at half-past nine in Trafalgar Square. He said that he was a detective, and he offered me two guineas if I would do exactly what he wanted all day and ask no questions. I was glad enough to agree. First we drove down to the Northumberland Hotel and waited there until two gentlemen came out and took a cab from the rank. We followed their cab until it pulled up somewhere near here."

"This very door," said Holmes.

"Well, I couldn't be sure of that, but I dare say my fare knew all about it. We pulled up halfway down the street and waited an hour and a half. Then the two gentlemen passed us, walking, and we followed down Baker Street and along——"

"I know," said Holmes.

"Until we got three-quarters down Regent Street. Then my gentleman threw up the trap, and he cried that I should drive right away to Waterloo Station as hard as I could go. I whipped up the mare and we were there under the ten minutes. Then he paid up his two guineas, like a good one, and away he went into the station. Only just as he was leaving he turned round and he said: 'It might interest you to know that you have been driving Mr. Sherlock Holmes.' That's how I come to know the name."

"I see. And you saw no more of him?"

"Not after he went into the station."

"And how would you describe Mr. Sherlock Holmes?"

The cabman scratched his head. "Well, he wasn't altogether such an easy gentleman to describe. I'd put him at forty years of age, and he was of a middle height, two or three inches shorter than you, sir. He was dressed like a toff, and he had a black beard, cut square at the end, and a pale face. I don't know as I could say more than that."

"Colour of his eyes?"

"No, I can't say that."

"Nothing more that you can remember?"

"No, sir; nothing."

"Well, then, here is your half-sovereign. There's another one waiting for you if you can bring any more information. Good-night!"

"Good-night, sir, and thank you!"

John Clayton departed chuckling, and Holmes turned to me with a shrug of his shoulders and a rueful smile.

"Snap goes our third thread, and we end where we began," said he. "The cunning rascal! He knew our number, knew that Sir Henry Baskerville had consulted me, spotted who I was in Regent Street, conjectured that I had got the number of the cab and would lay my hands on the driver, and so sent back this audacious message. I tell you, Watson, this time we have got a foeman who is worthy of our steel. I've been checkmated in London. I can only wish you better luck in Devonshire. But I'm not easy in my mind about it."

"About what?"

"About sending you. It's an ugly business, Watson, an ugly, dangerous business, and the more I see of it the less I like it. Yes, my dear fellow, you may laugh, but I give you my word that I shall be very glad to have you back safe and sound in Baker Street once more."

6   BASKERVILLE HALL

Sir Henry Baskerville and Dr. Mortimer were ready upon the appointed day, and we started as arranged for Devonshire. Mr. Sherlock Holmes drove with me to the station and gave me his last parting injunctions and advice.

"I will not bias your mind by suggesting theories or suspicions, Watson," said he; "I wish you simply to report facts in the fullest possible manner to me, and you can leave me to do the theorizing."

"What sort of facts?" I asked.

"Anything which may seem to have a bearing however indirect upon the case, and especially the relations between young Baskerville and his neighbours or any fresh particulars concerning the death of Sir Charles. I have made some inquiries myself in the last few days, but the results have, I fear, been negative. One thing only appears to be certain, and that is that Mr. James Desmond, who is the next heir, is an elderly gentleman of a very amiable disposition, so that this persecution does not arise from him. I really think that we may eliminate him entirely from our calculations. There remain the people who will actually surround Sir Henry Baskerville upon the moor."

"Would it not be well in the first place to get rid of this Barrymore couple?"

"By no means. You could not make a greater mistake. If they are innocent it would be a cruel injustice, and if they are guilty we should be giving up all chance of bringing it home to them. No, no, we will preserve them upon our list of suspects. Then there is a groom at the Hall, if I remember right. There are two moorland farmers. There is our friend Dr. Mortimer, whom I believe to be entirely honest, and there is his wife, of whom we know nothing. There is this naturalist, Stapleton, and there is his sister, who is said to be a young lady of attractions. There is Mr. Frankland, of Lafter Hall, who is also an unknown factor, and there are one or two other neighbours. These are the folk who must be your very special study."

"I will do my best."

"You have arms, I suppose?"

"Yes, I thought it as well to take them."

"Most certainly. Keep your revolver near you night and day, and never relax your precautions."

Our friends had already secured a first-class carriage and were waiting for us upon the platform.

"No, we have no news of any kind," said Dr. Mortimer in answer to my friend's questions. "I can swear to one thing, and that is that we have not been shadowed during the last two days. We have never gone out without keeping a sharp watch, and no one could have escaped our notice."

"You have always kept together, I presume?"

"Except yesterday afternoon. I usually give up one day to pure amusement when I come to town, so I spent it at the Museum of the College of Surgeons."

"And I went to look at the folk in the park," said Baskerville. "But we had no trouble of any kind."

"It was imprudent, all the same," said Holmes, shaking his head and looking very grave. "I beg, Sir Henry, that you will not go about alone. Some great misfortune will befall you if you do. Did you get your other boot?"

"No, sir, it is gone forever."

"Indeed. That is very interesting. Well, good-bye," he added as the train began to glide down the platform. "Bear in mind, Sir Henry, one of the phrases in that queer old legend which Dr. Mortimer has read to us and avoid the moor in those hours of darkness when the powers of evil are exalted."

I looked back at the platform when we had left it far behind and
saw the tall, austere figure of Holmes standing motionless and gazing
after us.

The journey was a swift and pleasant one, and I spent it in making
the more intimate acquaintance of my two companions and in playing
with Dr. Mortimer's spaniel. In a very few hours the brown earth had
become ruddy, the brick had changed to granite, and red cows grazed
in well-hedged fields where the lush grasses and more luxuriant vegetation spoke of a richer, if a damper, climate. Young Baskerville stared
eagerly out of the window and cried aloud with delight as he recognized
the familiar features of the Devon scenery.

"I've been over a good part of the world since I left it, Dr. Watson,"
said he; "but I have never seen a place to compare with it."

"I never saw a Devonshire man who did not swear by his county,"
I remarked.

"It depends upon the breed of men quite as much as on the county,"
said Dr. Mortimer. "A glance at our friend here reveals the rounded
head of the Celt, which carries inside it the Celtic enthusiasm and power
of attachment. Poor Sir Charles's head was of a very rare type, half
Gaelic, half Ivernian in its characteristics. But you were very young when
you last saw Baskerville Hall, were you not?"

"I was a boy in my teens at the time of my father's death and had
never seen the Hall, for he lived in a little cottage on the South Coast.
Thence I went straight to a friend in America. I tell you it is all as new
to me as it is to Dr. Watson, and I'm as keen as possible to see the moor."

"Are you? Then your wish is easily granted, for there is your first sight
of the moor," said Dr. Mortimer, pointing out of the carriage window.

Over the green squares of the fields and the low curve of a wood there
rose in the distance a gray, melancholy hill, with a strange jagged summit,
dim and vague in the distance, like some fantastic landscape in a dream.
Baskerville sat for a long time, his eyes fixed upon it, and I read upon
his eager face how much it meant to him, this first sight of that strange
spot where the men of his blood had held sway so long and left their
mark so deep. There he sat, with his tweed suit and his American accent,
in the corner of a prosaic railway-carriage, and yet as I looked at his
dark and expressive face I felt more than ever how true a descendant
he was of that long line of high-blooded, fiery, and masterful men. There
were pride, valour, and strength in his thick brows, his sensitive nostrils,
and his large hazel eyes. If on that forbidding moor a difficult and
dangerous quest should lie before us, this was at least a comrade for
whom one might venture to take a risk with the certainty that he would
bravely share it.

The train pulled up at a small wayside station and we all descended.
Outside, beyond the low, white fence, a wagonette with a pair of cobs

was waiting. Our coming was evidently a great event, for stationmaster and porters clustered round us to carry out our luggage. It was a sweet, simple country spot, but I was surprised to observe that by the gate there stood two soldierly men in dark uniforms who leaned upon their short rifles and glanced keenly at us as we passed. The coachman, a hard-faced, gnarled little fellow, saluted Sir Henry Baskerville, and in a few minutes we were flying swiftly down the broad, white road. Rolling pasture lands curved upward on either side of us, and old gabled houses peeped out from amid the thick green foliage, but behind the peaceful and sunlit countryside there rose ever, dark against the evening sky, the long, gloomy curve of the moor, broken by the jagged and sinister hills.

The wagonette swung round into a side road, and we curved upward through deep lanes worn by centuries of wheels, high banks on either side, heavy with dripping moss and fleshy hart's-tongue ferns. Bronzing bracken and mottled bramble gleamed in the light of the sinking sun. Still steadily rising, we passed over a narrow granite bridge and skirted a noisy stream which gushed swiftly down, foaming and roaring amid the gray boulders. Both road and stream wound up through a valley dense with scrub oak and fir. At every turn Baskerville gave an exclamation of delight, looking eagerly about him and asking countless questions. To his eyes all seemed beautiful, but to me a tinge of melancholy lay upon the countryside, which bore so clearly the mark of the waning year. Yellow leaves carpeted the lanes and fluttered down upon us as we passed. The rattle of our wheels died away as we drove through drifts of rotting vegetation—sad gifts, as it seemed to me, for Nature to throw before the carriage of the returning heir of the Baskervilles.

"Halloa!" cried Dr. Mortimer, "what is this?"

A steep curve of heath-clad land, an outlying spur of the moor, lay in front of us. On the summit, hard and clear like an equestrian statue upon its pedestal, was a mounted soldier, dark and stern, his rifle poised ready over his forearm. He was watching the road along which we travelled.

"What is this, Perkins?" asked Dr. Mortimer.

Our driver half turned in his seat.

"There's a convict escaped from Princetown, sir. He's been out three days now, and the warders watch every road and every station, but they've had no sight of him yet. The farmers about here don't like it, sir, and that's a fact."

"Well, I understand that they get five pounds if they can give information."

"Yes, sir, but the chance of five pounds is but a poor thing compared to the chance of having your throat cut. You see, it isn't like any ordinary convict. This is a man that would stick at nothing."

"Who is he, then?"

"It is Selden, the Notting Hill murderer."

I remembered the case well, for it was one in which Holmes had taken an interest on account of the peculiar ferocity of the crime and the wanton brutality which had marked all the actions of the assassin. The commutation of his death sentence had been due to some doubts as to his complete sanity, so atrocious was his conduct. Our wagonette had topped a rise and in front of us rose the huge expanse of the moor, mottled with gnarled and craggy cairns and tors. A cold wind swept down from it and set us shivering. Somewhere there, on that desolate plain, was lurking this fiendish man, hiding in a burrow like a wild beast, his heart full of malignancy against the whole race which had cast him out. It needed but this to complete the grim suggestiveness of the barren waste, the chilling wind, and the darkling sky. Even Baskerville fell silent and pulled his overcoat more closely around him.

We had left the fertile country behind and beneath us. We looked back on it now, the slanting rays of a low sun turning the streams to threads of gold and glowing on the red earth new turned by the plough and the broad tangle of the woodlands. The road in front of us grew bleaker and wilder over huge russet and olive slopes, sprinkled with giant boulders. Now and then we passed a moorland cottage, walled and roofed with stone, with no creeper to break its harsh outline. Suddenly we looked down into a cuplike depression, patched with stunted oaks and firs which had been twisted and bent by the fury of years of storm. Two high, narrow towers rose over the trees. The driver pointed with his whip.

"Baskerville Hall," said he.

Its master had risen and was staring with flushed cheeks and shining eyes. A few minutes later we had reached the lodge-gates, a maze of fantastic tracery in wrought iron, with weather-bitten pillars on either side, blotched with lichens, and surmounted by the boars' heads of the Baskervilles. The lodge was a ruin of black granite and bared ribs of rafters, but facing it was a new building, half constructed, the first fruit of Sir Charles's South African gold.

Through the gateway we passed into the avenue, where the wheels were again hushed amid the leaves, and the old trees shot their branches in a sombre tunnel over our heads. Baskerville shuddered as he looked up the long, dark drive to where the house glimmered like a ghost at the farther end.

"Was it here?" he asked in a low voice.

"No, no, the yew alley is on the other side."

The young heir glanced round with a gloomy face.

"It's no wonder my uncle felt as if trouble were coming on him in such a place as this," said he. "It's enough to scare any man. I'll have a row of electric lamps up here inside of six months, and you won't know it again, with a thousand candle-power Swan and Edison right here in front of the hall door."

The avenue opened into a broad expanse of turf, and the house lay before us. In the fading light I could see that the centre was a heavy block of building from which a porch projected. The whole front was draped in ivy, with a patch clipped bare here and there where a window or a coat of arms broke through the dark veil. From this central block rose the twin towers, ancient, crenellated, and pierced with many loopholes. To right and left of the turrets were more modern wings of black granite. A dull light shone through heavy mullioned windows, and from the high chimneys which rose from the steep, high-angled roof there sprang a single black column of smoke.

"Welcome, Sir Henry! Welcome to Baskerville Hall!"

A tall man had stepped from the shadow of the porch to open the door of the wagonette. The figure of a woman was silhouetted against the yellow light of the hall. She came out and helped the man to hand down our bags.

"You don't mind my driving straight home, Sir Henry?" said Dr. Mortimer. "My wife is expecting me."

"Surely you will stay and have some dinner?"

"No, I must go. I shall probably find some work awaiting me. I would stay to show you over the house, but Barrymore will be a better guide than I. Good-bye, and never hesitate night or day to send for me if I can be of service."

The wheels died away down the drive while Sir Henry and I turned into the hall, and the door clanged heavily behind us. It was a fine apartment in which we found ourselves, large, lofty, and heavily raftered with huge baulks of age-blackened oak. In the great old-fashioned fireplace behind the high iron dogs a log-fire crackled and snapped. Sir Henry and I held out our hands to it, for we were numb from our long drive. Then we gazed round us at the high, thin window of old stained glass, the oak panelling, the stags' heads, the coats of arms upon the walls, all dim and sombre in the subdued light of the central lamp.

"It's just as I imagined it," said Sir Henry. "Is it not the very picture of an old family home? To think that this should be the same hall in which for five hundred years my people have lived. It strikes me solemn to think of it."

I saw his dark face lit up with a boyish enthusiasm as he gazed about him. The light beat upon him where he stood, but long shadows trailed down the walls and hung like a black canopy above him. Barrymore had returned from taking our luggage to our rooms. He stood in front of us now with the subdued manner of a well-trained servant. He was a remarkable-looking man, tall, handsome, with a square black beard and pale, distinguished features.

"Would you wish dinner to be served at once, sir?"

"Is it ready?"

"In a very few minutes, sir. You will find hot water in your rooms. My wife and I will be happy, Sir Henry, to stay with you until you have made your fresh arrangements, but you will understand that under the new conditions this house will require a considerable staff."

"What new conditions?"

"I only meant, sir, that Sir Charles led a very retired life, and we were able to look after his wants. You would, naturally, wish to have more company, and so you will need changes in your household."

"Do you mean that your wife and you wish to leave?"

"Only when it is quite convenient to you, sir."

"But your family have been with us for several generations, have they not? I should be sorry to begin my life here by breaking an old family connection."

I seemed to discern some signs of emotion upon the butler's white face.

"I feel that also, sir, and so does my wife. But to tell the truth, sir, we were both very much attached to Sir Charles and his death gave us a shock and made these surroundings very painful to us. I fear that we shall never again be easy in our minds at Baskerville Hall."

"But what do you intend to do?"

"I have no doubt, sir, that we shall succeed in establishing ourselves in some business. Sir Charles's generosity has given us the means to do so. And now, sir, perhaps I had best show you to your rooms."

A square balustraded gallery ran round the top of the old hall, approached by a double stair. From this central point two long corridors extended the whole length of the building, from which all the bedrooms opened. My own was in the same wing as Baskerville's and almost next door to it. These rooms appeared to be much more modern than the central part of the house, and the bright paper and numerous candles did something to remove the sombre impression which our arrival had left upon my mind.

But the dining-room which opened out of the hall was a place of shadow and gloom. It was a long chamber with a step separating the dais where the family sat from the lower portion reserved for their dependents. At one end a minstrel's gallery overlooked it. Black beams shot across above our heads, with a smoke-darkened ceiling beyond them. With rows of flaring torches to light it up, and the colour and rude hilarity of an old-time banquet, it might have softened; but now, when two black-clothed gentlemen sat in the little circle of light thrown by a shaded lamp, one's voice became hushed and one's spirit subdued. A dim line of ancestors, in every variety of dress, from the Elizabethan knight to the buck of the Regency, stared down upon us and daunted us by their silent company. We talked little, and I for one was glad when the meal was over and we were able to retire into the modern billiard-room and smoke a cigarette.

"My word, it isn't a very cheerful place," said Sir Henry. "I suppose one can tone down to it, but I feel a bit out of the picture at present. I don't wonder that my uncle got a little jumpy if he lived all alone in such a house as this. However, if it suits you, we will retire early to-night, and perhaps things may seem more cheerful in the morning."

I drew aside my curtains before I went to bed and looked out from my window. It opened upon the grassy space which lay in front of the hall door. Beyond, two copses of trees moaned and swung in a rising wind. A half moon broke through the rifts of racing clouds. In its cold light I saw beyond the trees a broken fringe of rocks, and the long, low curve of the melancholy moor. I closed the curtain, feeling that my last impression was in keeping with the rest.

And yet it was not quite the last. I found myself weary and yet wakeful, tossing restlessly from side to side, seeking for the sleep which would not come. Far away a chiming clock struck out the quarters of the hours, but otherwise a deathly silence lay upon the old house. And then suddenly, in the very dead of the night, there came a sound to my ears, clear, resonant, and unmistakable. It was the sob of a woman, the muffled, strangling gasp of one who is torn by an uncontrollable sorrow. I sat up in bed and listened intently. The noise could not have been far away and was certainly in the house. For half an hour I waited with every nerve on the alert, but there came no other sound save the chiming clock and the rustle of the ivy on the wall.

7   THE STAPLETONS OF MERRIPIT HOUSE

The fresh beauty of the following morning did something to efface from our minds the grim and gray impression which had been left upon both of us by our first experience of Baskerville Hall. As Sir Henry and I sat at breakfast the sunlight flooded in through the high mullioned windows, throwing watery patches of colour from the coats of arms which covered them. The dark panelling glowed like bronze in the golden rays, and it was hard to realize that this was indeed the chamber which had struck such a gloom into our souls upon the evening before.

"I guess it is ourselves and not the house that we have to blame!" said the baronet. "We were tired with our journey and chilled by our drive, so we took a gray view of the place. Now we are fresh and well, so it is all cheerful once more."

"And yet it was not entirely a question of imagination," I answered. "Did you, for example, happen to hear someone, a woman I think, sobbing in the night?"

"That is curious, for I did when I was half asleep fancy that I heard something of the sort. I waited quite a time, but there was no more of it, so I concluded that it was all a dream."

"I heard it distinctly, and I am sure that it was really the sob of a woman."

"We must ask about this right away." He rang the bell and asked Barrymore whether he could account for our experience. It seemed to me that the pallid features of the butler turned a shade paler still as he listened to his master's question.

"There are only two women in the house, Sir Henry," he answered. "One is the scullery-maid, who sleeps in the other wing. The other is my wife, and I can answer for it that the sound could not have come from her."

And yet he lied as he said it, for it chanced that after breakfast I met Mrs. Barrymore in the long corridor with the sun full upon her face. She was a large, impassive, heavy-featured woman with a stern set expression of mouth. But her telltale eyes were red and glanced at me from between swollen lids. It was she, then, who wept in the night, and if she did so her husband must know it. Yet he had taken the obvious risk of discovery in declaring that it was not so. Why had he done this? And why did she weep so bitterly? Already round this pale-faced, handsome, black-bearded man there was gathering an atmosphere of mystery and of gloom. It was he who had been the first to discover the body of Sir Charles, and we had only his word for all the circumstances which led up to the old man's death. Was it possible that it was Barrymore, after all, whom we had seen in the cab in Regent Street? The beard might well have been the same. The cabman had described a somewhat shorter man, but such an impression might easily have been erroneous. How could I settle the point forever? Obviously the first thing to do was to see the Grimpen postmaster and find whether the test telegram had really been placed in Barrymore's own hands. Be the answer what it might, I should at least have something to report to Sherlock Holmes.

Sir Henry had numerous papers to examine after breakfast, so that the time was propitious for my excursion. It was a pleasant walk of four miles along the edge of the moor, leading me at last to a small gray hamlet, in which two larger buildings, which proved to be the inn and the house of Dr. Mortimer, stood high above the rest. The postmaster, who was also the village grocer, had a clear recollection of the telegram.

"Certainly, sir," said he, "I had the telegram delivered to Mr. Barrymore exactly as directed."

"Who delivered it?"

"My boy here. James, you delivered that telegram to Mr. Barrymore at the Hall last week, did you not?"

"Yes, father, I delivered it."

"Into his own hands?" I asked.

"Well, he was up in the loft at the time, so that I could not put it into his own hands, but I gave it into Mrs. Barrymore's hands, and she promised to deliver it at once."

"Did you see Mr. Barrymore?"

"No, sir; I tell you he was in the loft."

"If you didn't see him, how do you know he was in the loft?"

"Well, surely his own wife ought to know where he is," said the postmaster testily. "Didn't he get the telegram? If there is any mistake it is for Mr. Barrymore himself to complain."

It seemed hopeless to pursue the inquiry any farther, but it was clear that in spite of Holmes's ruse we had no proof that Barrymore had not been in London all the time. Suppose that it were so—suppose that the same man had been the last who had seen Sir Charles alive, and the first to dog the new heir when he returned to England. What then? Was he the agent of others or had he some sinister design of his own? What interest could he have in persecuting the Baskerville family? I thought of the strange warning clipped out of the leading article of the *Times*. Was that his work or was it possibly the doing of someone who was bent upon counteracting his schemes? The only conceivable motive was that which had been suggested by Sir Henry, that if the family could be scared away a comfortable and permanent home would be secured for the Barrymores. But surely such an explanation as that would be quite inadequate to account for the deep and subtle scheming which seemed to be weaving an invisible net round the young baronet. Holmes himself had said that no more complex case had come to him in all the long series of his sensational investigations. I prayed, as I walked back along the gray, lonely road, that my friend might soon be freed from his preoccupations and able to come down to take this heavy burden of responsibility from my shoulders.

Suddenly my thoughts were interrupted by the sound of running feet behind me and by a voice which called me by name. I turned, expecting to see Dr. Mortimer, but to my surprise it was a stranger who was pursuing me. He was a small, slim, clean-shaven, prim-faced man, flaxen-haired and lean-jawed, between thirty and forty years of age, dressed in a gray suit and wearing a straw hat. A tin box for botanical specimens hung over his shoulder and he carried a green butterfly-net in one of his hands.

"You will, I am sure, excuse my presumption, Dr. Watson," said he as he came panting up to where I stood. "Here on the moor we are homely folk and do not wait for formal introductions. You may possibly have heard my name from our mutual friend, Mortimer. I am Stapleton, of Merripit House."

"Your net and box would have told me as much," said I, "for I knew that Mr. Stapleton was a naturalist. But how did you know me?"

"I have been calling on Mortimer, and he pointed you out to me from the window of his surgery as you passed. As our road lay the same way I thought that I would overtake you and introduce myself. I trust that Sir Henry is none the worse for his journey?"

"He is very well, thank you."

"We were all rather afraid that after the sad death of Sir Charles the new baronet might refuse to live here. It is asking much of a wealthy man to come down and bury himself in a place of this kind, but I need not tell you that it means a very great deal to the countryside. Sir Henry has, I suppose, no superstitious fears in the matter?"

"I do not think that it is likely."

"Of course you know the legend of the fiend dog which haunts the family?"

"I have heard it."

"It is extraordinary how credulous the peasants are about here! Any number of them are ready to swear that they have seen such a creature upon the moor." He spoke with a smile, but I seemed to read in his eyes that he took the matter more seriously. "The story took a great hold upon the imagination of Sir Charles, and I have no doubt that it led to his tragic end."

"But how?"

"His nerves were so worked up that the appearance of any dog might have had a fatal effect upon his diseased heart. I fancy that he really did see something of the kind upon that last night in the yew alley. I feared that some disaster might occur, for I was very fond of the old man, and I knew that his heart was weak."

"How did you know that?"

"My friend Mortimer told me."

"You think, then, that some dog pursued Sir Charles, and that he died of fright in consequence?"

"Have you any better explanation?"

"I have not come to any conclusion."

"Has Mr. Sherlock Holmes?"

The words took away my breath for an instant, but a glance at the placid face and steadfast eyes of my companion showed that no surprise was intended.

"It is useless for us to pretend that we do not know you, Dr. Watson," said he. "The records of your detective have reached us here, and you could not celebrate him without being known yourself. When Mortimer told me your name he could not deny your identity. If you are here, then it follows that Mr. Sherlock Holmes is interesting himself in the matter, and I am naturally curious to know what view he may take."

"I am afraid that I cannot answer that question."

"May I ask if he is going to honour us with a visit himself?"

"He cannot leave town at present. He has other cases which engage his attention."

"What a pity! He might throw some light on that which is so dark to us. But as to your own researches, if there is any possible way in which I can be of service to you I trust that you will command me. If I had any indication of the nature of your suspicions or how you propose to investigate the case, I might perhaps even now give you some aid or advice."

"I assure you that I am simply here upon a visit to my friend, Sir Henry, and that I need no help of any kind."

"Excellent!" said Stapleton. "You are perfectly right to be wary and discreet. I am justly reproved for what I feel was an unjustifiable intrusion, and I promise you that I will not mention the matter again."

We had come to a point where a narrow grassy path struck off from the road and wound away across the moor. A steep, boulder-sprinkled hill lay upon the right which had in bygone days been cut into a granite quarry. The face which was turned towards us formed a dark cliff, with ferns and brambles growing in its niches. From over a distant rise there floated a gray plume of smoke.

"A moderate walk along this moor-path brings us to Merripit House," said he. "Perhaps you will spare an hour that I may have the pleasure of introducing you to my sister."

My first thought was that I should be by Sir Henry's side. But then I remembered the pile of papers and bills with which his study table was littered. It was certain that I could not help with those. And Holmes had expressly said that I should study the neighbours upon the moor. I accepted Stapleton's invitation, and we turned together down the path.

"It is a wonderful place, the moor," said he, looking round over the undulating downs, long green rollers, with crests of jagged granite foaming up into fantastic surges. "You never tire of the moor. You cannot think the wonderful secrets which it contains. It is so vast, and so barren, and so mysterious."

"You know it well, then?"

"I have only been here two years. The residents would call me a newcomer. We came shortly after Sir Charles settled. But my tastes led me to explore every part of the country round, and I should think that there are few men who know it better than I do."

"Is it hard to know?"

"Very hard. You see, for example, this great plain to the north here with the queer hills breaking out of it. Do you observe anything remarkable about that?"

"It would be a rare place for a gallop."

"You would naturally think so and the thought has cost several their lives before now. You notice those bright green spots scattered thickly over it?"

"Yes, they seem more fertile than the rest."

Stapleton laughed.

"That is the great Grimpen Mire," said he. "A false step yonder means death to man or beast. Only yesterday I saw one of the moor ponies wander into it. He never came out. I saw his head for quite a long time craning out of the bog-hole, but it sucked him down at last. Even in dry seasons it is a danger to cross it, but after these autumn rains it is an awful place. And yet I can find my way to the very heart of it and return alive. By George, there is another of those miserable ponies!"

Something brown was rolling and tossing among the green sedges. Then a long, agonized, writhing neck shot upward and a dreadful cry echoed over the moor. It turned me cold with horror, but my companion's nerves seemed to be stronger than mine.

"It's gone!" said he. "The mire has him. Two in two days, and many more, perhaps, for they get in the way of going there in the dry weather and never know the difference until the mire has them in its clutches. It's a bad place, the great Grimpen Mire."

"And you say you can penetrate it?"

"Yes, there are one or two paths which a very active man can take. I have found them out."

"But why should you wish to go into so horrible a place?"

"Well, you see the hills beyond? They are really islands cut off on all sides by the impassable mire, which has crawled round them in the course of years. That is where the rare plants and the butterflies are, if you have the wit to reach them."

"I shall try my luck some day."

He looked at me with a surprised face.

"For God's sake put such an idea out of your mind," said he. "Your blood would be upon my head. I assure you that there would not be the least chance of your coming back alive. It is only by remembering certain complex landmarks that I am able to do it."

"Halloa!" I cried. "What is that?"

A long, low moan, indescribably sad, swept over the moor. It filled the whole air, and yet it was impossible to say whence it came. From a dull murmur it swelled into a deep roar, and then sank back into a melancholy, throbbing murmur once again. Stapleton looked at me with a curious expression in his face.

"Queer place, the moor!" said he.

"But what is it?"

"The peasants say it is the Hound of the Baskervilles calling for its prey. I've heard it once or twice before, but never quite so loud."

I looked round, with a chill of fear in my heart, at the huge swelling plain, mottled with the green patches of rushes. Nothing stirred over the vast expanse save a pair of ravens, which croaked loudly from a tor behind us.

"You are an educated man. You don't believe such nonsense as that?" said I. "What do you think is the cause of so strange a sound?"

"Bogs make queer noises sometimes. It's the mud settling, or the water rising, or something."

"No, no, that was a living voice."

"Well, perhaps it was. Did you ever hear a bittern booming?"

"No, I never did."

"It's a very rare bird—practically extinct—in England now, but all things are possible upon the moor. Yes, I should not be surprised to learn that what we have heard is the cry of the last of the bitterns."

"It's the weirdest, strangest thing that ever I heard in my life."

"Yes, it's rather an uncanny place altogether. Look at the hillside yonder. What do you make of those?"

The whole steep slope was covered with gray circular rings of stone, a score of them at least.

"What are they? Sheep-pens?"

"No, they are the homes of our worthy ancestors. Prehistoric man lived thickly on the moor, and as no one in particular has lived there since, we find all his little arrangements exactly as he left them. These are his wigwams with the roofs off. You can even see his hearth and his couch if you have the curiosity to go inside."

"But it is quite a town. When was it inhabited?"

"Neolithic man—no date."

"What did he do?"

"He grazed his cattle on these slopes, and he learned to dig for tin when the bronze sword began to supersede the stone axe. Look at the great trench in the opposite hill. That is his mark. Yes, you will find some very singular points about the moor, Dr. Watson. Oh, excuse me an instant! It is surely Cyclopides."

A small fly or moth had fluttered across our path, and in an instant Stapleton was rushing with extraordinary energy and speed in pursuit of it. To my dismay the creature flew straight for the great mire, and my acquaintance never paused for an instant, bounding from tuft to tuft behind it, his green net waving in the air. His gray clothes and jerky, zigzag, irregular progress made him not unlike some huge moth himself. I was standing watching his pursuit with a mixture of admiration for his extraordinary activity and fear lest he should lose his footing in the treacherous mire when I heard the sound of steps and, turning round, found a woman near me upon the path. She had come from the direction in which the plume of smoke indicated the position of Merripit House, but the dip of the moor had hid her until she was quite close.

I could not doubt that this was the Miss Stapleton of whom I had been told, since ladies of any sort must be few upon the moor, and I remembered that I had heard someone describe her as being a beauty. The woman who approached me was certainly that, and of a most uncommon type. There could not have been a greater contrast between brother and sister, for Stapleton was neutral tinted, with light hair and gray eyes, while she was darker than any brunette whom I have seen in England—slim, elegant, and tall. She had a proud, finely cut face, so regular that it might have seemed impassive were it not for the sensitive mouth and the beautiful dark, eager eyes. With her perfect figure and elegant dress she was, indeed, a strange apparition upon a lonely moorland path. Her eyes were on her brother as I turned, and then she quickened her pace towards me. I had raised my hat and was about to make some explanatory remark when her own words turned all my thoughts into a new channel.

"Go back!" she said. "Go straight back to London, instantly."

I could only stare at her in stupid surprise. Her eyes blazed at me, and she tapped the ground impatiently with her foot.

"Why should I go back?" I asked.

"I cannot explain." She spoke in a low, eager voice, with a curious lisp in her utterance. "But for God's sake do what I ask you. Go back and never set foot upon the moor again."

"But I have only just come."

"Man, man!" she cried. "Can you not tell when a warning is for your own good? Go back to London! Start to-night! Get away from this place at all costs! Hush, my brother is coming! Not a word of what I have said. Would you mind getting that orchid for me among the mare's-tails yonder? We are very rich in orchids on the moor, though, of course, you are rather late to see the beauties of the place."

Stapleton had abandoned the chase and came back to us breathing hard and flushed with his exertions.

"Halloa, Beryl!" said he, and it seemed to me that the tone of his greeting was not altogether a cordial one.

"Well, Jack, you are very hot."

"Yes, I was chasing a Cyclopides. He is very rare and seldom found in the late autumn. What a pity that I should have missed him!" He spoke unconcernedly, but his small light eyes glanced incessantly from the girl to me.

"You have introduced yourselves, I can see."

"Yes. I was telling Sir Henry that it was rather late for him to see the true beauties of the moor."

"Why, who do you think this is?"

"I imagine that it must be Sir Henry Baskerville."

"No, no," said I. "Only a humble commoner, but his friend. My name is Dr. Watson."

A flush of vexation passed over her expressive face. "We have been talking at cross purposes," said she.

"Why, you had not very much time for talk," her brother remarked with the same questioning eyes.

"I talked as if Dr. Watson were a resident instead of being merely a visitor," said she. "It cannot much matter to him whether it is early or late for the orchids. But you will come on, will you not, and see Merripit House?"

A short walk brought us to it, a bleak moorland house, once the farm of some grazier in the old prosperous days, but now put into repair and turned into a modern dwelling. An orchard surrounded it, but the trees, as is usual upon the moor, were stunted and nipped, and the effect of the whole place was mean and melancholy. We were admitted by a strange, wizened, rusty-coated old manservant, who seemed in keeping with the house. Inside, however, there were large rooms furnished with an elegance in which I seemed to recognize the taste of the lady. As I looked from their windows at the interminable granite-flecked moor rolling unbroken to the farthest horizon I could not but marvel at what could have brought this highly educated man and this beautiful woman to live in such a place.

"Queer spot to choose, is it not?" said he as if in answer to my thought. "And yet we manage to make ourselves fairly happy, do we not, Beryl?"

"Quite happy," said she, but there was no ring of conviction in her words.

"I had a school," said Stapleton. "It was in the north country. The work to a man of my temperament was mechanical and uninteresting, but the privilege of living with youth, of helping to mould those young minds, and of impressing them with one's own character and ideals was very dear to me. However, the fates were against us. A serious epidemic broke out in the school and three of the boys died. It never recovered from the blow, and much of my capital was irretrievably swallowed up. And yet, if it were not for the loss of the charming companionship of the boys, I could rejoice over my own misfortune, for, with my strong tastes for botany and zoology, I find an unlimited field of work here, and my sister is as devoted to Nature as I am. All this, Dr. Watson, has been brought upon your head by your expression as you surveyed the moor out of our window."

"It certainly did cross my mind that it might be a little dull—less for you, perhaps, than for your sister."

"No, no, I am never dull," said she quickly.

"We have books, we have our studies, and we have interesting neighbours. Dr. Mortimer is a most learned man in his own line. Poor Sir Charles was also an admirable companion. We knew him well and miss him more than I can tell. Do you think that I should intrude if I were to call this afternoon and make the acquaintance of Sir Henry?"

"I am sure that he would be delighted."

"Then perhaps you would mention that I propose to do so. We may in our humble way do something to make things more easy for him until he becomes accustomed to his new surroundings. Will you come upstairs, Dr. Watson, and inspect my collection of *Lepidoptera?* I think it is the most complete one in the south-west of England. By the time that you have looked through them lunch will be almost ready."

But I was eager to get back to my charge. The melancholy of the moor, the death of the unfortunate pony, the weird sound which had been associated with the grim legend of the Baskervilles, all these things tinged my thoughts with sadness. Then on the top of these more or less vague impressions there had come the definite and distinct warning of Miss Stapleton, delivered with such intense earnestness that I could not doubt that some grave and deep reason lay behind it. I resisted all pressure to stay for lunch, and I set off at once upon my return journey, taking the grass-grown path by which we had come.

It seems, however, that there must have been some short cut for those who knew it, for before I had reached the road I was astounded to see Miss Stapleton sitting upon a rock by the side of the track. Her face was beautifully flushed with her exertions, and she held her hand to her side.

"I have run all the way in order to cut you off, Dr. Watson," said she. "I had not even time to put on my hat. I must not stop, or my brother may miss me. I wanted to say to you how sorry I am about the stupid mistake I made in thinking that you were Sir Henry. Please forget the words I said, which have no application whatever to you."

"But I can't forget them, Miss Stapleton," said I. "I am Sir Henry's friend, and his welfare is a very close concern of mine. Tell me why it was that you were so eager that Sir Henry should return to London."

"A woman's whim, Dr. Watson. When you know me better you will understand that I cannot always give reasons for what I say or do."

"No, no. I remember the thrill in your voice. I remember the look in your eyes. Please, please, be frank with me, Miss Stapleton, for ever since I have been here I have been conscious of shadows all round me. Life has become like that great Grimpen Mire, with little green patches everywhere into which one may sink and with no guide to point the track. Tell me then what it was that you meant, and I will promise to convey your warning to Sir Henry."

An expression of irresolution passed for an instant over her face, but her eyes had hardened again when she answered me.

"You make too much of it, Dr. Watson," said she. "My brother and I were very much shocked by the death of Sir Charles. We knew him very intimately, for his favourite walk was over the moor to our house. He was deeply impressed with the curse which hung over his family, and when this tragedy came I naturally felt that there must be some grounds for the fears which he had expressed. I was distressed therefore when another member of the family came down to live here, and I felt that he should be warned of the danger which he will run. That was all which I intended to convey."

"But what is the danger?"

"You know the story of the hound?"

"I do not believe in such nonsense."

"But I do. If you have any influence with Sir Henry, take him away from a place which has always been fatal to his family. The world is wide. Why should he wish to live at the place of danger?"

"Because it *is* the place of danger. That is Sir Henry's nature. I fear that unless you can give me some more definite information than this it would be impossible to get him to move."

"I cannot say anything definite, for I do not know anything definite."

"I would ask you one more question, Miss Stapleton. If you meant no more than this when you first spoke to me, why should you not wish your brother to overhear what you said? There is nothing to which he, or anyone else, could object."

"My brother is very anxious to have the Hall inhabited, for he thinks that it is for the good of the poor folk upon the moor. He would be very angry if he knew that I had said anything which might induce Sir Henry to go away. But I have done my duty now and I will say no more. I must get back, or he will miss me and suspect that I have seen you. Goodbye!" She turned and had disappeared in a few minutes among the scattered boulders, while I, with my soul full of vague fears, pursued my way to Baskerville Hall.

From this point onward I will follow the course of events by transcribing my own letters to Mr. Sherlock Holmes which lie before me on the table. One page is missing, but otherwise they are exactly as written and show my feelings and suspicions of the moment more accurately than my memory, clear as it is upon these tragic events, can possibly do.

Baskerville Hall, October 13th.

My dear Holmes:

My previous letters and telegrams have kept you pretty well up to date as to all that has occurred in this most God-forsaken corner of the world. The longer one stays here the more does the spirit of the moor sink into one's soul, its vastness, and also its grim charm. When you are once out upon its bosom you have left all traces of modern England behind you, but, on the other hand, you are conscious everywhere of the homes and the work of the prehistoric people. On all sides of you as you walk are the houses of these forgotten folk, with their graves and the huge monoliths which are supposed to have marked their temples. As you look at their gray stone huts against the scarred hillsides you leave your own age behind you, and if you were to see a skin-clad, hairy man crawl out from the low door, fitting a flint-tipped arrow on to the string of his bow, you would feel that his presence there was more natural than your own. The strange thing is that they should have lived so thickly on what must always have been most unfruitful soil. I am no antiquarian, but I could imagine that they were some unwarlike and harried race who were forced to accept that which none other would occupy.

All this, however is foreign to the mission on which you sent me and will probably be very uninteresting to your severely practical mind. I can still remember your complete indifference as to whether the sun moved round the earth or the earth round the sun. Let me, therefore, return to the facts concerning Sir Henry Baskerville.

If you have not had any report within the last few days it is because up to to-day there was nothing of importance to relate. Then a very surprising circumstance occurred, which I shall tell you in due course. But, first of all, I must keep you in touch with some of the other factors in the situation.

One of these, concerning which I have said little, is the escaped convict upon the moor. There is strong reason now to believe that he has got right away, which is a considerable relief to the lonely householders of this district. A fortnight has passed since his flight, during which he has not been seen and nothing has been heard of him. It is surely inconceivable that he could have held out upon the moor during all that time. Of course, so far as his concealment goes there is no difficulty at all. Any one of these stone huts would give him a hiding-place. But there is nothing to eat unless he were to catch and slaughter one of the moor sheep. We think, therefore, that he has gone, and the outlying farmers sleep the better in consequence.

We are four able-bodied men in this household, so that we could take good care of ourselves, but I confess that I have had uneasy moments when I have thought of the Stapletons. They live miles from any help. There are one maid, an old manservant, the sister, and the brother, the latter not a very strong man. They would be helpless in the hands of a desperate fellow like this Notting Hill criminal if he could once effect an entrance. Both Sir Henry and I were concerned at their situation, and it was suggested that Perkins the groom should go over to sleep there, but Stapleton would not hear of it.

The fact is that our friend, the baronet, begins to display a considerable interest in our fair neighbour. It is not to be wondered at, for time hangs heavily in this lonely spot to an active man like him, and she is a very fascinating and beautiful woman. There is something tropical and exotic about her which forms a singular contrast to her cool and unemotional brother. Yet he also gives the idea of hidden fires. He has certainly a very marked influence over her, for I have seen her continually glance at him as she talked as if seeking approbation for what she said. I trust that he is kind to her. There is a dry glitter in his eyes and a firm set of his thin lips, which goes with a positive and possibly a harsh nature. You would find him an interesting study.

He came over to call upon Baskerville on that first day, and the very next morning he took us both to show us the spot where the legend of the wicked Hugo is supposed to have had its origin. It was an excursion of some miles across the moor to a place which is so dismal that it might have suggested the story. We found a short valley between rugged tors which led to an open, grassy space flecked over with the white cotton grass. In the middle of it rose two great stones, worn and sharpened at the upper end until they looked like the huge corroding fangs of some monstrous beast. In every way it corresponded with the scene of the old tragedy. Sir Henry was much interested and asked Stapleton more than once whether he did really believe in the possibility of the interference of the supernatural in the affairs of men. He spoke lightly, but it was evident that he was very much in earnest. Stapleton was guarded in his replies, but it was easy to see that he said less than he might, and that he would not express his whole opinion out of consideration for the feelings of the baronet. He told us of similar cases, where families had suffered from some evil influence, and he left us with the impression that he shared the popular view upon the matter.

On our way back we stayed for lunch at Merripit House, and it was there that Sir Henry made the acquaintance of Miss Stapleton. From the first moment that he saw her he appeared to be strongly attracted by her, and I am much mistaken if the feeling was not mutual. He referred to her again and again on our walk home, and since then hardly a day has passed that we have not seen something of the brother and sister. They dine here to-night, and there is some talk of our going to them next week. One would imagine that such a match would be very welcome to Stapleton, and yet I have more than once caught a look of the strongest disapprobation in his face when Sir Henry has been paying some attention to his sister. He is much attached to her, no doubt, and would lead a lonely life without her, but it would seem the height of selfishness if he were to stand in the way of her making so brilliant a marriage. Yet I am certain that he does not wish their intimacy to ripen into love, and I have several times observed that he has taken pains to prevent them from being tête-à-tête. By the way, your instructions to me never to allow Sir Henry to go out alone will become very much more onerous if a love affair were to be added to our other difficulties. My popularity would soon suffer if I were to carry out your orders to the letter.

The other day—Thursday, to be more exact—Dr. Mortimer lunched with us. He has been excavating a barrow at Long Down and has got a prehistoric skull which fills him with great joy. Never was there such a single-minded enthusiast as he! The Stapletons came in afterwards, and the good doctor took us all to the yew alley at Sir Henry's request to show us exactly how everything occurred upon that fatal night. It is a long, dismal walk, the yew alley, between two high walls of clipped hedge, with a narrow band of grass upon either side. At the far end is an old tumble-down summer-house. Halfway down is the moor-gate, where the old gentleman left his cigar-ash. It is a white wooden gate with a latch. Beyond it lies the wide moor. I remembered your theory of the affair and tried to picture all that had occurred. As the old man stood there he saw something coming across the moor, something which terrified him so that he lost his wits and ran and ran until he died of sheer horror and exhaustion. There was the long gloomy tunnel down which he fled. And from what? A sheep-dog of the moor? Or a spectral hound, black, silent, and monstrous? Was there a human agency in the matter? Did the pale, watchful Barrymore know more than he cared to say? It was all dim and vague, but always there is the dark shadow of crime behind it.

One other neighbour I have met since I wrote last. This is Mr. Frankland, of Lafter Hall, who lives some four miles to the south of us. He is an elderly man, red-faced, white-haired, and choleric. His passion is for the British law, and he has spent a large fortune in litigation. He fights for the mere pleasure of fighting and is equally ready to take up either side of a question, so that it is no wonder that he has found it a costly amusement. Sometimes he will shut up a right of way and defy the parish to make him open it. At others he will with his own hands tear down some other man's gate and declare that a path has existed there from time immemorial, defying the owner to prosecute him for trespass. He is learned in old manorial and communal rights, and he applies his knowledge sometimes in favour of the villagers of Fernworthy and sometimes against them, so that he is periodically either carried in triumph down the village street or else burned in effigy, according to his latest exploit. He is said to have about seven lawsuits upon his hands at present, which will probably swallow up the remainder of his fortune and so draw his sting and leave him harmless for the future. Apart from the law he seems a kindly, good-natured person, and I only mention him because you were particular that I should send some description of the people who surround us. He is curiously employed at present, for, being an amateur astronomer, he has an excellent telescope, with which he lies upon the roof of his own house and sweeps the moor all day in the hope of catching a glimpse of the escaped convict. If he would confine his energies to this all would be well, but there are rumours that he intends to prosecute Dr. Mortimer for opening a grave without the consent of the next of kin because he dug up the neolithic skull in the barrow on Long Down. He helps to keep our lives from being monotonous and gives a little comic relief where it is badly needed.

And now, having brought you up to date in the escaped convict, the Stapletons, Dr. Mortimer, and Frankland, of Lafter Hall, let me end on that which is most important and tell you more about the Barrymores, and especially about the surprising development of last night.

First of all about the test telegram, which you sent from London in order to make sure that Barrymore was really here. I have already explained that the testimony of the postmaster shows that the test was worthless and that we have no proof one way or the other. I told Sir Henry how the matter stood, and he at once, in his downright fashion, had Barrymore up and asked him whether he had received the telegram himself. Barrymore said that he had.

"Did the boy deliver it into your own hands?" asked Sir Henry.

Barrymore looked surprised, and considered for a little time.

"No," said he, "I was in the box-room at the time, and my wife brought it up to me."

"Did you answer it yourself?"

"No; I told my wife what to answer and she went down to write it."

In the evening he recurred to the subject of his own accord.

"I could not quite understand the object of your questions this morning, Sir Henry," said he. "I trust that they do not mean that I have done anything to forfeit your confidence?"

Sir Henry had to assure him that it was not so and pacify him by giving him a considerable part of his old wardrobe, the London outfit having now all arrived.

Mrs. Barrymore is of interest to me. She is a heavy, solid person, very limited, intensely respectable, and inclined to be puritanical. You could hardly conceive a less emotional subject. Yet I have told you how, on the first night here, I heard her sobbing bitterly, and since then I have more than once observed traces of tears upon her face. Some deep sorrow gnaws ever at her heart. Sometimes I wonder if she has a guilty memory which haunts her, and sometimes I suspect Barrymore of being a domestic tyrant. I have always felt that there was something singular and questionable in this man's character, but the adventure of last night brings all my suspicions to a head.

And yet it may seem a small matter in itself. You are aware that I am not a very sound sleeper, and since I have been on guard in this house my slumbers have been lighter than ever. Last night, about two in the morning, I was aroused by a stealthy step passing my room. I rose, opened my door, and peeped out. A long black shadow was trailing down the corridor. It was thrown by a man who walked softly down the passage with a candle held in his hand. He was in shirt and trousers, with no covering to his feet. I could merely see the outline, but his height told me that it was Barrymore. He walked very slowly and circumspectly, and there was something indescribably guilty and furtive in his whole appearance.

I have told you that the corridor is broken by the balcony which runs round the hall, but that it is resumed upon the farther side. I waited until he had passed out of sight and then I followed him. When I came round the balcony he had reached the end of the farther corridor, and I could see from the glimmer of light through an open door that he had entered one of the rooms. Now, all these rooms are unfurnished and unoccupied, so that his expedition became more mysterious than ever. The light shone steadily as if he were standing motionless. I crept down the passage as noiselessly as I could and peeped round the corner of the door.

Barrymore was crouching at the window with the candle held against the glass. His profile was half turned towards me, and his face seemed to be rigid with expectation as he stared out into the blackness of the moor. For some minutes he stood watching intently. Then he gave a deep groan and with an impatient gesture he put out the light. Instantly I made my way back to my room, and very shortly came the stealthy steps passing once more upon their return journey. Long afterwards when I had fallen into a light sleep I heard a key turn somewhere in a lock, but I could not tell whence the sound came. What it all means I cannot guess, but there is some secret business going on in this house of gloom which sooner or later we shall get to the bottom of. I do not trouble you with my theories, for you asked me to furnish you only with facts. I have had a long talk with Sir Henry this morning, and we have made a plan of campaign founded upon my observations of last night. I will not speak about it just now, but it should make my next report interesting reading.

---

9   SECOND REPORT OF DR. WATSON: THE LIGHT UPON THE MOOR

Baskerville Hall, Oct. 15th.

My dear Holmes:

If I was compelled to leave you without much news during the early days of my mission you must acknowledge that I am making up for lost time, and that events are now crowding thick and fast upon us. In my last report I ended upon my top note with Barrymore at the window, and now I have quite a budget already which will, unless I am much mistaken, considerably surprise you. Things have taken a turn which I could not have anticipated. In some ways they have within the last forty-eight hours become much clearer and in some ways they have become more complicated. But I will tell you all and you shall judge for yourself.

Before breakfast on the morning following my adventure I went down the corridor and examined the room in which Barrymore had been on the night before. The western window through which he had stared so intently has, I noticed, one peculiarity above all other windows in the house—it commands the nearest outlook on to the moor. There is an opening between two trees which enables one from this point of view to look right down upon it, while from all the other windows it is only a distant glimpse which can be obtained. It follows, therefore, that Barrymore, since only this window would serve the purpose, must have been looking out for something or somebody upon the moor. The night was very dark, so that I can hardly imagine how he could have hoped to see anyone. It had struck me that it was possible that some love intrigue was on foot. That would have accounted for his stealthy movements and also for the uneasiness of his wife. The man is a striking-looking fellow, very well equipped to steal the heart of a country girl, so that this theory seemed to have something to support it. That opening of the door which I had heard after I had returned to my room might mean that he had gone out to keep some clandestine appointment. So I reasoned with myself in the morning, and I tell you the direction of my suspicions, however much the result may have shown that they were unfounded.

But whatever the true explanation of Barrymore's movements might be, I felt that the responsibility of keeping them to myself until I could explain them was more than I could bear. I had an interview with the baronet in his study after breakfast, and I told him all that I had seen. He was less surprised than I had expected.

"I knew that Barrymore walked about nights, and I had a mind to speak to him about it," said he. "Two or three times I have heard his steps in the passage, coming and going, just about the hour you name."

"Perhaps then he pays a visit every night to that particular window," I suggested.

"Perhaps he does. If so, we should be able to shadow him and see what it is that he is after. I wonder what your friend Holmes would do if he were here."

"I believe that he would do exactly what you now suggest," said I. "He would follow Barrymore and see what he did."

"Then we shall do it together."

"But surely he would hear us."

"The man is rather deaf, and in any case we must take our chance of that. We'll sit up in my room to-night and wait until he passes." Sir Henry rubbed his hands with pleasure, and it was evident that he hailed the adventure as a relief to his somewhat quiet life upon the moor.

The baronet has been in communication with the architect who prepared the plans for Sir Charles, and with a contractor from London, so that we may expect great changes to begin here soon. There have been decorators and furnishers up from Plymouth, and it is evident that our friend has large ideas and means to spare no pains or expense to restore the grandeur of his family. When the house is renovated and refurnished, all that he will need will be a wife to make it complete. Between ourselves there are pretty clear signs that this will not be wanting if the lady is willing, for I have seldom seen a man more infatuated with a woman than he is with our beautiful neighbour, Miss Stapleton. And yet the course of true love does not run quite as smoothly as one would under the circumstances expect. To-day, for example, its surface was broken by a very unexpected ripple, which has caused our friend considerable perplexity and annoyance.

After the conversation which I have quoted about Barrymore Sir Henry put on his hat and prepared to go out. As a matter of course I did the same.

"What, are *you* coming, Watson?" he asked, looking at me in a curious way.

"That depends on whether you are going on the moor," said I.

"Yes, I am."

"Well, you know what my instructions are. I am sorry to intrude, but you heard how earnestly Holmes insisted that I should not leave you, and especially that you should not go alone upon the moor."

Sir Henry put his hand upon my shoulder with a pleasant smile.

"My dear fellow," said he, "Holmes, with all his wisdom, did not foresee some things which have happened since I have been on the moor. You understand me? I am sure that you are the last man in the world who would wish to be a spoil-sport. I must go out alone."

It put me in a most awkward position. I was at a loss what to say or what to do, and before I had made up my mind he picked up his cane and was gone.

But when I came to think the matter over my conscience reproached me bitterly for having on any pretext allowed him to go out of my sight. I imagined what my feelings would be if I had to return to you and to confess that some misfortune had occurred through my disregard for your instructions. I assure you my cheeks flushed at the very thought. It might not even now be too late to overtake him, so I set off at once in the direction of Merripit House.

I hurried along the road at the top of my speed without seeing anything of Sir Henry, until I came to the point where the moor path branches off. There, fearing that perhaps I had come in the wrong direction after all, I mounted a hill from which I could command a view—the same hill which is cut into the dark quarry. Thence I saw him at once. He was on the moor path, about a quarter of a mile off, and a lady was by his side who could only be Miss Stapleton. It was clear that there was already an understanding between them and that they had met by appointment. They were walking slowly along in deep conversation, and I saw her making quick little movements of her hands as if she were very earnest in what she was saying, while he listened intently, and once or twice shook his head in strong dissent. I stood among the rocks watching them, very much puzzled as to what I should do next. To follow them and break into their intimate conversation seemed to be an outrage, and yet my clear duty was never for an instant to let him out of my sight. To act the spy upon a friend was a hateful task. Still, I could see no better course than to observe him from the hill, and to clear my conscience by confessing to him afterwards what I had done. It is true that if any sudden danger had threatened him I was too far away to be of use, and yet I am sure that you will agree with me that the position was very difficult, and that there was nothing more which I could do.

Our friend, Sir Henry, and the lady had halted on the path and were standing deeply absorbed in their conversation, when I was suddenly aware that I was not the only witness of their interview. A wisp of green floating in the air caught my eye, and another glance showed me that it was carried on a stick by a man who was moving among the broken ground. It was Stapleton with his butterfly-net. He was very much closer to the pair than I was, and he appeared to be moving in their direction. At this instant Sir Henry suddenly drew Miss Stapleton to his side. His arm was round her, but it seemed to me that she was straining away from him with her face averted. He stooped his head to hers, and she raised one hand as if in protest. Next moment I saw them spring apart and turn hurriedly round. Stapleton was the cause of the interruption. He was running wildly towards them, his absurd net dangling behind him. He gesticulated and almost danced with excitement in front of the lovers. What the scene meant I could not imagine, but it seemed to me that Stapleton was abusing Sir Henry, who offered explanations, which became more angry as the other refused to accept them. The lady stood by in haughty silence. Finally Stapleton turned upon his heel and beckoned in a peremptory way to his sister, who, after an irresolute glance at Sir Henry, walked off by the side of her brother. The naturalist's angry gestures showed that the lady was included in his displeasure. The baronet stood for a minute looking after them, and then he walked slowly back the way that he had come, his head hanging, the very picture of dejection.

What all this meant I could not imagine, but I was deeply ashamed to have witnessed so intimate a scene without my friend's knowledge. I ran down the hill therefore and met the baronet at the bottom. His face was flushed with anger and his brows were wrinkled, like one who is at his wit's ends what to do.

"Halloa, Watson! Where have you dropped from?" said he. "You don't mean to say that you came after me in spite of all?"

I explained everything to him: how I had found it impossible to remain behind, how I had followed him, and how I had witnessed all that had occurred. For an instant his eyes blazed at me, but my frankness disarmed his anger, and he broke at last into a rather rueful laugh.

"You would have thought the middle of that prairie a fairly safe place for a man to be private," said he, "but, by thunder, the whole countryside seems to have been out to see me do my wooing—and a mighty poor wooing at that! Where had you engaged a seat?"

"I was on that hill."

"Quite in the back row, eh? But her brother was well up to the front. Did you see him come out on us?"

"Yes, I did."

"Did he ever strike you as being crazy—this brother of hers?"

"I can't say that he ever did."

"I dare say not. I always thought him sane enough until to-day, but you can take it from me that either he or I ought to be in a strait-jacket. What's the matter with me, anyhow? You've lived near me for some weeks, Watson. Tell me straight, now! Is there anything that would prevent me from making a good husband to a woman that I loved?"

"I should say not."

"He can't object to my worldly position, so it must be myself that he has this down on. What has he against me? I never hurt man or woman in my life that I know of. And yet he would not so much as let me touch the tips of her fingers."

"Did he say so?"

"That, and a deal more. I tell you, Watson, I've only known her these few weeks, but from the first I just felt that she was made for me, and she, too—she was happy when she was with me, and that I'll swear. There's a light in a woman's eyes that speaks louder than words. But he has never let us get together, and it was only to-day for the first time that I saw a chance of having a few words with her alone. She was glad to meet me, but when she did it was not love that she would talk about, and she wouldn't have let me talk about it either if she could have stopped it. She kept coming back to it that this was a place of danger, and that she would never be happy until I had left it. I told her that since I had seen her I was in no hurry to leave it, and that if she really wanted me to go, the only way to work it was for her to arrange to go with me. With that I offered in as many words to marry her, but before she could answer, down came this brother of hers, running at us with a face on him like a madman. He was just white with rage, and those light eyes of his were blazing with fury. What was I doing with the lady? How dared I offer her attentions which were distasteful to her? Did I think that because I was a baronet I could do what I liked? If he had not been her brother I should have known better how to answer him. As it was I told him that my feelings towards his sister were such as I was not ashamed of, and that I hoped that she might honour me by becoming my wife. That seemed to make the matter no better, so then I lost my temper too, and I answered him rather more hotly than I should perhaps, considering that she was standing by. So it ended by his going off with her, as you saw, and here am I as badly puzzled a man as any in this county. Just tell me what it all means, Watson, and I'll owe you more than ever I can hope to pay."

I tried one or two explanations, but, indeed, I was completely puzzled myself. Our friend's title, his fortune, his age, his character, and his appearance are all in his favour, and I know nothing against him unless it be this dark fate which runs in his family. That his advances should be rejected so brusquely without any reference to the lady's own wishes and that the lady should accept the situation without protest is very amazing. However, our conjectures were set at rest by a visit from Stapleton himself that very afternoon. He had come to offer apologies for his rudeness of the morning, and after a long private interview with Sir Henry in his study the upshot of their conversation was that the breach is quite healed, and that we are to dine at Merripit House next Friday as a sign of it.

"I don't say now that he isn't a crazy man," said Sir Henry; "I can't forget the look in his eyes when he ran at me this morning, but I must allow that no man could make a more handsome apology than he has done."

"Did he give any explanation of his conduct?"

"His sister is everything in his life, he says. That is natural enough, and I am glad that he should understand her value. They have always been together, and according to his account he has been a very lonely man with only her as a companion, so that the thought of losing her was really terrible to him. He had not understood, he said, that I was becoming attached to her, but when he saw with his own eyes that it was really so, and that she might be taken away from him, it gave him such a shock that for a time he was not responsible for what he said or did. He was very sorry for all that had passed, and he recognized how foolish and how selfish it was that he should imagine that he could hold a beautiful woman like his sister to himself for her whole life. If she had to leave him he had rather it was to a neighbour like myself than to anyone else. But in any case it was a blow to him, and it would take him some time before he could prepare himself to meet it. He would withdraw all opposition upon his part if I would promise for three months to let the matter rest and to be content with cultivating the lady's friendship during that time without claiming her love. This I promised, and so the matter rests."

So there is one of our small mysteries cleared up. It is something to have touched bottom anywhere in this bog in which we are floundering. We know now why Stapleton looked with disfavour upon his sister's suitor—even when that suitor was so eligible a one as Sir Henry. And now I pass on to another thread which I have extricated out of the tangled skein, the mystery of the sobs in the night, of the tear-stained face of Mrs. Barrymore, of the secret journey of the butler to the western lattice window. Congratulate me, my dear Holmes, and tell me that I have not disappointed you as an agent—that you do not regret the confidence which you showed in me when you sent me down. All these things have by one night's work been thoroughly cleared.

I have said "by one night's work," but, in truth, it was by two nights' work, for on the first we drew entirely blank. I sat up with Sir Henry in his rooms until nearly three o'clock in the morning, but no sound of any sort did we hear except the chiming clock upon the stairs. It was a most melancholy vigil and ended by each of us falling asleep in our chairs. Fortunately we were not discouraged, and we determined to try again. The next night we lowered the lamp and sat smoking cigarettes without making the least sound. It was incredible how slowly the hours crawled by, and yet we were helped through it by the same sort of patient interest which the hunter must feel as he watches the trap into which he hopes the game may wander. One struck, and two, and we had almost for the second time given it up in despair when in an instant we both sat bolt upright in our chairs, with all our weary senses keenly on the alert once more. We had heard the creak of a step in the passage.

Very stealthily we heard it pass along until it died away in the distance. Then the baronet gently opened his door and we set out in pursuit. Already our man had gone round the gallery, and the corridor was all in darkness. Softly we stole along until we had come into the other wing. We were just in time to catch a glimpse of the tall, black-bearded figure, his shoulders rounded, as he tiptoed down the passage. Then he passed through the same door as before, and the light of the candle framed it in the darkness and shot one single yellow beam across the gloom of the corridor. We shuffled cautiously towards it, trying every plank before we dared to put our whole weight upon it. We had taken the precaution of leaving our boots behind us, but, even so, the old boards snapped and creaked beneath our tread. Sometimes it seemed impossible that he should fail to hear our approach. However, the man is fortunately rather deaf, and he was entirely preoccupied in that which he was doing. When at last we reached the door and peeped through we found him crouching at the window, candle in hand, his white, intent face pressed against the pane, exactly as I had seen him two nights before.

We had arranged no plan of campaign, but the baronet is a man to whom the most direct way is always the most natural. He walked into the room, and as he did so Barrymore sprang up from the window with a sharp hiss of his breath and stood, livid and trembling, before us. His dark eyes, glaring out of the white mask of his face, were full of horror and astonishment as he gazed from Sir Henry to me.

"What are you doing here, Barrymore?"

"Nothing, sir." His agitation was so great that he could hardly speak, and the shadows sprang up and down from the shaking of his candle. "It was the window, sir. I go round at night to see that they are fastened."

"On the second floor?"

"Yes, sir, all the windows."

"Look here, Barrymore," said Sir Henry sternly, "we have made up our minds to have the truth out of you, so it will save you trouble to tell it sooner rather than later. Come, now! No lies! What were you doing at that window?"

The fellow looked at us in a helpless way, and he wrung his hands together like one who is in the last extremity of doubt and misery.

"I was doing no harm, sir. I was holding a candle to the window."

"And why were you holding a candle to the window?"

"Don't ask me, Sir Henry—don't ask me! I give you my word, sir, that it is not my secret, and that I cannot tell it. If it concerned no one but myself I would not try to keep it from you."

A sudden idea occurred to me, and I took the candle from the trembling hand of the butler.

"He must have been holding it as a signal," said I. "Let us see if there is any answer." I held it as he had done, and stared out into the darkness of the night. Vaguely I could discern the black bank of the trees and the lighter expanse of the moor, for the moon was behind the clouds. And then I gave a cry of exultation, for a tiny pin-point of yellow light had suddenly transfixed the dark veil, and glowed steadily in the centre of the black square framed by the window.

"There it is!" I cried.

"No, no, sir, it is nothing—nothing at all!" the butler broke in; "I assure you, sir——"

"Move your light across the window, Watson!" cried the baronet. "See, the other moves also! Now, you rascal, do you deny that it is a signal? Come, speak up! Who is your confederate out yonder, and what is this conspiracy that is going on?"

The man's face became openly defiant.

"It is my business, and not yours. I will not tell."

"Then you leave my employment right away."

"Very good, sir. If I must I must."

"And you go in disgrace. By thunder, you may well be ashamed of yourself. Your family has lived with mine for over a hundred years under this roof, and here I find you deep in some dark plot against me."

"No, no, sir; no, not against you!" It was a woman's voice, and Mrs. Barrymore, paler and more horror-struck than her husband, was standing at the door. Her bulky figure in a shawl and skirt might have been comic were it not for the intensity of feeling upon her face.

"We have to go, Eliza. This is the end of it. You can pack our things," said the butler.

"Oh, John, John, have I brought you to this? It is my doing, Sir Henry —all mine. He has done nothing except for my sake, and because I asked him."

"Speak out, then! What does it mean?"

"My unhappy brother is starving on the moor. We cannot let him perish at our very gates. The light is a signal to him that food is ready for him, and his light out yonder is to show the spot to which to bring it."

"Then your brother is——"

"The escaped convict, sir—Selden, the criminal."

"That's the truth, sir," said Barrymore. "I said that it was not my secret and that I could not tell it to you. But now you have heard it, and you will see that if there was a plot it was not against you."

This, then, was the explanation of the stealthy expeditions at night and the light at the window. Sir Henry and I both stared at the woman in amazement. Was it possible that this stolidly respectable person was of the same blood as one of the most notorious criminals in the country?

"Yes, sir, my name was Selden, and he is my younger brother. We humoured him too much when he was a lad and gave him his own way in everything until he came to think that the world was made for his pleasure, and that he could do what he liked in it. Then as he grew older he met wicked companions, and the devil entered into him until he broke my mother's heart and dragged our name in the dirt. From crime to crime he sank lower and lower until it is only the mercy of God which has snatched him from the scaffold; but to me, sir, he was always the little curly-headed boy that I had nursed and played with as an elder sister would. That was why he broke prison, sir. He knew that I was here and that we could not refuse to help him. When he dragged himself here one night, weary and starving, with the warders hard at his heels, what could we do? We took him in and fed him and cared for him. Then you returned, sir, and my brother thought he would be safer on the moor than anywhere else until the hue and cry was over, so he lay in hiding there. But every second night we made sure if he was still there by putting a light in the window, and if there was an answer my husband took out some bread and meat to him. Every day we hoped that he was gone, but as long as he was there we could not desert him. That is the whole truth, as I am an honest Christian woman, and you will see that if there is blame in the matter it does not lie with my husband but with me, for whose sake he has done all that he has."

The woman's words came with an intense earnestness which carried conviction with them.

"Is this true, Barrymore?"

"Yes, Sir Henry. Every word of it."

"Well, I cannot blame you for standing by your own wife. Forget what I have said. Go to your room, you two, and we shall talk further about this matter in the morning."

When they were gone we looked out of the window again. Sir Henry had flung it open, and the cold night wind beat in upon our faces. Far away in the black distance there still glowed that one tiny point of yellow light.

"I wonder he dares," said Sir Henry.

"It may be so placed as to be only visible from here."

"Very likely. How far do you think it is?"

"Out by the Cleft Tor, I think."

"Not more than a mile or two off."

"Hardly that."

"Well, it cannot be far if Barrymore had to carry out the food to it. And he is waiting, this villain, beside that candle. By thunder, Watson, I am going out to take that man!"

The same thought had crossed my own mind. It was not as if the Barrymores had taken us into their confidence. Their secret had been forced from them. The man was a danger to the community, an unmitigated scoundrel for whom there was neither pity nor excuse. We were only doing our duty in taking this chance of putting him back where he could do no harm. With his brutal and violent nature, others would have to pay the price if we held our hands. Any night, for example, our neighbours the Stapletons might be attacked by him, and it may have been the thought of this which made Sir Henry so keen upon the adventure.

"I will come," said I.

"Then get your revolver and put on your boots. The sooner we start the better, as the fellow may put out his light and be off."

In five minutes we were outside the door, starting upon our expedition. We hurried through the dark shrubbery, amid the dull moaning of the autumn wind and the rustle of the falling leaves. The night air was heavy with the smell of damp and decay. Now and again the moon peeped out for an instant, but clouds were driving over the face of the sky, and just as we came out on the moor a thin rain began to fall. The light still burned steadily in front.

"Are you armed?" I asked.

"I have a hunting-crop."

"We must close in on him rapidly, for he is said to be a desperate fellow. We shall take him by surprise and have him at our mercy before he can resist."

"I say, Watson," said the baronet, "what would Holmes say to this? How about that hour of darkness in which the power of evil is exalted?"

As if in answer to his words there rose suddenly out of the vast gloom of the moor that strange cry which I had already heard upon the borders of the great Grimpen Mire. It came with the wind through the silence of the night, a long, deep mutter, then a rising howl, and then the sad moan in which it died away. Again and again it sounded, the whole air throbbing with it, strident, wild, and menacing. The baronet caught my sleeve and his face glimmered white through the darkness.

"My God, what's that, Watson?"

"I don't know. It's a sound they have on the moor. I heard it once before."

It died away, and an absolute silence closed in upon us. We stood straining our ears, but nothing came.

"Watson," said the baronet, "it was the cry of a hound."

My blood ran cold in my veins, for there was a break in his voice which told of the sudden horror which had seized him.

"What do they call this sound?" he asked.

"Who?"

"The folk on the countryside?"

"Oh, they are ignorant people. Why should you mind what they call it?"

"Tell me, Watson. What do they say of it?"

I hesitated but could not escape the question.

"They say it is the cry of the Hound of the Baskervilles."

He groaned and was silent for a few moments.

"A hound it was," he said at last, "but it seemed to come from miles away, over yonder, I think."

"It was hard to say whence it came."

"It rose and fell with the wind. Isn't that the direction of the great Grimpen Mire?"

"Yes, it is."

"Well, it was up there. Come now, Watson, didn't you think yourself that it was the cry of a hound? I am not a child. You need not fear to speak the truth."

"Stapleton was with me when I heard it last. He said that it might be the calling of a strange bird."

"No, no, it was a hound. My God, can there be some truth in all these stories? Is it possible that I am really in danger from so dark a cause? You don't believe it, do you, Watson?"

"No, no."

"And yet it was one thing to laugh about it in London, and it is another to stand out here in the darkness of the moor and to hear such a cry as that. And my uncle! There was the footprint of the hound beside him as he lay. It all fits together. I don't think that I am a coward, Watson, but that sound seemed to freeze my very blood. Feel my hand!"

It was as cold as a block of marble.

"You'll be all right to-morrow."

"I don't think I'll get that cry out of my head. What do you advise that we do now?"

"Shall we turn back?"

"No, by thunder; we have come out to get our man, and we will do it. We after the convict, and a hell-hound, as likely as not, after us. Come on! We'll see it through if all the fiends of the pit were loose upon the moor."

We stumbled slowly along in the darkness, with the black loom of the craggy hills around us, and the yellow speck of light burning steadily in front. There is nothing so deceptive as the distance of a light upon a pitch-dark night, and sometimes the glimmer seemed to be far away upon the horizon and sometimes it might have been within a few yards of us. But at last we could see whence it came, and then we knew that we were indeed very close. A guttering candle was stuck in a crevice of the rocks which flanked it on each side so as to keep the wind from it and also to prevent it from being visible, save in the direction of Baskerville Hall. A boulder of granite concealed our approach, and crouching behind it we gazed over it at the signal light. It was strange to see this single candle burning there in the middle of the moor, with no sign of life near it—just the one straight yellow flame and the gleam of the rock on each side of it.

"What shall we do now?" whispered Sir Henry.

"Wait here. He must be near his light. Let us see if we can get a glimpse of him."

The words were hardly out of my mouth when we both saw him. Over the rocks, in the crevice of which the candle burned, there was thrust out an evil yellow face, a terrible animal face, all seamed and scored with vile passions. Foul with mire, with a bristling beard, and hung with matted hair, it might well have belonged to one of those old savages who dwelt in the burrows on the hillsides. The light beneath him was reflected in his small, cunning eyes which peered fiercely to right and left through the darkness like a crafty and savage animal who has heard the steps of the hunters.

Something had evidently aroused his suspicions. It may have been that Barrymore had some private signal which we had neglected to give, or the fellow may have had some other reason for thinking that all was not well, but I could read his fears upon his wicked face. Any instant he might dash out the light and vanish in the darkness. I sprang forward therefore, and Sir Henry did the same. At the same moment the convict screamed out a curse at us and hurled a rock which splintered up against the boulder which had sheltered us. I caught one glimpse of his short, squat, strongly built figure as he sprang to his feet and turned to run. At the same moment by a lucky chance the moon broke through the clouds. We rushed over the brow of the hill, and there was our man running with great speed down the other side, springing over the stones in his way with the activity of a mountain goat. A lucky long shot of my revolver might have crippled him, but I had brought it only to defend myself if attacked and not to shoot an unarmed man who was running away.

We were both swift runners and in fairly good training, but we soon found that we had no chance of overtaking him. We saw him for a long time in the moonlight until he was only a small speck moving swiftly among the boulders upon the side of a distant hill. We ran and ran until we were completely blown, but the space between us grew ever wider. Finally we stopped and sat panting on two rocks, while we watched him disappearing in the distance.

And it was at this moment that there occurred a most strange and unexpected thing. We had risen from our rocks and were turning to go home, having abandoned the hopeless chase. The moon was low upon the right, and the jagged pinnacle of a granite tor stood up against the lower curve of its silver disc. There, outlined as black as an ebony statue on that shining background, I saw the figure of a man upon the tor. Do not think that it was a delusion, Holmes. I assure you that I have never in my life seen anything more clearly. As far as I could judge, the figure was that of a tall, thin man. He stood with his legs a little separated, his arms folded, his head bowed, as if he were brooding over that enormous wilderness of peat and granite which lay before him. He might have been the very spirit of that terrible place. It was not the convict. This man was far from the place where the latter had disappeared. Besides, he was a much taller man. With a cry of surprise I pointed him out to the baronet, but in the instant during which I had turned to grasp his arm the man was gone. There was the sharp pinnacle of granite still cutting the lower edge of the moon, but its peak bore no trace of that silent and motionless figure.

I wished to go in that direction and to search the tor, but it was some distance away. The baronet's nerves were still quivering from that cry, which recalled the dark story of his family, and he was not in the mood for fresh adventures. He had not seen this lonely man upon the tor and could not feel the thrill which his strange presence and his commanding attitude had given to me. "A warder, no doubt," said he. "The moor has been thick with them since this fellow escaped." Well, perhaps his explanation may be the right one, but I should like to have some further proof of it. To-day we mean to communicate to the Princetown people where they should look for their missing man, but it is hard lines that we have not actually had the triumph of bringing him back as our own prisoner. Such are the adventures of last night, and you must acknowledge, my dear Holmes, that I have done you very well in the matter of a report. Much of what I tell you is no doubt quite irrelevant, but still I feel that it is best that I should let you have all the facts and leave you to select for yourself those which will be of most service to you in helping you to your conclusions. We are certainly making some progress. So far as the Barrymores go we have found the motive of their actions, and that has cleared up the situation very much. But the moor with its mysteries and its strange inhabitants remains as inscrutable as ever. Perhaps in my next I may be able to throw some light upon this also. Best of all would it be if you could come down to us. In any case you will hear from me again in the course of the next few days.

---

10 EXTRACT FROM THE DIARY OF DR. WATSON

So far I have been able to quote from the reports which I have forwarded during these early days to Sherlock Holmes. Now, however, I have arrived at a point in my narrative where I am compelled to abandon this method and to trust once more to my recollections, aided by the diary which I kept at the time. A few extracts from the latter will carry me on to those scenes which are indelibly fixed in every detail upon my memory. I proceed, then, from the morning which followed our abortive chase of the convict and our other strange experiences upon the moor.

October 16th. A dull and foggy day with a drizzle of rain. The house is banked in with rolling clouds, which rise now and then to show the dreary curves of the moor, with thin, silver veins upon the sides of the hills, and the distant boulders gleaming where the light strikes upon their wet faces. It is melancholy outside and in. The baronet is in a black reaction after the excitements of the night. I am conscious myself of a weight at my heart and a feeling of impending danger—ever present danger, which is the more terrible because I am unable to define it.

And have I not cause for such a feeling? Consider the long sequence of incidents which have all pointed to some sinister influence which is at work around us. There is the death of the last occupant of the Hall, fulfilling so exactly the conditions of the family legend, and there are the repeated reports from peasants of the appearance of a strange creature upon the moor. Twice I have with my own ears heard the sound which resembled the distant baying of a hound. It is incredible, impossible, that it should really be outside the ordinary laws of nature. A spectral hound which leaves material footmarks and fills the air with its howling is surely not to be thought of. Stapleton may fall in with such a superstition, and Mortimer also; but if I have one quality upon earth it is common sense, and nothing will persuade me to believe in such a thing. To do so would be to descend to the level of these poor peasants, who are not content with a mere fiend dog but must needs describe him with hell-fire shooting from his mouth and eyes. Holmes would not listen to such fancies, and I am his agent. But facts are facts, and I have twice heard this crying upon the moor. Suppose that there were really some huge hound loose upon it; that would go far to explain everything. But where could such a hound lie concealed, where did it get its food, where did it come from, how was it that no one saw it by day? It must be confessed that the natural explanation offers almost as many difficulties as the other. And always, apart from the hound, there is the fact of the human agency in London, the man in the cab, and the letter which warned Sir Henry against the moor. This at least was real, but it might have been the work of a protecting friend as easily as of an enemy. Where is that friend or enemy now? Has he remained in London, or has he followed us down here? Could he—could he be the stranger whom I saw upon the tor?

It is true that I have had only the one glance at him, and yet there are some things to which I am ready to swear. He is no one whom I have seen down here, and I have now met all the neighbours. The figure was far taller than that of Stapleton, far thinner than that of Frankland. Barrymore it might possibly have been, but we had left him behind us, and I am certain that he could not have followed us. A stranger then is still dogging us, just as a stranger dogged us in London. We have never shaken him off. If I could lay my hands upon that man, then at last we might find ourselves at the end of all our difficulties. To this one purpose I must now devote all my energies.

My first impulse was to tell Sir Henry all my plans. My second and wisest one is to play my own game and speak as little as possible to anyone. He is silent and distrait. His nerves have been strangely shaken by that sound upon the moor. I will say nothing to add to his anxieties, but I will take my own steps to attain my own end.

We had a small scene this morning after breakfast. Barrymore asked leave to speak with Sir Henry, and they were closeted in his study some little time. Sitting in the billiard-room I more than once heard the sound of voices raised, and I had a pretty good idea what the point was which was under discussion. After a time the baronet opened his door and called for me.

"Barrymore considers that he has a grievance," he said. "He thinks that it was unfair on our part to hunt his brother-in-law down when he, of his own free will, had told us the secret."

The butler was standing very pale but very collected before us.

"I may have spoken too warmly, sir," said he, "and if I have, I am sure that I beg your pardon. At the same time, I was very much surprised when I heard you two gentlemen come back this morning and learned that you had been chasing Selden. The poor fellow has enough to fight against without my putting more upon his track."

"If you had told us of your own free will it would have been a different thing," said the baronet, "you only told us, or rather your wife only told us, when it was forced from you and you could not help yourself."

"I didn't think you would have taken advantage of it, Sir Henry—indeed I didn't."

"The man is a public danger. There are lonely houses scattered over the moor, and he is a fellow who would stick at nothing. You only want to get a glimpse of his face to see that. Look at Mr. Stapleton's house, for example, with no one but himself to defend it. There's no safety for anyone until he is under lock and key."

"He'll break into no house, sir. I give you my solemn word upon that. But he will never trouble anyone in this country again. I assure you, Sir Henry, that in a very few days the necessary arrangements will have been made and he will be on his way to South America. For God's sake, sir, I beg of you not to let the police know that he is still on the moor. They have given up the chase there, and he can lie quiet until the ship is ready for him. You can't tell on him without getting my wife and me into trouble. I beg you, sir, to say nothing to the police."

"What do you say, Watson?"

I shrugged my shoulders. "If he were safely out of the country it would relieve the tax-payer of a burden."

"But how about the chance of his holding someone up before he goes?"

"He would not do anything so mad, sir. We have provided him with all that he can want. To commit a crime would be to show where he was hiding."

"That is true," said Sir Henry. "Well, Barrymore——"

"God bless you, sir, and thank you from my heart! It would have killed my poor wife had he been taken again."

"I guess we are aiding and abetting a felony, Watson? But, after what we have heard, I don't feel as if I could give the man up, so there is an end of it. All right, Barrymore, you can go."

With a few broken words of gratitude the man turned, but he hesitated and then came back.

"You've been so kind to us, sir, that I should like to do the best I can for you in return. I know something, Sir Henry, and perhaps I should have said it before, but it was long after the inquest that I found it out.

I've never breathed a word about it yet to mortal man. It's about poor Sir Charles's death."

The baronet and I were both upon our feet. "Do you know how he died?"

"No, sir, I don't know that."

"What then?"

"I know why he was at the gate at that hour. It was to meet a woman."

"To meet a woman! He?"

"Yes, sir."

"And the woman's name?"

"I can't give you the name, sir, but I can give you the initials. Her initials were L. L."

"How do you know this, Barrymore?"

"Well, Sir Henry, your uncle had a letter that morning. He had usually a great many letters, for he was a public man and well known for his kind heart, so that everyone who was in trouble was glad to turn to him. But that morning, as it chanced, there was only this one letter, so I took the more notice of it. It was from Coombe Tracey, and it was addressed in a woman's hand."

"Well?"

"Well, sir, I thought no more of the matter, and never would have done had it not been for my wife. Only a few weeks ago she was cleaning out Sir Charles's study—it had never been touched since his death—and she found the ashes of a burned letter in the back of the grate. The greater part of it was charred to pieces, but one little slip, the end of a page, hung together, and the writing could still be read, though it was gray on a black ground. It seemed to us to be a postscript at the end of the letter, and it said: 'Please, please, as you are a gentleman, burn this letter, and be at the gate by ten o'clock.' Beneath it were signed the initials L. L."

"Have you got that slip?"

"No, sir, it crumbled all to bits after we moved it."

"Had Sir Charles received any other letters in the same writing?"

"Well, sir, I took no particular notice of his letters. I should not have noticed this one, only it happened to come alone."

"And you have no idea who L. L. is?"

"No, sir. No more than you have. But I expect if we could lay our hands upon that lady we should know more about Sir Charles's death."

"I cannot understand, Barrymore, how you came to conceal this important information."

"Well, sir, it was immediately after that our own trouble came to us. And then again, sir, we were both of us very fond of Sir Charles, as we well might be considering all that he has done for us. To rake this up couldn't help our poor master, and it's well to go carefully when there's a lady in the case. Even the best of us——"

"You thought it might injure his reputation?"

"Well, sir, I thought no good could come of it. But now you have been kind to us, and I feel as if it would be treating you unfairly not to tell you all that I know about the matter."

"Very good, Barrymore; you can go." When the butler had left us Sir Henry turned to me. "Well, Watson, what do you think of this new light?"

"It seems to leave the darkness rather blacker than before."

"So I think. But if we can only trace L. L. it should clear up the whole business. We have gained that much. We know that there is someone who has the facts if we can only find her. What do you think we should do?"

"Let Holmes know all about it at once. It will give him the clue for which he has been seeking. I am much mistaken if it does not bring him down."

I went at once to my room and drew up my report of the morning's conversation for Holmes. It was evident to me that he had been very busy of late, for the notes which I had from Baker Street were few and short, with no comments upon the information which I had supplied and hardly any reference to my mission. No doubt his blackmailing case is absorbing all his faculties. And yet this new factor must surely arrest his attention and renew his interest. I wish that he were here.

October 17th. All day to-day the rain poured down, rustling on the ivy and dripping from the eaves. I thought of the convict out upon the bleak, cold, shelterless moor. Poor devil! Whatever his crimes, he has suffered something to atone for them. And then I thought of that other one—the face in the cab, the figure against the moon. Was he also out in that deluge—the unseen watcher, the man of darkness? In the evening I put on my waterproof and I walked far upon the sodden moor, full of dark imaginings, the rain beating upon my face and the wind whistling about my ears. God help those who wander into the great mire now, for even the firm uplands are becoming a morass. I found the black tor upon which I had seen the solitary watcher, and from its craggy summit I looked out myself across the melancholy downs. Rain squalls drifted across their russet face, and the heavy, slate-coloured clouds hung low over the landscape, trailing in gray wreaths down the sides of the fantastic hills. In the distant hollow on the left, half hidden by the mist, the two thin towers of Baskerville Hall rose above the trees. They were the only signs of human life which I could see, save only those prehistoric huts which lay thickly upon the slopes of the hills. Nowhere was there any trace of that lonely man whom I had seen on the same spot two nights before.

As I walked back I was overtaken by Dr. Mortimer driving in his dog-cart over a rough moorland track which led from the outlying farmhouse of Foulmire. He has been very attentive to us, and hardly a day has passed that he has not called at the Hall to see how we were getting on. He insisted upon my climbing into his dog-cart, and he gave me a lift homeward. I found him much troubled over the disappearance of his little spaniel. It had wandered on to the moor and had never come back. I gave him such consolation as I might, but I thought of the pony on the Grimpen Mire, and I do not fancy that he will see his little dog again.

"By the way, Mortimer," said I as we jolted along the rough road. "I suppose there are few people living within driving distance of this whom you do not know?"

"Hardly any, I think."

"Can you, then, tell me the name of any woman whose initials are L. L.?"

He thought for a few minutes.

"No," said he. "There are a few gipsies and labouring folk for whom I can't answer, but among the farmers or gentry there is no one whose initials are those. Wait a bit though," he added after a pause. "There is Laura Lyons—her initials are L. L.—but she lives in Coombe Tracey."

"Who is she?" I asked.

"She is Frankland's daughter."

"What! Old Frankland the crank?"

"Exactly. She married an artist named Lyons, who came sketching on the moor. He proved to be a blackguard and deserted her. The fault from what I hear may not have been entirely on one side. Her father refused to have anything to do with her because she had married without his consent and perhaps for one or two other reasons as well. So, between the old sinner and the young one the girl has had a pretty bad time."

"How does she live?"

"I fancy old Frankland allows her a pittance, but it cannot be more, for his own affairs are considerably involved. Whatever she may have deserved one could not allow her to go hopelessly to the bad. Her story got about, and several of the people here did something to enable her to earn an honest living. Stapleton did for one, and Sir Charles for another. I gave a trifle myself. It was to set her up in a typewriting business."

He wanted to know the object of my inquiries, but I managed to satisfy his curiosity without telling him too much, for there is no reason why we should take anyone into our confidence. To-morrow morning I shall find my way to Coombe Tracey, and if I can see this Mrs. Laura Lyons, of equivocal reputation, a long step will have been made towards clearing one incident in this chain of mysteries. I am certainly developing the wisdom of the serpent, for when Mortimer pressed his questions to an inconvenient extent I asked him casually to what type Frankland's skull belonged, and so heard nothing but craniology for the rest of our drive. I have not lived for years with Sherlock Holmes for nothing.

I have only one other incident to record upon this tempestuous and melancholy day. This was my conversation with Barrymore just now, which gives me one more strong card which I can play in due time.

Mortimer had stayed to dinner, and he and the baronet played écarté afterwards. The butler brought me my coffee into the library, and I took the chance to ask him a few questions.

"Well," said I, "has this precious relation of yours departed, or is he still lurking out yonder?"

"I don't know, sir. I hope to Heaven that he has gone, for he has brought nothing but trouble here! I've not heard of him since I left out food for him last, and that was three days ago."

"Did you see him then?"

"No, sir, but the food was gone when next I went that way."

"Then he was certainly there?"

"So you would think, sir, unless it was the other man who took it."

I sat with my coffee-cup halfway to my lips and stared at Barrymore.

"You know that there is another man then?"

"Yes, sir; there is another man upon the moor."

"Have you seen him?"

"No, sir."

"How do you know of him then?"

"Selden told me of him, sir, a week ago or more. He's in hiding, too, but he's not a convict as far as I can make out. I don't like it, Dr. Watson —I tell you straight, sir, that I don't like it." He spoke with a sudden passion of earnestness.

"Now, listen to me, Barrymore! I have no interest in this matter but that of your master. I have come here with no object except to help him. Tell me, frankly, what it is that you don't like."

Barrymore hesitated for a moment, as if he regretted his outburst or found it difficult to express his own feelings in words.

"It's all these goings-on, sir," he cried at last, waving his hand towards the rain-lashed window which faced the moor. "There's foul play somewhere, and there's black villainy brewing, to that I'll swear! Very glad I should be, sir, to see Sir Henry on his way back to London again!"

"But what is it that alarms you?"

"Look at Sir Charles's death! That was bad enough, for all that the coroner said. Look at the noises on the moor at night. There's not a man would cross it after sundown if he was paid for it. Look at this stranger hiding out yonder, and watching and waiting! What's he waiting for? What does it mean? It means no good to anyone of the name of Baskerville, and very glad I shall be to be quit of it all on the day that Sir Henry's new servants are ready to take over the Hall."

"But about this stranger," said I. "Can you tell me anything about him? What did Selden say? Did he find out where he hid, or what he was doing?"

"He saw him once or twice, but he is a deep one and gives nothing away. At first he thought that he was the police, but soon he found that he had some lay of his own. A kind of gentleman he was, as far as he could see, but what he was doing he could not make out."

"And where did He say that he lived?"

"Among the old houses on the hillside—the stone huts where the old folk used to live."

"But how about his food?"

"Selden found out that he has got a lad who works for him and brings all he needs. I dare say he goes to Coombe Tracey for what he wants."

"Very good, Barrymore. We may talk further of this some other time." When the butler had gone I walked over to the black window, and I looked through a blurred pane at the driving clouds and at the tossing outline of the wind-swept trees. It is a wild night indoors, and what must it be in a stone hut upon the moor. What passion of hatred can it be which leads a man to lurk in such a place at such a time! And what deep and earnest purpose can he have which calls for such a trial! There, in that hut upon the moor, seems to lie the very centre of that problem which has vexed me so sorely. I swear that another day shall not have passed before I have done all that man can do to reach the heart of the mystery.

---

11 THE MAN ON THE TOR

The extract from my private diary which forms the last chapter has brought my narrative up to the eighteenth of October, a time when these strange events began to move swiftly towards their terrible conclusion. The incidents of the next few days are indelibly graven upon my recollection, and I can tell them without reference to the notes made at the time. I start them from the day which succeeded that upon which I had established two facts of great importance, the one that Mrs. Laura Lyons of Coombe Tracey had written to Sir Charles Baskerville and made an appointment with him at the very place and hour that he met his death, the other that the lurking man upon the moor was to be found among the stone huts upon the hillside. With these two facts in my possession I felt that either my intelligence or my courage must be deficient if I could not throw some further light upon these dark places.

I had no opportunity to tell the baronet what I had learned about Mrs. Lyons upon the evening before, for Dr. Mortimer remained with him at cards until it was very late. At breakfast, however, I informed him about my discovery and asked him whether he would care to accompany me to Coombe Tracey. At first he was very eager to come, but on second thoughts it seemed to both of us that if I went alone the results might be better. The more formal we made the visit the less information we might obtain. I left Sir Henry behind, therefore, not without some prickings of conscience, and drove off upon my new quest.

When I reached Coombe Tracey I told Perkins to put up the horses, and I made inquiries for the lady whom I had come to interrogate. I had no difficulty in finding her rooms, which were central and well appointed. A maid showed me in without ceremony, and as I entered the sitting-room a lady, who was sitting before a Remington typewriter, sprang up with a pleasant smile of welcome. Her face fell, however, when she saw that I was a stranger, and she sat down again and asked me the object of my visit.

The first impression left by Mrs. Lyons was one of extreme beauty. Her eyes and hair were of the same rich hazel colour, and her cheeks, though considerably freckled, were flushed with the exquisite bloom of the brunette, the dainty pink which lurks at the heart of the sulphur rose. Admiration was, I repeat, the first impression. But the second was criticism. There was something subtly wrong with the face, some coarseness of expression, some hardness, perhaps, of eye, some looseness of lip which marred its perfect beauty. But these, of course, are after-thoughts. At the moment I was simply conscious that I was in the presence of a very handsome woman, and that she was asking me the reasons for my visit. I had not quite understood until that instant how delicate my mission was.

"I have the pleasure," said I, "of knowing your father."

It was a clumsy introduction, and the lady made me feel it.

"There is nothing in common between my father and me," she said. "I owe him nothing, and his friends are not mine. If it were not for the late Sir Charles Baskerville and some other kind hearts I might have starved for all that my father cared."

"It was about the late Sir Charles Baskerville that I have come here to see you."

The freckles started out on the lady's face.

"What can I tell you about him?" she asked, and her fingers played nervously over the stops of her typewriter.

"You knew him, did you not?"

"I have already said that I owe a great deal to his kindness. If I am able to support myself it is largely due to the interest which he took in my unhappy situation."

"Did you correspond with him?"

The lady looked quickly up with an angry gleam in her hazel eyes.

"What is the object of these questions?" she asked sharply.

"The object is to avoid a public scandal. It is better that I should ask them here than that the matter should pass outside our control."

She was silent and her face was still very pale. At last she looked up with something reckless and defiant in her manner.

"Well, I'll answer," she said. "What are your questions?"

"Did you correspond with Sir Charles?"

"I certainly wrote to him once or twice to acknowledge his delicacy and his generosity."

"Have you the dates of those letters?"

"No."

"Have you ever met him?"

"Yes, once or twice, when he came into Coombe Tracey. He was a very retiring man, and he preferred to do good by stealth."

"But if you saw him so seldom and wrote so seldom, how did he know enough about your affairs to be able to help you, as you say that he has done?"

She met my difficulty with the utmost readiness.

"There were several gentlemen who knew my sad history and united to help me. One was Mr. Stapleton, a neighbour and intimate friend of Sir Charles's. He was exceedingly kind, and it was through him that Sir Charles learned about my affairs."

I knew already that Sir Charles Baskerville had made Stapleton his almoner upon several occasions, so the lady's statement bore the impress of truth upon it.

"Did you ever write to Sir Charles asking him to meet you?" I continued.

Mrs. Lyon flushed with anger again.

"Really, sir, this is a very extraordinary question."

"I am sorry, madam, but I must repeat it."

"Then I answer, certainly not."

"Not on the very day of Sir Charles's death?"

The flush had faded in an instant, and a deathly face was before me. Her dry lips could not speak the "No" which I saw rather than heard.

"Surely your memory deceives you," said I. "I could even quote a passage of your letter. It ran 'Please, please, as you are a gentleman, burn this letter, and be at the gate by ten o'clock.' "

I thought that she had fainted, but she recovered herself by a supreme effort.

"Is there no such thing as a gentleman?" she gasped.

"You do Sir Charles an injustice. He *did* burn the letter. But sometimes a letter may be legible even when burned. You acknowledge now that you wrote it?"

"Yes, I did write it," she cried, pouring out her soul in a torrent of words. "I did write it. Why should I deny it? I have no reason to be ashamed of it. I wished him to help me. I believed that if I had an interview I could gain his help, so I asked him to meet me."

"But why at such an hour?"

"Because I had only just learned that he was going to London next day and might be away for months. There were reasons why I could not get there earlier."

"But why a rendezvous in the garden instead of a visit to the house?"

"Do you think a woman could go alone at that hour to a bachelor's house?"

"Well, what happened when you did get there?"

"I never went."

"Mrs. Lyons!"

"No, I swear it to you on all I hold sacred. I never went. Something intervened to prevent my going."

"What was that?"

"That is a private matter. I cannot tell it."

"You acknowledge then that you made an appointment with Sir Charles at the very hour and place at which he met his death, but you deny that you kept the appointment."

"That is the truth."

Again and again I cross-questioned her, but I could never get past that point.

"Mrs. Lyons," said I as I rose from this long and inconclusive interview, "you are taking a very great responsibility and putting yourself in a very false position by not making an absolutely clean breast of all that you know. If I have to call in the aid of the police you will find how seriously you are compromised. If your position is innocent, why did you in the first instance deny having written to Sir Charles upon that date?"

"Because I feared that some false conclusion might be drawn from it and that I might find myself involved in a scandal."

"And why were you so pressing that Sir Charles should destroy your letter?"

"If you have read the letter you will know."

"I did not say that I had read all the letter."

"You quoted some of it."

"I quoted the postscript. The letter had, as I said, been burned and it was not all legible. I ask you once again why it was that you were so pressing that Sir Charles should destroy this letter which he received on the day of his death."

"The matter is a very private one."

"The more reason why you should avoid a public investigation."

"I will tell you, then. If you have heard anything of my unhappy history you will know that I made a rash marriage and had reason to regret it."

"I have heard so much."

"My life has been one incessant persecution from a husband whom I abhor. The law is upon his side, and every day I am faced by the possibility that he may force me to live with him. At the time that I wrote this letter to Sir Charles I had learned that there was a prospect of my regaining my freedom if certain expenses could be met. It meant everything to me—peace of mind, happiness, self-respect—everything. I knew Sir Charles's generosity, and I thought that if he heard the story from my own lips he would help me."

"Then how is it that you did not go?"

"Because I received help in the interval from another source."

"Why, then, did you not write to Sir Charles and explain this?"

"So I should have done had I not seen his death in the paper next morning."

The woman's story hung coherently together, and all my questions were unable to shake it. I could only check it by finding if she had, indeed, instituted divorce proceedings against her husband at or about the time of the tragedy.

It was unlikely that she would dare to say that she had not been to Baskerville Hall if she really had been, for a trap would be necessary to take her there, and could not have returned to Coombe Tracey until the early hours of the morning. Such an excursion could not be kept secret. The probability was, therefore, that she was telling the truth, or, at least, a part of the truth. I came away baffled and disheartened. Once again I had reached that dead wall which seemed to be built across every path by which I tried to get at the object of my mission. And yet the more I thought of the lady's face and of her manner the more I felt that something was being held back from me. Why should she turn so pale? Why should she fight against every admission until it was forced from her? Why should she have been so reticent at the time of the tragedy? Surely the explanation of all this could not be as innocent as she would have me believe. For the moment I could proceed no farther in that direction, but must turn back to that other clue which was to be sought for among the stone huts upon the moor.

And that was a most vague direction. I realized it as I drove back and noted how hill after hill showed traces of the ancient people. Barrymore's only indication had been that the stranger lived in one of these abandoned huts, and many hundreds of them are scattered throughout the length and breadth of the moor. But I had my own experience for a guide since it had shown me the man himself standing upon the summit of the Black Tor. That, then, should be the centre of my search. From there I should explore every hut upon the moor until I lighted upon the right one. If this man were inside it I should find out from his own lips, at the point of my revolver if necessary, who he was and why he had dogged us so long. He might slip away from us in the crowd of Regent Street, but it would puzzle him to do so upon the lonely moor. On the other hand, if I should find the hut and its tenant should not be within it I must remain there, however long the vigil, until he returned. Holmes had missed him in London. It would indeed be a triumph for me if I could run him to earth where my master had failed.

Luck had been against us again and again in this inquiry, but now at last it came to my aid. And the messenger of good fortune was none other than Mr. Frankland, who was standing, gray-whiskered and red-faced, outside the gate of his garden, which opened on to the highroad along which I travelled.

"Good-day, Dr. Watson," cried he with unwonted good humour, "you must really give your horses a rest and come in to have a glass of wine and to congratulate me."

My feelings toward him were very far from being friendly after what I had heard of his treatment of his daughter, but I was anxious to send Perkins and the wagonette home, and the opportunity was a good one. I alighted and sent a message to Sir Henry that I should walk over in time for dinner. Then I followed Frankland into his dining-room.

"It is a great day for me, sir—one of the red-letter days of my life," he cried with many chuckles. "I have brought off a double event. I mean to teach them in these parts that law is law, and that there is a man here who does not fear to invoke it. I have established a right of way through the centre of old Middleton's park, slap across it, sir, within a hundred yards of his own front door. What do you think of that? We'll teach these magnates that they cannot ride roughshod over the rights of the commoners, confound them! And I've closed the wood where the Fernworthy folk used to picnic. These infernal people seem to think that there are no rights of property, and that they can swarm where they like with their papers and their bottles. Both cases decided, Dr. Watson, and both in my favour. I haven't had such a day since I had Sir John Morland for trespass because he shot in his own warren."

"How on earth did you do that?"

"Look it up in the books, sir. It will repay reading—Frankland *v.*

Morland, Court of Queen's Bench. It cost me £200, but I got my verdict."

"Did it do you any good?"

"None, sir, none. I am proud to say that I had no interest in the matter. I act entirely from a sense of public duty. I have no doubt, for example, that the Fernworthy people will burn me in effigy to-night. I told the police last time they did it that they should stop these disgraceful exhibitions. The County Constabulary is in a scandalous state, sir, and it has not afforded me the protection to which I am entitled. The case of Frankland *v*. Regina will bring the matter before the attention of the public. I told them that they would have occasion to regret their treatment of me, and already my words have come true."

"How so?" I asked.

The old man put on a very knowing expression.

"Because I could tell them what they are dying to know; but nothing would induce me to help the rascals in any way."

I had been casting round for some excuse by which I could get away from his gossip, but now I began to wish to hear more of it. I had seen enough of the contrary nature of the old sinner to understand that any strong sign of interest would be the surest way to stop his confidences.

"Some poaching case, no doubt?" said I with an indifferent manner.

"Ha, ha, my boy, a very much more important matter than that! What about the convict on the moor?"

I started. "You don't mean that you know where he is?" said I.

"I may not know exactly where he is, but I am quite sure that I could help the police to lay their hands on him. Has it never struck you that the way to catch that man was to find out where he got his food and so trace it to him?"

He certainly seemed to be getting uncomfortably near the truth. "No doubt," said I; "but how do you know that he is anywhere upon the moor?"

"I know it because I have seen with my own eyes the messenger who takes him his food."

My heart sank for Barrymore. It was a serious thing to be in the power of this spiteful old busybody. But his next remark took a weight from my mind.

"You'll be surprised to hear that his food is taken to him by a child. I see him every day through my telescope upon the roof. He passes along the same path at the same hour, and to whom should he be going except to the convict?"

Here was luck indeed! And yet I suppressed all appearance of interest. A child! Barrymore had said that our unknown was supplied by a boy. It was on his track, and not upon the convict's, that Frankland had stumbled. If I could get his knowledge it might save me a long and weary hunt. But incredulity and indifference were evidently my strongest cards.

"I should say that it was much more likely that it was the son of one of the moorland shepherds taking out his father's dinner."

The least appearance of opposition struck fire out of the old autocrat. His eyes looked malignantly at me, and his gray whiskers bristled like those of an angry cat.

"Indeed, sir!" said he, pointing out over the wide-stretching moor. "Do you see that Black Tor over yonder? Well, do you see the low hill beyond with the thornbush upon it? It is the stoniest part of the whole moor. Is that a place where a shepherd would be likely to take his station? Your suggestion, sir, is a most absurd one."

I meekly answered that I had spoken without knowing all the facts. My submission pleased him and led him to further confidences.

"You may be sure, sir, that I have very good grounds before I come to an opinion. I have seen the boy again and again with his bundle. Every day, and sometimes twice a day, I have been able—but wait a moment, Dr. Watson. Do my eyes deceive me, or is there at the present moment something moving upon that hillside?"

It was several miles off, but I could distinctly see a small dark dot against the dull green and gray.

"Come, sir, come!" cried Frankland, rushing upstairs. "You will see with your own eyes and judge for yourself."

The telescope, a formidable instrument mounted upon a tripod, stood upon the flat leads of the house. Frankland clapped his eye to it and gave a cry of satisfaction.

"Quick, Dr. Watson, quick, before he passes over the hill!"

There he was, sure enough, a small urchin with a little bundle upon his shoulder, toiling slowly up the hill. When he reached the crest I saw the ragged uncouth figure outlined for an instant against the cold blue sky. He looked round him with a furtive and stealthy air, as one who dreads pursuit. Then he vanished over the hill.

"Well! Am I right?"

"Certainly, there is a boy who seems to have some secret errand."

"And what the errand is even a county constable could guess. But not one word shall they have from me, and I bind you to secrecy also, Dr. Watson. Not a word! You understand!"

"Just as you wish."

"They have treated me shamefully—shamefully. When the facts come out in Frankland v. Regina I venture to think that a thrill of indignation will run through the country. Nothing would induce me to help the police in any way. For all they cared it might have been me, instead of my effigy, which these rascals burned at the stake. Surely you are not going! You will help me to empty the decanter in honour of this great occasion!"

But I resisted all his solicitations and succeeded in dissuading him from his announced intention of walking home with me. I kept the road as long as his eye was on me, and then I struck off across the moor and made for the stony hill over which the boy had disappeared. Everything was working in my favour, and I swore that it should not be through lack of energy or perseverance that I should miss the chance which fortune had thrown in my way.

The sun was already sinking when I reached the summit of the hill, and the long slopes beneath me were all golden-green on one side and gray shadow on the other. A haze lay low upon the farthest sky-line, out of which jutted the fantastic shapes of Belliver and Vixen Tor. Over the wide expanse there was no sound and no movement. One great gray bird, a gull or curlew, soared aloft in the blue heaven. He and I seemed to be the only living things between the huge arch of the sky and the desert beneath it. The barren scene, the sense of loneliness, and the mystery and urgency of my task all struck a chill into my heart. The boy was nowhere to be seen. But down beneath me in a cleft of the hills there was a circle of the old stone huts, and in the middle of them there was one which retained sufficient roof to act as a screen against the weather. My heart leaped within me as I saw it. This must be the burrow where the stranger lurked. At last my foot was on the threshold of his hiding place—his secret was within my grasp.

As I approached the hut, walking as warily as Stapleton would do when with poised net he drew near the settled butterfly, I satisfied myself that the place had indeed been used as a habitation. A vague pathway among the boulders led to the dilapidated opening which served as a door. All was silent within. The unknown might be lurking there, or he might be prowling on the moor. My nerves tingled with the sense of adventure. Throwing aside my cigarette, I closed my hand upon the butt of my revolver and, walking swiftly up to the door, I looked in. The place was empty.

But there were ample signs that I had not come upon a false scent. This was certainly where the man lived. Some blankets rolled in a waterproof lay upon that very stone slab upon which neolithic man had once slumbered. The ashes of a fire were heaped in a rude grate. Beside it lay some cooking utensils and a bucket half-full of water. A litter of empty tins showed that the place had been occupied for some time, and I saw, as my eyes became accustomed to the checkered light, a pannikin and a half-full bottle of spirits standing in the corner. In the middle of the hut a flat stone served the purpose of a table, and upon this stood a small cloth bundle—the same, no doubt, which I had seen through the telescope upon the shoulder of the boy. It contained a loaf of bread, a tinned tongue, and two tins of preserved peaches. As I set it down again, after having examined it, my heart leaped to see that beneath it there lay a sheet of paper with writing upon it. I raised it, and this was what I read, roughly scrawled in pencil: "Dr. Watson has gone to Coombe Tracey."

For a minute I stood there with the paper in my hands thinking out the meaning of this curt message. It was I, then, and not Sir Henry, who was being dogged by this secret man. He had not followed me himself, but he had set an agent—the boy, perhaps—upon my track, and this was his report. Possibly I had taken no step since I had been upon the moor which had not been observed and reported. Always there was this feeling of an unseen force, a fine net drawn round us with infinite skill and delicacy, holding us so lightly that it was only at some supreme moment that one realized that one was indeed entangled in its meshes.

If there was one report there might be others, so I looked round the hut in search of them. There was no trace, however, of anything of the kind, nor could I discover any sign which might indicate the character or intentions of the man who lived in this singular place, save that he must be of Spartan habits and cared little for the comforts of life. When I thought of the heavy rains and looked at the gaping roof I understood how strong and immutable must be the purpose which had kept him in that inhospitable abode. Was he our malignant enemy, or was he by chance our guardian angel? I swore that I would not leave the hut until I knew.

Outside the sun was sinking low and the west was blazing with scarlet and gold. Its reflection was shot back in ruddy patches by the distant pools which lay amid the great Grimpen Mire. There were the two towers of Baskerville Hall, and there a distant blur of smoke which marked the village of Grimpen. Between the two, behind the hill, was the house of the Stapletons. All was sweet and mellow and peaceful in the golden evening light, and yet as I looked at them my soul shared none of the peace of Nature but quivered at the vagueness and the terror of that interview which every instant was bringing nearer. With tingling nerves but a fixed purpose, I sat in the dark recess of the hut and waited with sombre patience for the coming of its tenant.

And then at last I heard him. Far away came the sharp clink of a boot striking upon a stone. Then another and yet another, coming nearer and nearer. I shrank back into the darkest corner and cocked the pistol in my pocket, determined not to discover myself until I had an opportunity of seeing something of the stranger. There was a long pause which showed that he had stopped. Then once more the footsteps approached and a shadow fell across the opening of the hut.

"It is a lovely evening, my dear Watson," said a well-known voice. "I really think that you will be more comfortable outside than in."

For a moment or two I sat breathless, hardly able to believe my ears. Then my senses and my voice came back to me, while a crushing weight of responsibility seemed in an instant to be lifted from my soul. That cold, incisive, ironical voice could belong to but one man in all the world.

"Holmes!" I cried—"Holmes!"

"Come out," said he, "and please be careful with the revolver."

I stooped under the rude lintel, and there he sat upon a stone outside, his gray eyes dancing with amusement as they fell upon my astonished features. He was thin and worn, but clear and alert, his keen face bronzed by the sun and roughened by the wind. In his tweed suit and cloth cap he looked like any other tourist upon the moor, and he had contrived, with that catlike love of personal cleanliness which was one of his characteristics, that his chin should be as smooth and his linen as perfect as if he were in Baker Street.

"I never was more glad to see anyone in my life," said I as I wrung him by the hand.

"Or more astonished, eh?"

"Well, I must confess to it."

"The surprise was not all on one side, I assure you. I had no idea that you had found my occasional retreat, still less that you were inside it, until I was within twenty paces of the door."

"My footprint, I presume?"

"No, Watson; I fear that I could not undertake to recognize your footprint amid all the footprints of the world. If you seriously desire to deceive me you must change your tobacconist; for when I see the stub of a cigarette marked Bradley, Oxford Street, I know that my friend Watson is in the neighbourhood. You will see it there beside the path. You threw it down, no doubt, at that supreme moment when you charged into the empty hut."

"Exactly."

"I thought as much—and knowing your admirable tenacity I was convinced that you were sitting in ambush, a weapon within reach, waiting for the tenant to return. So you actually thought that I was the criminal?"

"I did not know who you were, but I was determined to find out."

"Excellent, Watson! And how did you localize me? You saw me, perhaps, on the night of the convict hunt, when I was so imprudent as to allow the moon to rise behind me?"

"Yes, I saw you then."

"And have no doubt searched all the huts until you came to this one?"

"No, your boy had been observed, and that gave me a guide where to look."

"The old gentleman with the telescope, no doubt. I could not make it out when first I saw the light flashing upon the lens." He rose and peeped into the hut. "Ha, I see that Cartwright has brought up some supplies. What's this paper? So you have been to Coombe Tracey, have you?"

"Yes."

"To see Mrs. Laura Lyons?"

"Exactly."

"Well done! Our researches have evidently been running on parallel lines, and when we unite our results I expect we shall have a fairly full knowledge of the case."

"Well, I am glad from my heart that you are here, for indeed the responsibility and the mystery were both becoming too much for my nerves. But how in the name of wonder did you come here, and what have you been doing? I thought that you were in Baker Street working out that case of blackmailing."

"That was what I wished you to think."

"Then you use me, and yet do not trust me!" I cried with some bitterness. "I think that I have deserved better at your hands, Holmes."

"My dear fellow, you have been invaluable to me in this as in many other cases, and I beg that you will forgive me if I have seemed to play a trick upon you. In truth, it was partly for your own sake that I did it, and it was my appreciation of the danger which you ran which led me to come down and examine the matter for myself. Had I been with Sir Henry and you it is confident that my point of view would have been the same as yours, and my presence would have warned our very formidable opponents to be on their guard. As it is, I have been able to get about as I could not possibly have done had I been living in the Hall, and I remain an unknown factor in the business, ready to throw in all my weight at a critical moment."

"But why keep me in the dark?"

"For you to know could not have helped us and might possibly have led to my discovery. You would have wished to tell me something, or in your kindness you would have brought me out some comfort or other, and so an unnecessary risk would be run. I brought Cartwright down with me—you remember the little chap at the express office—and he has seen after my simple wants: a loaf of bread and a clean collar. What does man want more? He has given me an extra pair of eyes upon a very active pair of feet, and both have been invaluable."

"Then my reports have all been wasted!"—My voice trembled as I recalled the pains and the pride with which I had composed them.

Holmes took a bundle of papers from his pocket.

"Here are your reports, my dear fellow, and very well thumbed, I assure you. I made excellent arrangements, and they are only delayed one day upon their way. I must compliment you exceedingly upon the zeal and the intelligence which you have shown over an extraordinarily difficult case."

I was still rather raw over the deception which had been practised upon me, but the warmth of Holmes's praise drove my anger from my mind. I felt also in my heart that he was right in what he said and that it was really best for our purpose that I should not have known that he was upon the moor.

"That's better," said he, seeing the shadow rise from my face. "And now tell me the result of your visit to Mrs. Laura Lyons—it was not difficult for me to guess that it was to see her that you had gone, for I am already aware that she is the one person in Coombe Tracey who might be of service to us in the matter. In fact, if you had not gone today it is exceedingly probable that I should have gone to-morrow."

The sun had set and dusk was settling over the moor. The air had turned chill and we withdrew into the hut for warmth. There, sitting together in the twilight, I told Holmes of my conversation with the lady. So interested was he that I had to repeat some of it twice before he was satisfied.

"This is most important," said he when I had concluded. "It fills up a gap which I had been unable to bridge in this most complex affair. You are aware, perhaps, that a close intimacy exists between this lady and the man Stapleton?"

"I did not know of a close intimacy."

"There can be no doubt about the matter. They meet, they write, there is a complete understanding between them. Now, this puts a very powerful weapon into our hands. If I could only use it to detach his wife——"

"His wife?"

"I am giving you some information now, in return for all that you have given me. The lady who has passed here as Miss Stapleton is in reality his wife."

"Good heavens, Holmes! Are you sure of what you say? How could he have permitted Sir Henry to fall in love with her?"

"Sir Henry's falling in love could do no harm to anyone except Sir Henry. He took particular care that Sir Henry did not *make* love to her, as you have yourself observed. I repeat that the lady is his wife and not his sister."

"But why this elaborate deception?"

"Because he foresaw that she would be very much more useful to him in the character of a free woman."

All my unspoken instincts, my vague suspicions, suddenly took shape and centred upon the naturalist. In that impassive, colourless man, with his straw hat and his butterfly-net, I seemed to see something terrible —a creature of infinite patience and craft, with a smiling face and a murderous heart.

"It is he, then, who is our enemy—it is he who dogged us in London?"

"So I read the riddle."

"And the warning—it must have come from her!"

"Exactly."

The shape of some monstrous villainy, half seen, half guessed, loomed through the darkness which had girt me so long.

"But are you sure of this, Holmes? How do you know that the woman is his wife?"

"Because he so far forgot himself as to tell you a true piece of autobiography upon the occasion when he first met you, and I dare say he has many a time regretted it since. He *was* once a schoolmaster in the north of England. Now, there is no one more easy to trace than a schoolmaster. There are scholastic agencies by which one may identify any man who has been in the profession. A little investigation showed me that a school had come to grief under atrocious circumstances, and that the man who had owned it—the name was different—had disappeared with his wife. The descriptions agreed. When I learned that the missing man was devoted to entomology the identification was complete."

The darkness was rising, but much was still hidden by the shadows.

"If this woman is in truth his wife, where does Mrs. Laura Lyons come in?" I asked.

"That is one of the points upon which your own researches have shed a light. Your interview with the lady has cleared the situation very much. I did not know about a projected divorce between herself and her husband. In that case, regarding Stapleton as an unmarried man, she counted no doubt upon becoming his wife."

"And when she is undeceived?"

"Why, then we may find the lady of service. It must be our first duty to see her—both of us—to-morrow. Don't you think, Watson, that you are away from your charge rather long? Your place should be at Baskerville Hall."

The last red streaks had faded away in the west and night had settled upon the moor. A few faint stars were gleaming in a violet sky.

"One last question, Holmes," I said as I rose. "Surely there is no need of secrecy between you and me. What is the meaning of it all? What is he after?"

Holmes's voice sank as he answered:

"It is murder, Watson—refined, cold-blooded, deliberate murder. Do not ask me for particulars. My nets are closing upon him, even as his are upon Sir Henry, and with your help he is already almost at my mercy. There is but one danger which can threaten us. It is that he should strike before we are ready to do so. Another day—two at the most—and I have my case complete, but until then guard your charge as closely as ever a fond mother watched her ailing child. Your mission to-day has justified itself, and yet I could almost wish that you had not left his side. Hark!"

A terrible scream—a prolonged yell of horror and anguish burst out of the silence of the moor. That frightful cry turned the blood to ice in my veins.

"Oh, my God!" I gasped. "What is it? What does it mean?"

Holmes had sprung to his feet, and I saw his dark, athletic outline at the door of the hut, his shoulders stooping, his head thrust forward, his face peering into the darkness.

"Hush!" he whispered. "Hush!"

The cry had been loud on account of its vehemence, but it had pealed out from somewhere far off on the shadowy plain. Now it burst upon our ears, nearer, louder, more urgent than before.

"Where is it?" Holmes whispered; and I knew from the thrill of his voice that he, the man of iron, was shaken to the soul. "Where is it, Watson?"

"There, I think." I pointed into the darkness.

"No, there!"

Again the agonized cry swept through the silent night, louder and much nearer than ever. And a new sound mingled with it, a deep, muttered rumble, musical and yet menacing, rising and falling like the low, constant murmur of the sea.

"The hound!" cried Holmes. "Come, Watson, come! Great heavens, if we are too late!"

He had started running swiftly over the moor, and I had followed at his heels. But now from somewhere among the broken ground immediately in front of us there came one last despairing yell, and then a dull, heavy thud. We halted and listened. Not another sound broke the heavy silence of the windless night.

I saw Holmes put his hand to his forehead like a man distracted. He stamped his feet upon the ground.

"He has beaten us, Watson. We are too late."

"No, no, surely not!"

"Fool that I was to hold my hand. And you, Watson, see what comes of abandoning your charge! But, by Heaven, if the worst has happened we'll avenge him!"

Blindly we ran through the gloom, blundering against boulders, forcing our way through gorse bushes, panting up hills and rushing down slopes, heading always in the direction whence those dreadful sounds had come. At every rise Holmes looked eagerly round him, but the shadows were thick upon the moor, and nothing moved upon its dreary face.

"Can you see anything?"

"Nothing."

"But, hark, what is that?"

A low moan had fallen upon our ears. There it was again upon our left! On that side a ridge of rocks ended in a sheer cliff which overlooked a stone-strewn slope. On its jagged face was spread-eagled some dark, irregular object. As we ran towards it the vague outline hardened into a definite shape. It was a prostrate man face downward upon the ground, the head doubled under him at a horrible angle, the shoulders rounded and the body hunched together as if in the act of throwing a somersault. So grotesque was the attitude that I could not for the instant realize that that moan had been the passing of his soul. Not a whisper, not a rustle, rose now from the dark figure over which we stooped. Holmes laid his hand upon him and held it up again with an exclamation of horror. The gleam of the match which he struck shone upon his clotted fingers and upon the ghastly pool which widened slowly from the crushed skull of the victim. And it shone upon something else which turned our hearts sick and faint within us—the body of Sir Henry Baskerville!

There was no chance of either of us forgetting that peculiar ruddy tweed suit—the very one which he had worn on the first morning that we had seen him in Baker Street. We caught the one clear glimpse of it, and then the match flickered and went out, even as the hope had gone out of our souls. Holmes groaned, and his face glimmered white through the darkness.

"The brute! the brute!" I cried with clenched hands. "Oh, Holmes, I shall never forgive myself for having left him to his fate."

"I am more to blame than you, Watson. In order to have my case well rounded and complete, I have thrown away the life of my client. It is the greatest blow which has befallen me in my career. But how could I know—how *could* I know—that he would risk his life alone upon the moor in the face of all my warnings?"

"That we should have heard his screams—my God, those screams!—and yet have been unable to save him! Where is this brute of a hound which drove him to his death? It may be lurking among these rocks at this instant. And Stapleton, where is he? He shall answer for this deed."

"He shall. I will see to that. Uncle and nephew have been murdered

—the one frightened to death by the very sight of a beast which he thought to be supernatural, the other driven to his end in his wild flight to escape from it. But now we have to prove the connection between the man and the beast. Save from what we heard, we cannot even swear to the existence of the latter, since Sir Henry has evidently died from the fall. But, by heavens, cunning as he is, the fellow shall be in my power before another day is past!"

We stood with bitter hearts on either side of the mangled body, overwhelmed by this sudden and irrevocable disaster which had brought all our long and weary labours to so piteous an end. Then as the moon rose we climbed to the top of the rocks over which our poor friend had fallen, and from the summit we gazed out over the shadowy moor, half silver and half gloom. Far away, miles off, in the direction of Grimpen, a single steady yellow light was shining. It could only come from the lonely abode of the Stapletons. With a bitter curse I shook my fist at it as I gazed.

"Why should we not seize him at once?"

"Our case is not complete. The fellow is wary and cunning to the last degree. It is not what we know, but what we can prove. If we make one false move the villain may escape us yet."

"What can we do?"

"There will be plenty for us to do to-morrow. To-night we can only perform the last offices to our poor friend."

Together we made our way down the precipitous slope and approached the body, black and clear against the silvered stones. The agony of those contorted limbs struck me with a spasm of pain and blurred my eyes with tears.

"We must send for help, Holmes! We cannot carry him all the way to the Hall. Good heavens, are you mad?"

He had uttered a cry and bent over the body. Now he was dancing and laughing and wringing my hand. Could this be my stern, self-contained friend? These were hidden fires, indeed!

"A beard! A beard! The man has a beard!"

"A beard?"

"It is not the baronet—it is—why, it is my neighbour, the convict!"

With feverish haste we had turned the body over, and that dripping beard was pointing up to the cold, clear moon. There could be no doubt about the beetling forehead, the sunken animal eyes. It was indeed the same face which had glared upon me in the light of the candle from over the rock—the face of Selden, the criminal.

Then in an instant it was all clear to me. I remembered how the baronet had told me that he had handed his old wardrobe to Barrymore. Barrymore had passed it on in order to help Selden in his escape. Boots, shirt, cap—it was all Sir Henry's. The tragedy was still black enough, but this man had at least deserved death by the laws of his country. I told Holmes how the matter stood, my heart bubbling over with thankfulness and joy.

"Then the clothes have been the poor devil's death," said he. "It is clear enough that the hound has been laid on from some article of Sir Henry's—the boot which was abstracted in the hotel, in all probability—and so ran this man down. There is one very singular thing, however: How came Selden, in the darkness, to know that the hound was on his trail?"

"He heard him."

"To hear a hound upon the moor would not work a hard man like this convict into such a paroxysm of terror that he would risk recapture by screaming wildly for help. By his cries he must have run a long way after he knew the animal was on his track. How did he know?"

"A greater mystery to me is why this hound, presuming that all our conjectures are correct——"

"I presume nothing."

"Well, then, why this hound should be loose to-night. I suppose that it does not always run loose upon the moor. Stapleton would not let it go unless he had reason to think that Sir Henry would be there."

"My difficulty is the more formidable of the two, for I think that we shall very shortly get an explanation of yours, while mine may remain forever a mystery. The question now is, what shall we do with this poor wretch's body? We cannot leave it here to the foxes and the ravens."

"I suggest that we put it in one of the huts until we can communicate with the police."

"Exactly. I have no doubt that you and I could carry it so far. Halloa, Watson, what's this? It's the man himself, by all that's wonderful and audacious! Not a word to show your suspicions—not a word, or my plans crumble to the ground."

A figure was approaching us over the moor, and I saw the dull red glow of a cigar. The moon shone upon him, and I could distinguish the dapper shape and jaunty walk of the naturalist. He stopped when he saw us, and then came on again.

"Why, Dr. Watson, that's not you, is it? You are the last man that I should have expected to see out on the moor at this time of night. But, dear me, what's this? Somebody hurt? Not—don't tell me that it is our friend Sir Henry!" He hurried past me and stooped over the dead man. I heard a sharp intake of his breath and the cigar fell from his fingers.

"Who—who's this?" he stammered.

"It is Selden, the man who escaped from Princetown."

Stapleton turned a ghastly face upon us, but by a supreme effort he had overcome his amazement and his disappointment. He looked sharply from Holmes to me.

"Dear me! What a very shocking affair! How did he die?"

"He appears to have broken his neck by falling over these rocks. My friend and I were strolling on the moor when we heard a cry."

"I heard a cry also. That was what brought me out. I was uneasy about Sir Henry."

"Why about Sir Henry in particular?" I could not help asking.

"Because I had suggested that he should come over. When he did not come I was surprised, and I naturally became alarmed for his safety when I heard cries upon the moor. By the way"—his eyes darted again from my face to Holmes's—"did you hear anything else besides a cry?"

"No," said Holmes; "did you?"

"No."

"What do you mean, then?"

"Oh, you know the stories that the peasants tell about a phantom hound, and so on. It is said to be heard at night upon the moor. I was wondering if there were any evidence of such a sound to-night."

"We heard nothing of the kind," said I.

"And what is your theory of this poor fellow's death?"

"I have no doubt that anxiety and exposure have driven him off his head. He has rushed about the moor in a crazy state and eventually fallen over here and broken his neck."

"That seems the most reasonable theory," said Stapleton, and he gave a sigh which I took to indicate his relief. "What do you think about it, Mr. Sherlock Holmes?"

My friend bowed his compliments.

"You are quick at identification," said he.

"We have been expecting you in these parts since Dr. Watson came down. You are in time to see a tragedy."

"Yes, indeed. I have no doubt that my friend's explanation will cover the facts. I will take an unpleasant remembrance back to London with me to-morrow."

"Oh, you return to-morrow?"

"That is my intention."

"I hope your visit has cast some light upon those occurrences which have puzzled us?"

Holmes shrugged his shoulders.

"One cannot always have the success for which one hopes. An investigator needs facts and not legends or rumours. It has not been a satisfactory case."

My friend spoke in his frankest and most unconcerned manner. Stapleton still looked hard at him. Then he turned to me.

"I would suggest carrying this poor fellow to my house, but it would give my sister such a fright that I do not feel justified in doing it. I think that if we put something over his face he will be safe until morning."

And so it was arranged. Resisting Stapleton's offer of hospitality, Holmes and I set off to Baskerville Hall, leaving the naturalist to return alone. Looking back we saw the figure moving slowly away over the broad moor, and behind him that one black smudge on the silvered slope which showed where the man was lying who had come so horribly to his end.

13   FIXING THE NETS

"We're at close grips at last," said Holmes as we walked together across the moor. "What a nerve the fellow has! How he pulled himself together in the face of what must have been a paralyzing shock when he found that the wrong man had fallen a victim to his plot. I told you in London, Watson, and I tell you now again, that we have never had a foeman more worthy of our steel."

"I am sorry that he has seen you."

"And so was I at first. But there was no getting out of it."

"What effect do you think it will have upon his plans now that he knows you are here?"

"It may cause him to be more cautious, or it may drive him to desperate measures at once. Like most clever criminals, he may be too confident in his own cleverness and imagine that he has completely deceived us."

"Why should we not arrest him at once?"

"My dear Watson, you were born to be a man of action. Your instinct is always to do something energetic. But supposing, for argument's sake, that we had him arrested to-night, what on earth the better off should we be for that? We could prove nothing against him. There's the devilish cunning of it! If he were acting through a human agent we could get some evidence, but if we were to drag this great dog to the light of day it would not help us in putting a rope round the neck of its master."

"Surely we have a case."

"Not a shadow of one—only surmise and conjecture. We should be laughed out of court if we came with such a story and such evidence."

"There is Sir Charles's death."

"Found dead without a mark upon him. You and I know that he died of sheer fright, and we know also what frightened him; but how are we to get twelve stolid jurymen to know it? What signs are there of a hound? Where are the marks of its fangs? Of course we know that a hound does not bite a dead body and that Sir Charles was dead before ever the brute overtook him. But we have to *prove* all this, and we are not in a position to do it."

"Well, then, to-night?"

"We are not much better off to-night. Again, there was no direct connection between the hound and the man's death. We never saw the hound. We heard it, but we could not prove that it was running upon this man's trail. There is a complete absence of motive. No, my dear fellow; we must reconcile ourselves to the fact that we have no case at present, and that it is worth our while to run any risk in order to establish one."

"And how do you propose to do so?"

"I have great hopes of what Mrs. Laura Lyons may do for us when the position of affairs is made clear to her. And I have my own plan as well. Sufficient for to-morrow is the evil thereof; but I hope before the day is past to have the upper hand at last."

I could draw nothing further from him, and he walked, lost in thought, as far as the Baskerville gates.

"Are you coming up?"

"Yes; I see no reason for further concealment. But one last word, Watson. Say nothing of the hound to Sir Henry. Let him think that Selden's death was as Stapleton would have us believe. He will have a better nerve for the ordeal which he will have to undergo to-morrow, when he is engaged, if I remember your report aright, to dine with these people."

"And so am I."

"Then you must excuse yourself and he must go alone. That will be easily arranged. And now, if we are too late for dinner, I think that we are both ready for our suppers."

Sir Henry was more pleased than surprised to see Sherlock Holmes, for he had for some days been expecting that recent events would bring him down from London. He did raise his eyebrows, however, when he found that my friend had neither any luggage nor any explanations for its absence. Between us we soon supplied his wants, and then over a belated supper we explained to the baronet as much of our experience as it seemed desirable that he should know. But first I had the unpleasant duty of breaking the news to Barrymore and his wife. To him it may have been an unmitigated relief, but she wept bitterly in her apron. To all the world he was the man of violence, half animal and half demon; but to her he always remained the little wilful boy of her own girlhood, the child who had clung to her hand. Evil indeed is the man who has not one woman to mourn him.

"I've been moping in the house all day since Watson went off in the morning," said the baronet. "I guess I should have some credit, for I have kept my promise. If I hadn't sworn not to go about alone I might have had a more lively evening, for I had a message from Stapleton asking me over there."

"I have no doubt that you would have had a more lively evening," said Holmes drily. "By the way, I don't suppose you appreciate that we have been mourning over you as having broken your neck?"

Sir Henry opened his eyes. "How was that?"

"This poor wretch was dressed in your clothes. I fear your servant who gave them to him may get into trouble with the police."

"That is unlikely. There was no mark on any of them, as far as I know."

"That's lucky for him—in fact, it's lucky for all of you, since you are all on the wrong side of the law in this matter. I am not sure that as a conscientious detective my first duty is not to arrest the whole household. Watson's reports are most incriminating documents."

"But how about the case?" asked the baronet. "Have you made anything out of the tangle? I don't know that Watson and I are much the wiser since we came down."

"I think that I shall be in a position to make the situation rather more clear to you before long. It has been an exceedingly difficult and most complicated business. There are several points upon which we still want light—but it is coming all the same."

"We've had one experience, as Watson has no doubt told you. We heard the hound on the moor, so I can swear that it is not all empty superstition. I had something to do with dogs when I was out West, and I know one when I hear one. If you can muzzle that one and put him on a chain I'll be ready to swear you are the greatest detective of all time."

"I think I will muzzle him and chain him all right if you will give me your help."

"Whatever you tell me to do I will do."

"Very good; and I will ask you also to do it blindly, without always asking the reason."

"Just as you like."

"If you will do this I think the chances are that our little problem will soon be solved. I have no doubt——"

He stopped suddenly and stared fixedly up over my head into the air. The lamp beat upon his face, and so intent was it and so still that it might have been that of a clear-cut classical statue, a personification of alertness and expectation.

"What is it?" we both cried.

I could see as he looked down that he was repressing some internal emotion. His features were still composed, but his eyes shone with amused exultation.

"Excuse the admiration of a connoisseur," said he as he waved his hand towards the line of portraits which covered the opposite wall. "Watson won't allow that I know anything of art, but that is mere jealousy because our views upon the subject differ. Now, these are a really very fine series of portraits."

"Well, I'm glad to hear you say so," said Sir Henry, glancing with some surprise at my friend. "I don't pretend to know much about these things, and I'd be a better judge of a horse or a steer than of a picture. I didn't know that you found time for such things."

"I know what is good when I see it, and I see it now. That's a Kneller, I'll swear, that lady in the blue silk over yonder, and the stout gentleman with the wig ought to be a Reynolds. They are all family portraits, I presume?"

"Every one."

"Do you know the names?"

"Barrymore has been coaching me in them, and I think I can say my lessons fairly well."

"Who is the gentleman with the telescope?"

"That is Rear-Admiral Baskerville, who served under Rodney in the West Indies. The man with the blue coat and the roll of paper is Sir William Baskerville, who was Chairman of Committees of the House of Commons under Pitt."

"And this Cavalier opposite to me—the one with the black velvet and the lace?"

"Ah, you have a right to know about him. That is the cause of all the mischief, the wicked Hugo, who started the Hound of the Baskervilles. We're not likely to forget him."

I gazed with interest and some surprise upon the portrait.

"Dear me!" said Holmes, "he seems a quiet, meek-mannered man enough, but I dare say that there was a lurking devil in his eyes. I had pictured him as a more robust and ruffianly person."

"There's no doubt about the authenticity, for the name and the date, 1647, are on the back of the canvas."

Holmes said little more, but the picture of the old roysterer seemed to have a fascination for him, and his eyes were continually fixed upon it during supper. It was not until later, when Sir Henry had gone to his room, that I was able to follow the trend of his thoughts. He led me back into the banqueting-hall, his bedroom candle in his hand, and he held it up against the time-stained portrait on the wall.

"Do you see anything there?"

I looked at the broad plumed hat, the curling love-locks, the white lace collar, and the straight, severe face which was framed between them. It was not a brutal countenance, but it was prim, hard, and stern, with a firm-set, thin-lipped mouth, and a coldly intolerant eye.

"Is it like anyone you know?"

"There is something of Sir Henry about the jaw."

"Just a suggestion, perhaps. But wait an instant!" He stood upon a chair, and, holding up the light in his left hand, he curved his right arm over the broad hat and round the long ringlets.

"Good heavens!" I cried in amazement.

The face of Stapleton had sprung out of the canvas.

"Ha, you see it now. My eyes have been trained to examine faces and not their trimmings. It is the first quality of a criminal investigator that he should see through a disguise."

"But this is marvellous. It might be his portrait."

"Yes, it is an interesting instance of a throwback, which appears to be both physical and spiritual. A study of family portraits is enough to convert a man to the doctrine of reincarnation. The fellow is a Baskerville —that is evident."

"With designs upon the succession."

"Exactly. This chance of the picture has supplied us with one of our most obvious missing links. We have him. Watson, we have him, and I dare swear that before to-morrow night he will be fluttering in our net as helpless as one of his own butterflies. A pin, a cork, and a card, and we add him to the Baker Street collection!" He burst into one of his rare fits of laughter as he turned away from the picture. I have not heard him laugh often, and it has always boded ill to somebody.

I was up betimes in the morning, but Holmes was afoot earlier still, for I saw him as I dressed, coming up the drive.

"Yes, we should have a full day to-day," he remarked, and he rubbed his hands with the joy of action. "The nets are all in place, and the drag is about to begin. We'll know before the day is out whether we have caught our big, lean-jawed pike, or whether he has got through the meshes."

"Have you been on the moor already?"

"I have sent a report from Grimpen to Princetown as to the death of Selden. I think I can promise that none of you will be troubled in the matter. And I have also communicated with my faithful Cartwright, who would certainly have pined away at the door of my hut, as a dog does at his master's grave, if I had not set his mind at rest about my safety."

"What is the next move?"

"To see Sir Henry. Ah, here he is!"

"Good-morning, Holmes," said the baronet. "You look like a general who is planning a battle with his chief of the staff."

"That is the exact situation. Watson was asking for orders."

"And so do I."

"Very good. You are engaged, as I understand, to dine with our friends the Stapletons to-night."

"I hope that you will come also. They are very hospitable people, and I am sure that they would be very glad to see you."

"I fear that Watson and I must go to London."

"To London?"

"Yes, I think that we should be more useful there at the present juncture."

The baronet's face perceptibly lengthened.

"I hoped that you were going to see me through this business. The Hall and the moor are not very pleasant places when one is alone."

"My dear fellow, you must trust me implicitly and do exactly what I tell you. You can tell your friends that we should have been happy to have come with you, but that urgent business required us to be in town. We hope very soon to return to Devonshire. Will you remember to give them that message?"

"If you insist upon it."

"There is no alternative, I assure you."

I saw by the baronet's clouded brow that he was deeply hurt by what he regarded as our desertion.

"When do you desire to go?" he asked coldly.

"Immediately after breakfast. We will drive in to Coombe Tracey, but Watson will leave his things as a pledge that he will come back to you. Watson, you will send a note to Stapleton to tell him that you regret that you cannot come."

"I have a good mind to go to London with you," said the baronet. "Why should I stay here alone?"

"Because it is your post of duty. Because you gave me your word that you would do as you were told, and I tell you to stay."

"All right, then, I'll stay."

"One more direction! I wish you to drive to Merripit House. Send back your trap, however, and let them know that you intend to walk home."

"To walk across the moor?"

"Yes."

"But that is the very thing which you have so often cautioned me not to do."

"This time you may do it with safety. If I had not every confidence in your nerve and courage I would not suggest it, but it is essential that you should do it."

"Then I will do it."

"And as you value your life do not go across the moor in any direction save along the straight path which leads from Merripit House to the Grimpen Road, and is your natural way home."

"I will do just what you say."

"Very good. I should be glad to get away as soon after breakfast as possible, so as to reach London in the afternoon."

I was much astounded by this programme, though I remembered that Holmes had said to Stapleton on the night before that his visit would terminate next day. It had not crossed my mind, however, that he would wish me to go with him, nor could I understand how we could both be absent at a moment which he himself declared to be critical. There was nothing for it, however, but implicit obedience; so we bade good-bye to our rueful friend, and a couple of hours afterwards we were at the station of Coombe Tracey and had dispatched the trap upon its return journey. A small boy was waiting upon the platform.

"Any orders, sir?"

"You will take this train to town, Cartwright. The moment you arrive you will send a wire to Sir Henry Baskerville, in my name, to say that if he finds the pocketbook which I have dropped he is to send it by registered post to Baker Street."

"Yes, sir."

"And ask at the station office if there is a message for me."

The boy returned with a telegram, which Holmes handed to me. It ran:

Wire received. Coming down with unsigned warrant. Arrive five-forty.
                                                    LESTRADE.

"That is in answer to mine of this morning. He is the best of the professionals, I think, and we may need his assistance. Now, Watson, I think that we cannot employ our time better than by calling upon your acquaintance, Mrs. Laura Lyons."

His plan of campaign was beginning to be evident. He would use the baronet in order to convince the Stapletons that we were really gone, while we should actually return at the instant when we were likely to be needed. That telegram from London, if mentioned by Sir Henry to the Stapletons, must remove the last suspicions from their minds. Already I seemed to see our nets drawing closer around that lean-jawed pike.

Mrs. Laura Lyons was in her office, and Sherlock Holmes opened his interview with a frankness and directness which considerably amazed her.

"I am investigating the circumstances which attended the death of the late Sir Charles Baskerville," said he. "My friend here, Dr. Watson, has informed me of what you have communicated, and also of what you have withheld in connection with that matter."

"What have I withheld?" she asked defiantly.

"You have confessed that you asked Sir Charles to be at the gate at ten o'clock. We know that that was the place and hour of his death. You have withheld what the connection is between these events."

"There is no connection."

"In that case the coincidence must indeed be an extraordinary one. But I think that we shall succeed in establishing a connection, after all. I wish to be perfectly frank with you, Mrs. Lyons. We regard this case as one of murder, and the evidence may implicate not only your friend Mr. Stapleton but his wife as well."

The lady sprang from her chair.

"His wife!" she cried.

"The fact is no longer a secret. The person who has passed for his sister is really his wife."

Mrs. Lyons had resumed her seat. Her hands were grasping the arms of her chair, and I saw that the pink nails had turned white with the pressure of her grip.

"His wife!" she said again. "His wife! He is not a married man."

Sherlock Holmes shrugged his shoulders.

"Prove it to me! Prove it to me! And if you can do so——!" The fierce flash of her eyes said more than any words.

"I have come prepared to do so," said Holmes, drawing several papers from his pocket. "Here is a photograph of the couple taken in York four years ago. It is indorsed 'Mr. and Mrs. Vandeleur,' but you will have no difficulty in recognizing him, and her also, if you know her by sight. Here are three written descriptions by trustworthy witnesses of Mr. and Mrs. Vandeleur, who at that time kept St. Oliver's private school. Read them and see if you can doubt the identity of these people."

She glanced at them, and then looked up at us with the set, rigid face of a desperate woman.

"Mr. Holmes," she said, "this man had offered me marriage on condition that I could get a divorce from my husband. He has lied to me, the villain, in every conceivable way. Not one word of truth has he ever told me. And why—why? I imagined that all was for my own sake. But now I see that I was never anything but a tool in his hands. Why should I preserve faith with him who never kept any with me? Why should I try to shield him from the consequences of his own wicked acts? Ask me what you like, and there is nothing which I shall hold back. One thing I swear to you, and that is that when I wrote the letter I never dreamed of any harm to the old gentleman, who had been my kindest friend."

"I entirely believe you, madam," said Sherlock Holmes. "The recital of these events must be very painful to you, and perhaps it will make it easier if I tell you what occurred, and you can check me if I make any material mistake. The sending of this letter was suggested to you by Stapleton?"

"He dictated it."

"I presume that the reason he gave was that you would receive help from Sir Charles for the legal expenses connected with your divorce?"

"Exactly."

"And then after you had sent the letter he dissuaded you from keeping the appointment?"

"He told me that it would hurt his self-respect that any other man should find the money for such an object, and that though he was a poor man himself he would devote his last penny to removing the obstacles which divided us."

"He appears to be a very consistent character. And then you heard nothing until you read the reports of the death in the paper?"

"No."

"And he made you swear to say nothing about your appointment with Sir Charles?"

"He did. He said that the death was a very mysterious one, and that I should certainly be suspected if the facts came out. He frightened me into remaining silent."

"Quite so. But you had your suspicions?"

She hesitated and looked down.

"I knew him," she said. "But if he had kept faith with me I should always have done so with him."

"I think that on the whole you have had a fortunate escape," said Sherlock Holmes. "You have had him in your power and he knew it, and yet you are alive. You have been walking for some months very near to the edge of a precipice. We must wish you good-morning now, Mrs. Lyons, and it is probable that you will very shortly hear from us again."

"Our case becomes rounded off, and difficulty after difficulty thins away in front of us," said Holmes as we stood waiting for the arrival of the express from town. "I shall soon be in the position of being able to put into a single connected narrative one of the most singular and sensational crimes of modern times. Students of criminology will remember the analogous incidents in Godno, in Little Russia, in the year '66, and of course there are the Anderson murders in North Carolina, but this case possesses some features which are entirely its own. Even now we have no clear case against this very wily man. But I shall be very much surprised if it is not clear enough before we go to bed this night."

The London express came roaring into the station, and a small, wiry bulldog of a man had sprung from a first-class carriage. We all three

shook hands, and I saw at once from the reverential way in which
Lestrade gazed at my companion that he had learned a good deal since
the days when they had first worked together. I could well remember
the scorn which the theories of the reasoner used then to excite in the
practical man.

"Anything good?" he asked.

"The biggest thing for years," said Holmes. "We have two hours before we need think of starting. I think we might employ it in getting
some dinner, and then, Lestrade, we will take the London fog out of
your throat by giving you a breath of the pure night air of Dartmoor.
Never been there? Ah, well, I don't suppose you will forget your first
visit."

14   THE HOUND OF THE BASKERVILLES

One of Sherlock Holmes's defects—if, indeed, one may call it a defect
—was that he was exceedingly loath to communicate his full plans to
any other person until the instant of their fulfilment. Partly it came no
doubt from his own masterful nature, which loved to dominate and surprise those who were around him. Partly also from his professional caution, which urged him never to take any chances. The result, however,
was very trying for those who were acting as his agents and assistants. I
had often suffered under it, but never more so than during that long
drive in the darkness. The great ordeal was in front of us; at last we
were about to make our final effort, and yet Holmes had said nothing,
and I could only surmise what his course of action would be. My nerves
thrilled with anticipation when at last the cold wind upon our faces and
the dark, void spaces on either side of the narrow road told me that we
were back upon the moor once again. Every stride of the horses and every turn of the wheels was taking us nearer to our supreme adventure.

Our conversation was hampered by the presence of the driver of the
hired wagonette, so that we were forced to talk of trivial matters when
our nerves were tense with emotion and anticipation. It was a relief to
me, after that unnatural restraint, when we at last passed Frankland's

house and knew that we were drawing near to the Hall and to the scene of action. We did not drive up to the door but got down near the gate of the avenue. The wagonette was paid off and ordered to return to Coombe Tracey forthwith, while we started to walk to Merripit House.

"Are you armed, Lestrade?"

The little detective smiled.

"As long as I have my trousers I have a hip-pocket, and as long as I have my hip-pocket I have something in it."

"Good! My friend and I are also ready for emergencies."

"You're mighty close about this affair, Mr. Holmes. What's the game now?"

"A waiting game."

"My word, it does not seem a very cheerful place," said the detective with a shiver, glancing round him at the gloomy slopes of the hill and at the huge lake of fog which lay over the Grimpen Mire. "I see the lights of a house ahead of us."

"That is Merripit House and the end of our journey. I must request you to walk on tiptoe and not to talk above a whisper."

We moved cautiously along the track as if we were bound for the house, but Holmes halted us when we were about two hundred yards from it.

"This will do," said he. "These rocks upon the right make an admirable screen."

"We are to wait here?"

"Yes, we shall make our little ambush here. Get into this hollow, Lestrade. You have been inside the house, have you not, Watson? Can you tell the position of the rooms? What are those latticed windows at this end?"

"I think they are the kitchen windows."

"And the one beyond, which shines so brightly?"

"That is certainly the dining-room."

"The blinds are up. You know the lie of the land best. Creep forward quietly and see what they are doing—but for heaven's sake don't let them know that they are watched!"

I tiptoed down the path and stooped behind the low wall which surrounded the stunted orchard. Creeping in its shadow I reached a point whence I could look straight through the uncurtained window.

There were only two men in the room, Sir Henry and Stapleton. They sat with their profiles towards me on either side of the round table. Both of them were smoking cigars, and coffee and wine were in front of them. Stapleton was talking with animation, but the baronet looked pale and distrait. Perhaps the thought of that lonely walk across the ill-omened moor was weighing heavily upon his mind.

As I watched them Stapleton rose and left the room, while Sir Henry filled his glass again and leaned back in his chair, puffing at his cigar. I heard the creak of a door and the crisp sound of boots upon gravel. The steps passed along the path on the other side of the wall under which I crouched. Looking over, I saw the naturalist pause at the door of an out-house in the corner of the orchard. A key turned in a lock, and as he passed in there was a curious scuffling noise from within. He was only a minute or so inside, and then I heard the key turn once more and he passed me and reëntered the house. I saw him rejoin his guest, and I crept quietly back to where my companions were waiting to tell them what I had seen.

"You say, Watson, that the lady is not there?" Holmes asked when I had finished my report.

"No."

"Where can she be, then, since there is no light in any other room except the kitchen?"

"I cannot think where she is."

I have said that over the great Grimpen Mire there hung a dense, white fog. It was drifting slowly in our direction and banked itself up like a wall on that side of us, low but thick and well defined. The moon shone on it, and it looked like a great shimmering ice-field, with the heads of the distant tors as rocks borne upon its surface. Holmes's face was turned towards it, and he muttered impatiently as he watched its sluggish drift.

"It's moving towards us, Watson."

"Is that serious?"

"Very serious, indeed—the one thing upon earth which could have disarranged my plans. He can't be very long, now. It is already ten o'clock. Our success and even his life may depend upon his coming out before the fog is over the path."

The night was clear and fine above us. The stars shone cold and bright, while a half-moon bathed the whole scene in a soft, uncertain light. Before us lay the dark bulk of the house, its serrated roof and bristling chimneys hard outlined against the silver-spangled sky. Broad bars of golden light from the lower windows stretched across the orchard and the moor. One of them was suddenly shut off. The servants had left the kitchen. There only remained the lamp in the dining-room where the two men, the murderous host and the unconscious guest, still chatted over their cigars.

Every minute that white woolly plain which covered one-half of the moor was drifting closer and closer to the house. Already the first thin wisps of it were curling across the golden square of the lighted window. The farther wall of the orchard was already invisible, and the trees were standing out of a swirl of white vapour. As we watched it the fog-wreaths came crawling round both corners of the house and rolled slowly into one dense bank, on which the upper floor and the roof floated like a strange ship upon a shadowy sea. Holmes struck his hand passionately upon the rock in front of us and stamped his feet in his impatience.

"If he isn't out in a quarter of an hour the path will be covered. In half an hour we won't be able to see our hands in front of us."

"Shall we move farther back upon higher ground?"

"Yes, I think it would be as well."

So as the fog-bank flowed onward we fell back before it until we were half a mile from the house, and still that dense white sea, with the moon silvering its upper edge, swept slowly and inexorably on.

"We are going too far," said Holmes. "We dare not take the chance of his being overtaken before he can reach us. At all costs we must hold our ground where we are." He dropped on his knees and clapped his ear to the ground. "Thank God, I think that I hear him coming."

A sound of quick steps broke the silence of the moor. Crouching among the stones we stared intently at the silver-tipped bank in front of us. The steps grew louder, and through the fog, as through a curtain, there stepped the man whom we were awaiting. He looked round him in surprise as he emerged into the clear, starlit night. Then he came swiftly along the path, passed close to where we lay, and went on up the long slope behind us. As he walked he glanced continually over either shoulder, like a man who is ill at ease.

"Hist!" cried Holmes, and I heard the sharp click of a cocking pistol. "Look out! It's coming!"

There was a thin, crisp, continuous patter from somewhere in the heart of that crawling bank. The cloud was within fifty yards of where we lay, and we glared at it, all three, uncertain what horror was about to break from the heart of it. I was at Holmes's elbow, and I glanced for an instant at his face. It was pale and exultant, his eyes shining brightly in the moonlight. But suddenly they started forward in a rigid, fixed stare, and his lips parted in amazement. At the same instant Lestrade gave a yell of terror and threw himself face downward upon the ground. I sprang to my feet, my inert hand grasping my pistol, my mind paralyzed by the dreadful shape which had sprung out upon us from the shadows of the fog. A hound it was, an enormous coal-black hound, but not such a hound as mortal eyes have ever seen. Fire burst from its open mouth, its eyes glowed with a smouldering glare, its muzzle and hackles and dewlap were outlined in flickering flame. Never in the delirious dream of a disordered brain could anything more savage, more appalling, more hellish be conceived than that dark form and savage face which broke upon us out of the wall of fog.

With long bounds the huge black creature was leaping down the track, following hard upon the footsteps of our friend. So paralyzed were we by the apparition that we allowed him to pass before we had recovered our nerve. Then Holmes and I both fired together, and the creature gave a hideous howl, which showed that one at least had hit him. He did not pause, however, but bounded onward. Far away on the path we saw Sir Henry looking back, his face white in the moonlight, his hands raised in horror, glaring helplessly at the frightful thing which was hunting him down.

But that cry of pain from the hound had blown all our fears to the winds. If he was vulnerable he was mortal, and if we could wound him we could kill him. Never have I seen a man run as Holmes ran that night. I am reckoned fleet of foot, but he outpaced me as much as I outpaced the little professional. In front of us as we flew up the track we heard scream after scream from Sir Henry and the deep roar of the hound. I was in time to see the beast spring upon its victim, hurl him to the ground, and worry at his throat. But the next instant Holmes had emptied five barrels of his revolver into the creature's flank. With a last howl of agony and a vicious snap in the air, it rolled upon its back, four feet pawing furiously, and then fell limp upon its side. I stooped, panting, and pressed my pistol to the dreadful, shimmering head, but it was useless to press the trigger. The giant hound was dead.

Sir Henry lay insensible where he had fallen. We tore away his collar, and Holmes breathed a prayer of gratitude when we saw that there was no sign of a wound and that the rescue had been in time. Already our friend's eyelids shivered and he made a feeble effort to move. Lestrade thrust his brandy-flask between the baronet's teeth, and two frightened eyes were looking up at us.

"My God!" he whispered. "What was it? What, in heaven's name, was it?"

"It's dead, whatever it is," said Holmes. "We've laid the family ghost once and forever."

In mere size and strength it was a terrible creature which was lying stretched before us. It was not a pure bloodhound and it was not a pure mastiff; but it appeared to be a combination of the two—gaunt, savage, and as large as a small lioness. Even now, in the stillness of death, the huge jaws seemed to be dripping with a bluish flame and the small, deep-set, cruel eyes were ringed with fire. I placed my hand upon the glowing muzzle, and as I held them up my own fingers smouldered and gleamed in the darkness.

"Phosphorus," I said.

"A cunning preparation of it," said Holmes, sniffing at the dead animal. "There is no smell which might have interfered with his power of scent. We owe you a deep apology, Sir Henry, for having exposed you to this fright. I was prepared for a hound, but not for such a creature as this. And the fog gave us little time to receive him."

"You have saved my life."

"Having first endangered it. Are you strong enough to stand?"

"Give me another mouthful of that brandy and I shall be ready for anything. So! Now, if you will help me up. What do you propose to do?"

"To leave you here. You are not fit for further adventures to-night. If you will wait, one or other of us will go back with you to the Hall."

He tried to stagger to his feet; but he was still ghastly pale and trembling in every limb. We helped him to a rock, where he sat shivering with his face buried in his hands.

"We must leave you now," said Holmes. "The rest of our work must be done, and every moment is of importance. We have our case, and now we only want our man.

"It's a thousand to one against our finding him at the house," he continued as we retraced our steps swiftly down the path. "Those shots must have told him that the game was up."

"We were some distance off, and this fog may have deadened them."

"He followed the hound to call him off—of that you may be certain. No, no, he's gone by this time! But we'll search the house and make sure."

The front door was open, so we rushed in and hurried from room to room to the amazement of a doddering old manservant, who met us in the passage. There was no light save in the dining-room, but Holmes caught up the lamp and left no corner of the house unexplored. No sign could we see of the man whom we were chasing. On the upper floor, however, one of the bedroom doors was locked.

"There's someone in here," cried Lestrade. "I can hear a movement. Open this door!"

A faint moaning and rustling came from within. Holmes struck the door just over the lock with the flat of his foot and it flew open. Pistol in hand, we all three rushed into the room.

But there was no sign within it of that desperate and defiant villain whom we expected to see. Instead we were faced by an object so strange and so unexpected that we stood for a moment staring at it in amazement.

The room had been fashioned into a small museum, and the walls were lined by a number of glass-topped cases full of that collection of butterflies and moths the formation of which had been the relaxation of this complex and dangerous man. In the centre of this room there was an upright beam, which had been placed at some period as a support for the old worm-eaten baulk of timber which spanned the roof. To this post a figure was tied, so swathed and muffled in the sheets which had been used to secure it that one could not for the moment tell whether it was that of a man or a woman. One towel passed round the throat and was secured at the back of the pillar. Another covered the lower part of the face, and over it two dark eyes—eyes full of grief and shame and a dreadful questioning—stared back at us. In a minute we had torn off the gag, unswathed the bonds, and Mrs. Stapleton sank upon the floor in front of us. As her beautiful head fell upon her chest I saw the clear red weal of a whiplash across her neck.

"The brute!" cried Holmes. "Here, Lestrade, your brandy-bottle! Put her in the chair! She has fainted from ill-usage and exhaustion."

She opened her eyes again.

"Is he safe?" she asked. "Has he escaped?"

"He cannot escape us, madam."

"No, no, I did not mean my husband. Sir Henry? Is he safe?"

"Yes."

"And the hound?"

"It is dead."

She gave a long sigh of satisfaction.

"Thank God! Thank God! Oh, this villain! See how he has treated me!" She shot her arms out from her sleeves, and we saw with horror that they were all mottled with bruises. "But this is nothing—nothing! It is my mind and soul that he has tortured and defiled. I could endure it all, ill-usage, solitude, a life of deception, everything, as long as I could still cling to the hope that I had his love, but now I know that in this also I have been his dupe and his tool." She broke into passionate sobbing as she spoke.

"You bear him no goodwill, madam," said Holmes. "Tell us then where we shall find him. If you have ever aided him in evil, help us now and so atone."

"There is but one place where he can have fled," she answered. "There is an old tin mine on an island in the heart of the mire. It was there that he kept his hound and there also he had made preparation so that he might have a refuge. That is where he would fly."

The fog-bank lay like white wool against the window. Holmes held the lamp towards it.

"See," said he. "No one could find his way into the Grimpen Mire to-night."

She laughed and clapped her hands. Her eyes and teeth gleamed with fierce merriment.

"He may find his way in, but never out," she cried. "How can he see the guiding wands to-night? We planted them together, he and I, to mark the pathway through the mire. Oh, if I could only have plucked them out to-day. Then indeed you would have had him at your mercy!"

It was evident to us that all pursuit was in vain until the fog had lifted. Meanwhile we left Lestrade in possession of the house while Holmes and I went back with the baronet to Baskerville Hall. The story of the Stapletons could no longer be withheld from him, but he took the blow bravely when he learned the truth about the woman whom he had loved. But the shock of the night's adventures had shattered his nerves, and before morning he lay delirious in a high fever under the care of Dr. Mortimer. The two of them were destined to travel together round the world before Sir Henry had become once more the hale, hearty man that he had been before he became master of that ill-omened estate.

And now I come rapidly to the conclusion of this singular narrative, in which I have tried to make the reader share those dark fears and vague surmises which clouded our lives so long and ended in so tragic a manner. On the morning after the death of the hound the fog had lifted and we were guided by Mrs. Stapleton to the point where they had found a pathway through the bog. It helped us to realize the horror of this woman's life when we saw the eagerness and joy with which she laid us on her husband's track. We left her standing upon the thin peninsula of firm, peaty soil which tapered out into the widespread bog. From the end of it a small wand planted here and there showed where the path zigzagged from tuft to tuft of rushes among those green-scummed pits and foul quagmires which barred the way to the stranger. Rank weeds and lush, slimy water-plants sent an odour of decay and a heavy miasmatic vapour onto our faces, while a false step plunged us more than once thigh-deep into the dark, quivering mire, which shook for yards in soft undulations around our feet. Its tenacious grip plucked at our heels as we walked, and when we sank into it it was as if some malignant hand was tugging us down into those obscene depths, so grim and purposeful was the clutch in which it held us. Once only we saw a trace that someone had passed that perilous way before us. From amid a tuft of cotton-grass which bore it up out of the slime some dark thing was projecting. Holmes sank to his waist as he stepped from the path to seize it, and had we not been there to drag him out he could never have set his foot upon firm land again. He held an old black boot in the air. "Meyers, Toronto," was printed on the leather inside.

"It is worth a mud bath," said he. "It is our friend Sir Henry's missing boot."

"Thrown there by Stapleton in his flight."

"Exactly. He retained it in his hand after using it to set the hound upon the track. He fled when he knew the game was up, still clutching it. And he hurled it away at this point of his flight. We know at least that he came so far in safety."

But more than that we were never destined to know, though there was much which we might surmise. There was no chance of finding footsteps in the mire, for the rising mud oozed swiftly in upon them, but as we at last reached firmer ground beyond the morass we all looked eagerly for them. But no slightest sign of them ever met our eyes. If the earth told a true story, then Stapleton never reached that island of refuge towards which he struggled through the fog upon that last night. Somewhere in the heart of the great Grimpen Mire, down in the foul slime of the huge morass which had sucked him in, this cold and cruel-hearted man is forever buried.

Many traces we found of him in the bog-girt island where he had hid his savage ally. A huge driving-wheel and a shaft half-filled with rubbish showed the position of an abandoned mine. Beside it were the crumbling remains of the cottages of the miners, driven away no doubt by the foul reek of the surrounding swamp. In one of these a staple and chain with a quantity of gnawed bones showed where the animal had been confined. A skeleton with a tangle of brown hair adhering to it lay among the débris.

"A dog!" said Holmes. "By Jove, a curly-haired spaniel. Poor Mortimer will never see his pet again. Well, I do not know that this place contains any secret which we have not already fathomed. He could hide his hound, but he could not hush its voice, and hence came those cries which even in daylight were not pleasant to hear. On an emergency he could keep the hound in the out-house at Merripit, but it was always a risk, and it was only on the supreme day, which he regarded as the end of all his efforts, that he dared do it. This paste in the tin is no doubt the luminous mixture with which the creature was daubed. It was suggested, of course, by the story of the family hell-hound, and by the desire to frighten old Sir Charles to death. No wonder the poor devil of a convict ran and screamed, even as our friend did, and as we ourselves might have done, when he saw such a creature bounding through the darkness of the moor upon his track. It was a cunning device, for, apart from the chance of driving your victim to his death, what peasant would venture to inquire too closely into such a creature should he get sight of it, as many have done, upon the moor? I said it in London, Watson, and I say it again now, that never yet have we helped to hunt down a more dangerous man than he who is lying yonder"—he swept his long arm towards the huge mottled expanse of green-splotched bog which stretched away until it merged into the russet slopes of the moor.

15 A RETROSPECTION

It was the end of November, and Holmes and I sat, upon a raw and foggy night, on either side of a blazing fire in our sitting-room in Baker Street. Since the tragic upshot of our visit to Devonshire he had been engaged in two affairs of the utmost importance, in the first of which he had exposed the atrocious conduct of Colonel Upwood in connection with the famous card scandal of the Nonpareil Club, while in the second he had defended the unfortunate Mme. Montpensier from the charge of murder which hung over her in connection with the death of her step-daughter, Mlle. Carère, the young lady who, as it will be remembered, was found six months later alive and married in New York. My friend was in excellent spirits over the success which had attended a succession of difficult and important cases, so that I was able to induce him to discuss the details of the Baskerville mystery. I had waited patiently for the opportunity, for I was aware that he would never permit cases to overlap, and that his clear and logical mind would not be drawn from its present work to dwell upon memories of the past. Sir Henry and Dr. Mortimer were, however, in London, on their way to that long voyage which had been recommended for the restoration of his shattered nerves. They had called upon us that very afternoon, so that it was natural that the subject should come up for discussion.

"The whole course of events," said Holmes, "from the point of view of the man who called himself Stapleton was simple and direct, although to us, who had no means in the beginning of knowing the motives of his actions and could only learn part of the facts, it all appeared exceedingly complex. I have had the advantage of two conversations with Mrs. Stapleton, and the case has now been so entirely cleared up that I am not aware that there is anything which has remained a secret to us. You will find a few notes upon the matter under the heading B in my indexed list of cases."

"Perhaps you would kindly give me a sketch of the course of events from memory."

"Certainly, though I cannot guarantee that I carry all the facts in my mind. Intense mental concentration has a curious way of blotting out what has passed. The barrister who has his case at his fingers' ends and is able to argue with an expert upon his own subject finds that a week or two of the courts will drive it all out of his head once more. So each of my cases displaces the last, and Mlle. Carère has blurred my recollection of Baskerville Hall. To-morrow some other little problem may be submitted to my notice which will in turn dispossess the fair Fench lady and the infamous Upwood. So far as the case of the hound goes, however, I will give you the course of events as nearly as I can, and you will suggest anything which I may have forgotten.

"My inquiries show beyond all question that the family portrait did not lie, and that this fellow was indeed a Baskerville. He was a son of that Rodger Baskerville, the younger brother of Sir Charles, who fled with a sinister reputation to South America, where he was said to have died unmarried. He did, as a matter of fact, marry, and had one child, this fellow, whose real name is the same as his father's. He married Beryl Garcia, one of the beauties of Costa Rica, and, having purloined a considerable sum of public money, he changed his name to Vandeleur and fled to England, where he established a school in the east of Yorkshire. His reason for attempting this special line of business was that he had struck up an acquaintance with a consumptive tutor upon the voyage home, and that he had used this man's ability to make the undertaking a success. Fraser, the tutor, died, however, and the school which had begun well sank from disrepute into infamy. The Vandeleurs found it convenient to change their name to Stapleton, and he brought the remains of his fortune, his schemes for the future, and his taste for entomology to the south of England. I learn at the British Museum that he was a recognized authority upon the subject, and that the name of Vandeleur has been permanently attached to a certain moth which he had, in his Yorkshire days, been the first to describe.

"We now come to that portion of his life which has proved to be of such intense interest to us. The fellow had evidently made inquiry and found that only two lives intervened between him and a valuable estate. When he went to Devonshire his plans were, I believe, exceedingly hazy, but that he meant mischief from the first is evident from the way in which he took his wife with him in the character of his sister. The idea of using her as a decoy was clearly already in his mind, though he may not have been certain how the details of his plot were to be arranged. He meant in the end to have the estate, and he was ready to use any tool or run any risk for that end. His first act was to establish himself as near to his ancestral home as he could, and his second was to cultivate a friendship with Sir Charles Baskerville and with the neighbours.

"The baronet himself told him about the family hound, and so prepared the way for his own death. Stapleton, as I will continue to call him, knew that the old man's heart was weak and that a shock would kill him. So much he had learned from Dr. Mortimer. He had heard also that Sir Charles was superstitious and had taken this grim legend very seriously. His ingenious mind instantly suggested a way by which the baronet could be done to death, and yet it would be hardly possible to bring home the guilt to the real murderer.

"Having conceived the idea he proceeded to carry it out with considerable finesse. An ordinary schemer would have been content to work with a savage hound. The use of artificial means to make the creature diabolical was a flash of genius upon his part. The dog he bought in London from Ross and Mangles, the dealers in Fulham Road. It was the strongest and most savage in their possession. He brought it down by the North Devon line and walked a great distance over the moor so as to get it home without exciting any remarks. He had already on his insect hunts learned to penetrate the Grimpen Mire, and so had found a safe hiding-place for the creature. Here he kennelled it and waited his chance.

"But it was some time coming. The old gentleman could not be decoyed outside of his grounds at night. Several times Stapleton lurked about with his hound, but without avail. It was during these fruitless quests that he, or rather his ally, was seen by peasants, and that the legend of the demon dog received a new confirmation. He had hoped that his wife might lure Sir Charles to his ruin, but here she proved unexpectedly independent. She would not endeavour to entangle the old gentleman in a sentimental attachment which might deliver him over to his enemy. Threats and even, I am sorry to say, blows refused to move her. She would have nothing to do with it, and for a time Stapleton was at a deadlock.

"He found a way out of his difficulties through the chance that Sir Charles, who had conceived a friendship for him, made him the minister of his charity in the case of this unfortunate woman, Mrs. Laura Lyons. By representing himself as a single man he acquired complete influence over her, and he gave her to understand that in the event of her obtaining a divorce from her husband he would marry her. His plans were suddenly brought to a head by his knowledge that Sir Charles was about to leave the Hall on the advice of Dr. Mortimer, with whose opinion he himself pretended to coincide. He must act at once, or his victim might get beyond his power. He therefore put pressure upon Mrs. Lyons to write this letter, imploring the old man to give her an interview on the evening before his departure for London. He then, by a specious argument, prevented her from going, and so had the chance for which he had waited.

Driving back in the evening from Coombe Tracey he was in time to get his hound, to treat it with his infernal paint, and to bring the beast round to the gate at which he had reason to expect that he would find the old gentleman waiting. The dog, incited by its master, sprang over the wicket-gate and pursued the unfortunate baronet, who fled screaming down the yew alley. In that gloomy tunnel it must indeed have been a dreadful sight to see that huge black creature, with its flaming jaws and blazing eyes, bounding after its victim. He fell dead at the end of the alley from heart disease and terror. The hound had kept upon the grassy border while the baronet had run down the path, so that no track but the man's was visible. On seeing him lying still the creature had probably approached to sniff at him, but finding him dead had turned away again. It was then that it left the print which was actually observed by Dr. Mortimer. The hound was called off and hurried away to its lair in the Grimpen Mire, and a mystery was left which puzzled the authorities, alarmed the countryside, and finally brought the case within the scope of our observation.

"So much for the death of Sir Charles Baskerville. You perceive the devilish cunning of it, for really it would be almost impossible to make a case against the real murderer. His only accomplice was one who could never give him away, and the grotesque, inconceivable nature of the device only served to make it more effective. Both of the women concerned in the case, Mrs. Stapleton and Mrs. Laura Lyons, were left with a strong suspicion against Stapleton. Mrs. Stapleton knew that he had designs upon the old man, and also of the existence of the hound. Mrs. Lyons knew neither of these things, but had been impressed by the death occurring at the time of an uncancelled appointment which was only known to him. However, both of them were under his influence, and he had nothing to fear from them. The first half of his task was successfully accomplished, but the more difficult still remained.

"It is possible that Stapleton did not know of the existence of an heir in Canada. In any case he would very soon learn it from his friend Dr. Mortimer, and he was told by the latter all details about the arrival of Henry Baskerville. Stapleton's first idea was that this young stranger from Canada might possibly be done to death in London without coming down to Devonshire at all. He distrusted his wife ever since she had refused to help him in laying a trap for the old man, and he dared not leave her long out of his sight for fear he should lose his influence over her. It was for this reason that he took her to London with him. They lodged, I find, at the Mexborough Private Hotel, in Craven Street, which was actually one of those called upon by my agent in search of evidence. Here he kept his wife imprisoned in her room while he, disguised in a beard, followed Dr. Mortimer to Baker Street and afterwards to the station and to the Northumberland Hotel. His wife had some inkling of his plans; but she had such a fear of her husband—a fear founded upon brutal ill-treatment—that she dare not write to warn the man whom she knew to be in danger. If the letter should fall into Stapleton's hands her own life would not be safe. Eventually, as we know, she adopted the expedient of cutting out the words which would form the message, and addressing the letter in a disguised hand. It reached the baronet, and gave him the first warning of his danger.

"It was very essential for Stapleton to get some article of Sir Henry's attire so that, in case he was driven to use the dog, he might always have the means of setting him upon his track. With characteristic promptness and audacity he set about this at once, and we cannot doubt that the boots or chamber-maid of the hotel was well bribed to help him in his design. By chance, however, the first boot which was procured for him was a new one and, therefore, useless for his purpose. He then had it returned and obtained another—a most instructive incident, since it proved conclusively to my mind that we were dealing with a real hound, as no other supposition could explain this anxiety to obtain an old boot and this indifference to a new one. The more *outré* and grotesque an incident is the more carefully it deserves to be examined, and the very point which appears to complicate a case is, when duly considered and scientifically handled, the one which is most likely to elucidate it.

"Then we had the visit from our friends next morning, shadowed always by Stapleton in the cab. From his knowledge of our rooms and of my appearance, as well as from his general conduct, I am inclined to think that Stapleton's career of crime has been by no means limited to this single Baskerville affair. It is suggestive that during the last three years there have been four considerable burglaries in the west country, for none of which was any criminal ever arrested. The last of these, at Folkestone Court, in May, was remarkable for the cold-blooded pistolling of the page, who surprised the masked and solitary burglar. I cannot doubt that Stapleton recruited his waning resources in this fashion, and that for years he has been a desperate and dangerous man.

"We had an example of his readiness of resource that morning when he got away from us so successfully, and also of his audacity in sending back my own name to me through the cabman. From that moment he understood that I had taken over the case in London, and that therefore there was no chance for him there. He returned to Dartmoor and awaited the arrival of the baronet."

"One moment!" said I. "You have, no doubt, described the sequence of events correctly, but there is one point which you have left unexplained. What became of the hound when its master was in London?"

"I have given some attention to this matter and it is undoubtedly of importance. There can be no question that Stapleton had a confidant, though it is unlikely that he ever placed himself in his power by sharing all his plans with him. There was an old manservant at Merripit House, whose name was Anthony. His connection with the Stapletons can be traced for several years, as far back as the schoolmastering days, so that he must have been aware that his master and mistress were really husband

and wife. This man has disappeared and has escaped from the country. It is suggestive that Anthony is not a common name in England, while Antonio is so in all Spanish or Spanish-American countries. The man, like Mrs. Stapleton herself, spoke good English, but with a curious lisping accent. I have myself seen this old man cross the Grimpen Mire by the path which Stapleton had marked out. It is very probable, therefore, that in the absence of his master it was he who cared for the hound, though he may never have known the purpose for which the beast was used.

"The Stapletons then went down to Devonshire, whither they were soon followed by Sir Henry and you. One word now as to how I stood myself at that time. It may possibly recur to your memory that when I examined the paper upon which the printed words were fastened I made a close inspection for the water-mark. In doing so I held it within a few inches of my eyes, and was conscious of a faint smell of the scent known as white jessamine. There are seventy-five perfumes, which it is very necessary that a criminal expert should be able to distinguish from each other, and cases have more than once within my own experience depended upon their prompt recognition. The scent suggested the presence of a lady, and already my thoughts began to turn towards the Stapletons. Thus I had made certain of the hound, and had guessed at the criminal before ever we went to the west country.

"It was my game to watch Stapleton. It was evident, however, that I could not do this if I were with you, since he would be keenly on his guard. I deceived everybody, therefore, yourself included, and I came down secretly when I was supposed to be in London. My hardships were not so great as you imagined, though such trifling details must never interfere with the investigation of a case. I stayed for the most part at Coombe Tracey, and only used the hut upon the moor when it was necessary to be near the scene of action. Cartwright had come down with me, and in his disguise as a country boy he was of great assistance to me. I was dependent upon him for food and clean linen. When I was watching Stapleton, Cartwright was frequently watching you, so that I was able to keep my hand upon all the strings.

"I have already told you that your reports reached me rapidly, being forwarded instantly from Baker Street to Coombe Tracey. They were of great service to me, and especially that one incidentally truthful piece of biography of Stapleton's. I was able to establish the identity of the man and the woman and knew at last exactly how I stood. The case had been considerably complicated through the incident of the escaped convict and the relations between him and the Barrymores. This also you cleared up in a very effective way, though I had already come to the same conclusions from my own observations.

"By the time that you discovered me upon the moor I had a complete knowledge of the whole business, but I had not a case which could go to a jury. Even Stapleton's attempt upon Sir Henry that night which ended in the death of the unfortunate convict did not help us much in proving murder against our man. There seemed to be no alternative but to catch him red-handed, and to do so we had to use Sir Henry, alone and apparently unprotected, as a bait. We did so, and at the cost of a severe shock to our client we succeeded in completing our case and driving Stapleton to his destruction. That Sir Henry should have been exposed to this is, I must confess, a reproach to my management of the case, but we had no means of foreseeing the terrible and paralyzing spectacle which the beast presented, nor could we predict the fog which enabled him to burst upon us at such short notice. We succeeded in our object at a cost which both the specialist and Dr. Mortimer assure me will be a temporary one. A long journey may enable our friend to recover not only from his shattered nerves but also from his wounded feelings. His love for the lady was deep and sincere, and to him the saddest part of all this black business was that he should have been deceived by her.

"It only remains to indicate the part which she had played throughout. There can be no doubt that Stapleton exercised an influence over her which may have been love or may have been fear, or very possibly both, since they are by no means incompatible emotions. It was, at least, absolutely effective. At his command she consented to pass as his sister, though he found the limits of his power over her when he endeavoured to make her the direct accessory to murder. She was ready to warn Sir Henry so far as she could without implicating her husband, and again and again she tried to do so. Stapleton himself seems to have been capable of jealousy, and when he saw the baronet paying court to the lady, even though it was part of his own plan, still he could not help interrupting with a passionate outburst which revealed the fiery soul which his self-contained manner so cleverly concealed. By encouraging the intimacy he made it certain that Sir Henry would frequently come to Merripit House and that he would sooner or later get the opportunity which he desired. On the day of the crisis, however, his wife turned suddenly against him. She had learned something of the death of the convict, and she knew that the hound was being kept in the out-house on the evening that Sir Henry was coming to dinner. She taxed her husband with his intended crime, and a furious scene followed in which he showed her for the first time that she had a rival in his love. Her fidelity turned in an instant to bitter hatred, and he saw that she would betray him. He tied her up, therefore, that she might have no chance of warning Sir Henry, and he hoped, no doubt, that when the whole countryside put down the baronet's death to the curse of his family, as they certainly would do, he could win his wife back to accept an accomplished fact and to keep silent upon what she knew. In this I fancy that in any case he made a miscalculation, and that, if we had not been there, his doom would none the less have been sealed. A woman of Spanish blood does not condone such an injury so lightly. And now, my dear Watson, without referring to my notes, I cannot give you a more detailed account of this curious case. I do not know that anything essential has been left unexplained."

"He could not hope to frighten Sir Henry to death as he had done the old uncle with his bogie hound."

"The beast was savage and half-starved. If its appearance did not frighten its victim to death, at least it would paralyze the resistance which might be offered."

"No doubt. There only remains one difficulty. If Stapleton came into the succession, how could he explain the fact that he, the heir, had been living unannounced under another name so close to the property? How could he claim it without causing suspicion and inquiry?"

"It is a formidable difficulty, and I fear that you ask too much when you expect me to solve it. The past and the present are within the field of my inquiry, but what a man may do in the future is a hard question to answer. Mrs. Stapleton has heard her husband discuss the problem on several occasions. There were three possible courses. He might claim the property from South America, establish his identity before the British authorities there, and so obtain the fortune without ever coming to England at all; or he might adopt an elaborate disguise during the short time that he need be in London; or, again, he might furnish an accomplice with the proofs and papers, putting him in as heir, and retaining a claim upon some proportion of his income. We cannot doubt from what we know of him that he would have found some way out of the difficulty. And now, my dear Watson, we have had some weeks of severe work, and for one evening, I think, we may turn our thoughts into more pleasant channels. I have a box for 'Les Huguenots.' Have you heard the De Reszkes? Might I trouble you then to be ready in half an hour, and we can stop at Marcini's for a little dinner on the way?"

THE END

"Ready for a deliciously different read? Something quirky, edgy, and utterly original? This novel's for you, girlfriend! *The Church Ladies* is laugh-out-loud funny one minute, soul-deep serious the next. Every character came alive for me; every struggle rang true. Loved it, loved it!"

LIZ CURTIS HIGGS

AUTHOR OF *BAD GIRLS OF THE BIBLE* AND *BOOKENDS*

"I absolutely loved this book! Lisa Samson's talent leaves me envious and awestruck."

TERRI BLACKSTOCK

AUTHOR OF *WORD OF HONOR* AND *TRIAL BY FIRE*

"As a twenty-year member of the 'church ladies sorority,' I applaud Lisa's fresh and insightful novel. This book made me laugh, cry, and, most importantly, think. I'm sure that God, who loves an honest, questioning heart, is smiling with approval on this marvelous work."

ANGELA ELWELL HUNT

AUTHOR OF *THE IMMORTAL* AND *THE NOTE*

"Lisa Samson may as well quit writing right now because I don't know how she will ever top *The Church Ladies.* Samson's irresistible town of Mount Oak is Mitford with a glorious edge; the characters who populate it are as familiar as the men and women who occupy pews beside you each Sunday. Perhaps, as I did, you'll even catch a glimpse of yourself within the pages of her novel! This captivating, precious story of grace could not be more beautifully told."

DEBORAH RANEY

AUTHOR OF *A VOW TO CHERISH* AND *IN THE STILL OF NIGHT*

"Lisa Samson's writing is literate, wise, whimsical. To those looking for a delightful surprise: Read *The Church Ladies* and be refreshed!"

JAMES SCOTT BELL

AUTHOR OF *BLIND JUSTICE* AND *THE DARWIN CONSPIRACY*

"Lisa Samson's *The Church Ladies* is a rollicking ride into the world of those tenuous yet strong ties that bind believers and families together. It runs the gamut from tears to laughter…to the point where I stop to examine my own life and the masks we Christians wear.…

"Samson's unique flair for language and voice make this a book you'll remember long after you close the cover. *The Church Ladies* is a must-read that bravely shows us Christians aren't perfect—just forgiven. Kudos to Lisa Samson for her willingness to show us the real face of redemption.

"*The Church Ladies* takes readers past the bounds of popular convention and straight into the spectacle of the flawed and quirky lives of the Fraser family. Poppy Fraser, guilt-consumed pastor's wife, heads up the parade as the reluctant matron of Highland Kirk Presbyterian. She's an unconventional woman who fulfills the role handed to her about as fitfully as a bat in a chandelier.

"Samson's writing effervesces with a perception of human nature beyond her years. You will believe you can order up a latte at Java Jane's and tête-à-tête with the eclectic cast of characters who enliven the streets of Mount Oak. Sample a slice of this delicious novel…a reviving exploration of family love, duplicity, and forgiveness—all served up with a side of abiding grace—and you won't stop till you've finished the whole pie. Lisa Samson writes like a dream!"

PATRICIA HICKMAN

AWARD-WINNING AUTHOR OF *KATRINA'S WINGS*

"Many authors write about life as it *should* be; Lisa Samson writes about life the way it truly is: fiery and fragile, tender and tragic, messy and magnificent. A stand-out novel in the sea of Christian fiction, *The Church Ladies* is penetrating, poignant, and astonishingly real."

SHARI MACDONALD

AUTHOR OF THE SALINGER SISTERS SERIES

A Novel

Lisa E. Samson

Multnomah®Publishers *Sisters, Oregon*

THE CHURCH LADIES
published by Multnomah Publishers, Inc.
© 2001 by Lisa E. Samson

International Standard Book Number: 1-57673-748-9

Cover photo by Robert E. Schwerzel/PictureQuest

Scripture quotations are from:
The Holy Bible, New International Version © 1973, 1984 by International Bible Society, used by permission of Zondervan Publishing House
The Holy Bible, King James Version (KJV)

Multnomah is a trademark of Multnomah Publishers, Inc.,
and is registered in the U.S. Patent and Trademark Office.
The colophon is a trademark of Multnomah Publishers, Inc.

Printed in the United States of America

For information:
MULTNOMAH PUBLISHERS, INC.•POST OFFICE BOX 1720•SISTERS, OREGON 97759

Library of Congress Cataloging–in–Publication Data
Samson, Lisa, 1964–
    The church ladies / by Lisa E. Samson.   p.cm.   ISBN 1-57673-748-9
1. Women–Religious life–Fiction. 2. City and town life–Fiction. 3. Church membership–Fiction.
    I. Title.
PS3569.A46673 C47 2001   813'.54—dc21   00–012265

02 03 04 05—10 9 8 7 6 5 4 3

To Jack Cavanaugh,
fellow wordsmith and trusted friend.
Thanks for telling me to "Go for it."
This one's for you.

❈

Special thanks to Bill Jensen for giving this book a place at Multnomah. To Karen Walker, Penny Whipps, and Steve Curley for their diligence. To my own little family, Will, Tyler, Jake, and Gwynneth, I know this one took a while, so thank you for your sacrifice and your patience. To my sister Lori, thanks for always being excited about my books, and thanks for actually thinking my writing matters. To my friends who encouraged me along the way, Miss Gloria, Jennifer, Heather, Chris, Karen, Marty, Jack C., you all are priceless. To my writing family in Chi Libris, it's a joy to take the writer's journey with the wonderful likes of you all, but I especially want to thank Athol Dickson, Deborah Raney, Colleen Coble, Angela Elwell Hunt, James Scott Bell, Terri Blackstock, Shari MacDonald, Patricia Hickman, and dear Liz Higgs for all their encouragement. A huge, heartfelt thanks to Doris Elaine "Till" Fell, who kept me sane with her understanding, her sympathy, and her wisdom. You, wonderful lady, are a gem. Thank you to attorneys Jim Bell and Douglas Fierberg. Thank you, Lord Jesus, for giving me the chance to serve You. I am in awe of Your grace.

I love to hear from my readers! Please email me at lesamson@hotmail.com.

How good and pleasant it is when brothers live together in unity! It is like precious oil poured on the head, running down on the beard, running down on Aaron's beard, down upon the collar of his robes.

It is as if the dew of Hermon were falling on Mount Zion. For there the LORD bestows his blessing, even life forevermore.

PSALM 133

As a prisoner for the Lord, then, I urge you to live a life worthy of the calling you have received. Be completely humble and gentle; be patient, bearing with one another in love. Make every effort to keep the unity of the Spirit through the bond of peace. There is one body and one Spirit—just as you were called to one hope when you were called—one Lord, one faith, one baptism; one God and Father of all, who is over all and through all and in all.

EPHESIANS 4:1–6

One

Many mornings I awaken thinking how much easier the men have it. Their Monday through Friday rolls by on well-worn ruts in a convoy of monosyllabic tasks. Wake, eat, work, eat, work, eat, sleep. Saturdays pass much the same with an extra "sleep" included in the afternoon. But Sunday mornings in particular cause me to call into question that ridiculous description of women as "the fairer sex," because there's nothing less fair than divvying up early morning tasks that first day of the week.

Scrambling around for children's church material and doling out cold Pop Tarts to anyone coherent enough to grab one, I sweat through my shower freshness even before the obligatory, understated string of pearls decorates my collar bones. A quick spritz of the sweet, flowery perfume the ladies' auxiliary gave me for Christmas last year accompanies the pantyhose runner check. And then, while the darkened sky still hovers over me like a Reformer's cloak, I scurry over to the church in the obligatory, understated pair of bone-colored pumps to mimeograph the bulletin, and, heaven help me, I always discover at least three typos, some embarrassing, some amusing, all sure to be exhumed by the hardly understated, censorious church maven, Miss Poole.

"Reverend Fraser needs three teams for the Mount Oak All-Church Spring Troubles Tennis Tournament in July." That typo deserved typo hall of fame status in the "Tell It Like It Really Is" category. But when the bulletin called for "sex volunteers to cover the tables at the town health fair" the board

7

had actually met, threatening to take away the "bulletin ministry" from me. I asked Duncan: husband, ruling elder, teaching elder, pastor, groundskeeper, and father of my three children, "So, is that a promise?" and heard nothing further.

Clearly I had put him in a difficult position. Clearly I breached any convention mentioned in *The Proper Christian Ladies' Handbook of Church Etiquette and Behavior,* chapter 15—"Church Authority." But the final clause at the end of the book, "And if you fail to uphold these statutes, ask God to forgive you, and He will," did leave room for maneuvering without eternal consequences. Of course, the guilt can last a lifetime.

I know a lot about guilt. My name is Poppy Fraser, and I've been living with guilt for a long time now.

Though I apologized to Duncan for jeopardizing his good standing with the elders and begged God's forgiveness for my belligerence and all, I've never stopped feeling sick when I see Elder Barnhouse handing out the bulletins. Surely, Sunday wasn't designed to be this way. I often think about persecuted Christians in flowing robes risking their lives to praise the Lord and learn His ways. Who cared about bulletins and typos when lives were staked upon one's own simple obedience?

I long for that kind of purity again.

Years ago I convinced myself that God could meet with me right in my breakfast nook. It's amazing what we can talk ourselves into. Not that God isn't able to meet a person anywhere, but that Scripture verse about forsaking not the assembly of the brethren is in there for a reason. Sometimes I think I liked my husband better as just a computer geek who worked too hard seven days a week. Who is this caring, preacherly guy he has become? And where does that leave me? I am suspicious, and it grieves me.

Life as I now am forced to live it is more than I bargained for back at the altar.

And Duncan's sermons feel more like sedation than inspiration. Just being honest. Although, if I am being totally honest, I have to wonder if his words bounce off of the invisible shield that materialized around me the day he announced our lives would change forever.

Most men's midlife crises seem to be a wild, awkward clutching at rejuvenation. The pathetic sports car. The pathetic mistress. The sudden, pathetic interest in handball or the like and all the pathetic gear that goes along with it. But not my husband. Oh no. Nothing could ever be that simple or pathetic with Duncan. He had to do the opposite. Batten down the hatches. Tighten the reigns. Slam on the brakes.

Oh, boy.

And there we were selling practically everything we could and going to seminary in the Midwest. Surely if God called Duncan to be a pastor, I would have experienced some kind of call to be a pastor's wife. Surely a sovereign God would know better than to put someone like me into such a position.

Maybe if I had been saved in the Jesus movement or something very California I'd have a better grasp of the first day of the week now that it's become the focus of the other six as well. But I'm an East Coast girl, and the guilty dread and heroic resolution that haunt me from 8 P.M. Saturday night forward haven't rendered the day any more attractive. Well, at least our church has the sense to hold their worship at nine-thirty. That way I can be home to cook a nice brunch. Some things I refuse to give up. Or maybe I just can't.

But now that Duncan had benedicted the service and most of the congregation had snorted awake from their morning naps, I rode alongside my husband in our van. My youngest child, Angus, began crying in the backseat, resonating much like the main soprano in the threadbare group the Highland Kirk calls a choir for lack of a more suitable term. Their rendition of "Jerusalem" that morning truly inspired awe amid the congregation. I had no idea that such a familiar song could be transmogrified into a dirge. But apparently anything can happen on Sunday. And at Highland Kirk, where contemporary means Honeytree, Vestal Goodman, or Dave Boyer, it didn't surprise me.

It was a pleasing song to have whirling over and over on the brain calliope, however. "Hosanna, in the highest! Hosanna to your king!" In my head I sing like an opera singer. Only not quite so loud. Back in Baltimore, back when we had money and prestige and clippings of our smiling faces in the Maryland section of the *Sunpaper,* I found myself at the opera frequently. Maybe in heaven I'll get to sing like that. Or maybe I'll just keep painting pictures. It's the only thing I've ever been good at anyway.

"Angus, honey, would you please stop crying?" I glanced over my shoulder at my five-year-old slumped down so far the top of his behind smashed the frayed maroon cording clinging by exhausted threads to the edge of the van's bench seat. "Here, maybe this will help you feel better." I untwisted the coat hanger that wires the glove box shut and fished around for the pack of cookies I always keep on hand for such emergencies. When did I place these things in here? I couldn't even begin to remember.

Oh, brother. Stale treats again. On the highway of motherhood I careen a few miles north of Peg Bundy and at least a hundred miles south of Elyse Keaton. Mrs. Brady zooms somewhere on the other side of planet earth in a large, sparkling new SUV, with Donna Reed singing "I've Been Working on the Railroad" at her side, a car that seats eight and still smells new, a car with a clean windshield…on the *inside,* and no crumbs jumping up at every bump in the road.

Shuffling through the contents of the glove box, I realize someone has been messing with my "mobile junk drawer" as my husband christened the space years ago.

Well, Angus didn't do it. Though clinically, verifiably a genius, he possesses the motor skills of a three-year-old. The hanger would have deterred him right away. Angus would have rightly deemed a paltry little box of bleached out cookies cast in some obscure animalian shape not worth such effort. Although, considering the fact that any runway model out there prances around with a higher body fat percentage than he does, I wished he *were* the culprit. His dark hair and anemic complexion only heightens the innocent vulnerability that drives most mothers to their knees beside their child's sleeping form. I am no exception to this nocturnal activity. And in the end, I can only rest in the fact that we are all in God's hands.

My two eldest children, hard-working young adults who own their own cars, would rather die the death of a thousand screams than stoop to a ride in the putty-patched van. They couldn't have possibly taken the cookies.

The raiding of my glove box seems to presuppose a certain level of intimacy. Thus, I complete the elimination process. "Duncan!"

His small, brown eyes, diminished by the thick lenses of his round, wire-rimmed glasses, glimmer like M&M's fresh out of the package. And he frowns below a mustache with much the same mottled coloring as an old Scottish terrier. It is softer than it appears. "Why are you always picking on me, Poppy? What do you think a grown man like me would have to do with a pack of processed, pasteurized kid food like that?"

"Why wouldn't I think it was you, Duncan?" I shut the glove box door and begin to twist the hanger. "You have that look on your face. The same one you got when we caught you eating up the candy bars Robbie was supposed to take to class for the seventh grade Christmas party."

Duncan cringed. "Oh, well, thanks for bringing that up, Popp. Not to mention that was over seven years ago."

"Hey, once you've earned a reputation, it's hard to live it down." Fact is, Duncan has a sweet tooth the size of Jim Carrey's incisors.

I held onto the door handle as our minivan lurched down the road on worn-out shocks. "Besides, I thought you didn't like the cinnamon kind with the white icing."

"They weren't cinnamon, they were—" His eyes closed briefly. "Crud, Poppy. Why do you always do that? Can't you save those tactics for the kids?"

Meanwhile, Angus had stopped crying, but how long ago, I couldn't say.

"I'm okay now." His rather tart tone accused. "If anybody really cares, that is. The mice ate through the cords, and Aslan came back to life."

I swatted Duncan with a rolled-up bulletin—only one typo today, thank God, and I literally meant that. "I told you he was too young for those books."

"The boy reads at a tenth grade level." Duncan defended his choice of reading material for his son.

"It's not all about I.Q."

I felt a sense of despair just then, as if they were all slipping away from me sooner than they ought to be—even little Angus, who by all rights should barely know his *ABC*s. He had let me down. It had been his job to keep me from feeling old and used up, from being the only one left on the Starship Enterprise, while those I loved glittered and sparkled and were transported away, leaving nothing behind but the circles on which they once stood.

"Let's just get home," I said.

I wanted to open up my kitchen drawers, slide out my old Henckel knives and start chopping away. I wanted to smell baking bread and browning butter, frying potatoes and crisping bacon, and strong, black coffee. I wanted to turn on the little CD player in my kitchen and put on the Mamas and the Papas and think about how summers used to be when songs like that played on the radio.

I wouldn't dream of leaving Duncan. Ever. *Ever.* Would I? Well, maybe not today. But a girl could dream. *Oh, God. How can I even think such thoughts?*

To obey is better than sacrifice, the Old Testament says. But sometimes obedience *is* a sacrifice. All the harder to be cheerful about it.

Angus squinted against the sunlight slipping through the rolled-down van window, the only mode of air conditioning the revolting, rusting vehicle could sustain for the past three summers. He began to read again as we bobbed our way down Church Street toward the IGA for the pound of bacon I forgot to buy the day before. No surprise there. One day I'll start making lists, but not yet. I don't want to admit the gray matter is beginning to droop a bit.

The words of C. S. Lewis remained in Angus's book this time, though, his mouth echoing the church signs.

"Free coffee at the Southern Baptists!"

Five second intervals lapsed between announcements. "Modern worship at Aunt Chris's church.... The United Methodists say their church is 'a place where you can be yourself—whomever you love.' What does that mean, Mama? And shouldn't that be *who*ever?"

I remembered the gossip my best friend Chris Knight told me regarding the new twilight gay/lesbian ministry at Centennial United Methodist. "I'll tell you when you're older."

"Oh, look, the Wesleyans have 'the old time religion for today's generation.' And the Episcopals want people to 'come as you are.' How can you come as anything else?"

I love it when his little brows go together like that, but I wish Angus would stop reading. Still, I can't help watching in fascination as his pale blue eyes skitter back and forth, rapidly bouncing from sign to sign. I loathe the standards, banners, and posters that honkey-tonk "the sacred side show" as the townspeople of Mt. Oak have rightly dubbed Church Street. The spirit of competition from the hotels, motels, and restaurants out by Lake Coventry has infected the religious community, and I don't like it one bit. It takes the dignity away, as though winning souls is a race to be won, a fight to be fought...well, okay, St. Paul couldn't have been wrong. But surely he didn't mean *this*.

"'When you're fightin' for souls, it takes no prisoners!'" I heard Harlan Hopewell, pastor of Port of Grace Assemblies of God Church and famous televangelist, boom this during the rebroadcast of the live, Sunday telecast last Thursday on SFBN—the Spirit-Filled Broadcasting Network. Hard to believe Mount Oak ground out such a glitzy, slick ministry like the *Port of Peace Hour.* The woman with the big, frizzy, red hairdo that sings and cries seems to be a caricature of sorts. But she loves Jesus. That fact couldn't be plainer. She wears her affection for "my Lord and Savior" as she always calls Him like a badge of honor. Which is more than I can say for myself. Maybe one day I'll give up this fight. Maybe one day I'll truly become a pastor's wife like that lady and not some half-rate actor trying to play the part.

Monstrous Mt. Oak First Presbyterian rolled by next. All brick construction, three-story Corinthian pillars looming with an air of disapproval over the Chippendale handrails angling up beside the brick steps. "Well, lookey there." Angus pointed to the crisp white letters arranged behind the locked glass door of the classically structured sign near the street. "'Sanctuary open 24 hours because you never know when the Spirit's going to move.' It looks like even the PCA Presbyterians think they've got themselves an angle now."

Statements like these frighten me the most. Suddenly my son's tears over Aslan's death on the stone table gave me a great deal of comfort. "Read your book, Angus."

"But didn't you just tell Dad—"

"Yeah, I did. And you can wipe that smirk off of your face right now, Right Reverend Fraser. I'll just run in for the bacon. Can you let me off at the door? The last thing I want is for this hair of mine to frizz up in the humidity."

Duncan pulled the van up in front of the IGA, and I bounded out.

"Hey!" he called.

Much to my chagrin, Duncan motioned me around to his window. If I didn't get that bread rising soon, we wouldn't eat before three. Maybe some prepared fresh dough would suffice just this once, the cinnamon kind with the white icing.

Ha! That sure would get Duncan's goat! I held back a chuckle as I leaned my forearms on his door.

He leaned forward, speaking softly. "I'm sorry. I know it's hard with the kids, and I know I don't always make things easier for you. But I love you. You do know that, don't you?"

I felt the familiar, unwanted flood of memory at his tender words. *Oh, Duncan, what have I done to us?*

He wasn't called Jody any longer; he was called Joseph. He had a degree from the University of Maryland, and he had filled out to man-sized proportions with beveled biceps and tanned legs ending in feet that looked good in rugged hiking sandals. He was apologizing that it was he who was going to oversee the remodeling of my kitchen and dressing room even though his degree was in architecture. I remembered that his father, Frank Callahan, had redone the kitchen seven years before when we moved into the gracious old house near the Maryland Golf and Country Club. He had done his best to live up to his nickname "The Casanova of Countertops," and his advances just plain gave me the willies. The job had gone three months over schedule and fifteen thousand dollars over budget. I wondered why this young man, Joseph, felt the need to apologize for his presence when I welcomed it, not only because he was already establishing a reputation for excellence but because he was even more beautiful in form and face than the bag boy down at Safeway. These days, with the way

Duncan constantly put in seventy to ninety hours a week with his computer firm, my eyes wandered more and more in the direction of bag boys and cabana boys, bag boys and life guards at the club, and bag boys. Joseph Callahan seemed like the height of maturity compared to my normal, safe fantasy fare, and he'd be remodeling my kitchen for the entire spring.

"No need to apologize at all, Joseph. Can I get you a cup of coffee?"

And a minute later when his callused yet sensitive fingers slid against mine as he took the mug, I knew a mixture of fear and excitement so potent I wondered if I should flee from it, confront it, or wear it like a peignoir from Victoria's Secret.

Even five years later, that feeling is easily recalled. The clarity of the memory, the way my pulse quickens and my color heightens frightens me. I honestly can't say I wouldn't make the same mistake again. Are there any nunneries left around these parts?

"Believe me, you don't have anything to apologize for, Duncan. I'm sorry I overreacted about the book. I'm sorry about everything." More sorry than a woman could be for this many years without the chivalrous aid of Prince Valium. Sometimes I envy those sixties ladies who took downers and didn't trim the fat off of their T-bones before pan frying them in butter.

I leaned in and felt his mouth on mine. Familiar lips, unexciting but reliable. Duncan said what he always says when I apologize to him. "There's nothing to be sorry for, sweetie." Only Duncan didn't know what he was really saying or he'd never say that or anything even close to it.

"You go ahead on in, babe. Wouldn't want that hair of yours to frizz."

I heard his words behind me as I stepped up my pace and rubbed the tickle above my lip, courtesy of his mustache.

So I bought the thick-sliced hickory bacon, my reward for surviving another service as the pastor's wife of Highland Kirk Presbyterian Church, U.S.A. What a frustrating position. Unpaid, too, mind you. Did IBM expect their managers' wives to do half the work just because she'd said "I do" over two decades before?

I think not!

Calm down, Poppy. Just calm yourself right down.

Two

I believe the worst part of being a pastor's wife is living up to that verse in the Bible that talks about an elder having his family in order. I'm trying hard. I really am and all I can say is, boy, am I glad people can't read my mind. It's one thing to act the part, but thinking it is another matter altogether. Talk about unruly. We were very up-front with the session regarding our family when Duncan interviewed. Our daughter, Paisley, had not yet made the decision to follow Christ. She still hasn't and is proud of that fact, claiming she isn't some mindless sheep like the rest of us.

The session knit their brows in concern and offered to pray for her. But it wasn't until Duncan said she'd already moved away from home that the board told us it wouldn't affect their decision to hire him. At first I thought, "Well!" and branded them hypocrites. Now, I just don't know. I mean nobody wants trouble, and who can blame them?

The worst part of the day awaited me, and my stomach soured as I grabbed another box of animal crackers for the glove box and jogged to the IGA checkout counter.

Paisley had arrived from Lynchburg for a visit the night before. The women's college graduate, with a fresh bachelor's degree, would be heading off to start her master's degree in three days. And she deigned to grace Mount Oak with her glorious presence, if she did say so herself, "But only for a few days, Mother."

Mother. Muh-therrr.

I cringe at the memory of Paisley's tone of voice. I don't remember my I.Q. dropping seventy-five points, but apparently Paisley has been informed otherwise. There was no way the twenty-two-year-old would have been talked into going to church with the family. And brunch with bacon? Out of the question. These days, Paisley doesn't put much more between her lips than dark green salads with a frightening amount of curly things. Where she gets her protein, I'll never know.

When we pulled up into the drive, Paisley was just swinging her final leg into her car. I closed my eyes. *Oh, God, give me strength. Help me not to open my mouth.* I never figured I'd ever feel dread at the sight of one of my children. And I've asked myself over and over how it ever got to this.

Paisley climbed back out.

Paisley wore those awful multipocketed hip-huggers sewn from an old army parachute, and a cropped black tank top she simply didn't have the shape for. Talk about ribs!

Duncan hopped out while I helped Angus climb down from his car booster. "Where you goin', sport?" he asked her.

Paisley slammed her door and skipped over to her father in that college girl way, fluid hair flashing an accordion shine as it bounced up and down. She put her arms around his neck. "Daddy!" She kissed his cheek. "I'm glad I caught you. Mitch is having a gig down in Greensboro tonight!"

Don't say ANYTHING!

"Heh." Duncan emitted a very fake chuckle. "That's great, hon."

Oh yeah, right, Duncan. What a crock! Our daughter is going to one of those smoky, drug-infested goofball clubs where the mediocre music blares so loudly it crackles the eardrums like tissue paper, and that's the best you can do?

"When will you be back?" I tried to stop the words midflow as they rushed out, but they seemed to come alive, losing all the characteristics they had been born with in my brain. Just a factual question, nothing more. But my vocal chords ignored the blueprint I'd drawn, creating a Frankenstein monster of accusation, come to live on its own to maim, destroy, and pick flowers with everyone but Paisley.

Duncan tried to run interference. "Popp, she's twenty-two."

Traitor.

"Preach it, Daddy." Paisley chipped at the red-black lacquer on her pinkie nail, digging away at the small amount of progress I felt I had made during my daughter's four years away at college. When I say liberal arts I mean *liberal* arts! And to think we paid all of that money to have her brainwashed. Only God Himself will get through to that child, and I want to be as far away as possible when the real battle seethes. Some things even a mother doesn't want to be around to witness. I think all of us know how much pain we can truly handle.

If only Paisley could see inside my heart. If only she could remember what it was like to be held in my arms the way I remember holding her. My firstborn. My baby girl.

Paisley quarried a nail clipper out of a small, molded, black plastic purse shaped like an eggplant. "Mother, can't I just go to a club, watch my boyfriend play, come home, and that be the end of it? I'm not going to drink. I'm not going to take drugs. And I promise I won't even have premarital sex tonight if it'll keep you quiet." She clipped her pinkie nail.

"Paisley, I was just wondering what time you were coming home. That's all. I wasn't telling you not to go. And I thought you and Mitch had broken up." I hated the defensive tone in my voice, the way my head shook back and forth like one of those Asian child dashboard ornaments. *I am the mother! The mother! Why do I always feel like I'm on trial?*

"Whatever." Paisley held her hand up like the people on trashy talk shows, giving me that "talk to the hand" garbage. So much for all I tried to teach her about respecting her elders.

I felt my face flush, and I clenched my fists, watching as my daughter chucked the nail clipper back into her purse.

Duncan's arm slipped around my waist at the precise moment I gagged down my frustration. "Go inside," he whispered into my ear. "You know whatever you say won't do any good."

Why did he have to aggravate the situation by making it "good cop, bad cop" all the time? *Don't I know what Paisley really needs? I am the female, right? Don't I have the inside scoop?*

"Come on, Gus, let's go." The fire inside of me lowered at the cool touch upon my little boy's bony, vulnerable shoulders. "How about if I read you some *Curious George?*"

"*Curious George?* Don't hold him back, Mother," Paisley ordered. "You're always trying to make him into something he's not." She yanked open her car door for the second time that day. "The child should be in a program for gifted children. We've got ourselves a living, breathing, genius and you feel you're qualified to do what's best for him. We learned all the drawbacks of homeschooling in Sociology of Education."

The sharpness of Paisley's voice assaulted the back of my head. Well, lah-dee-dah, Miss Twenty-Two-Year-Old educational authority of the universe. My own dissatisfaction with her abhors me. Maybe Duncan was right. Maybe I really should get inside and start the coffee. The Lord knew I needed a cup about now! I picked up my pace, determined to get to the kitchen before Paisley said another word.

"Now, Paisley," Duncan began, sounding like the *Father Knows Best* guy, Robert something or other. "Your mother is doing what we both think is best."

Oh, man. I felt the blush climb higher on my face and picked up my pace. Get inside, Popp!

"What *she* thinks is best." Paisley whipped her long, newly blackened hair into a ponytail.

"What do you mean?" Duncan asked in his typical naïve manner. "Your mother is one of the…"

But I tuned him out and continued my clipped pace to the house. I just couldn't listen to Paisley's never ending drone. Not now.

I yanked open the screen door.

If Paisley still lived at home, my quandary over whether or not to flee would be a no brainer. They say confession is good for the soul, but if I ever told Duncan about Jody…well, I can't even begin to guess how the conversation, much less the future, would turn out.

I followed Angus into the living room heading straight for *Curious George*. At least I could always count on *The Man with the Yellow Hat* to do the right thing by George. To just be nice. Why couldn't Paisley just be nice?

"She's not like you, Mama."

Angus's voice startled me. I had no idea I'd said the words out loud.

I heard Paisley's tires crunch the gravel of the drive as she drove away. Two minutes later the smell of bacon skirled in from the kitchen. After finishing the book, I went in to begin making a pot of coffee but saw that it was already brewing.

"What am I doing wrong, Duncan?" I began to peel potatoes for home fries, turning on a warm stream from the faucet.

"It's not just you, Popp. Paisley's responsible for her own actions now. She's an adult."

"I've failed her, though. Isn't it my responsibility as the mother to make sure that she learns how to be a woman?"

He shuffled the bacon on the griddle with a long fork. "You can only do so much, sweetie."

I adjusted the temperature of the running water, a bit cooler and it would be just right. "She thinks I'm a monster. And she thinks you're so nice. I feel unsupported by you, Duncan. Like I'm the only one who'll say it like it is with that child."

"I've always had a soft spot for her, Popp. You know that."

"But don't you worry about her?"

"All the time."

"You don't act like it." *Drat this peeler. I need to buy a new one, but I forget every time I'm in the store.* "And you never reprimand her."

"If we both jumped on her all the time, she'd never come home. And what good would that do?"

That was the truth. But it didn't seem like a tactic James Dobson would approve of!

I remember the times of my life when I wanted Jesus to hold off His coming just a little longer. Until the wedding. Until the baby was born. Until the house was finished. But these days, my own existence prompts me to cry out, "Come quickly, Lord Jesus." Oh, surely it's not that I feel I'm ready for His return, that I've redeemed my time in these evil days. I just want Him to save me from myself.

Three

Whoever said crickets brought good luck clearly was not a cricket.

I forced open my eyes in the 5 A.M. darkness, not quite ready for the search and destroy mission that normally compelled me from the warm nest of our bed. I once heard someone call crickets "nature's musicians." Good grief. If Jiminy Cricket scraped his back legs in my corner, I would cheerfully fwapp him with the white plastic sole of my Deerfoams, without a second thought. That little umbrella wouldn't fool me. A bug is a bug.

I rolled away the granular buildup from the base of my eyelashes. I never had sleepies until Angus's pregnancy, a heavyweight occurrence that threw my then forty-year-old body completely over the precipice of middle age, sent my youth flying over the wall of years like a blob of hot, bumpy tar, destined to splatter upon impact and burn out more quickly than its original design had intended. One day I had been a size seven with skinny arms, and the next the tags on my khakis mockingly pronounced me a size fourteen.

How Duncan can stand to even touch me now mystifies me. But there he stands every Monday night with that silly grin of romantic expectation on his face.

Settling my contacts over my corneas, I grumbled as I stood up. Like this walk was really going to do any good.

After tumbling into a pair of khaki shorts and squeezing my short, smashed, dark curls through the neck of a faded, navy blue T-shirt, I laced up my geriatric tan walking shoes and checked to make sure Paisley and Robbie had made it home and Angus still breathed.

Robbie, the middle child, my twenty-year-old water-skiing champion for two years running at Lake Coventry snored on the couch in the living room. The remote, magically still in hand, pointed toward the color bars on the television screen. He worked a late night. Closing down any fast-food joint isn't a task to be desired, but scrubbing the grill at Jeanelle's Juicy Burgers made cleaning out the fry daddy seem like wiping up Kool-Aid.

P.U., Rob. Couldn't you have taken a shower before you collapsed?

I couldn't help smoothing the light brown curls off of his forehead. So beautiful. Of all three children, Robbie has always understood me the most. And I've done my best not to play favorites, but Robbie has always sought out physical affection, hugs and kisses. He had snuggled in our bed in the morning before kindergarten, or woke me up by kissing my arm. Paisley shunned such expression, even as a tot. I should have reached out to her more.

I stay put here in Mount Oak for Robbie's sake. Angus's age, size, and lack of ability to make friends his own age classify him as carry-on luggage. Compact and ready to flee. But Robbie has a real life here. Robbie doesn't deserve the fallout my desertion would cause.

He opened his eyes. Though the dark of the room shadowed them, the same light blue as his little brother's looked up at me. "Off already, Mom?" His deep, sleepy voice muffled the words. "Want some company on your walk?"

"No, you got in late. Get some sleep."

His smooth jaw slackened before I even finished speaking. I kissed his prickly cheek, sighed, and stood up. Red and white uniform clothing trailed from the small bathroom down the hall, and a glass of Coke sat in a giant ring of water on the coffee table.

Definitely stuff to save for later.

I began the two-mile walk to the center of town. I do this every morning, bent on claiming first dibs to the only truly decent cup of coffee Mount Oak is capable of providing this early, a little place called Java Jane's.

Stainless steel, hardwoods, and purple leather cover every available surface. Pink velvet frames surrounding caricatures of local politicians add that confusing *je ne sais quoi* I admire in a town with little moxy.

I hopped down the stone steps of the house. The quaint bungalow shines with authentic, well-polished woodwork and built-in cabinetry from the arts and crafts movement. The church elder who ushered us on the tour of the house apologized for its old-fashioned ways, but since I was practically born with a paintbrush in my hand and coffee-table books about Degas, Braque, and Frank Lloyd Wright in my crib, I hooted with delight.

I pronounced it perfect, this little diamond in the woods, snugly set near the platinum waters of Lake Coventry. It filled a longing in my heart I hadn't previously known existed. Just two bedrooms, a living room, and a kitchen was all the real space the tiny house afforded, besides a sun porch and the attic that became Robbie's room. This sweet study of simplicity could have practically fit into the square footage of the family room of my old house by the country club in Maryland, the house I'd literally kissed good-bye when we left for St. Louis and seminary.

This, however, was simply home. A real home where people made it special, not gold faucets, granite counters, and dental molding on the bulkheads of the kitchen cabinets. A real home where the evidence of past families have been added to the traditions of our own. Angus's height will be recorded with children named Patty and Laurie and Beth, Heather and Wendy and Billy, children we'd never know but to whom he would compare himself until he either stopped growing or we moved away from the Highland Kirk.

Sometimes I think the Methodists have the right idea. Five or so years at one place and then, *YOU'RE OUTTA THERE!*

The area possesses an interesting history, Elder Barnhouse explained that first day. "Used to be, just 'bout ten years back Tweed Creek ran down the Coventry Valley just 'bout half a mile away. Then the power authority dammed it up near Dickerson's Pass, and Lake Coventry filled up the valley."

"So that's why the church is located right here by all the hotels and condos? Seemed like an unusual setup." Duncan's voice echoed from the glassed-in sunporch on the side of the house, the room I claimed immediately as my painting studio.

"Prime real estate now. Every square inch of the lot." Elder Barnhouse beamed like the jack-o-lanterns I imagined sitting on the stone posts at the bottom of the front steps. Do Presbyterians around here trick or treat, I wondered then.

Living on a lake seems too good to imagine, really—other than the dreadful "finding Angus drowned" factor that I live with every moment he isn't by my side. Everything is so painfully picturesque. The blues and greens glow so vividly my photos look fake. No one back in Maryland really believes such a place exists. They claim I embellish it all to make them jealous, to convince them I really made out by forsaking the high life, or worse, to entice them to come for a visit.

Heaven forbid.

So two hours after Duncan marched across the stage at Covenant Seminary to receive his diploma, we piled in the monstrous van and towed a U-Haul trailer all the way to Mount Oak. Three years ago.

Hurrying down the slate walk, I promised myself I'd finally dig up those malicious fountains of monkey grass this fall. I've hated the pernicious domes since the day we moved in. And they've been spreading ever since. My annuals had started to fade, and a month ago I stopped deadheading the red-and-white-striped petunias around the border of my flowerbeds. Poor little things. I know the little brown bungalow deserves perennials, but life isn't that certain. Not since we moved away from Baltimore. Not since Jody Callahan. Joe now. It was Joe now. And the thought of leaving the plants behind, plants that I had tended so carefully, season after season, year after year, brought on an unacceptable sadness.

I steer my feet to the gravel at the side of Lake Shore Drive. Not much activity from the vacationers this early. The B&Bs, inns, and motels I pass calmly huddle near the dark water. A few sprinkling systems busy themselves watering the gardens for which Lake Coventry is known. Hanging baskets garnish each doorway and window boxes seethe with white allysum and cascading blue lobelia. Bus groups on their way to D.C., the mountains, or the beach toured the border gardens surrounding most of the establishments.

I turn down Tweed Street, heading into town. Neon lights and transportable signs with big yellow arrows line this stretch between the wooded shores of the lake and the town square. Here the commercialism runs as thick as the start of the annual Mount Oak five kilometer run, and sprints at a rapid pace all summer long toward the finish line and that most coveted prize—three months in winter with nothing to do but worry about the coming season and complain about the previous one.

The first sign of life appears in front of Josef's, the only place offering haute cuisine. Josef himself stands out back watering his herbs. Guess they rise early in the old country. Forty strawberry pots curve their way up the side of his lot. He waves. I wave. And that pretty much is that. Josef knows little English, and I have it on fact that when he uses up the last of his tarragon, he resorts to Knorr's for his béarnaise sauce. I haven't found a better one myself.

I tromp past the neon signs that animate Tweed Street. Barnacle Bill's—owned by a retired accountant named Charlie Dickens, a member at Highland Kirk—displays a sign with a fish flapping its tail. Jeanelle's Juicy Burgers—flipped by Jeanelle herself, a New Age, chain smoking local with sun-leathered skin and a brassy blond braid that kisses the back of her thighs—sports a neon burger complete with lit up lettuce, onion, and ketchup. The Colonel's Kitchen—serving the finest creamed chipped beef and hash browns while the Colonel, a lapsed Catholic, stands guard at the cash register making sure the kids take only one lollipop apiece—has no neon lights. But a huge picture of General MacArthur has been bleaching itself in the front window for as long as I've been around. The great general now looks twenty years younger and sports light mocha-colored aviator sunglasses.

These are the high calorie money makers of Tweed Street.

But caffeine calls and I look forward to having my first clear thought of the day. Always the first customer of the jaunty little spot right on the town square, I push open the door. A string of tiny, oriental bells tinked against the glass.

"Good morning!" I peeled a copy of the day's *Washington Post* off the counter and sitting down in a club chair the color of crushed plums in the back corner, I flipped on a nearby floor lamp, sunk into the plush upholstery, and set the backs of my shoes onto the hammered stainless steel coffee table. The owners called a, "Good morning back atcha, Poppy," and resumed their preparations for the day.

If they had copies of the *Baltimore Sun,* I'd buy that. Sometimes my parents send me a copy, and I can travel home via newsprint for a bit. But the *Post* has to do in between times. My early morning ritual doesn't really have much to do with burning calories or staying healthy. It gives me escape from life down here. Tells me about things with which I am familiar. Eases the homesickness for a time.

The national news is pretty much the same as the *Richmond Times* and CNN. More scandal. More politicians unable to keep something shut. No surprise there. But I look at the pictures carefully, trying to see familiar landscape, enjoying the bit of Baltimore news allowed to denigrate *Post* pages.

Traffic is always big news. Road construction to help angry people get to jobs they hate sooner. Education is a familiar topic. No money, no learning. And how about them vouchers? Crime. Interesting but depressing. I skim news about the open-air drug market on C Street. How does that happen? Open-air? If the newspapers know about it, why aren't the metro police doing anything substantial?

Mount Oak's obvious advantages come to the fore during issues like this. Another good reason for dropping by.

Today, however, the conversation of the owners of Java Jane's proved too interesting, and I pretended to read the paper, a mere foil for eavesdropping on the two women who had been roommates at UNC-Chapel Hill. Ellen, a verbose redhead, speaks in colorful prose and hums like an actress singing at a pianoforte in a screen adaptation of a Jane Austen novel. She wears flowing things to go with her flowing hair and her flowing voice, and lots of embroidered vests and clunky shoes. She possesses a self-proclaimed penchant for handmade earrings that sway in time with her speech.

Margaret, skinny with bright blue eyes, sports Maria Shriver hair that probably weighs more than she does. She speaks at the front of her mouth and smiles with the point of her tongue between her teeth as if to show her sense of humor goes all the way down to the bottom. The same diamond posts glitter in her earlobes day after day.

"Sue Green wrote me yesterday." Margaret opened a large bag of espresso beans and poured them into the funnel-shaped bowl of the grinder. "Remember her?"

"Oh yes." Ellen nodded. "The pixielike, pointy-faced girl with the bandana penchant in your accounting class." She pulled a jug of 2 percent out of the fridge and began to fill the stainless steel carafe for those who like their coffee watered down that way.

"The one that refused to wear a bra, uh-huh."

"Wasn't she…?" Ellen's hand flattened out, an airplane dipping its wings quickly from side to side.

"Apparently not. She was engaged to a man, but now it's off."

Ellen started on the whole milk and shouted, "Why?" as Margaret ground the beans for my Red-Eye.

"Her fiancé was named Kevin Akers."

"So?"

I perked up. This sounded interesting. I've always disliked the name Kevin because I get it mixed up with the name Keith. So, invariably I call Kevins Keith and Keiths Kevin. Let your Kevins be Kevins and your Keiths be Keiths, I say, but my memory doesn't wish to cooperate.

"Well, she refused to give up her name or take his, and he insisted that if she loved him, she would at least hyphenate it, but she refused." Margaret crossed her arms and raised her eyebrows. "Sue Green, Brian Akers…"

Ellen's nostrils flared as the lightbulb flickered to life. "Oh, that's fabulous! Absolutely the most fabulous thing I've ever heard. Gloria Steinham would have been proud to know that a perfectly wonderful relationship had been sacrificed on the high altar of feminism."

Margaret began making two shots of espresso while Ellen pulled out a paper cup and filled it with the day's dark roast. "I can hear Bella applauding from here."

I couldn't help myself. "Not to mention Arnold Ziphal or Mr. Haney."

Ellen shook her head, her long, red hair flailing the air. She held out the cup while Margaret dropped the espresso into the brew. "When love and politics collide."

"Usually love wins out, but obviously not in this case," Margaret said. "It always did with me, though. Here you go, Poppy." She placed the coffee on the counter.

I slapped my shoes onto the floor, walked over, and grabbed the cup.

Sipping the strong, black liquid, in a whisper I proclaimed, "Perfect." Worth every step of the walk over.

"What do you think about that?" I sidled up to the grinder. "About that girl. Would you leave a guy over something like that?"

Both the women shook their heads. "Negative," said Ellen.

"Nah," Margaret agreed. "What about you, Poppy?"

I shrugged. "I don't think I'd leave a guy over something like that. Now, if he'd had an affair or something…"

"Absolutely," Ellen nodded as she spoke. "I wouldn't even want him haunting my attic!"

"I don't know…there's something to be said for forgiveness," Margaret said. "'To err is human—'"

Ellen waved that away. "Don't get me wrong; you can forgive, but it will never, ever be remotely the same." Ellen reached under the counter for a tray of fresh bagels and began to arrange them in an artsy willow basket. "It's like once you've eaten bad steak tartar, you never trust raw meat again."

"Would you tell?" I asked. "If you'd had an affair? Would you tell your husband?"

Ellen pursed her lips for several seconds. "Negative. Even though I've failed to hitch my wagon to a reliable paycheck, I can't ever see myself letting loose a corker like that!"

"I'd tell." Margaret arranged blondies on a plate destined to be covered with a glass dome. "I couldn't live with myself. It would be living a lie."

Yes. The Big Lie. The Masquerade.

Ellen snorted. "Oh, please, Mag. You sound like a soap opera that's lost its lather. All the psychologists say it's better not to tell. Once trust is broken it can never truly be made whole."

"I probably agree with you, Ellen." I put a lid on my coffee, checked my wristwatch, and realized the crew would soon be awake back at the bungalow. "Bye, girls. See ya tomorrow."

On my way home the delivery trucks had begun warming up, and joggers were doing much the same. I sipped on the coffee and hummed about fresh air, Times Square, and allergic smelling hay.

New York. Maybe that's where I'll go. Start doing abstracts, live in a small loft apartment in Soho, just me and Angus. Fruits and vegetables from the produce stands, bread from Zabar's, fresh flowers once a week, and a trip to Chinatown the first Wednesday of every month. We'd have to economize due to the high cost of living, but imagine the days we could spend at the museums: the Museum of Modern Art, the Guggenheim, or the Metropolitan. And all the little galleries!

But what about the roaches? Even worse than crickets. Maybe the roaches would be worth it, though. And Deerfoams worked just as well in New York City.

Oh no! I completely forgot!

Ladies Bible study was in three hours, and they'd scheduled me for refreshments. I ran over to the IGA, bought two boxes of lemon bar mix, brownie mix, a cantaloupe, and some grapes.

Mrs. Jergenson, with hands that live up to her name, leads the study from a book about Bible women that are so bad they make even someone like me think that maybe light will soon start shining at the end of my tunnel.

Do people suspect I am not all I am supposed to be? Do the members of Highland Kirk see my heart is bound by unwashed sheets, choked by secrets and lies, and aching to be set free?

Four

I flipped on the lamp clamped to my easel. At last. At last. Buttoning myself up into the tentlike recesses of my big shirt, I slid into my paint-splattered Keds and looked out the small window of my painting shed. Duncan's silhouette swayed at the kitchen window where he scrubbed the casserole dish. Me, I leave the pan to soak overnight, but Duncan takes baked-on cheese very seriously. Being a small man, Duncan isn't as strong as some and not as fast as others, but what Duncan possesses and what I've always admired about my husband is his endurance. Strong and fast are good, but it's endurance that matters in the long run. He runs for an hour every evening and stops only because an hour is all the time he has.

I'd sketched out the basic idea for the painting before supper, a watercolor I've been wanting to paint of my children for years. My mother had always said that children reach their peak of cuteness at two and a half years of age. Most family portraits I've seen capture the children at a certain year, ages varied. This painting, however, would show Paisley, Robbie, and Angus all at two and a half. I couldn't wait to see how it would turn out.

Duncan came in through the open door as soon as I had arranged my palette. "I brought you a cup of coffee."

"Thanks. Can you just put it there on the worktable?"

He did, gently moving some sketches and pencils aside to clear a spot. "Is there anything else I can get you?"

"Nope. I'm just so glad to be out here."

"I know." He looked uncomfortable. Duncan always seems uncomfortable in my studio. He just doesn't understand this side of me, and I don't expect him to. "I'm going to take Angus down to Bill D's for some pie."

"Okay."

"I'll just go running after he goes down."

"Okay."

"Are you sure you don't want anything else?"

"Yes, I'm fine."

"Because all you have to do is just say the word."

"Yes, Duncan, I'm sure. Now just get out of here!"

He laughed. "Just getting you back for the animal crackers." Then he kissed me on the cheek. A few minutes later I watched as he piled Angus into the van and drove off.

After masking the areas for the kids' faces, I dove my brush into the water and then some ultramarine and started on the sky. I'd rather paint natural surroundings than have to clutter up the picture with fireplaces and chairs. And why not make use of God's backdrop for the world? If it's good enough for Him, it's most certainly good enough for me.

I finished the sky by the time the phone rang. Not at all happy about it, but thinking it might be Rob telling me his junk heap car broke down or something, I punched the button and greeted the caller.

"Penny?" Only one person I know calls me by that name.

"Hi, Miss Poole."

"Is Reverend Fraser there?"

"No, Miss Poole."

"Where is he?"

I somehow knew that would be the next question, and that sinful side of my nature ignored it. "Can I help you with something?"

Silence. Then, "Well, since you're obviously refusing to tell me where he is, then you'll just have to do the job."

And the painting was coming along so well. "What is it?"

"I've got a 102 degree fever, and the executive committee meeting for the May Festival meets tonight."

Silent groan.

"Someone needs to be there to represent the church," she finished.

"Won't we just get steak-on-a-stick and face painting as usual?"

"I don't know. But if someone isn't there, we may just end up with something ghastly like sack races or cotton candy."

Strangely enough, I could actually see the woman's point. "What time does it begin?"

"Seven-thirty."

The clock on my wall said seven. "Down at the VFW hall?"

"Yes."

By 7:35 my khakis and I covered the seat of one of the folding chairs placed around two large tables someone had slid together. Hopefully, Duncan would see the note I left on the counter before he put Angus in bed and went running. Hopefully, he wouldn't just assume I was home, go running, and leave Angus by himself. Hopefully, one day I'll give him a little bit of credit.

Church folk and town folk alike gathered around the table. The smell of natural gas penetrates some of these older buildings, and the VFW hall was no exception. Folding chairs stood in stacks against the wall, and white linoleum tile covered the floor of the main meeting room. I could just picture veterans sitting around and chatting. I guess. What do they really do in these places?

A stylish young woman called the meeting to order. If I had known anyone there, I would have asked who this professional lady was. Instead I sat back and listened, taking mental notes for the grilling Miss Poole would give me later.

The Crazy Days of May, as the festival was renamed back in the eighties, is Mount Oak's major fundraiser. Talk about a bunch of complainers, nitpickers, and backbiters. And that was just the church people! I've never lived in a place where the rift between secular and sacred yawned so widely. Yawn is right. I looked at my watch hoping this meeting wouldn't last long, knowing I'd be lucky to be home by eleven.

Everybody had to have a say, at least three different ways. But even my ears perked up when Colonel Bougie of the Colonel's Kitchen spoke up.

"If I have to hear those ladies from Mount Zion Christian complain one more time about how much work the Boston cream pies are, I'm going to scream."

Well, amen to that.

Everybody agreed, and when the priest from St. Edmund's Episcopal reached into his briefcase and pulled out a bag of Hershey Miniatures, I figured maybe I could stay just a little bit longer.

Although he's nine months into his sixth year, Angus still can't pump himself on the swings. He doesn't like to go high either. Late one morning, I sat beside him, my hips screaming, squeezed painfully in the rubber belt that passes for a swing seat these days. The flat seats disappeared eons ago, those slabs of wood lacquered a high gloss green, painted over and over to a smooth finish. The flat seats vanished into some Bermuda Triangle of caution. The old-time swings had enabled me and my best friend Chrissy to stand firm, feet snug against the brackets that held the chains to the seat. Chains firmly in hand, we pumped for height with our entire bodies, swinging hard and comfortable and free. Hardly safe. We knew that. Back in those days, there was always someone home to run crying to, someone who didn't believe that safety and things equaled lots of love and lots of time.

I try to raise Angus like I had been raised, but he forever makes it difficult, asking questions I don't always know the answers to. So moments such as these filled with joy, joy, joy, these deep and wide moments of pure childhood are precious. Sometimes I hold Angus to myself, close, so close, and will myself to keep from screaming, "Stop, Angus. Just stop!"

I hadn't realized the luxury Paisley and Robbie had provided as regular kids who grew up on the right time schedule. I lived with no frantic sense of loss regarding them like I do with Angus. Like when I had lost my glasses in the ocean years before and my stolen sight prohibited me from looking for them. Rolling around in the water somewhere or buried beneath the sand, they weren't coming back. And neither is Angus, my baby. No pulling the wool over that child's eyes. No bribing. No deals.

Still, a lot of laddie remains in the little boy whose mind will leave me behind by the age of, oh, say eight. I don't keep up on the genius stuff anyway. If Angus's brain functions as well as everyone figures, he'll do fine without my intervention. But he still likes to sway gently back and forth on the swings while we sing Sunday school songs together.

He sang with me, "there's a fountain flowing deep and wide."

The quiet there by the swing set Duncan built soothed the troubled part inside me that shreds my peace of mind to bleeding ribbons.

Quiet in the dappled sunlight.

The apparatus rests in a grotto in the middle of a circle of pines that mulches the area with discarded needles. Blue sky slips through the protective heavy boughs. Sunshine mottles the child's perfect skin.

I don't know what I'd do without you, I thought, my love for this child a salve on my open sores. God gave him to me, this child of Duncan's. This I know.

"Rolled away, rolled away, rolled away," I began, remembering the words I'd learned as a child, one of the many songs sung while sitting in the second pew of the main sanctuary next to my best friend, my still best friend, Chrissy Vandervere, now Chris Knight. My memory always clothes us in sleeveless, yellow gauze dresses with white lace trim and pearl buttons sewn down the front. My mother purchased mine from Hutzler's in Towson, and Chrissy's mother had plucked hers from the missionary barrel in the storage closet of the church.

Chris's daddy was the pastor.

I've called Chris my best friend for over forty years now, though for a while I left my childhood friend behind. It was as if the dresses had been prophetic, a telling of what would become important to each of us. Chris, in her missionary barrel dresses, hand-me-down shoes, crocheted purses, and homemade prom gowns, had never deserted the faith. Chris never wandered down the seductive path of Mercedes and tennis bracelets and day spas. Chris kept her hand tucked firmly in between the wounds of Christ. Chris never wavered.

I wish I could say the same. But I met Duncan during a Campus Crusade meeting at Towson State. Gung ho for Jesus in those days. That was us. Singing praise songs with guitars, carrying our Bibles shamelessly with us while other people carried Nietzche. And then life kicked in soon after our wedding. Duncan began his business, and the only services we attended a few years after marrying were weddings, baptisms, funerals, and holidays. It went on like that for fifteen years. How does one find herself singing praise songs and reading the Bible faithfully one year and clinging to the doctrine of eternal security the next? If I knew the answer to that, I'd be a women's conference speaker, I guess.

Paisley is the casualty from that time of our lives. Robbie, quick to fall in line, lives his life as a testament to God's grace. At least as much as a twenty-year-old boy can. He reads his Bible every morning and always stops to help stranded motorists. What more could a mother ask? Spirituality and faith come easily to my son. I wish I could be more like him, like the young adult I myself was.

And now, Angus gives me the chance to do it right from the start. If I don't steal away with him some night. I pushed him harder on the swing. "Every burden of my heart rolled away," I finished, wishing it was that easy for me.

"My yoke is easy and my burden is light," Jesus says. But sometimes our burdens stink so badly the thought of handing such a package to the beautiful One who died willingly for us is hardly able to be contemplated. I want to ask Him if it's okay. I know He can handle such a burden, but does He *really* want to? Really? My head says yes. The Bible isn't a foreign book to me. I know about grace and redemption.

Maybe if I had been an unbeliever at the time of my fall, it would be different for me. I yearn for an easy explanation.

"Don't push me too high, Mama. Please."

I stopped the swing altogether, stood up and kissed his little mouth. The contact of those soft lips on mine intoxicated me, two seconds of woozy bliss, tender ecstasy, a feeling only a mother of an affectionate, sweet son knows. Those little hands on my shoulders. The impotent squeeze of short fingers.

He pulled back to look at his Batman watch. "I'd like for you to pick me up now. It's lunchtime."

I obeyed, lifting him easily, relishing the feel of his spindly legs gripping me tightly around the waist, his skinny arms around my shoulders.

I thrust my arms straight out from my sides as Angus hung onto me by his own strength like a koala on his tree. We twirled like a helicopter down the short path toward the kitchen door. "What shall we refuel with, Gus?"

"Tomato sandwiches."

I navigated our chopper through the screen door and set him down on the counter. "Did you know that Thomas Jefferson ate the first tomato in America? They thought it was poisonous before that." My arms folded against his response.

"I didn't *know* that! Cool." And he began to chant the song Duncan had taught him a while back. "George Washington, John Adams, Thomas Jefferson, James Madison, and James Monroe."

I joined in. "John Quincy Adams, Andrew Jackson, Martin Van Buren!"

A few things still remain that I can teach this kid. That satisfies me for now.

Ten minutes later the counter, tinted with tomato juice, textured by seeds and pulp, demanded a quick swipe of the dishrag. Angus's face deserved much the same treatment.

"I love tomato sandwiches," he cried, as I scraped the dishrag across his features.

Strange kid. Only his good eyesight saved him from complete misfithood. If he'd inherited my nearsightedness, he would have been positively stereotypical. Genius boy, thanks to Duncan. Thick glasses thanks to both of us. Could have been worse. I sat down and took a bite of my sandwich.

The juice dripped down my arm.

I sighed and got up from the table to get more napkins, grabbing a pile from the pottery bowl I made while getting my master's in fine art at the Maryland Institute. I love my tiny kitchen with its nicked butcher-block counters, scarred stone floors, and the massive hoosier with the pull-out table. I'd painted the walls with a garden mural and the ceiling sky blue. Clouds breezed across the blue expanse, ruffling the feathers of a couple of ornery-looking blue jays. It is always a nice day to eat in my kitchen, and I have the tummy to attest to that fact.

I wiped Angus's face again.

Duncan walked in. "Lunch ready?"

"Tomato sandwiches, Daddy." Angus's forearms dripped, so I wiped them, too.

Duncan grimaced, turning to me and rubbing his graying mustache. I held up my hands feeling like Mrs. Cleaver. "Don't worry. Egg salad for you."

"I'm going to change my shirt. Man, it's hot out there. Typical August."

I began making his sandwich. "Well, the tourist season officially ends tomorrow, and Monday night is the locals' post Labor Day dance down at the boathouse."

"Praise God it's over for another year." He shut his eyes tightly, took off his small wire-rimmed glasses, and rubbed the bridge of his nose. "We can shut down Creator's Corner until next June."

Highland Kirk had started Creator's Corner three summers before to provide a place for the children of vacationers to come when their parents wanted a vacation from vacation. We tell them about Jesus and assure them they are loved. But it's a hassle nonetheless, wiping off all of those Kool-Aid mustaches and changing diapers.

One's own kids' messes seem bad enough, but dealing with someone else's child's mess, well, surely that borders on sainthood. And if one can do it without gagging and with a smile, that woman will clearly receive an honorable mention at the back of the next year's edition of *The Proper Christian Ladies' Handbook of Church Etiquette and Behavior.*

But the tiny souls hidden beneath the smells, the tears, and the messes outweigh the inconvenience. One day some child will return to say thank you. This is eternal stuff going on here, and I have to remind myself of that every day. These kids will take "Allelu, Allelu, Allelu, Alleluias" right on home with them, and since God inhabits praise and all, who knows where it might lead?

Duncan reemerged a few minutes later wearing yard work clothing. He is, in fact, quite sexy in yard work clothing. Torn khaki and green grass stains frankly make me want to escort him into the bedroom right then and there. Not a normal occurrence to be sure. His lean, runner's frame, looking fit in shorts, at the same time reminds me that I probably weigh more than he does. Still, I like the feel of his spare stomach under my palms when I come up behind him in his half of the sunroom and lean down to see what he's typed into his computer.

I set his plate in front of him. Egg salad sandwich on whole wheat, Fritos, and a bunch of green grapes. The bedroom is quickly forgotten.

"I've got to mow the grounds today." He took a large bite.

It was one of the unexpected antikudos we had been hit with the day we moved in. And Duncan unwittingly inherited the bequest of the former pastor, a bachelor who left a legacy of emerald lawns and variegated this-and-thats Duncan neither wanted nor deserved.

I figure if he doesn't have the guts to stand up to the session and tell them to get someone else to take care of the grounds, he deserves it. But Duncan never complains. And what seems to bring him contentment in this life of serving others—sitting by sickbeds, holding puke pans and IV punc-tured hands, calling on shut-ins and praying, mulching and mowing and placating and hemming and hawing—has done exactly the opposite for me.

If I left, Duncan wouldn't be the only one picking up pieces. I realize this. Some women have it easy when they can't face their lives anymore. If they leave, well, hubby might have a bit of explaining to do. But if I go, it will ruin Duncan's career. I do not take this as lightly as it may seem. *May seem to whom?*

You, Lord? But You know what's in my heart anyway.

Duncan wiped his mouth. "I'm going to mulch as well."

I turned to Angus. "What about it, Gus? You want to help me mulch while Daddy mows the lawn?" I asked, completely out of guilt.

"Uh-huh."

Duncan ruffled his son's hair and mouthed the words "I love you" to me.

Jody measured the cabinets, measured the counters, and he did it all with such youthful grace, with such economical movements it reminded me of an animal in a way, going about its business without artifice or transaction. I watched, fascinated, feeling sexy all of a sudden, feeling womanly, desiring touch and tasting salt even as my mouth went dry, knowing it had been so long since I had felt desire, since I had been desired. Did he feel it, too, I wondered as he turned toward me and caught me staring at him, my eyes too wide, too full of wonder at this specimen of beauty and vigor and inexperience. I remembered how I had thought I would never in my entire life make love to anyone but Duncan, but now I wasn't so sure because these days I'M NOT SURE ABOUT MUCH. Only one thing: I'VE BEEN REARRANGING THE SAME CANS OF ROTTEN BEANS FOR YEARS NOW.

Jody winked, took off his cap and ran a hand through his thick, blond hair.

"Whatever I can do to make things a little easier." I felt my chin drop to my chest, hoping that with maybe yet another selfless act I might partially redeem the deeds of the past.

Maybe New England would be nice. With the leaves changing and all.

I slowly made my way to the bedroom to change into my scruffies, avoiding the dresser mirror as I did so.

Five

"Jack and Jill went up the hill to fetch a pail of water."' Mildred LaRue's voice skated gracefully around the notes of the old Glenn Miller tune with Olympian expertise. "'Jack fell down and broke his crown, because he boogie-woogied with the farmer's daughter.'"

Miss Mildred's phrasing spoke to me. And the little twitter of a vibrato she sometimes employed at the end of a verse bordered on magical.

The party atmosphere of the boathouse soaked into my skin as if the mottled flesh was nothing more than tattered Kleenex found in a winter coat pocket during the season's first wear. The smell of silk and linen and perfume embraced the odor of emotions heightened for various reasons: wheeling and dealing, partying hearty, or prowling unashamedly. Citizens "in the mood" circulated with the September breeze that slid off Lake Coventry like one of Mildred LaRue's plunges from middle C down to D-sharp.

Good-bye summer. Amen and amen. Better than socializing with the upper classes once again, better than sipping champagne, a certain relief hovered over the room. Even eating the strawberries that rotted serenely by an ice sculpture of a three-masted schooner at full sail paled in comparison to the fact that we all could breathe a little more freely.

I sipped my drink and watched the dance floor. The locals were jumpin' and jivin'. Gyrating with color, these folk around Mount Oak had money so old they didn't need to dress in black to prove themselves. As a general rule, I've always found the Southern gentry to be colorful. The octagonal pavilion that jutted out into Lake Coventry like a covered cul-de-sac vibrated with the pounding feet of the swing dancers. The older set, jitterbugging with a bit more panache, a comfy shuffle, and a bounce on the downbeat, seemed proud to have started the whole craze in the first place, although both feet never left the floor at the same time these days.

The church maven of Highland Kirk, the fearless typo-hunter herself, Miss Poole, wore long diamond earrings and a silver Nehru jacket quite the same color as her hair. She enthroned herself majestically at the head table closest to the ladies' room. This arrangement was certainly unusual for most gatherings, but Miss Poole's overactive bladder took precedence. I guess when one owns a veritable castle on Poole Point, one has a right to a basic enthronement of one's choice at the boathouse.

Miss Magda Poole owns more of Mount Oak than anyone else, and that includes the Broomhellers who own the IGA, the A-1 Dry Cleaners, and Krazy Kid Karts and Games out near the mall. Her "very late" father amassed compound millions with "his little trucks and trains" as she calls Poole Refrigerated Transport. She rules the Highland Kirk with a prover-bial iron fist, or as I would say, with an understated but well-manicured claw. The tyrant.

Until Duncan arrived.

And all is *not* well with the world there. I love it when Duncan takes a stand.

Trying to be supportive of my husband's ministry, hoping my "I'm not at all resentful" mask wouldn't slip, I smiled and waved at the woman who reminds me of my own mother. But with a lot more money and hipper taste in clothing.

She motioned me over. I hear and obey.

"How did the executive committee meeting go last night?" she asked.

I had been dreading the thought of this conversation, yet thankfulness that it was happening in a very public place filled my soul! "Well, some-one suggested giving Mount Zion Christian a break this year with the Boston cream pies."

"And you volunteered Highland?"

Nodding, I rushed to say, "I know it's going to be more difficult than steak-on-a-stick, but since our church is so far out of town and all, I was just trying to be helpful, boost up our profile a bit."

I may be mistaken, but I thought I saw a flicker of approval in her eyes. Yet her words revealed the opposite. "I guess I'll know next time to go myself come flood or famine."

I don't have to hang around for this, I thought and turned to go. "Excuse me but I need to find Duncan." Miss Poole waved me off. I hurried to my seat before someone took it. It was the best people-watching seat in the house by far.

Tuxedoed young bucks serve up double martinis and triple sec with a quadruple portion of happy sighs, commemorating the fact that we all actually survived another summer without a major lawsuit or loss of life or limb. Tomorrow the swankier, more exclusive enclaves such as the Coventry Meadows Resort or Tuckaway Manor Bed and Breakfast, for the more creative types, will begin preparing for the foliage viewers, a kinder, gentler sort of tourist. Then the Christmas lonelies who have no family to celebrate with arrive, or maybe they have families but regard a frigid lake as a bit more inviting.

Nibbling on a very sweet strawberry to freshen up my dark red lipstick, I watched Mildred LaRue intently. Miss Mildred who helps down at Creator's Corner on Thursday mornings has been a good friend for two years now. The woman weighs no more than a leg of lamb and stands at least five foot ten inches tall. Tonight she looked as if someone took a delicate African figurine and zapped it life-size with an expando ray gun, then bedecked it in a gown of iguana green sequins with a feathered neckline and tight-fitting chiffon sleeves. The feathered cuffs swirled and jumped with each flicker of her hand. And flickers abounded, palms flat toward the audience, all fingers pointing up like pickets in a privacy fence, thumbs relaxed, elbows bent, arms as fluid as the opening notes of Gershwin's "Rhapsody in Blue." Her hair, as black as it was ten years ago when she hit retirement age, flowed back from a broad forehead, pulled up in a high French twist thanks to Shamika down at the Braid Brigade, who can relax a bedspring if the price is right. Miss Mildred swears she doesn't color it, but I have to wonder. Even the most holy women aren't above a little *Lovin' Care*. Mildred loosened her vocal chords, slipping out of the peppy Glenn Miller number and rolling right into "All of Me." I swear Billie Holiday sung it no finer.

"'All of me. Why not take all of me?'" she crooned, as if anyone in his right mind would even need to be asked.

I've been inwardly asking that same question of Duncan for years. Duncan is so gentle and sweet, for the most part, and sometimes I just want him to take me like he feels he would die without me. But Duncan never wants me like that. Maybe Monday nights have become an obligatory occasion for him as well.

"Still keepin' the faith?"

I whirled around at the familiar greeting. Chris Knight, born Christine Anne Vandervere, raised Chrissy Vandervere, and voted by Mrs. Walston's second grade class as most likely to rotate a complete 360 degrees on the swing set at Hampton Elementary School, stood at my elbow. If Mrs. Robertson the principal hadn't decided to keep a vigil during our recesses that year, I know Chrissy would have gone where no boy from the sixth grade down had ever gone before. Chris had been like that then. She could run faster than anybody and stood mighty strong, mighty proud as the last kid out in Greek Dodge because she could catch Buddy English's hard throw without flinching.

Years ago, Chris had willingly taken on the role of wife to Gary, my favorite cousin and the new pastor over at Mount Oak Community Church: seeker-sensitive, contemporary, complete with a drama ministry, a heated baptistery hidden during regular services, and a coffee cart proudly serving Java Jane's finest. Normally she wears sundresses or jumpers and flip-flops, but tonight she had shimmied her way into a white, tea-length chiffon dress, accordion pleated, with an empire waist above a square, rhinestone buckle, surely an atrocity on anybody but Chris. I would be willing to place a sizeable bet that Chris had worn that very dress to her junior/senior banquet at the small Christian school she graduated from in 1972. Not that I went there. My parents, Fidge and John Heubner had me fully ensconced in a high-priced, mediocre school by the seventh grade. But, hey, they had horses there.

Chris's new, black church shoes still probably pinched the tiny corns on her smallest toes because she had taken them off, and, of course, looked utterly enchanting strolling around the pavilion in bare feet and a sloppy French twist.

"Hi, Chrissy."

"I hear the shrimp balls are wonderful." She set down her drink next to my tonic and lime.

"They are. I've eaten two dozen of them already."

Looking at this vision, the beautiful one of this best friendship, I wanted to fold myself up right then and jump into one of Duncan's tuxedo pockets. Instead, I swung my legs under the table, folding my arms into an *x* to hide my upper body. My hands, stretched by bony knuckles, seemed much too large just then, and why in the *world* had I chosen to go sleeveless?

"Have a seat," I invited, hating the way I always compare myself to Chris like that, especially considering that surely Chris never does that to me, that Chris would lay down across train tracks in front of the Cannonball Express for me. "Where's my Josh?"

Chris sat down and took a sip of her ginger ale. She reported the whereabouts of her only child. "Oh, he'll be here any minute. He was doing the final tear-down at the rental place, then he went home to shower, and he'll be here as soon as he can. Is Paisley coming?"

"Hardly. She's home on the phone while Mitch is trying to convince her to get back together with him."

Chris was too polite to sigh with relief regarding Paisley's absence, but I knew she wanted to by the way the small hands relaxed suddenly and the grayish green eyes cleared. She did take her job as second-cousin-in-law seriously, however. "How's Mitch's band doing?"

"The same."

"Any body parts newly pierced since we talked after lunch?"

"Nope, still going strong at twenty-five extra holes as far as I know."

No further updates needed. Chris always knew everything. Except about Jody. It was the only thing about me no one knew. Except for Jody....

Joe. Yes, he knew all about The Masquerade.

The cabinets remained doorless, and the slate floor felt cool to my bare feet when I entered the kitchen early that morning in my pajamas to find him already at work carving something on the island. He smiled sheepishly at the sight of me in my white satin tap pants and camisole, and I thought maybe I should put on a robe. But I had stepped on this bridge in my mind, a bridge spanning from behind me where Duncan stood with a laptop strapped around his neck like a cigar/cigarette tray to Jody in front of me, only Duncan looked really small and sickly and ghostlike, and Jody stood there like Spartacus or something with his feet apart, all muscular and with a pulse raging, looking at me in my tap pants and camisole. I placed a hand over my stomach and walked over and laid a hand on his arm and said, "What are you doing?" He shrugged, placing his youthful hand over mine and squeezing and keeping it there and said, "You said the woodwork beneath the granite was too plain, so I decided I'd carve you a couple of sparrows right here beneath the vegetable sink." I began to cry, and Jody quickly said, "It's a gift, I promise I won't charge you for my time on it. I'm just doing it because..." Then he stopped talking just as I looked up to see his beautiful face as he gathered his tools and left the room. So I kept my tap pants and camisole on all that day, and late that night before Duncan was due to steal quietly in, I turned on soft music, burned some candles, and I cried out to Duncan to see me, to save me. But when I awoke the next morning, the radio still played; the candles had burned down to nubs; and as I cleaned up the lumpy piles of wax on my dresser, my tears bounced off their contours. His side of the bed had been slept in, but Duncan was already gone. The next night I slipped into an old T-shirt and athletic shorts and fell asleep in front of reruns of The Mary Tyler Moore Show.

Three years ago, Jody married a sweet, supple thing from Worthington Valley. I still remember his fine anklebones and the way his hair bleached out to white only on the patches beside his forehead. Sometimes, before my brain can catch itself, I think it was worth it, most times I don't. I know that all of our sins nailed the Savior to the cross and that He would have died for the smallest of transgressions. But when I ponder my adultery in regards to the Crucifixion, I see a blow to the head that drives the crown of thorns deeper into flesh like mine, a place where a golden diadem should have rested instead.

"So Josh leaves tomorrow," I said.

"I can't believe it." Chris shook her head, the French twist sliding lower toward the nape of that long neck. "All that time and money we spent to conceive that boy, and he's already leaving us."

"Well, Johns Hopkins isn't all *that* far." I tried to be encouraging, but I have three children, not just one, and all of them inhabit the bungalow as of now. Not that Paisley's departure can happen soon enough.

Now that thought had guilt built right in.

Not a thought, according to *The Proper Christian Ladies' Handbook,* one should admit out loud. One should talk about her children as though everything were fine. Although, one was free to use words like "challenging" or "God must have *some* kind of plan for this one!" Up-speak allows for some measure of truth, but with a saving, optimistic slant.

Chris rolled her eyes. "It's a good five to six hours away, Popp. Besides, it's easy for you to say. You've still got Rob around."

Robbie had already begun his third year at the local community college, burning away the final dross of general education requirements and procuring an associate of arts degree in something absurdly general. Then next year he'd go on for his B.A. at some school out of town, out of state, out of the country, or perhaps off the continent of North America if he had his way. He'd talked about St. Andrews in Scotland for months, which of course made Duncan drag out the Fraser kilt and plaid while he prepared to make tatties and neeps and haggis which we all hate, except for Paisley, although now she doesn't touch the haggis on principle. The university accepted him for next fall, but he doesn't know yet if he is called to be a civil engineer or a youth pastor. I reason by the title alone they sound much like the same thing. But he applied to Covenant College as well, making sure to cover all the bases.

"Has Josh decided on a major yet?"

Chris began peeling apart the splits in her soft fingernails. "I think so.

He said he's going to go with premed, and then he can just stay at Hopkins for med school."

"You've got to be proud of him, Chrissy."

"I am! But I'd trade that all in a second to keep him home with me. I heard there was an opening up at the hydroelectric plant. But with that lacrosse scholarship…" She deposited her chin into her hand. "I guess it's silly of me, Popp, but I feel as if I'm giving him away. Like it's his wedding day or something, only he's the bride, and he's going to a new house, getting a new family, and leaving us behind forever."

"That's not silly."

"Yes, it is. It's too strong a feeling."

I rubbed the spot between Chris's protruding shoulder blades in a small circular pattern. I know that spot better than I know my own hands. "We'll go see him the weekend after classes start. I'll get my parents to watch Angus at their place, and we'll do the town together when Josh is busy. We'll see the sites, go down to the Inner Harbor, and we can even stay at one of those inns in Havre de Grace."

Chris frowned. "Poppy, I can't afford that."

I lifted my brows. "I'll take the money from the stash. Duncan won't mind."

"Are you sure?" Chris's eyes suddenly had the amazed look of a parent watching her kindergartener actually sing in the Christmas concert for the first time.

"Hey, we'll be out of town with nobody from around here to see us."

"Okay, I guess. You sure you want to use *the stash?*"

Those two words held great significance. Great riches. Literally. Well, maybe not *great riches* as in Sam Walton, Bill Gates kind of riches. But that account contains the money we made from the sale of our house, the sale of Duncan's computer firm, and my proceeds from my art. Also in the account sits the Jaguar convertible I'll never have, the vacation house in the Outer Banks I'll never have, and the membership to the country club we sold when Duncan got the call to minister.

"I'm sure. It's for a good cause. And if we were really all that altruistic and self-sacrificing and truly trusting God, we'd have given that money away a long time ago. Instead it's there, growing arms and legs and fangs, not to mention 12 percent interest, and because we drive around in a beat-up old van and haven't bought new clothes in years, we act like it's okay."

Chris put up her hands. "Yikes, Popp. Don't feel you have to beat yourself over the head for my sake. If anyone knows where your heart is it's me."

"That's truer than even you'd like to admit."

Chris lifted her glass in a small toast. "Faults and all."

"You said it, lady."

Then why am I always so jealous of her? No one loves me like Chris does. Not even Duncan. It is a clean love. A love with little expectation. A voluntarily blind love. Clean and neat and mature. And it is right here in Mount Oak.

Six

I don't know how Robbie managed to talk Duncan into buying a ski boat when we moved to the shores of Lake Coventry. Robbie emerged from the meeting "behind closed doors" with the smug grin of victory stretching his youthful male jowls. Duncan refused to talk about it, not one easily given to defeat however genial his demeanor. Duncan normally acts so happy and bright, and he'll do all the little things that I ask him to do. I never have to remind him to haul out the garbage or lug that pile of winter wear down to the cedar box in the basement. I never have to tell him it's mulching time or the van needs gas. But those big matters! He loathes losing. He hates it when his little patchwork quilt of a world sews a renegade square. Obviously, Robbie somehow stitched an appliqué of a speedboat over some preexisting log cabin motif.

Well, whatever he said, I thank him for it. The boat turned out to be a real source of satisfaction and escape. The first day of the off-season we flew across the water. Still warm. Still wet. But more wonderful than August water littered with tourists determined to have fun or else! Loaded with kids in bathing suits, the ancient Ski Nautique, inboard motor, time-tested boat for the serious skier—and only three thousand dollars very, very used—bounced across the water. Paisley, still fuming because I nixed the thong bikini idea, sat aft on a white towel reading *O Pioneers!* by Willa Cather, a surprise surely because didn't girls like her read Sylvia Plath or the works of Voltaire or something? I thought Paisley actually looked quite pretty in her old swim team suit I dug out of a storage box, but I knew Paisley felt otherwise. Hardly a surprise. But the next day we'd say good-bye until Christmas, something both Paisley and I agreed was a good thing for two entirely different reasons.

This time she had even hurt Duncan's feelings.

"Do you have any idea how embarrassing it is for me to tell people my father is a minister?" That particular barb shot out one evening at supper when Duncan talked about how important personal fulfillment and vision were when seeking out a vocation. He hadn't realized it until he went into the ministry.

Thus came the remark. Now, I'm not all that hepped up about being a pastor's wife, but I'm not *embarrassed* about it! The comment was over the line, even for Paisley. Duncan retreated into his work for the rest of the day. He must feel all alone at times in his choice of occupation. Well, Robbie thinks his Dad's dedication to God is cool and does what he can to support Duncan, so at least there's that. I've prayed so many times that I'd hop on board, and maybe one day I will. I don't know, though. If it means seeing Miss Poole more, well, I *know* I'm not even close to that level of spirituality.

I drove the boat while Robbie spotted for Josh Knight who signaled to up the speed of the boat. At least that's what Robbie yelled.

So I complied. Loved doing it, in fact. It satisfied that traveling yen that eats me up inside. At least for a brief while. I hollered a Bonanza-style whoop, Angus, Robbie, and Josh returning the call, and the boat sped forward.

After a few more runs we sat adrift in the middle of the lake eating tuna sandwiches and drinking grape soda. Even Paisley held a Nehi in her hand and laughed at Josh's corny one-liners. My heart sighed at the sight of those two together. Josh has always had a little crush on Paisley, despite the blood ties. And Paisley has always felt a sense of protectiveness toward her redheaded third cousin.

"So, Josh, you gonna miss this place when you go back to Baltimore?" Paisley reached into her beach bag, pulling out some chap stick.

"Nah! I'm finally escaping." His blue eyes reflected the flares of sunlight on the water. "Let me enjoy it for a while without having to think of Mount Oak."

Robbie bit off a huge chunk of sandwich, thrusting it into the side of his mouth the way boys do. "I don't blame you. Mount Oak is a great place to be *from.*"

"What do you mean?" I asked. "How could you not love it here?"

Paisley rolled her eyes. "Vacation spots are vacation spots for a reason, Mother."

Josh nodded. "You know, Aunt Popp, nice place to visit, but I—"

"—wouldn't wanna live there!" they all shouted together.

"I guess I'm just old." I wondered why I was so bent on defending the place.

Angus took my hand. "I like it here, Mama."

I smiled down at my son, feeling sad that at only five years old he had already accepted the job of being the family salve.

"Actually, I like it, too, Aunt Popp. But I'm saving it for a special girl."

Paisley's mouth dropped open. "You want to end up *here?*"

"Yeah. I really do. I may even buy this dumpy old boat from you, Aunt Popp, and take my own kids and nieces and nephews out on the lake."

"You're an only child, Josh," Robbie reminded him. "Where are you gonna get those nieces and nephews?"

"I'll rent them if I have to. But I'll have lots of kids. I'm not going to marry a girl that doesn't want a lot of kids."

"Figures," Paisley grumbled.

"No, really, Paise. It's not what you think. It's just my parents are so *quiet,* and my house was never loud and fun like yours was. Remember Christmas morning when I was twelve, and I got to spend the night on Christmas Eve? Man, that was great!"

I felt fondness wash over my heart. "Remember the way you guys used to practice running down the steps on Christmas Eve? Paisley could go from the top to the bottom in two swings. Remember the way you'd grab the banisters on either side, Paise, and then you'd swing out your legs?"

Paisley laughed, the hoop on the side of her bottom lip sliding half an inch to the left. "But Josh had to take it one step further. Remember how you rigged up that pulley thing from the ceiling, Josh? Dad was furious!"

"Until he tried it himself!" Robbie slapped the side of his thigh. "He flung himself halfway across the living room."

"Right onto my coffee table." I remembered how Josh had convinced Duncan to ride the contraption…with a red Superman cape from a long gone Halloween costume tied around his neck. Snapped the antique oak mission table right in two. But the memory of the sight of that feat redeems any furniture damage.

Angus started hopping up and down. "What about me, Mom? Was I there? Was I there?" He knew he wasn't, I suspected, but hated that he'd missed out on the hay days of the Fraser family.

Paisley pulled her little brother onto her lap. "No, Gussie. That was our last Christmas together in Maryland."

"It was the best day of my life," Josh said. "Even if the Superman cape did get ruined. And…it was loud that day! That's what I want my life to be like as soon as I'm old enough to make it happen."

I watched Paisley who looked very thoughtful as she kissed Angus on the cheek and played with his smooth, dark hair. That old bathing suit brought back a lot of memories.

I looked out over the meadow of the horse farm near the country club and watched as the grasses blew in the warm breeze of June, and I wondered what the kids were doing at camp just then because they might very well be riding horses or swimming or eating horrible pancakes, and I realized that I felt young again because I had two sparrows beneath my island counter, one with a wing protecting the other, one looking somehow female and adoring her male protector. And how did Jody get that adoring glint in the male sparrow's eye? I wondered as the gravel of the roadside crunched behind me, and there he was, the male bird in a black Ford pick-up truck, pulling up right behind my Range Rover. He got out calling, "Hi, Mrs. Fraser." My mouth opened, and I said, "Please call me Poppy, Joe, I'm not as old as I look." He smiled and said something like, "You're younger looking than most women your age…. So with your wisdom and experience, I'd say you have more going for you than the girls I left behind in Maryland." I knew there must have been plenty of those because Jody was so beautiful to me.

He stood beside me, close, and asked me if I liked the birds, his breath on my ear. I asked if there was a special meaning to the carving, and he grew red again in that endearing manner that gave me a feeling of power, power over such beauty, and all he said was, "I think you know."

A question has plagued me over the years and continues to swarm in my brain. If Duncan hadn't been enough to make me stay away from Jody, why hadn't Paisley been enough? Why not Robbie? And if they hadn't been enough to keep me from straying, why have they been enough to keep me from leaving?

There's that verse in the Bible that says God won't allow temptation to come your way that you're not capable of resisting. And I look back to those Jody days and think, *I could have resisted.* And because God had given me the strength to run away, I can't blame Him for not protecting me. His equipping should have been enough. But I chose not to exercise the muscles I had. Maybe that's what's happening now. Maybe I'm using muscles I didn't believe I had back then. If only I had the strength to come clean. Sometimes I feel like that crazy "Hang In There, Baby" cat on the poster. Hanging from a pole. Wanting to scramble up but afraid of slipping off completely with the effort of the climb.

We docked the boat by four o'clock. Robbie hurried off to get ready for work at Jeanelle's, and Paisley had to run to town to buy some of that expensive hair salon gel. Of course, my Dippity-Do wouldn't do even though it costs one-fourth the price. Not that I ever use it, but it seems like something a woman is supposed to have beneath the bathroom sink.

Angus slept soundly on the seat. I started to pick him up.

"Let me, Aunt Popp." Josh leaned down on his haunches and stared at Angus's pinched face for several seconds. Then he looked back up at me. "Hard to believe what's inside that little head, isn't it? I try to fathom what he must be thinking at times, but"—he looked back at his cousin—"it's impossible, isn't it?"

I wiped my sweaty palms on my shorts. "Yeah. I've stopped trying."

"It's hard having him, isn't it? Sometimes?"

I put my hand on Josh's head, my fingers kneading the soft orange curls.

"Yeah, it is. I—" How could I explain my feelings of loss to this eighteen-year-old boy?

"At least he's quiet about it. Not one of those precocious brats."

"Oh, I know! I'm doing my best to keep him from becoming one of those. Paisley thinks he should be in a special school with special teachers."

Josh looked up at me again, his blue eyes locking onto mine. "Who's more special than a mother? Especially a cool mom like you, Aunt Popp."

"That's what I keep trying to tell Paisley."

He slid his hands beneath Angus, gathered him close to his chest and stood easily to his feet. "Don't listen to her, Aunt Popp. I know she's your daughter and all, but...are you *sure* she's not adopted?"

I laughed. "I thought you always liked Paisley?"

"Oh, I do. I just don't think you should second-guess yourself about her that's all. You get so worried and wrinkled when she's around."

"Gee, thanks. That sounds like an attractive picture."

"No, really, Aunt Popp. If she can be herself around you, you should be yourself around her."

"She just always gets so mad at me, no matter what I say."

He cocked his head before stepping up out of the boat. "You still have the right to say it."

"I *know* that! I just like a little peace every once in a while."

"Paisley doesn't deserve that kind of consideration. Not any more. She's a college graduate now."

I began to tidy up the boat. "That's the magic age?"

"Yep."

"I'll keep it in mind."

"Want me to put Angus on his bed?"

"Yeah. That'd be good."

"I'll be right back to help you finish up with the boat."

"Oh no, buddy, you go on. You've got packing to do for tomorrow. The big day, college man!"

Josh walked up the small pier and took Angus into the house. He was back a minute later. "I'm going to help you with the boat."

I sighed and smiled at him. "Okay, hardhead. There's a trash bag right over there."

We finished the chores in a comfortable silence earned from years of comfortable conversation. I love this boy. I really do. And deep in my heart, I am glad he belongs to Chris. Chris deserves a good boy like Josh. Chris shouldn't have to reap what she hasn't sown.

We sat in the sunroom fifteen minutes later, playing solitaire on the computer.

"So you're set on joining a fraternity?" Good, I needed that ace of spades to get things rolling.

"Well, there's this guy in my church. He's going to be a junior this year, and he says he'd really push for me at Zeta Chi."

Two of hearts, and then the three. Yes. "What's his name?"

"Jason Harkens. You know him?"

"Didn't you and Robbie go on a ski trip with him last Christmas?"

"Yeah. Big guy. He plays lacrosse, too. Goalie."

"What's he majoring in?"

"Banking and finance. But don't let that fool you, he's really smart."

Good one. "Not everyone can be premed like you, buddy."

He grimaced. "I guess that came out wrong."

Ace of diamonds. Let's go, lady! "Is he someone you *really* look up to, though, Josh? I mean, when you pledge into a GLO, you're pledging for life."

"It sounds like a good fraternity, Aunt Popp. The alumni are still really involved and some of them even sponsor a guy or two for their years at school. Guys that have a lot of promise but not much cashola."

"That's pretty cool."

He pointed to the screen. "Seven of spades can go down there."

"Thanks."

"I can't believe you missed that, Aunt Popp."

I batted him on the arm. "He's going to be junior, you say?"

"Yeah. Jason is one of those supported guys. He got sponsored his sophomore year from some old man in Scarsborough."

"Do you think you could end up with a sponsor?"

He shrugged. "I don't know. There aren't many. But who knows? If I do well enough on the team, maybe there's some rotting old doctor who used to play lacrosse!"

I laughed. Josh did, too.

"I sure could use the money. The student loans are going to kill me after I graduate."

"What about that lacrosse scholarship?" I asked, thinking maybe the stash would come in handy after all, for Josh's sake.

"That was just tuition. A guy's gotta live."

"Man can't live by academia alone."

"Although judging by the smugness of some of the professors I met up at Hopkins, you'd think one could." Josh pointed at a three of hearts and a lonely four of clubs.

I clicked on the hearts. "Well, all I can say is, if I had to choose between having no more college professors or no more garbage collectors, I'd take the college professors every time!"

"What about doctors?"

"Only ones who don't think they're divine get to stay on Aunt Poppy's list of 'must have' occupations."

"Okay. Then that's the type of doctor I'll be someday." He stood to his feet. "Your coffeepot just stopped sputtering. Want me to fix you a cup?"

"That'd be great. Take one for yourself, too."

"I will. Whatever caffeine gene you've got ended up in me, too."

I watched him as he crossed the sunroom, his pale skin burned across the back and shoulders. His muscles sat close beneath his skin. All state lacrosse player. Offense. Fast and coordinated. I hoped those people at Johns Hopkins knew how lucky they were to get this kid!

Oh, man, there goes that nine of spades! Why didn't I see that before I clicked on the pile?

Man.

Mount Oak Community Church's young adult ministry hosted a barbecue in honor of all the kids leaving for college.

"Oh, come on, Poppy!" Chris harped into the phone. "Come on over. It's a good barbecue. Not just burgers and dogs."

"What else are they having?"

It all hinges on the food as far as I'm concerned, although seeing Chris definitely began to tip the scales in favor of the barbecue.

"Barbecue. Corn on the cob, roasted in a pit, I might add. And more pies than you can shake a stick at."

"You'd be surprised how many times I can shake a stick, Chrissy."

"Josh would be glad to see you."

"I'll be over in the morning to say good-bye, though."

"Come *on!*" Wow, did she sound like the fifth grade Chrissy or what?

"All right. What time?"

"Five."

So there I found myself in the heat at a nondenominational church sitting on a metal fold-out chair, balancing a plate of barbecue on my lap. It didn't begin to compare to Miss Mildred's Baptist barbecue, but then, not much compares to Mildred LaRue's food. Definitely worth the drive over, though.

I got to sit next to Josh and his friend Jason for a while. And they acted like typical jocks, throwing punches and the like. Whooo-hooo.

Right now they were out on the softball field throwing the lacrosse ball around, Jason sporting something protective along with his Samsonesque build. I could tell something brotherly rose to the surface during his interaction with Josh.

He'd be in good hands at Hopkins I hoped. And Chris said Jason's parents, founding members of Mount Oak Community, seemed like nice people. Owned the sporting goods store. Worked lots of hours, she said, and taught their son to do the same. Lots of brothers and sisters, too.

A few people from Highland Kirk had shown up to support relatives. I waved to Elder Barnhouse's wife. Bercie is one of the few ladies at church I have actually connected with. I know I should get more emotionally involved with the parishioners, but, well, most of them have so many years to their credit, I just don't relate. Except with Bercie.

Bercie does sculpture.

Bercie hurried over. "I just want you to know that I bought the bread for communion on Sunday, and it's in the freezer down in the kitchen."

"You won't be there?"

The beautiful older woman with a beige blond bob and browned, tennis player legs shook her head. "Gerald's taking me to Asheville for the weekend!" She blushed.

Now that sure was a pretty sight.

I waved a hand. "Then you just leave everything to me, Miss Bercie."

"Now, I usually take the bread out to thaw during Sunday school, then I go down just before the sermon's over and put it in the plate, and then take it up through the side door near the organ during the prayer at the end of the message."

"Really? I never noticed you doing that!"

Bercie winked. "You must actually keep your eyes closed during prayer."

"It's one of the few moments of peace and quiet I get all week!"

"That's motherhood for you. And it gears you up for all the greetings afterwards, too, I'll bet."

"That, too."

"You sure you don't mind doing this?"

"Not at all; you just have a good time with Elder Barnhouse."

Then Bercie scooted off with a thanks and a wave, and she rejoined a group of native Mount Oakers, the tennis crowd at the local country club. I sighed, remembering those days and how easy life had been. What Jesus said about the broad gate and the narrow gate? Well, it must be so.

Chris floated around the grounds with a tea pitcher and a genuine smile. The perfect pastor's wife. Really. Not just an act. She loved this life so much.

I heard the steeple clock at St. Edmund's Episcopal chime eight times. Time to go. Angus's new "Only Mommy can put me to bed" phase drove Duncan crazy. I'd be nice so he wouldn't have to go through another difficult bedtime.

As I left, I pulled Jason Harkens aside. "Now don't you let anything happen to my favorite cousin, you hear?"

He scratched his blond hair, the bulk of it pulled back into a short ponytail. "Don't worry, Mrs. Fraser."

"Seriously, bud. I was in a sorority. Try to keep him from too much drinking. You know how it is."

"I do. Don't worry; I'll watch him like a hawk."

"And don't you *dare* tell him I had this conversation with you."

He laughed. "Don't worry about that either. I've never seen Josh drink, so I don't think you have much to worry about, and I'm not a drinker either. Can't hold it well at all. Not worth it."

"But you're a big guy."

He shrugged. "That's the way it is. And to be honest I'm not at all sorry about it. When the other guys are passed out, *I'm* talking to the ladies and showing them how a gentleman acts."

"The coherent ones, anyway."

"The self-respecting kind, I would say."

Smart kid. Now if he was for real and not being an Eddie Haskell, well, only time would tell for sure.

When I climbed in bed that night I asked Duncan about it. "Do you think that's what's wrong with kids today? That they're not self-respecting?"

"Oh, sure. Remember when we were teenagers and everything was about freedom of expression, sexuality, and everything else?"

"Uh-huh." I began my nightly ritual of cracking my knuckles.

"Well, now they have so much freedom to say yes that they don't know that no is really an option anymore."

"You right-wing freak."

He kissed me softly on the cheek. "That's freak*azoid,* thank you very much. Have to keep up with the times, you know, if you want to be effective in the ministry."

"Well, goodnight, Pastor Freakazoid."

"Goodnight, Mrs. Freakazoid."

The darkness thickened with sooncoming sleep, and I laid a hand on his arm.

"What is it, sweetie?" he asked.

"I can't believe it."

"What?"

"I actually said the words 'what's wrong with kids these days?'"

He chuckled. "You old thing you."

"It's disgusting."

"Not if you're right."

I kissed him on the cheek.

"We're doing all right, Poppy, aren't we?"

"Yeah," I said. "Yeah."

I sat cross-legged on the floor by the carving of the sparrows, and I drew an outline of the birds, capturing their expressions perfectly on the block of watercolor paper I'd bought just for the drawing because I realized I had to place my own hands around this. I had to create this for myself, at my own easel, with my own tools, so that with each stroke I might yearn for what I would never have again, what I never, in truth, possessed at all. For Duncan would have never even thought to carve a pair of sparrows even if he'd had the wherewithal to do it. So I painted the birds, my heart crying silently out to my husband, knowing that even now, even with so much fantasy and emotion invested, Duncan could really save me if he wanted to. But it had to be something he did on his own, not of my own machination, or it wouldn't mean a thing.

Seven

decided the three-mile walk to Chris's house would be a morally responsible decision. Better than getting into that van with a cracked dashboard, cracked vinyl upholstery, and cracked inside walls. The whole thing reminded me of a suspicious egg one is not sure whether or not to replace before moving on to the yogurt section at the grocery store, the kind of egg with the spidery fissures shadowed beneath the main shell that might spell out e. coli. Better to walk and get some exercise than be mad at Duncan the entire way over.

I could stop by Java Jane's on my way back home for my morning cup of coffee, good to the last eavesdrop. That settled the matter. Maybe more episodes of Green-Akers had been scheduled.

The 4 A.M. misty morning possessed that close smell of a barely decaying summer. A few leaves had started to yellow and corkscrew down, pasted onto the wet black roadway. Honking Vs began arrowing farther south now. The air breathed differently, too. I proclaimed it autumn because September had come.

One less autumn after this one's over.

I didn't take much notice of the lack of activity around Lake Coventry this morning. The time had arrived to think about mortality. Again. And I wondered why I had been cursed with a very loud life-clock ticking inside. *All right, so I'm forty-five now, which means if I double that it makes ninety. Since there's longevity on my side of the family, I just might make it to that age, which means I still have as many autumns left as I've already lived.*

Next year the count would be up to ninety-two. I hate the fact that for every one year you live, the mortality scale ups you by two. Death looming, plans need to be made and shoved aside.

In autumn I lean toward cremation. In fact, in most seasons I want to be cremated. Ashes scattered into the Chesapeake Bay, and that would be that. Some people hate the fact that after a couple of generations we are remembered no more. I take a great deal of comfort from it.

I navigated the dark roads. A few lamplights cast halos, and when I pulled my glasses away from my field of vision down onto the lower portion of my nose, they looked like small, smoky eclipses lining the street. Too early for contacts this morning. An especially heavy patch of fog blanketed the Mount Oak town square as I hurried toward it. I replayed my favorite memories of the boy I was helping to send off to college. I love Josh almost as much as I love Robbie. I feel that turgid blood tie between us, that bond of countless family gatherings, lots of movies viewed together, and shared glasses of warm soda in plastic cups.

Joshua Reynolds Knight. We called him Reynolds Wrap for the first month of his life because he liked to be cocooned tightly in his receiving blanket. Then we switched to Wrappy until he turned one, at which time Gary forced us to go with just Josh. "Just Josh" he called himself until he reached three.

And now Johns Hopkins University waited for him, back in Baltimore, back near Charles Village and Roland Park and all those apartment buildings like the ones into which my folks had eventually retired.

I thought of the way Josh worshiped Robbie for years and closed my eyes briefly against the memory of Robbie spurning him when he turned twelve and Josh was only ten. Before then, the two boys had played together all the time. But Josh was small and had to wait for puberty longer than most kids. Robbie had practically been born with a deep voice, started shaving by thirteen, in fact. Josh had been an innocent. Still was in many ways. I felt my heart fold painfully around the recollection of the day Robbie walked away from a teary-eyed Josh, who couldn't understand why Robbie didn't want to play G.I. Joes with him anymore. Sure, even Josh himself had been too old to play with dolls, but Robbie didn't have to call him a stupid baby.

Of course, Chris forgave Robbie when I made him go back and apologize, and she never blamed anybody for the incident and never brought it up again. In fact, Chris probably forgot all about it. But I never did. And at that moment, as I passed the churches of Mount Oak, their contentious signs and banners shrouded in the dark morning fog, I felt glad Josh was going to be the doctor. Let him show Robbie up for once.

Gary slammed the hatchback of the station wagon as I walked up the driveway of the small stone rancher. A softball jersey hung from a hanger hooked over his fingers.

"Gary!" My loud voice echoed in the still of morning.

He turned and I waved. Gary's Irishness, inherited from his father, the relative I don't share, never wanes in its overall impact: that red hair, those freckles, those short, yet powerful soccer player legs. The only thing that stands between him and a perfect impersonation of the Lucky Charms guy is the accent. Strictly Baltimore. "Heya, Popp!"

"Hey, Gare. You going to play softball up there today?"

"You know me, hon. Can't stand a warm day without pitching at least one game." He snapped the handle of the hanger onto the hook inside the back passenger side door. "Actually, I've got one final game this evening after we get back. There won't be time to get back here to change."

Church league stuff. "The finals?"

"Yeah. We're gonna cream those Pentecostals."

"I see the boys of summer in their ruin." *Thank you, Dylan Thomas.* I don't know why the churches don't get together and build a sandlot and thereby completely resurrect the feeling for which they are searching.

Thankfully, Chris emerged from the house. "Nothing like a little friendly competition," she said beneath a Kleenex, blowing away her morning allergies. She set a bag of snacks on the front seat.

I reached in and grabbed a handful of corn pops.

Gary remained cheerful. "Be thankful that it gets us outta you guys' hair for three hours a week."

I followed Chris back into the house. "There is that."

"You said it." Chris walked back to the kitchen. "I've got coffee. It's not Java Jane's, but it's got caffeine."

"Lead the way, lady."

The kitchen was a mess. Chris's kitchen is always a mess. It is so famous for its messiness that whenever the Fraser kitchen gets out of hand we call it a "Knight Kitchen." The sink burgeoned with dirty dishes; the counters buckled beneath pots, muffin tins, and thirteen-by-nine-inch baking pans begging for a bath. Piles of mail, packages of napkins, rotting bananas, a huge crate of zucchini and tomatoes, which I knew would get thrown out eventually, hid the sparkly sixties countertop. Open drawers grinned with an underbite; the dishwasher was clean but unemptied. And talk about crumbs!

So much for Java Jane's, I decided, pouring a cup of coffee. I knew I wouldn't step foot on the road back home until I had cleaned my friend's kitchen. No one should have to come home to this after taking their only son off to college. I started picking up items that could go directly into the trash can. Besides, Gary would appreciate it, too, and I owe him a lot. He'd always been there for me when we were growing up as some sort of payment since he'd lucked out and got Lucy Palmer as a mother and not Fidge Palmer. Lucy was the cool one. The older one. The one who let us have picnics up on her king-sized bed while we watched *Hogan's Heroes*.

"Don't even think about it, Aunt Popp."

Up from his room in the little rancher's basement stood the child we literally prayed into existence. I viewed him afresh. Oh, man! Who had set our clocks years ahead of where they should have been? Who had taken this small, redheaded boy and stretched him to five foot eight? Who had snatched the G.I. Joe doll out of his hands, and where had that boomerang he had been trying to learn to throw for years suddenly gone? And those big feet! Where did they come from? "I don't know what you're talking about, Josh."

"Oh, come on. You're going to stay behind and clean the kitchen. The question is"—he pulled me into a gentle embrace—"why couldn't you have done it two days ago so my last days at home would have been less cluttered?"

I hugged him to me hard. "You ready?" I pulled away, patting his shoulders.

"Ready for anything, I think. Mom's worried, though."

Chris stepped into the kitchen, arms full of towels with the tags still on. "I'm worried! So what? You know what that kind of life is like, Popp. Am I being paranoid?"

I held up my hands. "You sure you want me to answer, blood being thicker than water and all?"

"Okay, just forget I said anything then."

Josh put an arm around his mother. They stood eye to eye. He looked so much like his dad it threw me back to the past, remembering how proud Gary had been the day this guy arrived via the miracles of reproductive medicine. It looked like Gary standing next to his wife, a Gary that had day-tripped to the fountain of youth and all Chris got was a stupid T-shirt.

"I'll be fine, Mom. You'll be glad to be rid of me!"

Chris turned him around toward the door. "Get out of this house and get on your way."

We walked to the car, the air inside the vehicle swarming with Gary's muttered complaints about all of his son's paraphernalia. "How much stuff does one kid need anyway?" His grumblings, a time honored tradition of fathers with college-bound children everywhere, reminded me of my own father when I left home, as well as Duncan when we all bid adieu to Paisley with a guilty sigh of relief.

"What kind of doctor do you want to be anyway, Josh?"

"A gerontologist," he said with a wide grin. "That way I can take care of you right away, Aunt Popp."

Chris said from her seat in the car, "He's got plenty of time to decide."

I kissed Josh good-bye, hugging him again. "Love you, Reynolds Wrap," I whispered.

"I love you, too, Aunt Popp." He kissed my cheek, got in the station wagon, and shut the door as Gary started the engine.

All three of them waved as Gary backed out onto the street.

The window rolled down, and the college-bound boy stuck out his face. "And it's just Josh!"

I waved them out of sight.

And the black drive stood empty, the moist street lay still, and the clouded sky had begun to thin. A nice little family was taking their only child off to college.

I waved again to no one, forced back the tears I felt gathering inside of me, and shuffled inside to clean up the kitchen. Clean up the mess, Poppy. Just clean up the mess and go home.

Eight

Normalcy returned as autumn spread its warm rainbow across the broadleaf trees. And even as the foliage raged then died, the programs at Highland renewed themselves with a springtime vigor. Ladies Bible study one morning a week. Workplace Women every Thursday night. Duncan resumed the men's prayer breakfast at Bill D's restaurant on Tuesday mornings at seven. We'd even experienced an influx of families with children which called for the planning of Harvest Night at the end of October. Thanksgiving brought Josh home…yes…and our two families celebrated together with Gary and Duncan doing the turkey breasts on the grill. Chrissy and I stayed inside and made oyster dressing, sweet potato casserole, and that soupy, green bean casserole Gary insisted on having.

December saw the annual church bazaar and pancake breakfast, the culminations of four Saturdays of making crafts. And then we decorated the sanctuary for Christmas. Now, I have to admit, Highland Kirk knows how to decorate. Williamsburg has nothing on these ladies. Garlands, swags, and wreaths filled the sanctuary with the smell of greens and citrus fruits. Real candles burned at the Christmas Eve service. Afterwards, Josh joined the Frasers for our yearly ritual beginning with sliding on a new pair of pajamas and congregating around the tree to open one gift.

Christmas Eve and midnight had just chimed its way to December 25. But it still felt like Christmas Eve, stars crisply silver in an ink blue sky and air so thin and clear it almost hurt to breathe. Walking home from the ten o'clock service, I'd bundled Angus inside of my coat. We kept each other warm and hummed "O Little Town of Bethlehem."

"A silent star goes by."

Isn't that one of the loveliest phrases ever written? I love the variety of God: heavenly hosts scaring shepherds, a silent star shining on the babe, swaddling clothes, kings in purple on a journey. Finery made more so by nearby rudeness. Rudeness made breathlessly simple by nearby finery. It's easy to think of Jesus as the babe of Christmas.

What does He look like now? How does that hair as white as wool really appear from His seat at the right side of the Father? When I'm sad, I think of the shepherd Jesus. But when I'm angry at injustice and cruelty, I remember the way Jesus is now.

Even so, come quickly. Make this the best Christmas ever, Lord.

Wait. Find Paisley first, okay?

"Oh, man, Aunt Popp, this is the coolest!" Josh jumped to his feet from his seat on our living room floor, his present hanging from his fingers. "Thanks!"

All I can say is, the boy knows how to give a hug.

Robbie, wearing a tattered Santa hat, let out a laugh and clapped. "Superman!"

"Shhh! Angus is asleep!" I scolded.

Josh flung the new cape around his shoulders. "Here I go!" Josh ran for the narrow flight of steps that joined the attic to the rest of the house.

I laughed, remembering the day I bought it at one of those temporary Halloween stores with cheap costumes and fake everythings. Chris and I tried on masks and wigs, laughing so hard we wore ourselves out. A trip to The Sweet Stop remedied that, however.

Josh's big feet clattered up the stairs, his shoes visible at the top. He growled a primordial holler, and gripping the opening into the attic propelled himself ten feet through the air and onto the couch with a sturdy thump.

Duncan ran in from his study where he had busied himself on the final touches of his Sunday sermon the day after Christmas. "What was that noise?"

"Oh, man," Josh said in a "dude" voice, "you gotta try this."

So much for Angus sleeping.

The activity lasted until 1 A.M. when I zipped in with some hot cider in mismatched mugs. Even Duncan made sure he took his turn every third time, although this time he refused to wear the cape. "A man's got to keep his dignity."

"What little you have left, Dad."

Robbie and Duncan punched each other.

"Cretins," I said, all the while enjoying their utterly male exchange.

Angus slept on, unfortunately, because he woke up the next morning at five o'clock, and only Duncan and I could rouse enough to watch him open his presents. And then Duncan fell back asleep on the couch.

Such is the life of the baby of the family.

Josh, always an early riser much to his mother's chagrin, was the first of the Christmas Eve revelers to awaken. He shared some Christmas Blend coffee with me in the kitchen while Angus played with his new Nintendo set in the living room.

"How's school, Josh?"

"Pretty good."

"Did you like your classes this semester?"

"They were okay. General education stuff. A little boring to be honest. You know."

"Actually, I don't. I had to study a lot." I hate to admit that, but it's true. Today they'd probably say I have a learning disability, but for some reason, when I read a book, I have to repeat the sentences several times before they sink in.

"Well, it's what you do with what you have that counts."

"Josh, you're priceless."

He spooned some more sugar into his coffee. "I've made some friends, though. So that's good."

"Did you find that Christian athletic group I told you about?"

"Yeah, thanks, I did. They're a good bunch."

"What do you guys do?"

"Oh, you know. Instead of alcohol, they get their kicks out of rock climbing and stuff."

I thought about getting out some orange juice, but decided against it just then. "Have you gone on any climbs with them?"

He got up and opened the refrigerator door. "Yeah. Went down to the Peaks of Otter on the Blueridge Parkway one weekend." Pouring more milk into his coffee, he said, "It's really something being up high like that. What a way to view the world! Talk about being close to God." He sat back down. "We take our Bibles sometimes and share. It's cool."

"More power to you, Josh. I prefer to keep my feet on the ground."

Angus called out, "Wanna play with me, Josh?"

"I'd love it," Josh hollered back, then raised his brows above a wide smile. "Duty calls."

A minute later he sat cross-legged on the floor with his little cousin, letting Angus beat the tar out of him.

He really should be a pediatrician, I thought. He'd make a great pediatrician.

Surprisingly, Paisley called at eight to wish us all a Merry Christmas. She stayed in Massachusetts over the holiday with her new live-in boyfriend...a stockbroker named Phillip, of all things.

Phillip—a Bible name.

I swallowed against the nausea, blinked against the stinging of my eyes. Oh, Paisley. My child, my child. I pictured her caught by her long hair in the branches of a tree as the mule she rode kept going without her, just lumbering on in stupidity while his burden flailed her body in a voluntary seizure against the surrounding air.

Swallowing again, I remembered a houseful of people who loved me, people I hadn't yet ruined, awaited breakfast.

Chris and Gary came over for brunch after the church services ended. Gary brought his guitar, and we sang carols. This was the way Christmas was supposed to be.

Talk about food! Eggs benedict with crabmeat instead of Canadian bacon, Chris's famous home fries with caramelized onion and cups of cheese, pastries and baked goods, french toast with strawberries and real whipped cream. And, bless Mother's heart, Starbuck's coffee cast a wide net of aroma all through the downstairs, fishing everyone else out of bed by 10 A.M. I have to admit that every once in a while my mother comes through. In fact she'd sent five pounds of Guatemala in an ornate, needle-point stocking.

Whoa, Fidge lady!

The remains of Christmas that had waited for a week out by the road for pick-up by the trash men were long gone. The bottom of the last bag of coffee lurked just an inch below the beans now. I'd gained eight pounds since the cold settled in, and the walks to Java Jane's waned down to nothing more than a guilty memory. Size sixteens loomed on my horizon if I didn't do something soon. Well, to be honest, they had arrived, but I refused to go buy new pants. I'd thought about dragging my pregnancy jeans out of storage, but the thought horrified me so much I decided I'd rather go around with constricting waistbands and short rises.

But it was a Weather Channel morning today.

I sat in the living room, the only source of light radiating from the television. Robbie's head lay in my lap. Another night sleeping on the couch, poor guy. He's so keyed up when he gets home from work. I wanted to walk, really, but an ice storm pelted the town. It had been licking Mount Oak for three hours now, stinging the tin roof of the bungalow, lulling everyone but me into a late sleep. The streetlight down by the Best Western illuminated a world coated in light corn syrup, and the superintendent of the county schools pronounced them closed.

Good thing I'd gone grocery shopping yesterday.

Yeah, definitely a good thing. I'd met a nice girl at the checkout line. Seemed like a child, really, but she was married to the new interim pastor over at Oak Grove Baptist Bible Church. Independent. Fundamental. King James Version only. At least that's what it says on their sign. Her name tag said Sunny. Aptly named, apparently. Unless she turned off that sweet smile when she left work.

She kept saying, "Yes, ma'am" this and "Yes, ma'am" that, which kind of bugged me. And I can't blame the culture down here. Baltimorean kids say ma'am at the checkout, too. It is a pride thing, pure and simple.

Gliding music announced *Local on the Eights,* and although I had been viewing for an hour, I still felt a responsibility to see if anything had changed. Duncan never watches *Local on the Eights*. He is one of those people who only watches during a hurricane along the coast or when tornados "are ravaging the Midwest." Hardly a devoted weather fan.

Vivaldi's "Winter" played, and after the precipitation radar screen disappeared, dependable weather woman Phoebe appeared in her trim yellow suit and perfect black bob, telling me to "stay tuned" because the Travel Wise report would be coming up next.

Oh, good.

I love the travel report, all those interstates and state lines just spread out at a glance. Cloud cover over the Great Plains. Cold up in Minnesota. No surprise there. It satisfies that pent up feeling I've been nurturing since leaving Jody Callahan's arms. Seeing all those roads, knowing each mile has its very own vista, its very own smell, its very own combination of green and brown and gray and blue, knowing that if I wanted to I could hop in the van...

The *van?*

Well, see. Frustrated again. Maybe Robbie *doesn't* keep me from leaving. Maybe the van does. How in the world could I leave in that rattletrap? How could I jump in with a suitcase for myself and one for Angus and leave? A picture of New York City iced up the screen. Sludge City looked more like it. Maybe New York wasn't such a good idea after all; maybe someplace warm like Arizona might be better.

Maybe that was too warm.

I pointed my remote at the screen. Sunny in Colorado today. I'd have to think more about the Rockies as a possible location.

The screen blackened, and darkness surrounded me. I shuffled into the kitchen to make a pot of coffee. When I yanked off the filter basket, to my surprise it weighed more than expected. I held it up to my nose in the darkness and sniffed the last of the Starbuck's. Yep, the coffeemaker needed nothing but a click of the button. Duncan sure doesn't make things easy for me. The nice things he does feel like lemonade on a cold sore. And yet, what if he acted like a pig? Would I be more prone to stay, thinking it just penance?

I flipped on the light, blinking against the brightness.

As the coffee dripped, I scribbled a note to Duncan that said—

You've got Angus today. I'm going to paint.

With men, it is best to leave no room to maneuver. Coffee notwithstanding.

I searched under the kitchen sink for the ugly green vigilante thermos, knocking over Mr. Clean and the scrubbing bubbles in the process. After filling the dented thermos, I screwed on the inner lid, rued the day I misplaced the outer cap, and grabbed the lopsided, mauve pottery mug Paisley had fashioned in the fifth grade.

The screen door slammed behind me as I slipped my way down the precarious, icy pathway.

God created me to paint, I reasoned, unlocking the studio, wondering why I always feel I have to justify my artwork.

"Penelope, the Lord told me to come here and say a prayer."

I let a soaking wet Mildred LaRue into my studio. Even covered in freezing rain, the woman couldn't have weighed more than ninety pounds. Somehow she'd managed to keep her makeup in place.

I took a grocery bag from Mildred's arms. "Did He also tell you to bring food?"

"The Lord doesn't have to *tell* me to bring food, child. He *made* me to bring food." She began scraping off her slick, bright green coat. "Just like He made you to paint. Mmm, mmm. You been busy, I see."

Mildred LaRue is the only person in the world, besides Angus, allowed to view my unfinished work. I myself don't understand it, but with Miss Mildred, history doesn't play into it much, and Mildred herself says she's always wanted to have good hands and be an "artiste." I figure if this woman could be so transparent and mean it, well, letting her into my pigmented world of paint in hopes that Mildred will someday let me into her own pigmented world seems like a good idea. Not that Miss Mildred has done that. We never talk about black or white things. I don't know how to ask the questions I've always had without coming off as offensive.

Like why do black women age so much slower, and how come their young girls always wear all of those pigtails, and is it hard to find base makeup that really is the perfect shade of brown? And those are just the superficial questions.

"I like that little green dot there on that skipjack," Mildred said, pulling out her own thermos—a little plastic Campbell's soup kind that immediately sucked me back to first grade and the day my mother packed Chicken and Stars for the first time in my Sleeping Beauty lunch box.

"What have you got in there?"

"Just Liptons. Got some monkey bread in the bag, too."

"Smells nice."

"Still warm, too."

I squeezed more white onto my plastic, cubbyholed pallet, a good sign that the painting wouldn't end up with the temperament of a Flannery O'Connor novel. Although the idea of putting sharp things in my shoes sounded like a good form of penance—painful, constant, unseen. "So what are you supposed to pray about with me?"

"Strength to do what is right." She took out a funnel cake pan and a knife. The aroma of cinnamon and butter filled the space between us.

This woman looked beautiful sitting there in a fluffy seawater green sweater and black velvet pants. Miss Mildred possesses those gentle kind of eyes. Soft yet strong. As if they choose to be soft, choose to be vulnerable so that a little bit of God shows through. "All right, then," I said. I put down my paintbrush and held out my hand.

"Let's pray." Mildred set the knife on top of the bread. "Father God, give Penelope the strength to do what is right. I know You, Lord, and I know You don't like people to suffer needlessly. You died for her, Jesus, just like You did for me and all. Help her to believe it all the way in. Help her to rest in Your love and to let You take those extra fool burdens she insists on lugging around. Life is hard enough as it is. For Your yoke is easy and Your burden is light. Amen."

"That's it?"

"That's all there is. Seems to me that about says everything needing to be said. Any more might just as well qualify as vain repetition. Now, you got one of those mugs for me, too?" Mildred pointed to Paisley's creation.

"Hold on." I climbed down from my stool and rinsed out a *Maryland Is for Crabs* mug, transferred my coffee into it, then rinsed out the pottery mug for Miss Mildred. "Paisley made me that mug years ago."

Mildred poured from her thermos. "That big boy of yours didn't make you a mug, too?" She swallowed a large gulp of tea.

"Nope. Too busy for stuff like art."

Mildred's eyes danced. "He does all the stuff you wished you could do when you were little, doesn't he?"

I thought about it. "I guess I wanted to be coordinated like that."

"That best friend of yours, she good at sports?"

"Yeah. All state women's field hockey and basketball."

"I *see.*" Mildred topped off her tea.

I smiled and reached out to rub the bony upper arm of Mildred LaRue. Wow. Real cashmere. "I know you do. Would you like to stay for lunch?"

"Depends on what you're having, Penelope."

"Whatever it takes to keep you here."

Miss Mildred's presence works like triple antibiotic ointment on a nagging rash. She knows I have an infected itch and knows what treatment it needs. But she has no idea what caused the rash in the first place and has never asked although I know she is dying to find out.

"Tell you what, Penelope. *I'll* make us some lunch. Still got some of that whiting in the freezer my Herman caught in August?"

"Yep, in there behind the ice cream from Angus's birthday party in September."

Mildred shook her head and rolled her eyes. "Now I know what that prayer was for. The Lord was telling you to clean out your freezer." Chuckling at her own joke, she slid off her stool and eased back into her coat. "First I'm going to put some potatoes in the oven. Then after a while we'll have us a fish fry."

I could hear the sound of the crumb-coated fish dropping into the fry daddy. Yep, Mildred LaRue always knew just what I needed, when I needed it, and how.

And how.

"How are you going to make it down the walk in those high-heeled boots of yours, Miss Mildred?"

"I got here, didn't I? I'll be back in a few minutes to sing to you while you work."

"That a promise?"

"I never make a promise I can't keep."

I painted better to Mildred's voice. Though the sky promised nothing but more of the same icy drizzle, it was turning out to be a good morning.

Three hours later we sat down to eat. Duncan offered up an official sounding prayer with *Thees* and *Thous* and *arts* and *Thines,* and Angus fidgeted in his seat because he loves fish so much, and he loves Miss Mildred's fish the best.

After the amen we stabbed our forks through the crumb-covered whiting, and Mildred started laughing. For a woman that skinny she has a laugh that borders on obesity.

"Are you gonna tell us a story, Mother LaRue?" Angus asked.

"Are you up for one, boy?"

"I sure am."

"I figured as much." Mildred heaped a mound of buttered yams onto Angus's plate. "Well, more than a few years back, when the Reverend Jesse David LaRue, God rest his soul, was both my pastor and my husband, we used to have fish fries at church. To raise money, you know."

I did know. Just a few months before we'd had a ham supper to raise money for a new roof for the church. We were thirsty for a week afterwards.

"Well, we usually didn't have them in the summer, but that year we did because the church bus broke down and needed fixing, and there wasn't money in the treasury for it, you know. So it was hot as blazes in the church hall, and the kitchen was just filled with us women dipping the fish in the crumbs and dropping them in the fat—"

"What else did you have?" Duncan readied a mound of spinach greens on his fork.

"Corn bread, greens, I think. It was a while ago, Pastor Fraser, and the point of the story isn't the food anyway. Pass me that applesauce, will you?"

I reached for the bowl feeling a keen disappointment. I love stories about food. My eyes met Duncan's. He does, too.

"The point of this story is the hornets."

Angus scrunched up his face. "I don't like flying insects, Mother LaRue. Especially ones with stingers."

"So you like flies then?" I asked him.

He scrunched up his face again.

"I *hate* flies!" Mildred said. "Hate 'em! The way they're all black and buzzy and just hang around your head just looking for trouble. My Jesse David could really swat flies. Mmm! He was a fly's worst nightmare."

Duncan's eyes twinkled. "What about the hornets then, Miss Mildred?"

Duncan and I always call anybody who is old enough to be our mother Miss. The Baltimore City way. The ladies at Highland Kirk love it.

"Well, it was hot as blazes in that church hall. I thought the plastic forks would melt, and we just filled the water pitchers with ice because it melted so fast. So my Jesse David got two of the deacons to bring in the fans from the sanctuary. That was before the days of air conditioning, Angus."

Duncan smiled. "When all the ladies carried little China fans in their pocketbooks."

"That's right, Pastor Fraser. So anyway, they wheeled these big old fans into the room."

"The kind on the tall stands?" Duncan asked.

"Goodness gracious, you Frasers ask a lot of questions!"

"Did they have lots of dusty globs hanging from the wire?" I asked just to be ornery.

Mildred hooted. "They were so disgusting nobody would volunteer to clean them!"

I took my first bite of fish, and I'd been about to say, "We had those at my church growing up," but I opted for another bite of fish instead.

"So the deacons put them on either side of the room. One near a window and the other near the door. But what no one knew, not even my Jesse

David, was that there was a hornet's nest right outside the window, and the sexton, Mr. Hall, had forgotten to put the screen in that window in the spring."

I got up to turn on the coffeepot.

"That regular or decaf, Penelope?"

"Regular."

"Good. Cause I'm coming back out with you to your studio. You're going to finish that painting tonight."

"I am?"

"Yep. The Lord told me that, too."

"Okay." No sense in putting up a fuss since I was going to lose anyway. And if the Lord told her that, who was I to argue?

"But what about the hornets?" Angus's voice sounded too strident in the same room as a good fish supper.

"Well, you know how a fan works. It sucks the air in from behind. And these fans were so big, they sucked more than just air. They sucked in those hornets and started shooting them all over the room!"

"Did any of them make it through the blades alive?"

"Most of them. One shot down into Brother Tyree's potatoes, and he was the lucky one. Poor Missus Purnell got one down her blouse, and let me tell you, hornets can sting more than once, or at least that one could!"

With a twinkle in her eye, Mildred picked at her fish. "I tell you what, we were hopping down in that hall more than at any service we ever had. Even my Herman Winfred, who wasn't *my* Herman in those days, had a hornet after him, and he was running in circles with his hands up in the air shouting, 'Glory! Glory!'"

"So who turned off the fan?" Angus asked.

"Not me! I was having too much fun watching from my place at the deep fat fryer. Finally my Jesse David went over and pulled the plug. Just pulled the plug. Hornets swarming around like...well, like a swarm of bees."

"Sometimes it's up to the pastor to keep his head," Duncan said.

"You're telling me. He was a good man, my Jesse David. A good man. I miss him. Those were the hay days of our church."

"How long has he been gone?" Duncan reached for his glass of Coke. The pastor in him came out in a way that I had to admire. His sermons may be shredded wheat, but his shepherding is Red Velvet cake with cream cheese icing and decorations that don't make one wince from too much sugar.

"Ten years now."

"I wish I could have met him."

"Me, too. He'd tell you how to straighten out that Miss Poole!"

Duncan shook his head. "I don't know if even the Right Reverend Jesse David LaRue could do that. Now she's threatening all manner of things about that stained glass window behind the choir loft."

How come he hadn't told me this before now? "What do you mean?" Oh, that's right. It was the old "wait until someone else is around" tactic.

"The stained glass window is leaking terribly. Something happened when they repaired the roof." Duncan took off his glasses and rubbed his nose. "I suggested that maybe we'd want to replace it with plate glass. The view is beautiful, Poppy. Looks right out over the lake."

I suddenly wondered what on earth I had in common with the man I married. How could someone in his right mind equate stained glass with plate glass? "But there's always been a stained glass window there, Duncan. It's a magnificent piece."

"Do you realize how much it will cost to have it restored? Almost five times as much as replacing the window. And it will look out over the lake, for cryin' out loud."

"But, Duncan—"

"Look, I know you're all artsy and everything, but we're talking twenty thousand dollars. What do you think, Miss Mildred?"

The jazz singer held up her hands, the fingers fluttering. "Uh-uh, Pastor Fraser. Don't be asking me that. You know I'll side with my sister in Christ no matter what the matter is." She winked at me. "It's a man's world here in the church, baby. We ladies have to stick together."

"You said it," I agreed.

Duncan brightened his voice. "We can talk about it later."

"I think the woman's said all she needs to say," Mildred said decisively, obviously using her age to her advantage.

Angus finished up the last of his applesauce. "Can I have some more?"

"Aren't you going to eat your other piece of fish?" I asked.

"No. I'm not as hungry as I thought."

Duncan stabbed the fish with his fork and lifted it over to his own plate.

Drat! I wished Herman Winfred had caught more fish. Typical of Duncan to just take it without asking if I wanted any.

I watched as his fork descended down sideways and cut the **piece** in two. The biggest half ended up on my plate. His eyes twinkled into mine, and I knew my thoughts hadn't been lost on him.

School had ended two days before, and now the kids were off to camp because I sent them off at the beginning of the summer. I needed that break after all the running around I did during the school year. So the silent sunshine that spilled across the new countertops and warmed the polished granite seemed luxurious. I thought of Jody and looked at the sparrows on the woodwork underneath the top of the island, thinking they were a message to me now that I was all alone and the kitchen was almost finished with only the cabinet doors needing to be hung.

He came through the door without knocking, his hair sweaty and curled, and his eyes fell on me boldly, those eyes that made me feel like warm tomato aspic ran through my veins, pumped through my veins, thudded like Indian war drums through my veins. When he set down his toolbox, I offered him coffee with my mouth and offered him so much more with my eyes, and he held out his hand, his big callused hand that was just like the one that reached up and lightly touched my temple.

Nine

he screen door of the kitchen slammed behind Robbie. My heart leapt. I hate to admit that—that my son's presence thrills me like it does. But my infidelity gave birth to a severe honesty. I can't deny that Robbie needs me more than Duncan does, and he gives back more than Duncan does. He still kisses me when he comes into the kitchen for breakfast, and here on February 14, 11 P.M., he arrived home from his shift at Jeanelle's Juicy Burgers. I hadn't heard anything from Duncan since lunch, heard nothing about sweethearts, seen no paper cards, and tasted no chocolate candies. Only an hour remained until Valentine's Day bid adieu for another year. Against my better judgment, I always hold out hope for the holiday.

Robbie dangled a Jeanelle's bag. "Mayo with fried onions."

From behind his back he whipped out a green glass vase of three pink rose buds he'd probably gotten from the refrigerator florist at Broomheller's IGA before work. The three little blossoms looked wilted and greasy, and I knew they'd never bloom. The poor darlings were the prettiest flowers I'd ever seen. "Happy Valentine's Day, Mom. I forgot to put them in the fridge at work."

I pulled him into my arms, eyes blurring with tears. He is so beautiful, too. My eyes closed, and tears spilled quickly down my cheeks. "Thanks, Rob."

"Shoot, Mom. It's only a burger and three dead flowers."

His voice resonated deep now. Like a real man's. I cleared my throat, opened my eyes. "I'll just get a plate. "

Three minutes later he shuffled up to the attic with a bowl of Magic Stars, ready to study for an algebra test. I consumed the burger and figured half a pint of Ben and Jerry's would be fitting as long as I was gorfing. Bloated and filled with five different kinds of fat, I stared at the back door waiting for Duncan to skulk in. He promised this career would be different. He said Christians understood the importance of family. I suspected he left out the word *supposedly* on that one. Because I realized that the word *supposedly* should have been uttered a lot and it wasn't. If he'd said *supposedly* about those things, my expectations might have been subconsciously lowered. But as it stood, I expected the life of Father Tim and Cindy and her cat from Mitford. Yes, the folks of Mount Oak were quirky and kind, and it was such a beautiful town, but I brought me along for the ride. Even with all that niceness and beauty crammed down my throat, it failed to erase that part of me that I suppress every day, the part that dreams of flight and is jealous of her best friend's beauty and goodness. The part that tries its best to stay hidden from the church people.

So I decided that eating the remaining half-pint of ice cream would give me something to do as I watched the kitchen door and waited for Duncan to walk in. He finally did at 1 A.M., just after I admitted to myself I'd gone over the edge into a size sixteen and called up a twenty-four hour catalogue's eight hundred number to order a pair of jeans and two new pairs of khakis.

He rubbed the bridge of his nose and turned away from me. "Hiya, Popp."

"It's Valentine's Day."

"I know. But we had session meeting, and I thought tomorrow we'd go out for a nice dinner. Just the two of us."

"Robbie's working. Did you get a babysitter for Angus then?"

"Uh—no."

"No, you didn't because you just now thought about that dinner, and you're trying to placate me. You're trying to make me think this is something you've been chewing on all day, that you couldn't wait to get home and take me to bed."

He just stared at me, saying nothing. Not too late to take the high road.

"This is the third night in a row you've been home after midnight, Duncan." So much for the high road.

Was it really starting all over again?

"I'm sorry, babe. With the window controversy and all...and Miss Poole has been horrible. We had so much on our agenda tonight. It seems the fact that I spent four hours with her yesterday evening made no difference."

I was too frightened to feel sorry for him. One of those moments pounced down when I thought if I had to live exactly like this for the rest of my life, well, I might just as well close my foot in a bear trap or something. Yes, I couldn't find a nicer guy than Duncan. But being a nice guy didn't always cut it. Didn't he realize our marriage had shifted, that he was once again living with a walking time bomb?

"Poppy, please. I can't help it when stuff like this comes up. It comes with the territory."

"That's the problem. It doesn't matter where we are; the territory starts to look the same. You promised me that once you graduated you'd have more time for us. Do you think because you walk across the lawn and spend thirty minutes eating lunch with us that's enough?"

"Come on, Popp. I'm tired. I don't need this right now."

I felt a hysteria bubble expand my throat. "Are you even capable of needing us?"

He set his briefcase down on the butcher block with a loud thunk. "Look, I'm keyed up right now. It was a long night. I was expecting you to have a little pity or, wishful thinking, that maybe you'd be asleep! But here you are, barking on your chain as usual. I'm going running."

"There's a cold rain out there."

"No different than in here. Just go to bed, why don't you, Poppy?"

He walked by me. Just walked by me. Stunned and sheepish and feeling stupid and petty and exactly like that kind of female no self-respecting woman admits she is, I seethed with fresh anger. Duncan had never talked to me like that before. Yes, he'd been upset with me. But he'd never said anything so mean. Had never used canine expressions. It must have been some meeting, but that didn't excuse his conduct. The creep.

My hands shook as I rinsed out the ice cream bowl, and I felt needy and wanting again. Why does he have that kind of control over me? Whenever he gets miffed at me, I feel like I'm suddenly losing him, and I agree to all sorts of things.

Well, not this time. I couldn't afford to just let him walk all over me again. I wouldn't sit still while he turned this career into just another excuse for workaholism, and a holy excuse at that.

Duncan slammed out of the front door, avoiding me as I stood in the doorway in between the kitchen and the living room. He wore the running shoes I bought him for Christmas as well as the green, waterproof jogging suit with reflective patches. Well, at least he wouldn't be hit by a car before he got back. I wouldn't have to feel guilty about that!

Maybe Duncan had a point about my being in bed.

Tiptoeing to Angus's room, I checked to see if he was covered and sure enough, he'd kicked off the blankets, and his feet felt like cooler packs with toes. So I tucked him in again and said a prayer for him because life can be a curse as well as a blessing. Jesus already lives inside of his heart, so I knew he wouldn't be alone in his trials. But sometimes Jesus doesn't speak too loudly, and when a person is deaf like me, it can make things difficult. So I prayed for good ears for him, and maybe while God worked on his ears, He'd sharpen up mine a little, too.

In the bathroom, I took off my clothes and threw them in the hamper. In the darkness of my bedroom I scraped open my top dresser drawer and put on an old pair of boxers and a T-shirt. Duncan's castoffs. Soft and spare.

The fire left me.

As I turned to get in bed, my foot kicked my suitcase. I lugged it out and stared at the fine leather.

Duncan watched me packing. The kids were home from camp now, and I had to get away—now—now—now. Jody had been everything I thought Duncan would be, and I had been a fool after that first time to think the end would come, and we would just leave it at that. But after our times together he would really talk to me and laugh with me and trace my jawline with his index finger and say how he always thought I was so pretty, even when he'd been helping his father on my first kitchen years before. I'd calculated that the last time Duncan told me I was pretty was at my brother's wedding three years earlier when I wore this horrible apricot taffeta affair, affair definitely being the wrong word because gowns weren't affairs, and neither were receptions and elegant gatherings. Affairs "happened," and then they were planned, and soon one was so caught up in the excitement and the glory and the need. The need was an amazing thing to be taken along in, and it was a wonderful need like a ride in a 1963 Triumph TR3 convertible over the Bay Bridge. I wasn't going to stop that car as long as I lingered in Hunt Valley and Jody breathed and ate and slept only five minutes away and called me from his car phone just to say sweet things and tell me I was pretty, truthfully, to have someone so beautiful think I was pretty meant more than I wanted to admit, but it wasn't worth this.

Not anymore.

Three weeks of unadulterated adultery had to be enough, or this would become a way of life, and I'd start rationalizing and making it everyone else's fault. Or worse, I'd leave everything else behind just to be with Jody, to lie in his arms and feel admired like one of those sexy women in the movies or on TV, a woman whose smile meant something to somebody.

"I'll just be gone a couple of weeks, Duncan."

"But all the way down to the Outer Banks?"

"Look, I've paid for the rental house out of my own money."

"It's not about the money."

"It can't be about me."

"How can you say that?"

"Look at me! Do you even think I'm pretty anymore?"

"What are you talking about?"

"I've got to go."

I kept telling myself it had been about the sex, all about the sex.

I lived out of that suitcase for the rest of that summer away in North Carolina. Two weeks stretched into four, and then two months crawled by on bloody knees there at the dark brown house up at the northern stretch of the beach, nestled behind dunes covered in sea oats. Only I knew I paid for the entire summer in advance. Josh and Chris had come down for a couple of weeks, and I never told my best friend why I stayed away from home until school started again. So I painted all those lighthouses down there, pretending to the world that's why I had come. I refused to wear sunblock, burning my skin to blisters at first, baking it to leather by the end of August, only to come home to Duncan's spiritual revival.

The old radiator clicked beside me.

What did you just do, Poppy? Why should he want to come home when you're acting like such a shrew? What bride ever dreams she'll turn into a shrew? Not me. As a new bride I thought, *I'll rise above all that. I'm not a typical woman at all! I'm not marrying because I need to. I'm marrying because I want to.* And then the years go by, and you find yourself losing any patience you'd ever had. You find yourself being silent on the phone when he calls to tell you he'll be late when, really, not many husbands even bother to call. You find that you're feeling sorry for yourself when, really, you've got a nice roof overhead, decent clothing, and food on the table. And sweet kisses on the cheek, temple, forehead, and mouth.

If I had been able to catch up to Duncan then, who ran like wind with hair, I would have. My mind filled with the picture of him running, running. Breathing fully, freely, eating up the miles of road beneath his feet. Was he running from me?

I decided to set out the mug filled with Hersey's Kisses I bought him at Java Jane's that morning. My own desperation filled me with dread.

Am I alone in these feelings? Do I simply expect too much?

The phone rang. I scooped it up before it finished the first jangle, praying nothing had happened to Paisley.

"Mrs. Fraser?"

"Yes?"

"It's Keith Haring. From over at Mount Oak Community?"

"Oh yes. One of the deacons I think Chris said?"

"Yes. Chris wanted me to call you." He paused. "I don't know how else to tell you this, Mrs. Fraser, but Josh is dead."

I gasped, almost dropping the phone.

"Yeah, he died about three hours ago."

"What happened?" My hands, filling with heat as they gripped the receiver, began to shake.

"A hazing accident. It's all I was told."

"Is she there?"

"They've left already."

"I'll go, too. If you hear from her, tell her I'll be there as quickly as possible."

I hung up the phone and opened the suitcase, my heart beating wildly, my face flushing as I sought release. It didn't matter what I took to wear, I guessed, throwing in only some underpants, a bra, and a pair of jeans. Did this even require a suitcase? We were just going up to make arrangements to bring the body home.

The body? Oh, God. The body. Not the body. Josh. Just Josh. The horrible fact dropped from my head to my heart. My stomach heaved, and my eyes finally overflowed as I shook from each joint.

Pelting sobs erupted, saline tears squeezed upon my hands as I ground my palms into my eyes and knelt down beside the suitcase.

Oh, Josh!

"Poppy!" Duncan ran into the room. He pushed the suitcase aside. "What's going on? It was just a little fight, sweetie. I didn't mean anything by what I said."

I couldn't look at him. Somehow I managed to grunt, "Josh is dead."

"What?"

I couldn't say anything else. The phone rang again. Duncan caught it, and a conversation ensued for the next few minutes. "I'll tell her. Yes, I'll tell her that, too. And, Gary, I'm so sorry. We'll be waiting at the house when you get there."

He hung up the phone softly.

"Did Gary tell you what happened?"

He moved the suitcase to the floor, sat down next to me, and put his arms around me. "Yeah. Apparently Josh climbed up the tower on Television Hill. He slipped."

I wailed.

Duncan wiped the back of his hand across his eyes. "They think he was dead well before he hit the ground."

"What was he doing up there?"

"Maybe a fraternity thing. Several of the guys watched it happen. But there wasn't anything they could do."

"Was he drunk?"

"Nobody knows yet. The autopsy is this morning. Gary wants us to be at his house tomorrow morning when they come back. He also asked if you and I could begin to arrange the funeral."

"So they don't want me to come up then?"

He shook his head. "Poor Josh."

"Yeah." I got up and found a Kleenex. I should be doing something. "Should we tell Robbie now or in the morning?"

"I'll tell him now. He'd be upset if we waited." He swallowed his emotions, I could tell, by the way his nostrils flared and he squeezed his eyes closed for two brief seconds. And I let Duncan take over wondering how my friend was dealing with this right now. Trying to picture her there in the car or at the airport or wherever. I didn't even know how they were getting up to Baltimore. She was crying now, though. I knew that. Chrissy never had been the type to force down emotions.

Chris doesn't deserve this. She doesn't, Lord.

And Gary. My cousin. His only son gone in an instant. One minute they'd been sleeping, the next their son had died. No transition. No "You'd better get to the hospital quick."

After unpacking the hastily thrown together suitcase, I sat on the edge of the bed and wept some more, then felt the sudden emptiness that a death brings. No more picnics or fun times with Josh. No vacations at the beach. No more watching him and his dad throw the lacrosse ball around and hearing Chris shout, "Hey, you guys!" when the ball knocked over the pitcher of red-dyed Kool-Aid she inevitably brought along.

I've always thought of a death as a sudden dent in the universe, a concave emptiness in the atmosphere you couldn't see, but you knew was there. I think it takes the world a little while to fill in the dent, to smooth out the giant wrinkle one human life, when snuffed out, leaves. And for some, it takes longer than others.

With hands still shaky and eyes still blurred, I made another pot of coffee and sat at the kitchen table. Robbie didn't come down, but I heard his restless pacing, and I heard stifled wails. I tried to pray as I sat there, but just then I realized that sometimes it's okay to just lean on the everlasting arms, that at times like these God comes to you and not the other way around.

The sun began to rise several hours later, and I watched as Duncan prayed on his knees in his office, elbows bent and digging into the padding of his desk chair. He tugged at my heart then, so skinny and pale, bright pink patches of grief on the cheek facing me.

"How's Robbie?"

He just shook his head. "I don't know. I stayed up there. But then he asked if he could be by himself a while. I think I'll have a cup of coffee if you don't mind."

"I'll make another pot."

"Okay, I'll just be a little longer."

And he placed his face back into his palms.

Duncan had taken over, thank God, and I meant that more literally than ever before, a new appreciation for my spouse settling my nerves.

The IGA would open in a few hours, and I'd pick up the ingredients for a chicken divan casserole. Nothing spicy would do for a grieving family; something creamy and bland was the proper accompaniment to grief. According to *The Proper Christian Ladies' Handbook,* chapter 11, "Sorrow," anything else seems disrespectful. And to some extent, I must agree.

Ten

ou been so busy taking care of that family that someone's got to take care of yours." Mildred LaRue began pulling Gladware containers out of a grocery bag. "I'm on my way out to a gig for the weekend, but this should see you all through supperwise until I'm back."

"You don't have to feed us, Miss Mildred." I took a sip of my coffee. "There's plenty of casseroles left over from the Knight's house."

"Well, that's a big church. And he is the pastor. That best friend of yours say anything yet?"

"Not really." I shook my head and examined the cheerful walls of my kitchen. They mocked me now, and I thought maybe an antique white might give everyone a fresh start. The funeral took place a week ago; all family members on both sides had come and had already returned to Maryland. Due to the autopsy, Josh had been dead over a week by the time we laid him in the modern cemetery out near the mall. As promised, we met Chris and Gary when they came back from Baltimore, but Chris just said, "I'm sorry, Poppy," and ran to the basement of her house—to Josh's room. Gary just cried and cried.

When a strong man weeps, it is a terrifying thing to behold.

Mildred placed the last tub of food in the freezer. "Shame she's cut herself off from the people who love her. Can't blame her, though. I've been praying."

"Thanks, Miss Mildred."

"Well, these knees aren't what they used to be, but they work well enough. Herman's waiting outside in the Impala."

"Atlantic City this weekend you said?"

"Uh-huh. Some little dive somewheres. But I'm hoping people from Caesar's come on in. Maybe they'll like what they see."

I stood up and put my arms around Miss Mildred's long neck. "Maybe?"

Mildred held me close. "Yeah, well, you take care of yourself this weekend, baby. And eat up that good food. I even made chicken-fried steak for you. Those other casseroles will sit fine in the freezer."

Mildred's soft kiss on my cheek felt like lotion on December hands. I waved my friend away from the front porch. The crocuses had just started to bloom. Purple crocuses. Guess spring decided on an early arrival this year.

I poured another cup of coffee, walked down to the dock and sat in the hard breeze, trying my best to believe Paul actually penned Romans 8:28 for situations like this: "And we know that in all things God works for the good of those who love him, who have been called according to his purpose." Josh knew better than I did about that now. Josh sat with the heavenly host while his mother sat in his old bedroom bearing a weight of a grief I couldn't begin to imagine.

Duncan's face wore a wearier expression than usual as he let the screen door bang behind him. As he set his briefcase and a small white bag on the butcher block, I noted that the gray in his hair had thickened even since Christmas.

"You've got to stop sitting at that table, Popp. You haven't schooled Angus for almost three weeks."

"I know. It's just so hard. If Chris would talk to me, maybe I could do something. But I just feel paralyzed by the fact that she's over there in that little house all by herself. And poor Gary. It's not like he doesn't have his own grief to deal with."

"Yeah. But at least he's talking."

"To you."

"Yeah. I'm worried about Chris, though."

"Is she eating?" I asked.

"Not much."

"I should take her a latte from Java Jane's. She'll drink those."

"Maybe that would be a good idea."

I glanced at the clock. Six-thirty. The girls at Java Jane's had already closed up for the night and were probably busy leading cool, funkily dressed lives. Dinner party with friends, perhaps, each bringing an odd ingredient like jicama or ugly fruit. Or perhaps right now they sat in an old theater in Richmond listening to Nanci Griffith strum her guitar with the Blue Moon Orchestra. What had once seemed so free and fun three weeks ago had turned to Ecclesiastes in a matter of seconds.

"What are you doing home so early?" I asked, careful to intone my voice so he knew it made me glad.

He picked up the bag. "I'm tired of casseroles. I got a pound of crab-meat from Barnacle Bill's." Charlie Dickens lets Duncan have anything for half price—one of the kudos of having church members who owned busi-nesses like Barnacle Bill's.

"You want me to make you some crab cakes?"

"No. I'll do it. Why don't you go out to your studio this evening?"

"I don't feel like painting."

"That's why you need to go. Go on, Popp. Even if you don't paint, at least get out of the kitchen."

I looked down at the cold coffee in my mug. "I guess a change of scenery wouldn't hurt."

"I'll bring your dinner out to you."

But I didn't paint anything. Not even a sky. Just sat some more and lis-tened to the transistor radio I'd duct taped to my easel years before. I never could get into the preachers or the roundtable discussions with the token woman on board. Chris loves those shows. I desperately want to.

However, just then the Christian station played a soft, panpipe arrangement of one of the old tunes I recognized from the hymnbooks of my childhood. *I'd rather have Jesus than anything.*

I stared at the bland block of paper before me and could think of nothing that would improve the rough white expanse. And after eating my crab cake and complimenting Duncan on his cooking, which has always been good, I stood under the shower, washed my hair with ivory soap because I hadn't been to the store since I'd run out of shampoo, then went to find Angus.

He and Robbie were laid back on Robbie's bed up in the attic. Both boys jumped with surprise and sat up straight. Robbie set the book aside they'd been reading. Some science fiction book that they both knew would give Angus bad dreams.

"Tomorrow things will be different, okay?"

Angus nodded. "Can I sleep with Robbie again tonight?"

Robbie put his arm around his little brother's neck. "Fine with me, Mom."

"All right."

I turned to go and made it to the door. I looked back at my sons. "Robbie, you'll say prayers with him?"

"Sure."

I set my alarm for five-thirty. I'd start my walks again tomorrow, too. Stop by Java Jane's and make that two. And maybe Chris would open up and talk, or maybe she'd just drink her latte in silence. That would be okay, too.

But the next morning I hit the snooze twice and finally turned off the alarm altogether.

Miss Poole inched toward me on feet that overlapped the tops of her pumps in fluid pillows of flesh. Potstickers in shoes. I have to admit the woman has style. She doesn't sway beneath hats with jiggling floral appendages or squeeze herself into QE2 suits in shades of aqua or robin's egg blue. She doesn't hang pocketbooks from the crook of her arm or clip sparkly beaded earrings from 1964 to her soft lobes. This woman inched toward me with a diamond dragonfly clip in her smooth silver pageboy, a fringed black shawl draped over a severe black pencil dress, and a little

Bohemian, beaded, drawstring bag looped around her fragile wrist. Only her shoes gave her away. Boots, of course, would have completed the outfit perfectly, but I'd heard that Miss Poole never wore them. I'd never heard why, and honestly, some things I'd just rather not know.

Her servant, Ira, an older gentleman with the build of farm equipment, stood to the side, pretending to read an outdated issue of *Our Daily Bread*. His height went right along with his build. I gauged him to be at least six foot five, which, when he was a teen back in the late thirties, must have been astoundingly tall. He doesn't serve officially as a deacon or an elder or anything, but Ira always helps put away the chairs and tables in the rec hall downstairs, and he always arrives first at the town festivals to set up our booth.

Ira is the kind of man who helps move the piano when a local family needs help loading the moving van. He doesn't grab a small box of nonperishables every five minutes and drink coffee the other four.

Duncan is that kind of guy, too. I have always been proud that he moves pianos and highboys, and doesn't balk at the Maytags or Frigidaires either. To my thinking, that says more about a man than almost anything.

"Penny!" the hip maven shouted, waving a bulletin. "Have I heard correctly?"

I straightened my pearls and felt my left earlobe to see if I should be embarrassed by my earrings. No, just the little pearl drops hung there today. "It depends on what you've heard, Miss Poole."

"That we actually agree on something."

"Are you talking about the window?"

"Of course! Now, Penny, I want you to do all you can to convince Duncan to let me pay for the restoration."

"You mean you've offered to pay for it?" I'd kill Duncan at brunch. The headline of the *Mount Oak Sentinel* would read "Local Minister Slain at Home. Wife Flees in Putty-Patched Van!"

"I certainly have! It would be a tragedy to let that go! It's been there since I was a little girl."

"Maybe you could try negotiating with him, Miss Poole. What if he says yes to the window, and you say you won't interfere with getting new hymnbooks?"

Miss Poole looked thoughtful. "I'll have to think about that. But I do know we can't let the PCA Presbyterians downtown have beautiful windows and us just have plate glass! I mean, they're the ones that pulled out of the denomination in the first place!"

"They've got new hymnbooks."

"Really?" Miss Poole regathered her shawl around her shoulders. "Well, fine job on the bulletin today. No typos."

And she walked into the sanctuary on her polelike legs, stiffened by arthritis and black support hose.

Sometimes I actually like the woman. I sighed and made my way to the fifth pew on the left by the window aisle. The choir filed into their seats up at the front. What selection would they sing today? I opened up the bulletin and silently groaned.

"And He Shall Feed His Flock" by Handel. Oh, brother, another wonderful song being led like a lamb to the slaughter.

Eleven

can't get through to her. I've been over there every day for three weeks, and she won't see me."

"Robbie's still alive is why." Mildred LaRue's eyes saddened and drooped more than the underdrawers on my clothesline. "Poor baby." She looked older today for some reason, and I couldn't tell why. Memphis housed Mildred LaRue and the Star Spangled Jammers for a week-long engagement at some rib house and now we sat at the hoosier sharing a rack Miss Mildred brought home with her. Dry ribs. I will never truly enjoy sloppy bones again.

Mildred wiped her fingers. "You got to give her time, Penelope."

"But this isn't good for her."

"I know. At least I guess I know. I've never even had a child to lose."

I drummed my fingers on the table. Miss Mildred and I talked a lot, but one never knew who she could really voice big doubts to: the big, eternal scary you-shouldn't-even-be-*thinking*-such-things-let-alone-talking-about-them kind of doubts. "How could God do that to a nice boy like Josh? And to parents like that who've sacrificed their entire lives to serve Him?"

"That's the big question, Penelope."

"It doesn't make me think very kindly of God." I looked up for some kind of lightning bolt.

"Maybe God respects us enough to let our decisions be our own."

Miss Mildred believes in free will. I'm more of a predestination type of gal. I make it a rule never to discuss theology with her because she knows her Bible, that woman. And although I can remember what verses say, I couldn't begin to tell you what book they're found in.

"If you saw your child running toward the edge of a cliff, wouldn't you stop him?" I asked.

"Or climbing up a TV tower?"

"Yeah." My eyes burned with tears.

"I'm not God, baby. All I know is that there is pain and suffering in the world. The first step to dealing with it is to accept it as a fact of life."

Angus looked up. "Jesus suffered on the cross."

I pictured the scene in the Garden of Gethsemane: Jesus praying, His beautiful face torn by anguish, glistening with a mixture of sweat and blood. *Not My will, but Thine.* Even Jesus asked if it were possible that God would take the cup of suffering away from Him. And God said no.

I sat here at my kitchen table questioning His love because of that refusal.

"'He spared not His own son,'" Mildred quoted.

"But it seems so easy to say because God spared not His own son that it's okay for Him to take Chris's away from her."

"Is Josh in heaven?" Angus asked.

"Yes," I answered.

"That's good," he said.

I wished Chris and Gary could say the same. It's such a frightening world at times, filled with questions, mysteries, and wonders. And there are times when only faith gets me through, when I have to stop asking questions for just a moment, long enough to catch my breath and remember that God is good. We are His children, and He really does know what is best.

Each day I awaken and pray for grace and wisdom and enough faith to keep me from losing the very same.

"'I believe,'" I whispered. "'Lord, help thou my unbelief.'"

"That verse is in there for a reason, baby." Mildred reached out and put her hand on my shoulder. "It's in there so we know those kind of feelings are normal. So we know that our humanity is understood by God, that He can handle any question we've got."

I wiped my moistened eyes with a corner of my napkin. "So where is the line between honest questions and disrespect?"

She pointed a finger and rested it on my heart. "In there."

I cried again. Deep groans of deeper doubt and utter helplessness. "I need to do something, Miss Mildred. Just something. I don't know what."

"I guess all we can do is pray."

"I've been doing that."

"Me, too, Penelope."

Angus looked up from his chair and away from *The Voyage of the Dawn Treader.* "What's that verse Dad always says before prayer meetings? 'Where two or three are gathered together—'"

Mildred smiled at him as she finished. "'There am I in your midst.' That boy is right, Penelope. We need to be praying together for your friend."

I scrutinized the two faces before me, both skinny, different colors and different ages, and I wondered two things as I blew my nose and dried my eyes once again. How did my five-year-old child have more sense than I did? And why did a wise woman like Mildred LaRue call a foolish woman like me her friend?

"I'm leaving for Nags Head tomorrow morning for a five-day gig. I'll be back on Monday. That night good for you?" Mildred asked.

I ran my finger over the stippled curve of an orange in a fruit bowl on the hoosier. "Yeah. What time?" I sniffed the freshness of the peel.

"Six-thirty. And come hungry."

"Food, too, as well as prayer?"

Mildred stood to her feet and grabbed her coat from the rack by the door. "Haven't got the leading to start fasting yet, Penelope."

"Where you up and going to?" I asked. Hardly a surprise, though, because Mildred always left abruptly.

Mildred waved a graceful hand. "To church. The pastor's wife is in a tizzy. Seems some of the ladies have been gossiping about her."

"In church?" I let out a melodramatic gasp.

"Hard to believe, isn't it? Well, the woman wears her hair much too short and acts like some queen, so she's got it coming to her."

"What are you going to say?"

"I have no idea."

So Mildred went off in a flurry of green clothes and righteous indignation.

During the Beatles' era, I had been a "John girl" and Chris had been a "Paul girl." It pretty much described our differences in character and personality, for while Chris has always been a fan of the obvious, I prefer the obscure. But not the downright weird. The "Ringo girl" ruled that territory. The only "Ringo girl" I ever knew had been the sole and founding member of the Cryptogram and Word Search Puzzler Club and was named Samantha Regina—pronounced with a long i. The fact that Chris couldn't understand why I proclaimed myself a "John girl" always picked at me. I could see the appeal of Paul, straight up. Cute, pleasingly crooked teeth, that mop of brown hair and those droopy eyes that said, "Love, love me do." But Chris could only say John's "nose looks like an arrow pointing straight down to an angry, sneering mouth."

Chris never forgave him for his spiritual influence on the time. Although she truly did feel sad that someone murdered him. I had to give her that. "He was your guy, Poppy," Chris had said the day she'd heard the news and called to check on me.

"Yeah. He was." But I didn't feel as sad as I thought I should have. Some people are destined to quickly blister, then pop. But a sense of completion prevails, a sense of destiny contained like a serum within the whole blistery situation And then a healing could begin, leaving a callus. Like Princess Diana—now that death came as a shock to me, yes, but then it ceased to be surprising. Or James Dean. Or John Bonham. Marilyn Monroe. Same thing.

But not Josh. No, he didn't fit this category at all. He wasn't supposed to be dead yet. Josh never acted like some shooting star, some burning bush. Josh grew up regular, a nice kid who would have made a wonderful father, wouldn't have minded mowing the lawn every Saturday as long as he could sit and watch the Hopkins game undisturbed for the latter part of the afternoon. Josh would have sat at the dinner table with his youngest child on his lap, balancing his buttered peas on his fork so they didn't drop into freshly washed, feathery hair.

Miss Mildred said God has enough respect for us to let us suffer the consequences of our free decisions. All well and good in theory, I say. But what about the drunks that walk away from the accidents they've caused, while some innocent wife is groping around the scene desperately feeling for a pulse on her baby trapped in its carseat, or hollering at her husband with tearful cries of, "Say something, Phil! Oh, God, please say something!" So Josh did a stupid thing. He climbed up a tower, lost his footing, and died.

Did his guardian angel fall down on the job? Did God forget that verse about bearing us up lest we dash our foot against a stone?

I shoved the questions from my mind, unable to bear the contemplation just then.

The day felt warm for a March Wednesday. Sixty degrees at noon. I pulled on some leggings, a T-shirt, a nylon anorak, and my walking shoes. After stuffing a five-dollar-bill in the pouch pocket on my front, I grabbed Angus's windbreaker and walked into the sunroom. "Wanna go be with Daddy a little while?"

"Okay." He got up looking five years old. He always looked his age when his mouth stayed shut. "Can I take my book?" His hand clutched *The House with a Clock in its Walls*.

"I'm sure that would make Daddy happy."

Duncan appeared far from pleased after I walked across the expanse from house to church. But he knew better than to cross me, I guessed. I had pasted that look on me face, that "Think twice, Bucko" expression I'd learned from my mother, who'd learned it from my grandmother—all too familiar with that set to the eyes that stubborn women inherit from stubborn women. He merely clenched his jaw, refused to look me in the eye, and asked what he should fix for lunch.

"Hot dogs. And I'm one of your parishioners, too, you know, Duncan."

He knew when he married me I was like this, my German maiden name being the giveaway. Fair warning and all. I'm careful not to abuse the privilege, though.

"Duncan?"

"Yeah, babe."

"That verse about 'giving His angels charge over thee to keep thee in all thy ways,' and the 'lest thou dash thy foot against a stone' part?"

"Uh-huh. Do you have a question about that?"

I nodded. "Isn't that some kind of promise to us believers?"

His ire faded instantly, and he shook his head. "No, hon. That verse is talking about the Messiah. The Bible never promises we won't have pain and suffering."

"But what about the hairs of your head verse? And the lilies and the sparrows?"

Angus tugged on my jacket. "Can I go down to the nursery and play with the toys?"

"Sure, buddy," Duncan said, and he took my hand. "Babe, if the Bible really did promise us no pain, and if God's love was measured by the amount of pain we suffered, this would be a really lousy religion and one that fails all the time."

"I know."

"God never promised we wouldn't suffer. We all wish He would have, but He really never did. And even that verse about the sparrow. What is it that He's watching the sparrow do?"

"Fall."

I closed my eyes and wept once more.

Duncan folded me into his arms and whispered. "If He sees the sparrows fall, Popp, He saw Josh fall, too." He pulled back and looked into my eyes. "The Lord was there with Josh, Poppy. He was. 'Precious in the sight of the Lord is the death of His saints.'"

The crying felt good, cleansing, and powerful and so I took advantage of the church pastor and stayed within the circle of his arms for the next ten minutes.

So I walked alone along Lake Shore Drive, waving to parishioners as they passed by in their really nice, nonputtied, noncoathangered cars. I ignored everything else. Java Jane's and two lattes. That was my destination, and then I would think about what to say after that. What would Chris think, me just barging in with my key, espresso drinks in hand? It didn't matter. The time to act like a *best* friend arrived. Not just a friend who respectfully stood back and let her best friend isolate herself because that's what she says she wants. No, that's not what *best* friends do. *Best* friends scream and yell and jerk their friends by the throat with a roaring "Stop it! Say something! Anything!"

Don't they?

How come I couldn't read Chris like I used to? Why didn't I know what to do instinctively now?

No, those thoughts would save until after Java Jane's. I'd think about it in a few minutes.

Margaret tended the coffee shop by herself. "A latte? Really?" she asked when I placed the order. "You hardly ever get lattes, Poppy. Must be a special day."

"Just trying to cheer up a friend."

"Oh, good choice then."

Margaret, her mane of brown hair swept back in a ponytail, began to make the drink, banging the little filter basket. "You haven't been here in a while. Everything okay?"

"Yeah. I'll get back to my routine now that it's warmer. You all doing okay?"

"Uh-huh. Ellen's away for a week, though. Gone on a cruise down in the Caribbean. She goes away by herself every once in a while. Likes the Norwegian cruise line."

"I hear they've got the best looking attendants."

Margaret shrugged. "If you like blondes."

"Been busy?"

"No more than usual. So, this friend of yours, will she need a good scone too? I baked apricot ones this morning."

"I don't think so. It's really a tragedy she's gone through. A latte will do."

"Got ya."

Margaret handed me the drinks. "See you tomorrow morning then? It's supposed to be another nice one."

"Okay."

Hoping that commitment possessed enough potency to get me out of bed at 5 A.M., I resumed my mission.

The drinks felt good in my hands, warm, smooth, and tidy beneath their dependable lids. But their questionable nature remained, and a feeling of unsurety settled in the pit of my stomach as I wondered just how Chris would react.

Chris refused the latte. "How can I? With Josh gone and all?"

I let mine get cold, too. How do you drink your own latte after that? But Chris had let me in, and that could definitely be considered progress. She looked horrible. But she didn't smell that way, so at least she had enough strength to shower. "Are you eating?"

"Some."

"Okay. How's Gary?"

"I'm not sure. He doesn't come down here much."

We sat together in Josh's room. His school trunks had been mailed back home and were stacked near the door. Big labels, with clumsy, El-Marko lettering screaming his parents' names. No longer Josh's things, but not really theirs either.

Chris looked up, the hollows of her eyes made darker by the gloom of the room. Only the desk light cast its jaundiced rays upon the green blotter. A sicklier light I couldn't imagine. The dehumidifier hummed, but the room smelled discarded somehow.

"They found out he was drinking," Chris said and laid back on the pillow. "That's what the autopsy showed. I didn't know how to even tell you that."

"Have you been sleeping down here, too?"

"Yeah."

I sat some more, looking around. The room was still as neat as Josh had probably left it. "I'm going to go clean the kitchen."

"Okay. That would be nice." Chris turned and faced the wall. "Didn't you hear what I said?" she called as I moved toward the threshold.

"Yeah. Josh was drinking."

"So who's to blame then? Us or him?"

I said nothing. Just went up the stairs.

scoured the kitchen, lugged laundry from the first floor to the basement, then back again. After vacuuming the wood floors and the carpets, even the disquieting square footage beneath the colonial blue living room sofa, I arranged the shoes at the bottom of Chris's closet.

And pass the Kleenex!

Dust now coated the black church shoes, inside and out. Chris felt so proud and excited about those shoes. Ninety-eight dollars reduced down to twenty-four. Cole Haans. Thick, shiny kind of leather. Not rube shoes. Two-inch heels. Substantial leather soles.

The latte visit had been four days ago. And every day since I'd spent time trying to get Chris's house back to normal while Angus did his school-work at the kitchen table. Well, my definition of normal, anyway. Once I finished, the place would be cleaner than the day they moved in. Chris now spent her time in the kitchen doing cryptograms like a Ringo girl, thank God, and I literally meant that. So now, after hurrying through my Red-Eye, I stopped at Broomheller's IGA and picked up the latest edition of *Pencil Puzzles and Word Games*. Once again, that checkout girl named Sunny lived up to her name. Every day she did, the sweet thing. I have never been described as sweet. Of course I never looked like Sunny either. Long, straight blond hair and a wide, perfect face. Green eyes, too. At six-teen, I would have given anything for green eyes when Mother forced me to go to the school mixers. Girls with green eyes seemed to get asked to dance more than plain old, brown-eyed girls.

I knew I should read up on helping someone deal with grief, climb through the Internet, find out about the various stages. But I couldn't. I couldn't reduce Chris to that. I couldn't start second-guessing what stage she was actually in, gauge whether she had, indeed, gone from one stage to the other, or whether she had reverted back to a previous one. I was no psychologist. I didn't want to be a psychologist; I didn't want that kind of responsibility. I only wanted to be a friend, to do the dishes, to vacuum, to launder, to keep the kind of things going that I knew how to keep going.

And what right did I have to give advice to anybody anyway? Especially Chris. Now all those chummy conversations with Josh about Greek campus life sickened me. Even the most innocent of conversations can turn around and spew mace at your heart.

Gary arrived home from the Sunday night service at Mount Oak Community. He kept himself moving, handling it all so much differently than his wife. Not yet preaching, he attended all the services, even the repeats, sitting in the back with those deep purple circles under his eyes. He talked to Duncan and his deacons, and he yelled at God at 2 A.M. Or at least that's what the nosy neighbor next door said when I arrived after cleaning up my Sunday brunch earlier that afternoon. I just rolled my eyes and let myself inside. After I cleaned the bathroom, I ran a nice hot foaming bath for Chris, lit a couple of Gardenia scented candles, and told my friend to go soak for a while.

"So is it true, Gare?" I asked him when he walked into the kitchen, laying a hand on his very wrinkled, long-sleeved polo shirt. "You really yelling at God in the middle of the night and all?" I'd definitely take home some ironing.

"Minnie-Belle telling tales again?" You could tell he tried his best not to let his feelings out, but his hoarse voice was stiffer than a trampoline spring.

"Thought I'd better make sure it's true." I handed him a cup of decaf and began to slice up a vine-ripened tomato: $3.99 a pound at the IGA. For a tomato!

He cleared his throat and sat down at the kitchen table. "Thanks. Nah,

Popp. It's not true. I feel like it, though." He set down the cup after taking a sip.

I salted the slices. "I guess so."

"I been watching a lot of TV real late. Didn't think I had it loud enough for the neighbors to hear. And Minnie-Belle would have complained if it were."

"Yeah." I sat down with the plate of tomatoes and slid them over to Gary. With the way Angus eats, subversive nutrition is my specialty. "I want to ask all sorts of questions, Gare. And I want to say all sorts of things, but everything that comes to mind sounds wrong. Maybe I should just blurt it out without thinking first."

"I know. I'm a preacher, remember? I've sat in your chair more than my own." He put a slice of tomato in his mouth.

"Yeah."

Gary placed a hand on my forearm as he swallowed. "You're just here. That's enough. Chris has been a lot better without the housework wearing down on her. I did all I could, but I'm only one person."

"I don't know what else to do."

"It's a lot." He quickly ate another slice.

"I wish I were altruistic about it. The fact is, it makes me feel better."

"Good."

"How was church tonight?"

"Fine. But I find myself tearing up during the musical numbers now. Remember"—he released a strangled little chuckle—"how Josh always loved to play the guitar up there?"

"Yeah." I did. "He'd really get into it."

"I miss him."

"I know. Me, too."

"And every day something new pops up, a memory that I hadn't thought of before. And each new memory brings on the flood all over again."

I took his hand and squeezed. "I dreamed about him the other night, and it was so real."

Gary eagerly jumped on that, picking up another slice of tomato. "That's happened to me a lot. Two nights ago I dreamed we were sitting on the couch in front of the TV eating cereal and laughing at Bugs Bunny, both in our flannel boxers. And suddenly I looked over at him, and I said, 'But you're dead, Josh,' and he started to fade away. I cried out, 'No,' and he reached out and just said, 'Dad.' That was all, just 'Dad.'" His voice, abraded by pain, lowered. "I awoke feeling like I had been given a gift. Like I'd had him back again for just a little while."

I reached back to the counter, grabbed the coffeepot and topped off my drink. Gary downed the final slice, took three large gulps of his coffee, and held out the cup for some more. "How's Robbie doing with it all?" he asked.

"He's taken on six extra hours this quarter and another job, working the security desk at the Best Western until midnight on weekends."

"I'd heard it got broken into."

"Yeah. He's doing his best to keep busy." To be honest, I could have litanized about how Robbie's job made the very cells of my body run scared, but it seemed a petty worry when compared to their plight. That verse in the Bible about casting all your cares on Him is one that's always been easier said than done for me. But Josh's death somehow made giving Robbie's job over to Jesus a little easier than usual. And anyway, how much help would I be if some armed robber broke into the Best Western?

"I saw a post from him on a grief Web site last night," Gary said.

"Really?"

He nodded. "You might want to talk to him more about it, Popp."

I promised I would.

Chris called down from the bedroom. "Gary, is that you?"

"Yeah, honey! Just drinking coffee with Popp!"

The bedroom door slammed.

A spent sigh escaped him. "She thinks I'm terrible now. Everything I do is wrong. Like I'm supposed to stop functioning or something."

"She wouldn't even drink a latte."

"That doesn't surprise me. Well"—he gulped down the hot coffee, wincing at the heat—"I'd better go upstairs."

He stood to his feet and tried to straighten out his shirt. "Remember that first day you brought her to our house? How old were you guys?"

"Tenth grade."

"Man, wasn't she something? Tanned skin and that long, blond hair. And she'd never even kissed a guy until me."

"Chris is like that."

"Yeah, she still is, Popp. You'll never find anybody more loyal than Chris. It's probably why she's acting like she is."

I leaned over and hugged Gary. "I love you, buddy."

"I love you, too, Popp. I don't know what I'd do right now without you guys."

I kissed his cheek. "She'll come around."

"She has to." He walked toward the door and turned back around. "Doesn't she?"

I sat in the kitchen for several more minutes and finished my coffee. Wiping down the counter one last time, I turned off the coffeemaker, then called up Duncan. "Can you come get me? I don't feel like walking home, and I've got some laundry."

"I'll be right there," he said without hesitation.

The entire way home he did nothing but try to convince me to change my mind about the plate glass window.

He can really be a jerk sometimes.

The scene outside the front window on Monday evening should have delighted me, would have delighted me on a different day. Today it made my stomach feel as though I'd eaten too many raw oysters. The sky steadily littered the grass with an ambitious load of flakes on the diagonal. And here I thought spring had come for good. Drat. I'd have to drive in it out to Miss Mildred's for prayer, recounting the entire way the only accident I'd ever had, the accident in a January snowstorm. Well, maybe I'd give her a call first; maybe Miss Mildred would give me an out.

"I don't even think so, Penelope *Heubner!*" Mildred's voice assaulted my phone ear. "I've got a pork roast waiting, and the skin is brown and crispy. And you know how you like my biscuits. They rose an extra half inch tonight just for you. And if you don't get here soon, they'll get cold."

"But the weather!" Wow, that was a first-class whine even if I did say so myself. Sheesh.

"It's the perfect night for a cup of my grandmother's hot cider. We can warm our hands on the mugs while we pray. I've been looking forward to this all day."

"Miss Mildred, you're not being kind here. I really want to get out of this."

"I know, baby. And I'm just not going to let you. You need this as much as Chris does. Besides, I thought you knew me better than that."

"I do. I was just hoping to catch you during an off moment."

"Mildred LaRue doesn't have off moments."

I could say "Amen to that," but didn't.

And so, knuckles glowing ghostly white atop the steering wheel, I found myself sliding downtown, up Church Street and out onto Route 45 to Miss Mildred's family farmstead. Mildred, the only daughter of Cyrus and Urvana has lived there all of her life. Her great-great-grandfather's manumission papers hang in a dime-store frame on the dining room wall. She does just enough maintenance to keep the house from disrepair. See, Mildred LaRue has more sense than to spend family money and singing money on "fool knickknacks" as she calls anything that doesn't hang in her closet.

But I know it's about more than preference. How much does a jazz singer really make once she subtracts travel expenses, salaries, and costumes from the pay? Just another example of a preacher's widow being sent out to pasture and left to grow her own grass.

And Miss Mildred has it good, from the horror stories I hear around the presbyteries. Esteemed wife one day, widow the next with nothing to show for years and years of service, not to mention utter aggravation. If pure Christianity and undefiled is visiting the widows and fatherless in their afflictions, someone is really missing the boat! I hear lots of horrible tales in the ministry of terminally ill pastors being let go because the medical expenses would be too much for the church. God doesn't bless that kind of thinking, I do know this.

Will I end up like Miss Mildred and so many others? Then I remember the stash and think perhaps Duncan has the right idea after all!

I slid up to the latticed porch and breathed deeply to calm my stuttering heart. No use thinking about the drive home! I'd walk if I had to, so letting the dread of the obvious spoil the evening with Miss Mildred would be just plain stupid.

A large, jagged-lipped hole gaped open in the middle of the front lawn, halfway between the front porch and the pasture fence. A shovel lay on the ground nearby. I walked over and peered down. Four feet wide approximately, five feet deep so far, and what in the world could it mean?

Mildred threw the side door open. "Around here, Penelope!"

The aroma of roasted pork spirited away the snappy chill as I stepped up onto the boards. "Man! That smells so good."

"And you didn't want to go out into the snow! Hurry up, you're letting out the heat!"

Mildred, wearing black, crushed-velvet pants and a green sweater with sparkly, sequined blue and green argyles, ushered me into the warm kitchen, her large hands leaving heated spots on my back. I always suspected that Miss Mildred's mother had it remodeled back in the early sixties. The metal cabinets had been painted sea foam—precursor to avocado green. And why did decades of kitchen décor always denote themselves by a particular shade of green? Hunter green in the eighties. Celery/sage in the nineties.

The stainless steel cooktop supported a steaming pot or two, and underneath a gingerbread hooded window, the single-welled sink, also stainless, overflowed with crockery. The linoleum tiled floor flowed underfoot in stripes of sea foam, white, and that dry, chalky yellow.

"What's that hole outside for?"

Mildred let out a disgusted grunt. "Herman's digging."

"For what?"

"He heard a radio broadcast from one of those crazy people that believe in UFOs and pyramids and the Lord knows what else. And some man wrote a book about tunnels that are filled with gold. From the Civil War."

With a loud laugh, I pared off my coat. "And he thinks you may have one in your yard?"

"Yes, he does! Didn't even ask my permission to start digging."

Mildred took my coat, and I followed her to the small closet in the hallway outside the kitchen.

"Well, at least the snowstorm stopped him for a while."

"Big, old, ugly pit out there for me to look at when I pull up now," Mildred complained as I followed like a three-year-old back to the kitchen. "Go ahead and sit down, Penelope. You're worse than my own shadow."

"Why does he think you've got tunnels here?"

"My ancestor was very successful. He'd been freed quite some time before the war, and Herman says that if he had been my great-great-grand-father, he would have hid his money in the ground during the war, so it stands to reason that Grandpop did just that, and it's there just waiting to be found by Herman Winfred."

"I'm sure his wealth was tied up in his land, though, wasn't it?" I sat down on a rickety wooden chair and watched her fill the serving dishes.

"I'd suspect so. But there's no telling Herman about that sort of thing. That man goes all over the place in his thinking. And he does it with such business, too."

"Well, at least it keeps him out of your hair."

"There is that."

A crispy roast of pork, browned potatoes, and onions communed together on a large oval platter with a chipped lip. Two mismatched place settings waited to be loaded up.

"And here's some greens." Mildred spooned them into a white porce-lain bowl. "Let's eat."

Mildred closed her eyes, and her brown hand cradled mine. "Bless this food, Lord. Bless us all. Amen."

"No sauerkraut, Miss Mildred?"

"Oh, for heaven's sake!" Mildred threw up her hands. "You Germans. Just hold on a second and I'll heat up a can. But you'd better start eating the other stuff beforehand. Don't want it to get cold."

I wouldn't have uttered the fact that bagged sauerkraut tasted so much better than canned if my life had depended on it. "So you're going to let Herman continue his holes?"

"Like you said, it keeps him out of my hair when we're not out on the road, so I guess there's something to say for it."

Herman plays a fine guitar.

The meal made worthwhile every heart-stuttering slip on the way over. I shouldn't have eaten the skin but Miss Mildred did and was no worse for the wear at seventy-two, so I figured why not. I'd never experienced the wonder of greens up in Baltimore County, but with a little vinegar sprinkled on the cooked-down leaves, it spoke to that German in me at which Miss Mildred always poked fun.

Penelope *Heubner,* indeed.

True to Miss Mildred's word, we ended up the meal with mugs of cider and sat in the turret area of the parlor. Two chairs outlined with rows of upholstery pins and partially covered with quilts looked more than prepared to welcome our derrieres, no matter what size the derriere happened to be.

"You seen Chris today?" Mildred asked.

"Yeah. For a little while." Man, that cider was good.

"Still doin' stuff over there?"

"As much as I can." I wondered what kind of spices she used.

"What about at your house?"

"Duncan's still pitching in." It sure beat the boxed mix I'd always used.

"He's a good man, Penelope. I don't know why you can't appreciate that to its fullest."

"It's not about him, Miss Mildred."

She waved that away. "Of course it is. Back in the day, we didn't think like that. But"—she sighed—"that wasn't the way we were raised to think. We were raised to count our blessings and focus on them. And, since you're obviously not going to fill me in on why your heart is so sore, I guess we'd better do what we came to do."

We prayed.

I love to pray with Mildred LaRue.

God's Spirit descended into the room, settling peacefully to listen to our prayers said in the name of God's Son.

Angus sure had the right idea.

I prayed aloud, too, feeling myself transcended, feeling the words slip forth from my throat like milk and honey. Flowing out. Flowing up. Rich. Back and forth we pleaded for God's mercy, God's peace. Two things He is especially equipped to give.

God doesn't qualify as some divine magician, making trials disappear in a puff of smoke and a holy abracadabra. He is a friend to help us through. If people realized that, maybe they wouldn't be so bitter at the way the world is turning out. Maybe they'd hold on tight to the good things lest the disillusionment and the disappointment snatch those away, too. Like I could talk.

"Oh, Lord Jesus," I prayed. "Shine a light on Chrissy tonight. Give her a space of peace in which to curl up. Let her sleep peacefully and fully and maybe tomorrow, when she wakes up, she'll be ready to take a step forward. We don't ask for her to start running, Lord, just a baby step, a step that says 'I need to keep going'."

"And I agree with my sister," Mildred spoke up. "Lord, that family needs to know You're there. Father God, send them Your Spirit to heal and comfort. You said You would send us a Comforter, Father. And now we claim Your loving promise, Jesus, that You will never leave us nor forsake us. You haven't forsaken our dear sister, Christine. But maybe she feels that way, Lord. Maybe she feels lost and alone and forsaken. Touch her tonight, dear Lord Jesus. Touch her in a way only You can."

We uttered the final amen together.

Miss Mildred's eyes glowed from deep inside, and as she reached forward and set down her mug beside my own she looked younger for the time she'd spend in the Spirit's presence. "The Spirit told me to sing to you Poppy, and here's the song."

Her deep voice began the words of an old hymn I had sung countless times. "'Grace, grace, God's grace. Grace that will pardon and cleanse within. Grace, grace, God's grace. Grace that is greater than all our sins.'"

The tune glazed my eyes with tears.

"You got that, Penelope? You're struggling, and God has already granted you grace. It's big enough for whatever it is that's fighting inside of you."

"I know that."

"You don't act like it. Take hold of it. Grab it and hold it as tightly as you can."

"It's not that easy, Miss Mildred."

Her eyebrows raised. "It's not? Hmm. I guess that whole 'cast your cares on Him' thing is a myth then?"

"I can't let go, Miss Mildred. Sometimes I can, but then it always ends up back in my lap."

"Let me just ask you one question, Penelope. Is it guilt you're dealing with?"

"Yes."

"Then it's about knowing who to put your trust in, baby."

"I trust God, Miss Mildred."

"You can say that, but I know this about guilt…. When you hang onto it, stroke it and use it for penance, what you're really doing is taking the crucifixion much too lightly."

I didn't get what she meant exactly.

"He died once for all sins, baby. All sins. Would you dare to stand before His face and say, 'Your pain and suffering was *almost* enough for me, but not quite'?"

The thought horrified me. "Of course not."

"But that's exactly what you're doing."

"I'm scared if I let go, I'll fall right back and do it all over again."

"That's the crux of it all, isn't it?"

"Yes, Miss Mildred, it is."

I felt annoyed. I didn't come here for a soul examination.

"So, when I say it's all about knowing who to put your trust in, you know exactly what I'm saying?" Her eyes held mine in a prison of understanding. It hurt. Violently.

"Yes."

"Good." Mildred transitioned as beautifully as she did up on stage between numbers. "But what you *also* know is that one, skinny old woman like me is not going to do all that pork roast justice. I'll give you some food to take home."

I prayed all the way home, forgetting about the ice on the road, letting my guardian angel lead me on. *Have I looked on Your cross frivolously? I asked Jesus. Have I sacrificed the beauty of Your horrible death, Your obedient sacrifice, by my own fear?*

Oh, dear Lord, forgive me.

You died for my sins. I've heard that all of my life. Now I need to let You keep me from them, take away the veil that keeps me from seeing Your precious blood covering them, erasing them. I need to see You for the Savior You truly are and shall always be.

Gary broke down in my arms the next day. And we cried together over that little boy with the G.I. Joes and the boomerang. And my tears spilled not for Josh anymore, Josh in the bosom of Jesus, but for his parents. Gary cried for himself, and I cried for him. And Chris stood at the kitchen door weeping, but not joining in our circle of sorrow.

I've thought about death a lot during the years I've walked the earth in disquiet. I've thought about what it will be like to transcend space and time. And I've come to the conclusion that the apostle Paul was right when he says it's far better to be with Christ.

If only we didn't have to die to get there.

Thirteen

ngus's eyes swelled to the size of peppermints. The television projected tiny scenes of *The Wizard of Oz*—before the tornado—onto his eyes. Stealing looks at him while checking my e-mail at Duncan's computer, I hurried through them all and then found one from my mother. Dreaded those. Especially the instructional ones. "You need to start taking St. John's Wort," began the latest lesson. "It keeps you emotionally balanced, Poppy."

It made me wonder if Duncan had been talking to her behind my back.

"Hey!" Angus hollered. "Well, lookey there!" His small finger, jammed up against the glass of the screen, bent backwards at the first knuckle. "Look, Mama! Look! Come here; you gotta see this. Hurry!"

I jumped up from the desk. "All right."

"Look!" He stood to his feet now, dancing as though his bladder had filled to capacity, pointing to the three farm hands in succession. "*Those* guys...those *guys*...they're the guys from Oz! He"—his finger pressed Ray Bolger's nose—"is the scarecrow. That guy is the cowardly lion, and *he's* the tin man! Right?"

Sure enough, he'd touched Burt Larr and then Jack Haley.

I sat down next to him, cross-legged, and pulled him into a hug. "I remember when I realized that, Gus." I purposely failed to divulge the fact that I'd already seen my tenth birthday by the time I'd experienced that particular rite of passage. "It's cool, isn't it?"

"Yeah. Like her friends were guiding her all along."

"Good friends do that. Even if they have to make fools out of themselves."

He turned around, sat in my Indian-style legs, and leaned back against my abdomen. "Wanna watch the rest with me?"

I could do a million other things with my time. I'd seen *The Wizard of Oz* at least eight times since we bought him the video for his fifth birthday, the birthday he asked for what he called "a scientific skeleton."

"Let me go get my coffee, bud."

So I watched and sipped, while Angus sat in the "mommy chair" and told me everything that was coming next. The time on the VCR flashed twelve o'clock over and over.

All the phrases that eventually became sayings slid past my ears. "Pay no attention to that man behind the curtain!" "The size of a man's heart isn't determined by how much he loves, but by how much he is loved by others." "There's no place like home."

Yeah, yeah, yeah.

"I wonder what happened to Dorothy's parents that she had to go live with Auntie Em?" Angus asked, his voice quiet.

I shook my head. "Maybe it was a previous tornado. I'll get Daddy to buy you the book. Maybe that'll say."

"And why couldn't they hear her pounding the cellar door with her hard shoe. It wasn't as loud in the storm cellar as it was outside, was it, Mama? They could have heard that banging down there. And they *knew* she was outside. Wouldn't they have been listening for her?"

"Look, here comes that horrible Miss Gulch!"

"I can't stand her!"

"Me neither."

But the crabby old woman on the bicycle stole his attention even as she stole Dorothy's dog, and I kept thinking about hard shoes and cellar doors. Duncan was much like Aunt Em and the gang, I supposed. He'd kept on working late, and then he started acting so stressed out all of the time, complaining about his employees, complaining about everything. Our conversations were nothing more than gripe sessions, and, well, that's when the bag boys began to take on a whole new aura.

But Duncan would have never cheated on me had the situation been reversed.

My watch said eight o'clock. And Duncan? Still not home. See?

Lucky for me the only bag boys they hired here at the IGA were retirees, thank God, and I literally meant that.

"I feel like a milkshake. How about you, Gus?"

"Sure." He sighed. "Do I have to go with you to the store?"

"Nope. Robbie's upstairs studying."

"Okay."

I climbed up the attic stairs. "Rob?"

"Yeah, Mom."

"Can I come in?"

"Sure."

I entered the room. As neat as Josh had been, Robbie was exactly the opposite. Now I have always kept a clean house, and Chris and I often joked that if the boys hadn't been two years apart, we would have sworn someone switched them at birth. It wasn't that the room held a wide variety of items, for Robbie kept his interests limited. Clothes shrouded most surfaces, and copies of *Sports Illustrated* had been slapped down all around the bed. Many times I had managed some variation of skating on Robbie's floor, all of those slick pages sliding beneath my socks. I stayed near the door just to play it safe. "I'm going out to get some ice cream to make milkshakes. Gus is watching *Wizard of Oz.*"

"Okay."

"You want anything?"

"Nah. I grabbed a sub on the way back from Jeanelle's."

"Six inch?"

"No. Twelve."

"Oh...okay, well..."

I wanted to talk about Josh, but I couldn't think of how to start. How would Elyse Keaton have started if she'd gone up to talk to Alex P. Keaton? It isn't that TV moms always say just the right thing. But they sure know how to start up a conversation with succinctness and understanding. And the looks they paste on their faces hold the perfect combination of tenderness and concern. They never look scared to death or queasy, and they never open the conversation by screaming something like, "You're not going to do something stupid like that, too, are you?"

Maybe I needed a writer to slip me scripts for all occasions.

"Rob?"

"Yeah, Mom."

"Are you okay?"

He nodded.

"Really?" I asked.

"Yeah, you know. Just..."

"Do you want to talk to me about Josh?"

He shook his head. "Mom, what is there to say?"

"Well, are you wondering why it happened? Anything like that?"

Robbie, sitting on the bed with his legs out in front of him, crossed at the ankles, started to bob his feet back and forth, jitters of movement. "What's the point in wondering why it happened, Mom? People die. People die young. It happens every day. So wondering why that happens is like wondering why there's a food chain, why black widows eat their mates, why giraffe babies have to learn to run right away."

"I don't think I'm following you on this one, buddy."

His face petrified. "It's like we can accept all the cruelties in the animal world and say 'that's the way God made it,' and then it's like, whoa, if it happens to us. Why do volcanoes erupt and kill with hot lava? And what about that tsunami thing that wipes out entire villages? So, no, I'm not asking why because I'm not that stupid. It happens! Stuff like this happens all the time!" He paled and shuffled through his papers. "Okay? Okay! Is that what you wanted to hear?"

I maneuvered over the magazines and sat next to him. I tried to take him into my arms but he resisted, pushing gently against me. "No, Mom. Man, I'm not a little kid anymore."

Sucking in my breath, the most profound sense of awkwardness I'd ever experienced ricocheted inside of me. Awkwardness and loneliness and a deep, groaning sorrow flooded my sinking heart. Tears filled my eyes, and I jumped off the bed, slid across the floor, and ran down the stairs.

"Mom!" Robbie called after me, but I ran into the kitchen, grabbed my keys off the counter, and yanked open the pantry to lift my windbreaker off the hook.

"Mom!"

I wanted to run right outside, but I stopped, remembering I was the parent. Right? "Yeah, Rob?"

Turning, I saw him standing there in a pair of large boxer shorts and a gray T-shirt with the mange. "I didn't mean I don't love you any more, Mom. I just meant I can fight my own battles now. I really can."

I nodded. "I know, buddy. I'm just a little emotional about stuff right now. I'm sorry, too."

He leaned back on the counter. "Sometimes a guy is forced to see all the sides of God. And sometimes it takes some doing to accept them. You know?"

Boy did I. "Yeah, I do."

"And then you feel so wrong and shallow and shortsighted even for having the nerve to actually judge God."

"Is that what's happening now?"

He nodded and looked down at the floor. "I've been asking Him a lot of questions lately."

"Have you talked to Dad about them?"

"Yeah. But there comes a time in a man's life when he's got to find out the answers on his own."

A man's life.

Robbie saw himself as a man now. That was good.

"I miss Josh, Mom."

The words were so soft I barely heard them, but I watched with a breaking heart as his face crumbled and his tears poured forth. I rushed over and held him in my arms. My Robbie. My son, weeping. When he gained his composure a few minutes later, he said, "There's so many moments I wish I could go back to and live all over again." And he cleared his throat, wiped the reddened wet of his face with a flat, horizontal hand.

"You go on to the store before it gets too late."

"It'll get easier, Rob."

"I hope so, Mom." He disengaged from my embrace and walked out of the kitchen leaving a void I knew I couldn't fill. Only one person could, and there was more than enough of Him to go around. And that was my prayer as I walked out in the misty darkness.

With the amount of snow that had fallen a few nights ago when I'd gone to Miss Mildred's, there still should have been more left than there was, but the thermometer had climbed back up to a regular spring day. I did what I intended to do in the first place, climbed into the van and turned the ignition key.

The radio blared a praise song. And I sang along, knowing that verse in the Bible about God inhabiting the praise of His people was true. I gave Rob over to Him for the millionth time since he'd been born. Peace visited me, ushering me along the dark road, and as I mindlessly drove the familiar ribbon of asphalt, a light rain began to fall, dissolving the cottony puddles of snow spring was overtaking.

I ran into the store, veered past the produce, past the dairy section, and right into frozen foods. The price of ice cream alone was enough to bring me to the proverbial screeching halt. Good grief, Breyer's was expensive these days! Five bucks for a half gallon of vanilla bean? Principle alone propelled me to choose some cheap, plastic bucket variety instead. Just vanilla would have to do. I'd get some Oreos as well and make blizzardy things. The boys would like that.

And there she stood, sunny, young Sunny, a vision of pert, glossy-haired, young womanhood up there scanning items at the checkout, wearing a fisherman's sweater and a knee-length, black polyester skirt. With hose and church shoes. "Hi!" she called out to me when I got in the short line. "Late night run?"

I held up the ice cream and cookies in reply and waited until a blushing guy with batteries, a pack of Coor's, and a box of Tampax was rung through, as well as a suited, middle-aged man with a Healthy Choice chicken dinner and a bottle of Snapple.

"How you doing?" I asked Sunny after the man left with his lonely, heart smart supper.

"Oh, all right, I guess. A little tired."

"Long day?"

"Yes, ma'am. Been here since noon."

I looked at my watch. Eight-thirty. "You on until closing?"

"Yes, ma'am…. Um, ma'am?" Sunny hesitated. "Y'all are friends with the Knights, aren't you? Over at Mount Oak Community?"

"Yeah. Chris is my friend."

"I heard about their son."

"The whole town has, I guess."

"Yes, ma'am. It's not like I'm prone to talebear or be a gossip or such, but I wanted you to tell them that I've been praying regularly for them."

"Where do you go to church?" I asked as Sunny put the items into a blue, crackly store bag. I knew, of course, from the general gossip, but I didn't want Sunny to think I was prone to talebear or such.

"My husband, Mark, is the interim pastor over at Oak Grove Baptist Bible Church."

I smiled. "Out on Route 29?"

"Yes, ma'am."

Naturally, I also heard about the troubles they had six months ago. If one could compare church tribulations to the offerings down at The Sweet Stop on the square downtown, the troubles at Baptist Bible would be akin to a Banana Split Royale. For five. Served in a trough. "You like it here so far in Mount Oak?"

"Yes, ma'am. We're sort of new to town. A coupla' months. That'll be $4.68, by the way."

I looked behind me. No line. Good. This girl intrigued me for some reason. I pulled my wallet out of my purse and dug out a five. Ha-hahh, Breyers people. Ice cream *and* Oreos for less than a half gallon of your over-priced stuff. "Where're you from originally, Sunny?"

"Bainbridge, Georgia."

"Where's Bainbridge?"

Sunny took the bill and began to make change. "Southwest corner. Not too far from Dothan, Alabama, and about an hour from Tallahassee, Florida."

"Convenient to everywhere, eh?"

"Yes, ma'am."

I meant that as a joke. "Well, welcome to Mount Oak, Sunny. I'm Poppy Fraser."

"That's a nice name."

"I'm a pastor's wife, too. My husband, Duncan, is the pastor up at the Highland Kirk."

She handed me the change. "What kinda church is that?"

"Presbyterian."

"Oh." She looked down. "Don't know much about Presbyterians."

"Well"—I gathered the two handles of the bag—"we don't bite."

"No, ma'am, I don't guess y'all do."

"Heyyy, sunny Sunny!" A loud voice, sweet and smooth like pecan syrup and more flowery than magnolia perfume, sang from behind my back.

I jumped.

Sunny gave a little wave. "Hey, Mrs. Hopewell!"

I turned my head to see a face smack up to mine. Charmaine Hopewell, wife of the Reverend Harlan Hopewell, singing star of the *Port of Peace Hour,* stood right behind me at the IGA without a stitch of makeup on her face. And the woman's cart burgeoned with nothing but prepackaged junk! That went a long way for me. Nice to know a TV personality like Charmaine Hopewell had her downfalls like the rest of us regular gals. And when she smiled, an orthodontic retainer glimmered.

"How are you doing, Sunny?" She turned to me. "Isn't she just a peach? Makes coming to the grocery store a little more...sunny!" Her laughter should have annoyed a woman like me, but it didn't. It made me smile. "So what are y'all talking about?" Charmaine asked.

"I was just telling Mrs. Fraser here—"

"Call me Poppy, please."

"Oh, I know!" Charmaine Hopewell laid a comfortable hand on my arm. "All those 'missuses' and 'yes, ma'ams' make you feel like a patriarch's wife, don't they?"

I laughed. Back in Maryland, the charity organizations I served with would bring in celebrities from time to time for their galas. Usually politely distant, they did nothing whatsoever that made me want to say, *Let's hang out.* But Charmaine, loved by hundreds of thousands all over the South, seemed like the type you could invite over for a chicken dinner and ask to get the bottled salad dressing out of your scary refrigerator while you plated up the food on your everyday dishes. "I sure don't need any extra help in feeling old," I said.

Sunny turned red. "Yes, ma'am, but I was just saying how sorry I was about Josh Knight, because I remember how Mrs. Fraser and his mother used to come in here together when I first started working here, so I figured they were friends and all."

Charmaine Hopewell's face dropped with a genuine sadness. "We've been praying over at our church, too. How's the boy's parents doing?"

"Gary's holding up, but Chris…" I set down my bag. "I mean, how do you get over something like that?"

Charmaine leaned against the counter. "I don't think you can. I mean, you go on, especially if you've got other children—"

"He was the only one," I said.

"Then I just don't know. You've got to keep praying, though. I know that much."

I looked at the two pretty faces before me, both so different. The fact that they really did care about perfect strangers amazed me in a way. "Do you all know Mildred LaRue?" I asked.

"Oh yes! Love her! You know, she's sung with me on the *Port of Peace Hour* several times."

Sunny shook her head. "I don't think I know who y'all mean."

Charmaine took over. "Real skinny black lady, always wearing green."

"Drives that big green Impala?"

"Yep, that's her."

I said, "Well, she and I get together Monday nights to pray for Chris. She lives out on Route 45, across from Tweed Road."

Charmaine nodded her head of huge auburn hair. "Been there a couple of times myself."

"Well, you're both welcome to join us. Around six o'clock. She makes dinner, too."

Charmaine pushed off the counter. "Monday night's a good night for me. And it'll keep me from suggesting we eat out for supper...*again!* Harlan hates it when I spend money even if it is the money I make myself with my CD's. After the televangelist scandals of the eighties..." She rolled her eyes. "Anyway, I'll be there. How about you, Sunny? You want to go, too? I'll give you a ride."

She shook her head. "No, ma'am, I don't believe I can." She didn't bother to give an explanation as to why, so I didn't ask.

I doubted whether a glitzy TV personality like Charmaine Hopewell would really show up anyway.

Fourteen

ngus still danced around when he had to go to the potty badly, which provided some consolation to me. I'd take my warm moments when and where I could get them these days. It wasn't that life didn't have its joys anymore. But a cloud definitely shadowed my relationship with my sons. Josh's cloud, a gray rain falling from its gloom, seemed to taint the ease with which I had always loved my boys. It wasn't easy anymore, not when you really, *really* knew they could be snatched up at a moment's notice.

There's that verse in the Bible that says the death of a saint is precious in the eyes of the Lord. It's easy to picture Jesus welcoming Josh into heaven, and if it was true that he died before he hit the ground, well, I guess he was just swooped right up. One second he was falling in fear, the other he was flying with the Lord, right up to a place where he'd still be precious indeed. If we could see what is really happening during the death of a Jesus child, we'd view the whole thing differently. But we can't. I can imagine, though. And because it's true, it comforts me. I'll see Josh again. I'll see him again because Jesus died for him and opened up the pathway to heaven for all who believe in Him. Jesus' death covered it all.

There's an old song that says "Calvary covers it all." The word *all* is a beautiful word. It's definite. It can't mean anything less.

Angus tugged on my hand as we hurried to the car from the last of the day's errands. Mondays always ended up like this. You'd think after three years, I'd take Monday as my Sabbath. I have the best of intentions Sunday night. But Monday morning when the milk is low, and the bread is down to two heels kissing, my best plans are laid to waste because as long as I'm out getting milk, I might as well...breathe, Poppy, breathe.

"Please, Mom, I really gotta go."

"But we'll be home in five minutes, Gus."

"Please, Mom!"

"Oh, all *right!*" I snapped, pulling him roughly back into the IGA, his skinny arm stretched tautly as I yanked him along. I watched my own *Mommie Dearest* moment in horror. Those quick, black waves of anger that burst out every so often scared me.

Angus jerked his hand free and ran to the back of the store. Waiting for him outside the men's room, I felt more guilt crawling like worms all through me. I gave myself credit for one thing, though. I wasn't beyond an apology. Poor Angus. He didn't deserve this.

Calvary covered this, too.

He exited the bathroom thirty seconds later looking down at his shoes. I set down the bag of groceries and kneeled on the floor in front of him. Sitting back on my heels, I took him into my arms and pulled him down on my lap, his little legs draping over either side. So warm and sweet. "Sorry, buddy. It's been a long day."

"Okay," he said and struggled free. "Can I have one of those Tootsie Pops when I get home?"

"Yeah." I laughed and wondered just who the sucker was here.

We slid into the gravel driveway at four-thirty, both Angus and I determined to take a little nap. He'd fallen asleep on the short drive home, actually, and refused to stir. So I hauled him into his room, depositing him on the bed in his coat, and then brought in the bag of perishables.

Shoving the entire sack into the refrigerator, I decided to take a shower first, then lay down for a bit before getting ready for prayer at Miss Mildred's. I just needed a few minutes to refresh myself before entering a room full of beautiful women. Miss Mildred and Charmaine. Great, just great. Now, not only guilt would be present with me during my prayers, but jealousy as well.

It felt good when I laid myself down. Five-forty was the last call to give me enough time to dampen my bangs after being mashed in the towel, cover up the bags and circles under my eyes, and get dressed. I'd be surprised if I get more than three or four naps a year, so forty-five minutes of sleep seemed like a gift sent straight from God.

I counted my blessings as I drifted off. Duncan was a good man, and there was hope yet for Paisley if the conversion of St. Paul gave me any indication. I really needed to pray more for the child. Angus. Robbie. A pretty little house. Good coffee in the morning. Prismacolors. Small feet. Tootsie Pops. Toilet paper. The Weather Channel. Cordless phones.

Cordless ringing phones. Ringing phones.

My eyes opened. Ringing phone!

I sat up in the bed and reached for the shrill mechanism on the nightstand. Shoot, I'd just fallen asleep. It had better not be Duncan calling to say he couldn't watch Angus, or this Monday night would be really barren!

"Frasers."

"Penelope Anne Huebner, what on God's green earth are you doing right now?"

"Miss Mildred? What's the matter?"

"It's 6:01, girl, and you're still not here."

I panicked, pulled the towel off my hair and sprang out of bed. "I'm just leaving, Miss Mildred. Got a little behind, that's all."

"And you forgot to tell me we'd have one more."

"Charmaine Hopewell's there?" I ran over to the closet and pulled down a white shirt and a pair of khaki pants, quickly grabbing the jangling hangers, halting their clang so Miss Mildred wouldn't hear. If I could keep her talking while I dressed, the timing would be perfect. I'd hang up, get on the road, and arrive at the house on Route 45 with no one the wiser.

"Uh-huh. Looking like a dreamboat, no less. And here I am in flat shoes and palazzo pants."

"What's wrong with palazzo pants?" I shoved my feet into my own pants.

"Just a little on the casual side."

"Oh, Miss Mildred, it's just us girls."

"I know that, but I made a fancy meal."

Groaning, I swirled the blouse around and stabbed my arms into the armholes. "Will it be spoiled because of me?"

"If you don't get here soon, it will be. Now hurry up and get on your shoes now that you've got your other clothes on."

"How did—"

"And I hope you had a good nap." Her voice warmed. "See you in a few minutes, baby."

Mildred hung up. That woman. That wonderful, skinny old woman. Sometimes love for another human being bursts your heart with happiness. My father and I used to call them "bursts of love."

I kissed Duncan on the cheek as he sat at his computer, grabbed my coat, and hurried through the kitchen.

"Poppy!" he called. "Wait a sec!"

But I didn't stop to listen; I only heard him say something about some loud bangs or such. Probably more trouble with that blasted window in the sanctuary. Or maybe they'd decided what to do, and workmen had started already.

In any case, it would keep. Miss Mildred had made a fancy meal, and I didn't want to spoil it.

There are some times in a woman's life when she should actually stop and take the time to listen to her husband, because some of those times he's speaking in her best interest. And I realized, much too late, mind, that I should have heeded Duncan and not slammed out of the kitchen in a big, fat, stupid hurry.

I'd laughed and eaten and had such a good time with Miss Mildred and Charmaine. The star attraction of the *Port of Peace Hour* had stuffed her small self into even smaller jeans and a red sweater with a big cowl neck. She wore high heeled, red suede boots, the swashbuckler kind with rounded lips that shielded her knees. Her lips matched her sweater, and her sweater matched her hair, that riotous red, a color Charles Revson would have sold his gas-guzzling yacht to have created. No other makeup covered her face, however.

The food was astonishing. French cooking no less. Fancy French cooking. A *foie gras* and spinach terrine molded in the shape of a curving fish, started us off right. It was such fun sitting there, talking about men (Herman had dug four new holes in the yard) and hair and makeup and diets and books. Charmaine proved to be a wonderful conversationalist, a girly girl. And she listened, too, letting us have our say, which surprised me. Her perfectly plucked brows scrunched together as she concentrated on every word spoken, looking as though her brain cells were busy taking mental notes, especially when the conversation turned to disciplining children.

"My three are horrible!" she said after asking me if I had ever resorted to spanking. "Just terrible. They don't listen to a word I say."

"It's all in how you say it," Mildred said. "Not that I can really talk."

I spoke up. "I've always wanted to ask you why you never had children, Miss Mildred. You're so good with Angus and all."

Mildred got up from the table. And I readied myself for some story-telling, because Miss Mildred always told her big stories as she moved around: like how Jesse David died of diabetes, and why she had come to live with her grandmother at the age of seven, and even the time she developed vocal nodules. "I didn't want children at first. I had a good career singing, going with the Star Spangled Jammers at good clubs in St. Louis, and New Orleans. High class clubs. And then I met Jesse David." She began to clear off the dishes, casting a warning glance in my direction, and bobbing a greasy fork up and down when I rose to help.

I sat back down.

"Was he a preacher then?" Charmaine asked.

"Yes, he was. A good one, too."

Not like Duncan, I thought. Duncan categorized himself as a teacher, not a preacher.

"What is it about preachers?" Charmaine asked. "Why are women so attracted to them? Harlan has women throwing themselves at him, and, although I love him dearly, he ain't no Mel Gibson."

I shook my head. "I don't know. Duncan doesn't seem to have that kind of problem." Now there was food for thought.

"Not yet." Mildred kept up her plate gathering. "Just give him time in the ministry."

"He hasn't seasoned yet." Charmaine's eyes met Mildred's, and they laughed.

I remained clueless.

"You'll get it one day, baby," Mildred assured me. "Some of these church women, they look on the preacher as some kind of Jesus substitute here on earth."

Charmaine nodded. "That's right. All over the pastor, looking to him like he's got *all* the answers."

"Which he doesn't," Mildred said.

"Nope. Little do they know the man can't keep an eye on his own keys and loses his wallet at least once a month."

That, I could relate to.

"Duncan hasn't been in it long enough to develop that authoritative patina," Mildred said with a smirk.

"Did the women fawn all over your husband, Sister LaRue?" Charmaine asked.

"They sure did! And with good reason!"

Charmaine fiddled with her napkin. "I guess I find it hard to complain about Harlan's groupies. I was one of them a decade ago. How did you handle that?" she asked Mildred.

"I didn't have to handle anything! My Jesse David did all the handling that needed to be done. He was always kind and concerned about his women members, but honey, he let me know in no uncertain terms that he was all mine!"

We laughed together. Miss Mildred would expect no less of her man.

"Now," Mildred said, "if I can only get our current pastor's wife to stop acting so jealous all the time, I'll be doing something."

"Does she have anything to be jealous about?" I asked, knowing that even nice people got sucked into adultery, too.

Mildred shrugged. "Maybe Pastor Phelps is a little too familiar acting. I don't know. But she doesn't help matters any the way she slinks her arm through his and gazes up at him all googly-eyed and broadcasting for all to hear how *wonderful* their marriage is all the time."

"Yuck," I said.

Charmaine said, "It's like my grandma always said, 'If you've got to flaunt it, you really haven't got it.'"

Oooh, I liked that one. I'd write it down as soon as I got home. "So anyway, Miss Mildred. What was it you were saying about your career and all?" I definitely didn't want this conversation to change course for good.

"Well, I met my Jesse David just as things were really heating up for me and my singing. In fact, it was on the train to New York that we met. I took one look at that man, and my heart"—she placed a long, bony hand against her breast—"it just jumped up into my throat. That man looked good in pinstripes is all I can say!" She closed her eyes and inhaled through her nose to calm herself.

"So…," I prompted.

"So I sat right next to him and started up a conversation. We laughed the entire time north, and when we got to Penn Station I told him where I'd be singing, and he showed up that night wearing that same suit and a big smile. Mmm. That man, so tall and proud looking, made heads turn, I can tell you."

"You must have been a striking couple," Charmaine added. "Harlan and I look as mismatched as a pepper shaker with a powdered sugar duster."

Mildred wiped the counters in ambitious, hard circles. "I told him that night after the show, when we were eating cheesecake over in Times Square, that I couldn't have children. Told him all sorts of stuff like that, like how it had grieved me for years, like how it made me such a good blues singer."

I closed my eyes briefly. "Miss Mildred, I'm sorry for bringing that up. I didn't—"

Charmaine laid her hand on my arm. "Now, Poppy, you couldn't have known."

Mildred started to chuckle as she poured three mugs of coffee.

"What's so funny?" I asked.

"You are. The both of you. If you'd have let me finish, I would have told you that all of that was nothing but lies!" She sat down, sliding a mug to each woman. "As far as I knew then, I could have children like everybody else. But I was scared that night. Scared of the way that man had eaten his way into my soul in such a short time, like some sweet acid that only burned away the rotten parts."

She took a sip of her coffee. "Mmm, that's good. Chickory in there. My own blend."

"No Chock Full of Nuts for you, Miss Mildred," I said.

Mildred reached behind her to the counter and grabbed a plate of cookies. Store bought. "Sorry about these. Didn't have time to do a fancy dessert."

I grabbed two; Charmaine just sipped on her coffee and smiled apologetically. Well, I had started walking again, so how much could a little dessert hurt? "So you lied? Why?"

"It was that preacher thing! I wanted him to feel sorry for me for some reason. To give him a reason to reach out to me."

"And it backfired, didn't it?" Charmaine asked.

"It sure did. I never could tell him the truth."

"Oh, Miss Mildred, why?" I felt my stomach turn.

"Don't know. I tried to gather nerve, letting him soothe my supposed aching soul. He'd even pray loud and hard in prayer meetings about it. I felt so ashamed. Finally, menopause hit, and then it was just too late."

"That's terrible," Charmaine said. "Didn't you get pregnant, though? Just naturally? I know with me, Harlan only had to look at me with a glimmer in his eye and I was pregnant!"

"I never had any trouble along those lines either," I said. "I got pregnant on the first month with Paisley, the second month with Robbie, and Angus without even trying."

Mildred spooned some sugar into her coffee. "I know. It just never really happened. I guess what I had said in New York had turned out to be the truth." Mildred's face fell in a way I'd never seen before. I knew I needed to extend some comfort. But what does one say after a revelation like this? My hand found hers, and thankfully, Charmaine rolled her eyes and said, "Well, motherhood isn't all it's cracked up to be. Sometimes I wish I had stayed single. I'd probably have a Grammy by now and bigger 'you know whats' to go along with it!"

Laughter spilled from each of us. Yep, Charmaine would fit in just fine!

"Let's go do what we came to do," Mildred said, and we obeyed, picking up our mugs and walking into the parlor.

I passed an old mirror, big and dim and dotted with black flecks, but it was clear enough to see my reflection, the reflection of a middle-aged female with the worst case of towel bangs ever known to womankind.

Why didn't Duncan chase me down? Shaking my head, I grabbed an afghan from the couch on the way to the turret room.

"What are you doing that for?" Mildred asked when we sat down and I draped the blanket over my head and shoulders, dressed up like a Bible woman.

"Just cold, I guess."

This was great. Now I had to pray looking like the sheik of Arabi and feeling utterly embarrassed and jealous while two slim, gorgeous, highly talented women freely petitioned the throne of grace. Just great.

It amazes me how Satan works sometimes. How he'll take something little like bangs and enlist them into thievery. Well, they wouldn't steal my joy tonight. I let the afghan slip, muttered an apology about my hair, and felt a peculiar happiness and relief when Charmaine said, "God doesn't even see your hair, Poppy."

Well, amen to that.

Fifteen

A week later I repeated the scene, but with better hair. Charmaine came again, this time bringing the dessert. "Sunny filled me in on how much you love your sweets, Poppy, so I made my mama's hot milk cake for you. I even brought some strawberries to put on top."

Sunny filled her in. Oh, that was classic. Maybe I should curb my evening runs to the IGA for a while, lest the mayor, the newspaper editor, or the surgeon general find out.

"Where did you find the strawberries this time of year?" Mildred asked as she ushered the flamboyant church lady into the kitchen. "And where did you find that green scarf, child!"

"The Green Grocer over on Mortimer Street for the strawberries, came from South America or something. And y'all should have seen the tomatoes! And the scarf I got at that little place on the square. That gift shop owned by the woman who used to be married to the chief of staff over at Memorial, until he had that affair with that cute little waitress at Barnacle Bill's."

Affairs again. Sheesh. I pushed the thought from my head and decided to concentrate on the superficial, namely their clothing. A great topic for rumination, second only to hair.

I had dressed up for the occasion, wearing a pair of black, wool, crepe pants and a real cashmere sweater I'd paid a fortune for in the old days, a blush color, almost pink, almost not, imbued the fuzzy threads. The shoes looked good, too, crisp black loafers with a modern heel. Duncan actually bought them for me when we went to the mall one day for the monthly toiletries run during Big B's sale.

Charmaine rubbed my arm. "You sure look pretty tonight, Poppy. I love that sweater." She smiled into my eyes, so I knew she spoke the truth as she saw it.

Mildred took my light jacket as I sat down. "Let's face it, we all look pretty fine tonight."

"And no men to spoil it," Charmaine said.

I raised my glass of water. "I'll drink to that."

"You know, y'all, if our husbands talked about us like we do about them, well, I'd just be so hurt!"

"Me, too, Charmaine."

Mildred flickered her fingers. "Oh, don't worry about that. I can tell you they don't. They don't think about us much when we're not with them. You can trust me on this one."

I had always figured as much. Most women do figure as much. But it wasn't something I wanted to admit out loud like Miss Mildred did.

A breeze caught at the kitchen curtains forcing the sheers farther into the room. It delivered the scent of spring and a freshly cut lawn some-where nearby. Duncan would be resuming his groundskeeper role soon. But I wasn't going to complain about the weather. It had given me a boost. Chris, too. "I meant to tell you on the phone, Miss Mildred. Chris came out of the house with me two days ago for a walk."

"Praise God from whom all blessings flow!" Mildred raised a hand.

"Thank You, Jesus," Charmaine cried.

I wondered briefly what planet I suddenly inhabited. Presbyterians didn't act like this, for goodness' sake. We didn't even shout "Amen!" But it touched a place within me, a place I might never really learn to locate on my own, but one I respected when so easily exhibited in someone else.

"How did Chris cope with it?" Mildred asked.

"Well, we went at 4:30 A.M. because she didn't want to run into any-one and have to hear condolences."

"I don't blame her," Charmaine said. "The poor thing."

"That little boy of yours was right, Penelope. We should have been praying a long time ago."

I shrugged. "Well, I'm Calvinistic enough to believe we started just when we were supposed to."

I completely disobeyed *The Proper Christian Ladies' Handbook* and the chapter on appropriate uses of systematic theology. Only in Bible studies are such uncomfortable doctrines to be mentioned and usually only in the presence of those like-minded. If I had to bet money, Charmaine was a free-will type like Miss Mildred.

To my limited knowledge, *The Handbook for Christian Men* has no such regulation.

Charmaine suddenly sat up straight and stiff in her chair. See? Said the wrong thing again, Poppy!

"Did you hear that?" she asked, eyes so round I thought she might blacken her eyebrows with some of the nutty brown mascara brushed carefully on her lashes.

I braced myself for the coming onslaught.

"What?" Mildred asked. "You hear something other than Poppy's Calvinism?"

"Uh-huh. Sounded like it came from the porch."

I felt the hair follicles on the nape of my neck bunch together. "You think someone is out there?" I whispered. I never lasted through the night at slumber parties. When they started telling stories like the man with the golden arm, or thump-thump-scratch, I was out of there, running for the phone to call home.

Mildred stood to her feet. "Calm down, girls. I'll go see who it is."

A definite thump shook the floorboards now.

"I know I'm a scaredy-cat," Charmaine said. "But one time we had a burglar, and now I jump at the least little thing."

Mildred pulled open the kitchen door and hollered into the darkness, "Who's there?"

"We just came to pray!" a youthful, female voice cried.

"It's all right, ladies," she said from the porch. "It's just that sweet little blond girl from down at the IGA."

"Sunny?" I stood up.

"And who you got with you?" Mildred ushered the newcomers into the warm kitchen.

"This is India Clemmings," Sunny said.

I had never seen the new woman before. If one could have taken Sunny and turned her upside down and inside out, this woman would have resulted.

I was happy, however, that *someone* else in the kitchen sported a bigger waist than I possessed. It didn't seem to matter that the woman was at least fifteen years younger with glowing, ruddy skin and impossibly huge brown eyes. She tripped over the threshold as she walked into the room, but caught herself immediately. Laughing a nervous laugh, she held up a foot entombed in a biker boot with a sole thicker than a top-of-the-line porterhouse. "Someday I'm going to give up my boots, but for now, I guess I'll just keep tripping everywhere I go." The nervous laugh sounded again. Her warm, mellow voice belonged to an opera singer or something, not this girl whose garb proclaimed that she had alternative music and frappachinos pumping through her veins.

She shoved a pair of sunglasses into her pocket.

I liked her right away. "Come on in. Miss Mildred just made some coffee. And for the record, I think your boots are very cool. That jacket is great, too." Leather. Hip length. And hand painted with pictures of long dead composers.

Mildred pulled down mugs while I scraped in an extra chair from the dining room and made introductions. "Have a seat. I'm Poppy Fraser, and this is Mrs. Mildred LaRue."

Mildred offered a quick flicker of a wave.

"And I'm Charmaine Hopewell." Charmaine started slicing up the hot milk cake.

Sunny pulled out the remaining kitchen chair. "India's the music minister over at St. Edmund's Episcopal."

Episcopal? I thought, as I spooned strawberries onto the cake slices. When I thought "Episcopal," nothing registered but robes and well... robes. How sad was this?

"Seems we got more than our fair share of church ladies here tonight," Mildred said. "And musical ones, too."

"Not me." Sunny lowered her lithe body into her chair and set her white vinyl purse in her lap just so. I stole a look under the table. White shoes, too. Now where did that child's mother go when fashion etiquette needs began to surface? Good heavens, she was wearing black panty hose with them. Well, just because a person was saved from the fires of hell did not mean she was saved from her own poor taste.

Oh, brother, Poppy.

And what does it really matter anyway? Sometimes I hated my own snobbery. For someone who hated legalism, I sure had a lot of rules! But it seemed that Mother had never stopped sitting on my shoulder pointing out faux pas.

As Charmaine said before, God doesn't see that stuff. You know, I think He put that verse in the Bible about His not looking on the outward appearance to free us—and to prick at us when we find ourselves judging someone by something as insignificant as her clothing. Some church women judge clothes on the quality, others judge it by whether or not there's one place to put your legs or two.

Charmaine, not exactly tasteful in that purple, leopard print satin blouse tucked into purple leather pants, not to mention the green scarf with coordinating high-heeled boots, jumped right in. "I'm so excited to meet you, India. I was over at the Christmas handbell concert y'all did a few months ago. You wrote some of the music, didn't you? I remember seeing the name India beside some of the pieces, and I recalled thinking about India somebody-or-other in *Gone with the Wind* and all."

India ran her hand through extremely short brown hair. "A few of them. It was a good autumn for me, creatively speaking. I've seen you on TV."

Charmaine waved one of her beautifully manicured hands. "Oh, please. Don't mention that."

Sunny took a cup of coffee from Mildred. "I met India two months ago at the grocery store. She drives the cutest little car you ever saw."

"What is it?" I asked, knowing I would be mortified when I viewed it next to my heap of a van out there at the front of the house.

"It's a red Volkswagen with black dots!" Sunny said. "It looks just like a ladybug."

Wow, a girl who writes handbell pieces, wears biker boots, and drives a Volkswagen that looks like a ladybug. Now Paisley could take lessons from this girl on how to be unique without being sullen. How to be child-like not childish.

"I just like ladybugs," India said.

"That's nice." Mildred handed her a glass of water. "I like humming-birds myself."

"I hope you don't mind me bringing India along," Sunny said. "But I was walking up the road, and she was passing by—"

"You *walked* here?" Charmaine said, clearly horrified.

"Well, yes, ma'am. You see we don't have but one car and—"

"—*and* her husband doesn't know she's coming," India supplied, set-ting her left foot on her right knee. "He's out of town tonight and tomor-row."

"He's still in school over at Valley Baptist Seminary," Sunny explained. "That's when he goes."

Mildred crossed her arms and leaned against the counter. "Why are you sneakin' here, child?"

Sunny's glance at India filled up with something very, well, very cloudy. "Mark isn't much inclined to what he calls 'ecumenical nonsense.'"

"Oh," Mildred said. "So why are you disobeying him then?"

The girl looked up, straight into Miss Mildred's gaze. "I don't know."

"An honest woman. Good for you, child." Mildred took a plate of dessert from Charmaine who, I noticed, didn't cut a piece for her svelte, TV self.

Mildred waved her fork at the lot of us. "Eat up, girls. We need to be about the Lord's business now."

India didn't pray, and she watched the entire while, I realized, sneak-ing glances from time to time. But her face was sad, and I prayed silently for her, somehow able to feel the desolation so obviously present in this young woman with a ladybug for a car.

We stormed heaven that night with our prayers. We broke down walls of fear and doubt and claimed promises on behalf of Chrissy, and in the claiming for her we remembered that they were given to us as well.

"Oh, my loving Father," Charmaine had begun, and goosebumps spread themselves out on my limbs as she took us all before the throne of grace. She prayed with such passionate intimacy with God, such childlike devotion. He wasn't just her Father, He was her Daddy. She reminded us all through her prayers that Jesus sent the Holy Ghost to comfort us in situations like this and to guide us through them.

The Holy Ghost, the Holy Spirit, whatever name He is called by, was called upon frequently that night. And I felt Him there, really there in our midst, and there were times I dared not open my eyes in fear of sending Him away by my own sinfulness. *Thank You, God,* my heart frequently raised the words. *Thank You for letting us meet with You here.*

Sunny's soft voice began, her words belying her youth, and she called upon God, entering the throne room of prayer as someone very familiar with the chamber, very comfortable with her surroundings, yet still in awe, still aware that she talked to the King of kings and Lord of lords. "Dear Heavenly Father, we thank Thee for listening to our prayers and petitions," she began. "We thank Thee for giving us the words to say and the voices with which to speak them where we are gathered, more than two or three, Lord, in Thy midst."

Isn't it wonderful, that verse that says, "Draw nigh to God, and He will draw nigh to you?" God comes near. We don't have to go to some special prayer building in some special city in some special country. God comes near to us, right where we are.

We stayed long into the night, Sunny and I asking questions of Miss Mildred and Charmaine, the veteran pastor's wives. When Sunny asked, "How do you let all the criticism roll off your back?" Mildred replied, "It's like anything else, baby. You just get used to it, take it as part of the job."

"That's not encouraging, Miss Mildred," I said. "It could take years."

"Oh, it does take years! Believe me!" Charmaine's eyes softened. "But after a while you really do realize that if you don't let them roll off, they'll chip away at your heart until there's nothing left. It's all about whether you really want to love people or not, Poppy."

I remembered that verse in the Bible about loving those who don't love you. How it basically says, So what's the big deal if you love those who bless you? Even sinners do that! But loving those who curse you, criticize you, examine every little thing you do while wearing a pair of negative glasses, well, that is, as Charmaine might say, "A whole nother matter."

"Besides," said Mildred. "Harboring it all just makes you bitter. And that never helps anyone, least of all you."

Bitterness. That sure hit the mark.

"Do you feel you have to be friends with the women in your church?" I asked Charmaine.

"Friendship has many levels, Poppy. I may not have this kind of conversation with many of the church women, but I love them in Jesus."

Mildred said, "Mmn-hmn. Never underestimate the value of that."

Back in the late seventies I heard a song where the writer was begging Jesus to let him see the world through His eyes. On the way home I prayed that prayer much the same, but my version exchanged the words *church ladies* in place of the word *world*. And why in heaven's name did I think I was so much better than they were, anyway?

I pulled into Highland Kirk's parking lot, stared at the dark mass of building against a sky of backlit indigo. Does love have to *feel* like love to *be* love? Is obedience to God *ever* hypocritical? I would ask Duncan, but there are some things a girl has to find out for herself.

I almost asked Duncan, "How long has it been since we've done this?" but successfully bit it back before it popped out. I seemed to have a more highly developed ability in the speech control department when eating at Josef's French Country with Duncan than in driveways with Paisley. I wanted nothing to come out incriminating or house Frau-like. I wanted him to know I appreciated tonight because it hadn't been a spontaneous measure on his part. It had been in the works for at least a week.

I knew this because he'd snuck his navy blue pinstripe to the A-1 Dry Cleaners, and the lady there had given me his order, too, when I went in to pick up the linens I'd dropped off just after Christmas. Thank God, and I literally meant that, I had enough foresight to fill the woman in on the situation, girl talk style, and told her to button her lip and save the suit for Duncan.

Josef's is a compact, rustic little restaurant. Only about ten or twelve tables, *prix fixe* menu, and talk about desserts! Not only is their sugar content probably more than two back-to-back cans of Coca-Cola, but they're so lacy and artistic, one almost hates to eat them. Almost.

Duncan sipped on his water. "I don't know why we don't do stuff like this more often."

I successfully bit back the obvious retort. "I'm glad we're here, though."

It was a good moment for me, just then. Duncan looked so nice, his peppered, thinning hair combed perfectly and, now that it was warmer, his tanned neck contrasting with a beautiful blue, starched button-down. I adored button-downs, thought them sexy on the right guy.

I forcefully shoved Jody aside, but not before realizing a blue oxford button-down would have looked ludicrous on him. Wow, quite a revelation! I concentrated on my husband instead. "So tell me about your day, and by the way, the tie looks good."

"Yeah." He smiled and lifted the pointed end, examining the fine pattern on the ice green tie. "Fidge came through this year, didn't she?"

I lifted my glass. "Here's to my mother then."

His brows lifted. "You must be in a good mood."

"I am," I confessed. "I really am."

There must have been something to that St. John's Wort thing after all. Maybe I should listen to Mother more often. Or maybe I'm not giving credit where it is due. Life's loads had certainly become a little easier to bear since the Monday night prayer meetings had begun.

The sweet thing about Duncan is that he doesn't take me to a nice restaurant to relay some important news, to soft sell some big change he wants to foist upon me. He takes me out to be with me, and he concentrates on me completely.

Unfortunately it only happens once or twice a year. But if it happened more often, I'd feel more guilty about The Masquerade, so maybe it is for the best. Maintenance is what it is, truth be told. Why do married couples let themselves get so busy they only have time for maintenance? And, shoot, I am just as guilty as Duncan. Well, almost, anyway. I cannot award him the upper hand completely.

We ordered something horribly expensive for two and talked about our lives.

As we pulled into the driveway, Duncan turned to me and said, "Close your eyes, Popp. I've got a surprise for you."

"Okay."

He stopped the van, turned off the engine, and came around to my side. The door opened with a loud groan, and I felt his hand on my arm.

"Okay, get out and put your other hand on my arm. I'll walk you over."

This was different. Especially for Duncan.

We slowly walked together to the front of the van and a little bit beyond. Hard to tell, really.

"Okay, you can open your eyes now."

I did. There before me sat a brand-new car, a glistening green Subaru wagon. A darling car. A four-wheel drive, ride through rivers and fields and look cute but understated, classy but frugal car. A wonderful car for traveling far and wide.

I turned to Duncan, tears in my eyes. "Thank you," I whispered.

Robbie and Angus bounded out of the house, clapping and hollering.

"I told you she'd cry, Dad!" Angus shouted.

"Yep, Dad." Robbie thumped his father on the back. "Tears of joy."

Sixteen

hris's cheeks held color for the first time in weeks. April was winding down now, and the high rarely dipped below the mid-seventies these days. We had taken several rides in the ski boat together. Jesus called Himself the living water, and I can see why He did. Water is so flowing and free and so needed. Hold it in your own little container and keep it there and it'll stagnate. I've tried so desperately to figure Jesus out in my mind, and one of these days I may stop seeking to place Him in my own Jesus-shaped cistern and just go with the flow of Living Water, moving in faith that I'm not paddling down the river Styx, but sailing free and clear down the Jordon with no one at the helm but the Spirit of God.

"I come so that you might have life and have it more abundantly," Jesus said. Drink up, Poppy. For heaven's sake, drink until you cannot drink any more.

I prayed the same for everybody I loved just then, going down a quick checklist in my mind. I prayed for Chris, too, as we sped along the surface of the water, not saying much of anything. Chris drove sometimes, standing, letting the air scour her bronzing skin.

"I'm coming alive again," she told me that April day.

"If you're going to survive this, Chrissy, it has to begin somewhere."

"It scares me, though."

I covered up a napping Angus with a towel. "It doesn't mean you don't still love Josh...if that's what you're worried about, Chrissy."

"Gary got me to go on the Internet last night. Did you know that other boys have died in hazings?"

"Yeah." I had been all over the Internet when it first happened. Alcohol poisoning killed a lot of college kids on hell night and other nights, too. And reading how much booze it actually took to get to that state boggled my already baffled mind. I read about a blood alcohol content of .68, on a female no less, and wondered how much she must have drank to get there, and how fast she drank it.

Man, had things changed since I was in college. The kids drank, sure, but not so fast like they do now. They gave their minds enough time to get the signal it was time to stop, time to pass out so no more alcohol could get in. But these days, it didn't work like that.

"I checked out Maryland's hazing laws, Popp. If I pressed charges, those boys will only pay five hundred dollars and spend six months in prison."

"That can't be right, Chris. Wouldn't they at least get manslaughter? Are you sure those statutes aren't just for hazing, you know, when the person hazed survives or something?"

"Maybe." Chris pushed the old boat faster. "I need to find out more, I guess."

"Yeah. Maybe you do." I wasn't going to try to talk her out of it. Stitched up with purpose, crusader's boots walked the path of pain with a bit more cushion.

"Would you tell me what it was like for you, Popp? In the sorority and stuff?"

I slipped a pair of sunglasses and some sunblock out of my boat bag, thinking it ludicrous how one went out for a day in the sun and then did everything imaginable to avoid it. "What do you mean? I never went through a hazing. Not like that."

"Okay, hardhead. Your initiation then. Tell me about that."

I thought about my hell night experience and began to laugh. "It was really just silly, Chris."

"Were you drunk?"

"No. Just one beer. It wasn't like today, all that binge drinking they do now." I began to slather on the lotion, comparing my freckled, rounded shoulders to Chris's tanned, sculptured ones. I pulled down my sunglasses and looked frankly at my friend. "Why do you want to know this? Are you sure you want to hear all of this? Maybe you had better slow the boat down and let us drift for a while."

Chris nodded and did as I suggested. She sat down, fingers still tripping along the steering wheel. "I don't know why I want to know, Popp. Maybe I'm trying to reconstruct his last minutes on earth; maybe I'm trying to understand why he'd subject himself to all that. If it was good, I want to know that, too. I'm just trying to answer a few of the thousands and thousands of questions that won't stop running through my mind."

Dropping the sunblock back in the bag, I pulled out two bottles of Nestea, opened mine and handed one to Chris. "Well, I'd be lying if I said hell night wasn't scary, Chrissy."

She unscrewed the cap, the metal lid popping as air rushed beneath it. "What did you have to do?"

I felt sick to my stomach, remembering the embarrassment, wondering what Chris would think of me after I told her. I'd always been proud I'd been a sorority girl, but hadn't ever divulged the facts surrounding my initiation. Well, here goes, I thought, remembering how I'd said to Chris, over and over again, if you need *anything*, I'm here. "It was stupid, I guess. We had to go to the bathroom of the sorority house and strip down."

"Naked?"

I nodded, feeling even more ridiculous. I'd had a sweet, lithe, pert body back then, but I couldn't help remembering the scene as though I possessed my present, more dimply state. "They threw cans of fruit and soup and well, anything canned all over us."

"Soup?" Chris's face wrinkled. "Are you sure?"

"Yeah. I know that because I remember a blob of cream of celery condensed hitting me right on the forehead."

Chris nodded and sipped her tea. "I've always wondered why you hated cream of celery."

"Yeah, well, that's why. So in between the food and all, they doused us in ice water."

"That must have been the worst."

I shook my head. "No, the food was worse. And when you're naked..." I let that sink in. "All slimy and stuff. I was actually relieved when a good bucketful hit me."

"So you were scared?"

"Yeah, I was. Because I knew it was the first pass, and there was more to come."

Chris gripped the steering wheel. "You know, I guess the question we outsiders always ask is, why? Why would you try to get into a sorority in the first place if you knew you'd have to be embarrassed like that?"

"I guess it's because it's an honor to be in a sorority. It's exclusive by its very nature. We were only able to be humiliated because the house thought we could cut it."

"I don't understand that kind of thing." Chris shook her head. "Maybe it's a rich girl thing."

"Oh, Chris..." I sighed.

"Sorry. But you *are* a snob, Popp." Chris grinned. "So what did they do next?"

"Well, we were allowed to get on our bras and underpants, and one at a time we went down to the basement and sat on tubs of ice. And they screamed obscenities at us and ridiculed us."

Chris's mouth dropped open. "Wasn't it horrible?"

"Yes! A couple of the girls were really mean about it, too. They were sophomores." I winked.

Chris laughed. "Now *that* I understand."

"Didn't you experience *any*thing this excruciating at Liberty?"

"Yeah." Chris nodded. "Having to listen to the LBC Singers week after week in chapel." She rolled her eyes and looked like herself for the first time in months.

I stood up and hugged her. "Oh, Chrissy," I whispered. "I love you."

"Well, I love you, too, Poppy."

"Was their singing that bad?"

"Oh no. They sang great! It just looked like their features were doing gymnastics, they tried to put so much expression on them. Like, what does a nineteen-year-old *really* know about grace?"

"I guess we all have our trials."

Chris slugged down the remainder of her tea. "So did it work?"

"What, hell night and all?"

"Yeah. I mean, what was the upside to it?"

"The next morning we were all sisters. The girls that had been so mean threw a big party, and we dressed up and danced, and it was wonderful. And we pledge sisters had really bonded in our adversity."

"I still don't understand it, Popp. I guess I probably won't. How could you not feel animosity toward those who had ridiculed you?"

"Maybe it was because they had gone through it, too. I don't know. Thing is, Chrissy, some girls and boys can take that sort of thing, **and** others can't. I'm not sure why that is."

"I guess it's like anything." Chris threw her bottle into the trash bag. "Can I drive fast again?"

"Go on, lady."

Chris sped the boat around the lake until the gas meter sagged low against the left side of the dial.

"You wanna go down to Java Jane's for a latte?" I asked.

Chris stiffened and turned on me. "Good grief, Poppy. What makes you think I'm ready for a latte?"

Chris's comment haunted me the rest of the day. *What does a nineteen-year-old really know about grace?* I guess it's true overall, but if I look back at myself at age nineteen and compare it to myself right now, I think I knew more about grace then. I trusted more, and I was willing to give of myself freely and with joy.

There's that verse in the Bible that says we are justified freely by the grace of Jesus through the redemption He provided. I've heard the saying "the greater the sin, the greater the grace." I used to believe it. But now, I believe grace is always great. It can't be made lesser because we've acted a little bit better than someone else. Does Chrissy still hold fast to grace like she did before? I don't know how she feels about it now. And I'm afraid to ask.

God's grace is manifested everyday, though. I know that. When I picked up Angus at the church, I asked Duncan if there was anything I

could do to help him. The overt surprise in his eyes was my shame, the
delight that replaced it my glory. Well, God's glory. Only His grace would
have made it possible for me to even ask the question. So he asked me if
I could address the cards he had to send out that week. My goodness! I
had no idea. Birthday, anniversary, get-well, sympathy to a member's
mother on the West Coast, and a couple of congratulations cards.

I read each note penned inside by my husband's hand. Talk about
grace.

Duncan certainly knew what he was doing in buying me the Subaru.
Angus loved being able to climb in easily, Robbie rode along with us more
often, and Duncan suggested drives now.

Every morning when I left for my walk, I'd pat the little green car on
its hood and be on my way. Chris joined me now, post Java Jane's. Though
I walked twice as far now, I ate twice as much. Always behind the weight
curve.

Man.

Tomorrow, May began, always a milestone for me, like spring had
finally stuck. I slugged down my coffee and met Chris in the town square.
It was the first time for such open walking. Usually we'd go down Route
45, past Miss Mildred's homestead and on up Tweed Road toward
Highland Kirk. But today I suggested we meet at six-thirty, walk for a
while, and eat breakfast at Bill D's. Chris had surprisingly agreed.

It would be her first meal out.

She looked beautiful walking across the park to where I sat on the
steps of the octagonal bandstand. The yellow sundress Chris wore pierced
the dimness of the early morning, echoing the first bit of sunrise. It
promised to be a pale sunrise today, not raging or glorious. Just regular and
nice. I have a lot to say for regular and nice.

She waved from about ten yards away. "Hi, Poppy!"

I got up. "Ready?"

She breathed in deeply. "Yeah."

"Big step."

"I know."

So we began to walk.

"Can we still go out Route 45 and just end up in town this time?" Chris asked.

"Yeah. But you're not going to back out on breakfast are you?"

"No. I promise. I just don't want to run into any church people. Or not many, anyway. They won't understand how I can be out walking and still not coming to services."

"Forget about them," I said with a laugh.

Chris shook her head. "One day you're going to accept the parameters of your position as a pastor's wife, Poppy."

"I don't think so. I don't see how I can. Not like that, anyway." I thought about that duck with the water rolling off its back. Like that would ever happen!

Ten minutes later we walked along Route 45, a two-lane road with farms on either side. Some woods, too.

"Who's going to watch Angus during breakfast?"

"Robbie. He doesn't have class until eleven today. Duncan will get him his breakfast and all before he leaves."

"Okay."

I understood her concern. Chris was still a mother, but without someone to worry about. If she wanted Angus for that, well, fine with me.

Mildred LaRue suddenly blew by us in her green Impala. She slammed the brakes on the cyclone, the car screeching in response. And then she backed up with a jammed down accelerator. It took all of my self-control not to jump into the ditch beside the road.

"Hey, Miss Mildred!" I called as the passenger side window of the iguana-mobile rolled smoothly down.

"Hey there, you all. Hey, Christine. How you doing?"

"Hi, Miss Mildred. I'm doing all right."

Chris knew Miss Mildred from Creator's Corner.

"We been praying."

"Yeah, I know, thanks. Poppy told me."

"Maybe you want to come along with Penelope sometimes. It's good to hear the prayers firsthand. You know?"

Chris smiled. "Yeah, maybe I'll just do that sometime."

Mildred cocked an eyebrow at me. "Doesn't sound like much commitment in that remark, does it, Penelope?"

"Nope."

"You listen here, Christine. Penelope here can't push you much, you being her best friend and all, but I'm telling you this, you need to allow yourself some more support."

"Yes, Miss Mildred."

"I mean it!"

"So where you heading off to, Miss Mildred?" I asked.

Mildred shook her head and jerked a thumb at me. "There she goes, changing the subject on me again. I'm headed down to church. Ladies meeting with the Reverend Mrs. Thing leading. Talking about submitting to authority. And guess who's the authority? I'm gonna try and put out any fires before they hit full blaze."

"Good luck."

Mildred leaned forward. "Will you be there tonight?"

It was Monday. "Of course."

Mildred shook a finger at Chris. "You should listen to me. I'm not this old for nothing. What's your favorite dinner?"

"Roast beef with mashed potatoes and green beans," Chris said.

"Well, funny you should say that, because that's what's for dinner. Six o'clock!" She sped away, rolling up her window as she went, dust puffing from underneath the wheels.

"If my memory serves me correctly," Chris said, "that woman doesn't quite know how to take no for an answer, does she?"

"You got that right."

"And if I don't come, she may very well be on my doorstep at 6:10 asking why I'm not there yet."

"You're right there, too."

Chris sighed and we walked on. "Maybe it would be good to come. Do you think Gary would mind?"

"I think he'd do back handsprings."

Chris laughed. "He could, too, you know. He can still do all that stuff."

"I know."

Silence enfolded us. There had been a lot of silence the past few months, but this felt different. It was back to the same quiet togetherness we'd known since we were three years old.

"Chrissy?" I asked later at Bill D's where we sat in the deserted back room.

"Yeah."

"What do you think of God now?"

She stared at me for a moment. "I know I should say the spiritually mature thing here, Popp. But it would be a lie. Have you ever read the book of Job?"

I nodded.

"Well, you know how he curses everything *but* God? The day he was born, the light, the this, the that?"

"Yeah."

"That's me."

"I'm sorry for asking, but—"

"It's okay. But from anyone else but you or Gary or Duncan, I would have been offended."

I knew what she meant. Only a lot of years earned anyone the right to ask questions like that. "Does it scare you that you may always feel this way?"

"Sometimes. But there are more books than Job, Poppy. And even Job's life is restored tenfold." She pushed away her half-eaten plate of food. "You want to know the only thing that gives me any comfort these days?"

"Yeah," I nodded.

"It's that I'll see him again. I'll see Josh again. I know that as surely as I know he isn't here with me now."

Heaven must be a wonderful place, I've always reasoned. I've got a list a mile long of saints I want to have a conversation with during eternity. David, Paul, Peter, Jonah (I really relate to Jonah), Pascal, John Calvin, C. S. Lewis, and especially Rembrandt. And now I've got Josh to add to this list. Eternity is a long time. We'll have many more conversations together, me and Josh. If only I could talk to him now and have so many of my questions answered.

Seventeen

picked Chris up at five-forty-five, tooling along to an old Billy Joel CD. One of the kudos of the new car I had failed to foresee was the renewed ability to belt out my favorite songs at the top of my lungs. It had never really been about having the technological capacity for such an activity so much as not looking like an idiot. Who wants to scream out "Allentown" in a putty-patched van? I certainly didn't, but now, well, I'd taken my little zippered CD case out of my studio and put it in the Subaru.

The studio was little used anyway these days.

Jesus said, "Take up your cross and follow Me." But sometimes I think taking up our cross means laying something else down. Like paints and brushes. Who was I trying to fool anyway? Yes, I'd laid down my paints, but the cross I carried was pretend, for show even.

Of course, all the women welcomed Chris, and she became the star that night, and well she should have been. India still didn't pray, but she did bring along a friend, a friend with a white Saab convertible.

Oh, well, it wasn't as if my Subaru ever had anything over the ladybug.

"This is Joanna," India said when Chris and I walked into the room.

Joanna held out a slender hand from where she sat at the dining room table. Good, we'd outgrown the kitchen. I noticed the nails brushed with a very soft, pearlescent pink. Understated yet feminine. Definitely the work of the Korean man down at Love Nails in the tiny strip shopping center across from the mall. "Joanna Jones-Fletcher. And you must be Poppy Fraser. India's told me a lot about you."

I couldn't imagine what that could be. "It's good you could come." I turned to face the rest of the women. "Everybody, this is Chris."

Chris gave a little wave, her face reddening. "Thanks, you guys," she said softly. "For praying and everything."

"Of course you know Miss Mildred. This is Charmaine Hopewell."

Charmaine squeezed Chris's forearm. "Hey, Chris. Praise the Lord you're here with us tonight."

"This is Sunny."

"Hey, ma'am."

Chris turned to me at the "ma'am."

"This is India."

India stood to her feet, her chair falling back onto the floor. "Oh, brother!" she cried cheerfully and bent to pick it up. "I'm a klutz. Nice to meet you."

Chris shook her hand. "I hear you compose music."

"I sure do."

"What a wonderful gift."

India sat back down. "Can't sing well, though. I leave that to Mrs. LaRue and Charmaine. Not that they'd ever sing *my* kind of music."

"And you've just met Joanna," I said.

Mildred stood at the head of the table. "Sit down now, everyone. It's time to eat."

Chris hardly said a word during the meal, but I had never seen her eat so much food at one time. She packed away at least four pieces of roast beef, two helpings of mashed potatoes, and one and a half mounds of green beans.

"Did you know that Joanna is a church lady, too?" Mildred asked me. "No."

"Uh-huh. Her husband's the pastor over at Centennial United Methodist."

The twilight gay/lesbian ministry church. Well, apparently the pastor wasn't living an alternative lifestyle! Trying to picture a meeting night of the twilight group in Mount Oak, well, I figured maybe three people might show up. Tops.

Joanna wiped her mouth, set her napkin by her plate, and pushed out her chair a little. Crossing one leg casually over the other, she wore gorgeous cream-colored linen slacks so impeccably cut they could only have been tailored just for her. She picked up her water goblet as though it were a wine glass and said, "Well, if that's all one needs to qualify as a church lady, I suppose I fill the bill."

Oh yes! She chaired that meeting for the May festival last fall.

"Joanna was on Wall Street for years," India said, obviously impressed.

"How did you meet your husband then?" Mildred asked.

"Oh, I used to summer at Lake Coventry. A solitary vacation, mind you. And he was a lifeguard. It was the summer before his last year at seminary."

"You must miss life in the big city," I said.

She flipped one side of her dark brown pageboy back over her shoulder. "I do. Very much."

"So, what brought you here tonight?" Mildred asked, sitting back down with a topped-off potato bowl.

"India brought me along. She said we both could use the support of other women involved in the church, and it was a good cause."

Chris shifted in her seat.

A good cause, eh?

My eyes met Mildred's. *Change the subject!* I tried to vibe her. *Change the blasted subject!* Mildred nodded.

"Well, let's go pray then."

And so we did, Charmaine and Miss Mildred and Sunny really getting into it.

"Thank You, God, for preserving Chris this far," Mildred began.

"Yes, Lord!" Charmaine said. "Once again we don't understand, for although You've lavished upon us so many things, we know You never promised we'd always understand."

Sunny jumped in. "But that's what makes faith faith, Lord Jesus."

"Amen!" Mildred raised a hand. "'Without faith it is impossible to please Him.'"

"We believe that, Lord," I told Him. "We believe that in the light of eternity this will all make sense. And if we can't see that as ever being a possibility, help us to know that it's true. That you can take any situation and beautify it with Your holiness."

I held Chris's hand and watched from beneath half-shuddered eyes. India still examined each woman present, and Joanna Jones-Fletcher fell asleep. Mildred took up the prayer, and I listened as Charmaine mumbled something I didn't understand, softly very softly. And Chris cried, but she muttered, "Yes, Lord. Yes, Father," and I had to believe that God was using us just then to strengthen His child, His Christine. And I looked around the room after the final amen was said and counted myself privileged, no *blessed*, to be in the same room as these women.

"So what did you think?" I asked Chris on the drive home. We'd stayed late with Miss Mildred, hearing all about the uppity pastor's wife and the upcoming gigs. Mildred even mentioned Herman Winfred, saying that maybe she needed to make him a more permanent part of her life, that maybe the other side of the porch swing needed a regular rear end to cover it.

Fat chance, I thought. Miss Mildred give up her independence? Yeah, right. Unless Herman was a Milquetoast, and he didn't seem like a Milquetoast. Milquetoasts stayed away from strong-willed women like Mildred Grace LaRue.

"I'm glad I went," Chris said. "I didn't get a real feel for that Joanna girl. Or India either, for that matter. But the others really seem to care."

"Oh, they do."

"Although if that Sunny girl had called me ma'am one more time..."

"I'm with you, lady."

In order to get from Miss Mildred's home to Chris's, a trip through town was necessary. The IGA would close in five minutes. "Would you mind if I stopped at the grocery store?" I asked.

"Okay."

"You want to come in or wait in the car?"

"I'll wait here."

I hurried into the store, ignoring the dirty look from the cashier, and ran back to the Slim Fast aisle. After being with all of those slender, beautiful women, I realized it was time to do something definite about my weight. Something proven. Something mindless.

The dark chocolate looked like a flavor that would keep my interest over the long haul. I wasn't all that great at diets. I knew this going in and had no delusions of grandeur.

I paid the $4.20 and went back to the car.

"What'd you get?" Chris asked.

"Slim Fast."

"Oh, Poppy. Why?"

"I'm a size sixteen, Chrissy. I've never been a size sixteen in my life."

"Who cares about what size you are when you've got big brown eyes and thick, dark curly hair?"

Yeah, right. I started the engine. "But you've got to admit it. I've gained some weight."

"I can't tell the difference. Honestly."

"You wouldn't be able to see it if somebody paid you to. You're not an outward appearance type of woman."

"Is that a compliment?"

"A huge one."

"Good," she said.

I pulled out of the parking space and sped across the empty lot. This was a great car.

We drove the mile to Chris's in silence. When I pulled up into the drive, Chris cleared her throat. "I called a lawyer today."

"How come?"

"I think I might press charges."

"Against who? The boys? The fraternity?"

"I'm not sure yet. I just want to find out what my options are."

"Okay."

Chris picked up her purse and drove her vision into my gaze. "I know it won't bring Josh back, so you don't have to say anything like that."

"Okay. Is it an inner soothing thing, though, Chris? Something to concentrate on to help the pain?" *I mean, is that what grieving women do?*

"I don't know what it's about, actually. I just can't let things lie the way they are right now." She put her hand on the handle and opened the car door. "Will you take me up to Baltimore soon?"

"Name the day."

"Okay. Thanks, Popp."

I would have said something like, "That's what friends are for," but it sounded wrong in my mind, so I knew it would sound triply wrong hanging in the air between me and Chris.

"If I can keep one other set of parents from suffering like this, don't you think I should?"

"Yes, Chrissy, I do."

"Don't you think that's only right?"

"I think you have to do it if you think you should."

"Okay. Well, thanks for tonight."

"Sure."

"I really didn't want to go, you know."

"I know. But you did, and it took a lot of strength," I said. "You wanna walk tomorrow morning?"

Chris nodded. "I may just meet you at Java Jane's."

"Really?"

"Yeah. But I'm just getting regular coffee."

"That's all I usually get in the mornings." Well, sort of.

She slid a leg out of the car, her sandaled foot resting on the blacktop of the driveway. "Good. Okay, well, see ya."

"Bye."

I watched her as she negotiated the walk, the light by the door catching her blond hair. Yeah, she was coming back to life all right, but it was sad because her life had changed. There are some things we can never completely drive out of our minds as long as we live.

Chrissy's eyes had changed forever. Part of the light in them had passed on to the next world with Josh.

I drove myself to the lake, pulled up to the boathouse, and walked out to the end of the pier. There, with the moonlight silvering the lake, I downed all four diet shakes, crushing each can, one by one, and throwing them into the trashcan.

❦

I looked at myself in the mirror. I examined the lines around my eyes, the way the corners of my mouth drooped a little, and realized that yes indeed, I looked my age. I didn't used to. The thought depressed me almost as much as the day I looked down at my hands and saw Mother's there holding the paintbrush. A lot of women say they seem to be turning into their mothers, but I refuse to admit any such thing. And there is nothing to admit because Fidge is still a social-climbing creature, a butterfly who's given herself wings of gold, wings that glimmer expensively but weigh her down considerably.

At least that's what I say.

What would my mother have been like had she learned to be content with her life? I had no idea. Maybe she would have been like my Aunt Lucy, Gary's mom, who still lived in Hamilton and owned cats.

I twirled the few stray curls around my face and pursed my mouth. I realized years ago I would actually go through my entire life having never really seen my face. Sure, I'd spot my reflection in the mirror, in windows, in clean plates, and on the spout of the bathtub. I'd catch myself in the polished top of my dresser and sometimes even in the back of a spoon, but they were only images, moving snapshots. I'd see myself in photos, too. But I'd never actually *see* my face. Perhaps the closest I might ever come to it would be if I bent down and saw myself reflected in the eyes of Angus or Robbie or Paisley. But only if the light was right.

I backed away from the mirror.

Time to clench my way through the task at hand. The annual Mount Oak Crazy Days of May all committee meeting would begin shortly. Of course, the various committees had been meeting since January, but I was only called to this meeting to give a report of the progress of Highland Kirk's booth. We'd been discussing whether or not to sponsor the goldfish game this year along with the Boston cream pie setup. Miss Poole thought "the change of pace might be nice, dear."

I wanted to say, "Okay, but only if you'll swallow one alive." However, knowing Miss Poole's drive to get her own way, she might have taken me up on it.

The good thing about tonight, however, was that Miss Mildred had to go, too, since she was providing the music. It was the town's bicentennial year, after all. Two hundred years of Mount Oak.

Yikes.

The phone rang. Miss Mildred was in a panic. At least for Miss Mildred. "So, since me and the Jammers are going to be the entertainment, do you think I should go against my normal green and wear something red, white, and blue?"

"For tonight?"

"No, for seven o'clock tomorrow morning! Of course tonight!"

"It's just a meeting, Miss Mildred. I doubt if it'll matter much. You always look nice no matter what you wear."

"I'm just trying to keep professional. If I'm wearing red, white, and blue sequins at the gig, I'm thinking I should be wearing red, white, and blue at the committee meeting." Her throat was opening wide again, I realized.

"Yes, then. You should. Do you have a white jacket?"

"Sure do."

"Okay. If you've got a blue skirt and a red blouse, I've got a wonderful scarf you can borrow."

Silence.

"What is it, Miss Mildred?"

"I'm not used to borrowing things, Penelope Heubner. You should know better than to even ask."

I felt my heart sink. First Chris. Now Miss Mildred. Seemed I'd become an expert at offending people without trying. "Okay. I'm sorry."

"What's it look like? It's not something equestrian or with golf non-sense on it, is it? I know you used to be one of those country club, horsey types, and I'm wondering if I should trust one of your scarves."

I laughed at the heavy doubt weighing down Miss Mildred's tone. "What if I told you it was just like a flag, but the stars were embroidered with pearlescent threads, and the stripes were outlined with coordinating sequins?"

"You kidding me?"

"Nope. Paisley was *Aunt Sam* as she called it, for a figure skating routine when she was ten. In fact, you can have it if you want, and then there won't be any borrowing factor."

"You sure you won't wear it yourself?"

This time I was silent.

A warm, Mildredy chuckle caressed my ear. "I'll be over to your house at a quarter after seven to get it."

"You want to ride together?"

"I was wondering when you were going to take me for a ride in your sassy new automobile."

After I hung up, I found Duncan in his study. "Got some Mildred LaRue style CDs for the car?"

"You know it, baby."

A stuffed vinyl CD holder was ready and waiting by the kitchen door ten minutes later.

Eighteen

The smell of cut grass lined the breeze, and flowers hefted up new perfume into the air. The freshness of a well-wintered lake coming to life once more brought a twitter of excitement to my heart. I don't know why I don't just give up the charade and admit I love this place, all committee meetings notwithstanding.

Lake Coventry parades its finest in the month of May. The flowers had not yet grown gangly. The grass, now a darker green than during its initial rise from dormancy, grew thick and lush, bolstering itself for the intense heat July and August promised. And the stems of the columbines that most Mount Oakers seemed to adore still grew short. I hate when they get so long by the end of the summer, overeager somehow, the blooms trying to get somewhere they aren't supposed to go. Columbines can be devious flowers if one truly gets to know them. Sure, they seem fanciful, perhaps even lifted from the pages of a storybook, but I suspect they know exactly what they are doing.

I backed out of my driveway, shoving the gearshift quickly into first.

Late. And it was all Miss Mildred's fault. I love Miss Mildred with all my heart, but being late really gets my socks in a twist.

I have many sins. Nonpunctuality is not one of them, although it does lead to an extreme judgmentalism in the direction of those who can't seem to get their act together in a timely manner.

Miss Mildred, not a particularly punctual person to begin with, had wavered and waffled over whether or not to wear the scarf. The conversation extended into the drive over. "You're from Baltimore, Penelope. What would Francis Scott Key have thought of this scarf?"

"Miss Mildred! You've got to be kidding! Francis Scott Key?"

"Well, him writing about 'the flag was still there' and all. I don't think he had a sequined scarf in mind."

"I know he didn't, but that doesn't mean he wouldn't have approved. And besides, what in the world difference does it make if he wouldn't have?"

Mildred studied me. "I have a kinship with Francis Scott Key, Penelope. He named the poem "The Star Spangled Banner," and my band is called The Star Spangled Jammers, and therefore, I feel I owe something to the man. You've got to admit that using the word *spangled* was genius on his part. It could have been the star spotted banner or the star dotted banner. It could have even been the star littered banner, which would have been a downright awful name for a jazz singer's band."

"But he's been dead for years, Miss Mildred." We passed by Josef, bent over his strawberry pots. He didn't wave. Must not have recognized my new car.

"Well, so has Moses, but people still go to temple."

I laughed. "Oh, come on! You can't compare Francis Scott Key to Moses!"

"Why not?"

"Miss Mildred! Moses was…well Moses! Leader of the nation of Israel. Deliverer from slavery."

"God delivered them from slavery, Miss Heubner."

"Well, yeah, through Moses though. Don't get touchy now, Miss Mildred. I mean, Moses is looked upon as the founder of the law, the—" I heard a snort beside me.

Mildred laughed silently but deeply, tears streaming down her wrinkled cheeks.

I blew out a sigh. "That was not nice and you know it. Leading me on like that. Francis Scott Key, eh?" I allowed the right side of my mouth to lift. "I'll show you Francis Scott Key, Madame LaRue. And speaking of rue—" I almost ran into a phone booth near the Exxon.

"Calm down, Penelope. I was just having a little fun with you. I can't believe I strung you along for so long with this one. Francis Scott Key! What did that man ever do for me?"

"He gave you the name for your band," I said, concentrating on my driving a bit more. "You said so yourself."

"Okay. That is true." Mildred leaned forward and turned on the stereo.

"And don't you go razzing on Francis Scott! Fort McHenry is my favorite place in the world. It's where Daniel Peverly kissed me on my ninth grade field trip. My first kiss right there in the dungeon!"

"I thought you went to an all girls' school?"

"I did. His class from public school was there the same day. He went to our church."

"Any other kisses from him after that?"

"No. Yuck."

"Yeah, first kisses are usually like that. What CDs you got? Herman Winfred keeps telling me we got to get us a CD player in the Impala."

"Have a look through the case. Duncan made sure you'd be happy right before we left."

Her wide smile dazzled me. Mildred's smiles are like gift-wrapped little packages from the Almighty, sent down as if to say, "See, as long as people are smiling like this, how bad can it be?"

Gosh, I love that woman.

"Mmm, mmm. Billy Holiday. Sarah Vaughn. Don't feel like listening to those *other* women. What else we got?" Her fingers flipped the discs. "Oh yes. Oh yes, here is the one. *Cookin' with the Miles Davis Quintet.*" She slid it out of the sleeve and opened the glove box, the still clean glove box. "Now where in the name of heaven do you put this thing in?"

I began to chuckle.

"What are you laughing at?" Mildred asked.

"I'm not laughing. I'm basking in the moment."

"What for?"

"I think this is the first time that you've got the question and I've got the answer."

"Well, enjoy it then." Mildred shut the glove box. "But don't get so happy you forget about this CD."

I took it from her and slid it into the narrow, horizontal slit just above the radio's face.

The sweet trilling piano began to speak, a soft base undergirding its mellow dialect. And then the tenor sax arrived and took over the conversation. "My Funny Valentine." Soft, candied strains of love. Taffy notes, chocolate timing, conversation hearts all wrapped up in a papered box with a bow the size of St. Louis.

Mildred oozed back into the seat. "Now this, Penelope Huebner, is what I call classical music."

The piano responded again to the sax. I love you, too, baby.

The sax was still emoting when we arrived at the boathouse. The lot brimmed with cars and trucks, and other stragglers scurried in with blank faces designed to hide sheepish embarrassment.

Mildred made us finish out the song. "You don't just leave off in the middle of 'My Funny Valentine,' Penelope," she said. "It's like playing a seven-note scale."

The Crazy Days of May ushered in the tourist season. Sort of. Summer locals from around the state who came to clean up their condos and air out their vacation houses before the renters began trickling in during early June spent a lot of dough at Crazy Days. Travel agencies scheduled bus trips around the festival as well. Twenty-thousand attendees would mill around during the day. The town clogged with people; the streets seethed with visitors. But the local churches and businesses raised big money, with 15 percent of the proceeds going to a selected charity. This year we'd chosen Parents without Partners. A few of the more legalistic churches had raised a fit at that particular planning meeting last fall. Thankfully, Miss Poole had felt good that day, and I didn't have to sit through it alone.

"Why should we condone divorce?" the wife of the pastor at Oakwood Road Holiness said.

The priest from the Episcopals, India's boss, had shot the dissenters down in a very sixties, hippie manner as he stood up in his hiking sandals and climbing shorts, crowned with a priestly shirt. Talk about a fashion faux pas. But the "Hey, mans" and the "social justice" bit seemed somewhat over the top. The guy desperately needed a vocabulary overhaul, judging by the look on the old-timers' faces, who seemed to have no earthly idea what he was even talking about.

When they'd tallied the votes, the majority went for Parents without Partners anyway.

As Mildred and I walked into the meeting room, the sun setting over Lake Coventry enflamed the sky to a fuming hue. I love that brilliant, glowing shade of red-orange more than any other I ever use for my paintings. It speaks to my soul, matches the fire, the agitation. But yet, it is a God color, so it soothes in a way, telling me God loves me even at my most difficult. It tells me that God actually uses difficult, sore colors like bloody reds and bruised purples to His glory, so why couldn't He use people like that?

He could. I saw evidence all the time that I was being used by Him despite my appalling attitude and my secret sins. So why were the Holiness people any different? When that verse talks about vessels used for dishonor and vessels used for honor, it doesn't say the honorable use vessels are necessarily gorgeous, and we know for sure, since there are none righteous, no not one, they aren't perfect either.

Of course the room had been set up backwards, so we walked in just behind the podium. Good grief. All eyes fell upon us as we entered the room.

The entire "who's who" of Mount Oak suddenly stared at us as we slithered in late! Talk about humbling.

Miss Poole glared at me, plunking down her cavernous, black woven leather purse on the empty seat next to her. Why she didn't inhabit one of the chairs behind the podium, I didn't know, but I knew by the set of the maven's jaw that she was clearly unhappy about it. To make matters worse, the chairs of honor supported Methodists, a sure thing to put Highland Kirk's hip resident control freak into a real old-fashioned tizzy.

Joanna Jones-Fletcher sat facing the group, wearing something very Talbotish in charcoal gray. She winked smoothly at us.

Mildred, of course, walked in like the Queen of Sheba making half the people in the room feel as if they had been too early. Too bad she'd chosen a scarf and not a boa. If I had half her panache, I'd be selling at galleries in New York.

"Is that Jeanelle up at the podium?" I asked Mildred as we sat down.

"Sure is."

"She got all of her hair cut off this winter. Now why didn't Robbie tell me that?"

"Because he's a twenty-one-year-old boy?" Mildred whispered.

A practical woman in a flared aqua skirt and a white polo shirt, the lady who ran the dunking booth the year before for the Catholic church, turned around and shushed us. *Oh, shush, yourself. This isn't a national summit or anything.*

"I'll read out who's doing what," said Jeanelle, in charge of the food stands this year. "Barnacle Bill's will be doing crab cakes again. I'm doing burgers and dogs, of course. Josef is going to do French pastries and croque monsieur." She pronounced it mon-sire. "And two churches asked to do the Boston cream pies."

Asked?

I could smell trouble burning like dried leaves in a rusty old barrel.

A buzz erupted within the group of ladies from Mount Zion Christian Church. *What could this woman be saying,* I imagined their inner thoughts. *We've been doing the Boston cream pies for twenty-five years!* Or however long it had been.

Jeanelle, a self-proclaimed New Ager, cleared her throat. "I've always thought change isn't a bad thing. So I've given the chance to do the Boston cream pies to the Highland Kirk."

What? Given the chance? This wasn't some competition! I thought we were just being nice! I thought I was doing the Christian thing back in September when I volunteered Highland to take the food stand with the most grueling preparation. I felt my heart speed up, and I stole a look at Miss Poole, whose chin had tilted up, a smug smile pulling her mouth down.

"Oh, for heaven's sake," I mumbled. "She's actually enjoying it."

Mildred chuckled.

"Yeah, you go ahead and laugh, Mildred LaRue. Just you wait until you find out the Hallelujah Baptist has been bumped from doing the fried chicken!"

"They wouldn't dare!" Mildred whispered harshly.

A minute later Jeanelle said, "And since the ladies at Hallelujah can make the best fried chicken this side of the Mason Dixon, we'll keep them just where they are."

That, naturally, made one of the Mount Zion members spring to her feet. I couldn't believe no one had given them a heads up. The tiny woman with a case of severe scoliosis and hair the color of old snow in a coal town, cried in a New York City accent, "So then, you're saying we didn't do a good job on the Boston cream pies last year? Is that what you're saying?"

Wow. How in the world did this woman end up in Mount Oak?

"No, Miss Betty," Jeanelle said, "I'm not. It's just that I thought it was time for you all to get a little break—"

"But the Hallelujah ladies have been doing fried chicken for just the same amount of time! Am I right or am I right, Missus LaRue?"

And she sounded like a female mafia don, too.

Mildred said, "Mmn, hmn."

Jeanelle reddened, her fingers clearly itching for a cigarette. "Look, we had our reasons. Nothing you should take personal offense over."

"Well, how else are we supposed to take this?" the little lady said. She turned and pointed a finger at me. "You should be ashamed of yourself! Stealing people's booths like that. It just figures the Presbyterians would do something like that! You think that just because God chose you, you can walk all over people!"

I felt my eyes swell to the size of lemons. Doctrinal accusations in a public forum! And in front of nonbelievers to boot! I looked at Mildred with a "What in the world do I do now?" expression. Mildred laid a strong hand on my arm.

"Now, ladies," Jeanelle said. "This isn't the time or the place."

Colonel Bougie of the Colonel's Kitchen stood to his feet and swept an arm over the entire group. "I don't know why we have to have the churches involved at all! It's the same thing *every single YEAR!* These people are nothing more than a four-star pain in the patooty. You people are more trouble than you're worth, that's for sure."

"Now just a minute, Colonel," the hip Episcopalian said. India's boss man. "To castigate the entire Christian community of Mount Oak because some misguided women—"

"Misguided!" yelled Lady Mount Zion of New York. "Well, who gave you the right to judge?"

Joanna Jones-Fletcher stood to her feet and politely moved Jeanelle aside. "Excuse me, folks." Her voice was modulated with a womanly firmness. "I know how competitive the churches are around here, but this is for a good cause. If we could maybe just put aside our differences for an hour, please? Remember, this is all for a *very* good cause."

I felt sick.

And then Marc Tipton stood to his feet. "I'd just like to say something on that note," he requested respectfully.

Joanna pointed to him. "Yes, Marc." Then she shuffled her notes.

I gazed at him in wonder. Just plain huge, this guy weighed in at a good three hundred and fifty pounds at least. And I couldn't take my eyes off of him. I had pictured Sunny's husband along the Southern, athletic boy kind of line.

"A few of us more conservative churches have gotten together and discussed the possibility of our proceeds going to a different charity besides Parents without Partners."

"I'm sorry." Joanna shook her head. "But that really isn't possible. We've already discussed this."

"What about Big Brothers and Sisters?" he asked, and I had to give him credit for at least trying.

"It will be twice the paperwork, and quite frankly, Marc, I have to wonder whether or not you all can actually agree on an alternative charity anyway."

Colonel Bougie clapped, and several others joined in.

"Preach it!" someone yelled from behind me.

Oh, brother. Kingdom living at its finest.

Marc stood to his feet. "Well, then," he said with a sigh, "I guess we won't be participating this year."

"Us either." The pastor from Calvary Independent spoke. "I don't mean to cause such friction, but it's just a matter of principle. I hope there aren't any hard feelings, y'all."

They walked out a minute later, their wives trailing behind, red faced and looking down at their sensible shoes. Poor Sunny. I don't know how she bore the embarrassment. Unless of course, she agreed with Marc and felt if she didn't take a stand now, when would she?

"What do you think of that?" I whispered to Mildred.

"It doesn't matter what I think, baby. And that's just the fact."

When I walked out later hearing some guy holding a motorcycle helmet say, "I wish those church people would just butt out of the public domain," I almost yelled a hearty, "Amen to that!" I whispered it to Mildred instead.

But Mildred wiped away a small tear. "People got a right to live by their consciences, Penelope. Just 'cause you think you're right doesn't give you the right to disrespect your brothers and sisters in the Lord."

"But they're dragging us all down with them!"

"No, they're not. The only person that can drag you down is yourself. If the town decides to use a broad brush to paint us all, that's their own narrow-mindedness. Narrow-mindedness works both ways, Penelope."

Well, that sure enough was God's honest truth, and I literally meant that.

It all still made me mad, though.

When I pulled into the drive, Mildred laid a hand on my arm. "'Do not think of yourself more highly than you ought,'" she quoted, "'but rather think of yourself with sober judgment.'"

"Where's that found?"

"Romans 12:3."

See, Miss Mildred knows where verses are found, which pretty much explains why she was the one telling me what God wanted me to hear.

I persuaded her to come in for a cup of Lipton tea and some slice and bake Toll House cookies. Duncan joined us in the living room, taking a cookie from the plate as he sat down on the couch next to Miss Mildred. "So you survived, huh?"

"Barely. Want some tea?" I asked him as I poured out a cup for Mildred.

A chuckle from Mildred accompanied his nod. "What happened?"

We told him.

"How come you're not up there on the executive committee, Miss Mildred?" he asked. "You've been in Mount Oak all your life."

Mildred set down her cup. "Did you see any black folk up there, Penelope?"

"No." I set down mine. "None."

"And you won't either."

"But you're an institution around here," Duncan said.

"That doesn't matter. There's an old guard here in Mount Oak, Pastor Fraser. And I'm not going to beat my head against a wall trying to sink to their level."

Go, Miss Mildred.

"How come you've never moved away? To Memphis or New Orleans or someplace?" I asked.

"This is home. Grandpop didn't leave Mount Oak, and he had good reason to. If he could stick it out, so can I."

"Don't you feel like fighting, though, sometimes?"

"Sometimes standing firm is fighting, Popp," Duncan said.

"You got that right, Pastor Fraser."

It's hard for me to imagine anyone disrespecting Mrs. Mildred LaRue. And it's hard for me to imagine anyone consciously deciding not to make good use of her wisdom. Surely it was their loss. But not mine. God spoke to me through Miss Mildred's wisdom, and I wouldn't trade her friendship to sit next to anyone in this world, but Jesus.

Nineteen

o say that the Crazy Days of May went downhill from there would be like saying Picabo Street does a little skiing. The Highland Kirk woke up two mornings after the meeting with its new plate glass window dulled by a patina of egg.

I couldn't imagine the Mount Zion people resorting to such mischief. Not even Don Betty.

"I think it was Miss Poole's doing," Duncan said with a glint in his eye.

Arranging grapes on his plate, next to the Fritos of course, I said, "Oh, Duncan, get serious for a minute."

He winked. "She's always been against that window, Popp."

"Well, so have I, but that doesn't mean I threw a bunch of eggs at it."

"Hmm. Now that you mention that, I guess you are a viable suspect."

I set the plate down in front of him and yanked open the refrigerator door. It just wasn't a tuna salad day for me. Duncan loved it, and normally I did, too, but...ah, there it sat behind the Nestles Qwik, a Styrofoam container of chili, laced with sour cream and grated cheese and some chopped green onion for color. Duncan had taken Angus out to Chuckie Cheese the night before so I had gone over to the IGA's hot food bar. I'd run into Sunny, as I hoped I would, and the two of us ended up having coffee and pie at Bill D's.

Duncan shoved at least seven Fritos in his mouth as I shoved the chili into the microwave.

"But you gotta admit, the timing is just too perfect." Duncan carefully

175

picked up his sandwich so the tuna salad wouldn't fall out. "She just jumped on the chance to do it and have it seem like it came from an outside source."

I crossed my arms in front of my chest and laughed. "Can you just picture Magda and Ira out there winding up? But when it comes right down to it, does it really matter who did it? I would think that the best scenario would be Miss Poole."

"Why is that?"

"Because then it means our entire town isn't beyond hope."

Duncan took a big bite of sandwich and pushed it into the side of his mouth. "I heard things were a little tense yesterday at the softball game between Mount Zion and St. Edmund's Episcopal. And Gary told me it wasn't much better at their game with the Methodists."

"Really?"

"Yeah. One guy pushed the catcher on Gary's team."

"What was that all about?"

Duncan shrugged. "He told me the two were sports rivals going all the way back to junior high school."

"Still."

"I know."

"I've never much cared for church league sports anyway." I watched the cheese beginning to melt into the chili. "I'm not quite sure of the reasoning behind their existence."

"Just allows for some camaraderie, I guess. A place to set aside doctrinal differences and just fellowship. It's not much different than you ladies getting together for dinner and such."

"Maybe I just don't understand it because I'm not the athletic type."

"Don't be too harsh on it. Church league is the kind of place where a guy who can't play ball really well can drive up from work, get out on the diamond in his hard shoes and find some acceptance."

"Too bad the world can't see that then."

"Now city league, that's the cutthroat place."

I shook my head. "Maybe we should just pull out of the festival altogether."

Angus walked into the room, trailing a silky scarf behind him. "Is my lunch ready?" He stuck his thumb in his mouth. Never mind that he'd never been a thumb sucker before this. Oh, well.

"Yep." I reached into the fridge and pulled out a plate of grapes and cheese cubes. "Sit down, buddy. I'll pour you some milk." It was my newest mission. The "Get Protein inside Angus" crusade.

"I don't think we should pull out," Duncan said. "But I do have a mind to go to Mount Zion and tell them we'd love for them to have the Boston cream pies back."

"Isn't that something to bring before the session?"

"It should be. But you know Calvin Jesters is right there in Miss Poole's back pocket. And George May is his best friend."

Man, I thought.

We Presbyterians are always so proud of our church government, but at times like this, well, I wished for a more Baptist, patriarchal kind of system. I wished Duncan had some ex cathedra kind of power, possessed blazing, intimidating eyes, a strong voice, and weak deacons. And hair swept up in a pompadour wouldn't be all bad either. "Are you willing to take a risk like that? You've always been so careful."

And he looked up at me then, his eyes peering into mine, then widening, then going back to normal. The right side of his mouth lifted a bit, and he took my hand. "I'll be okay."

"It could mean your job."

"Maybe. But I've been around the block a few times, babe. This one isn't a field they'll be willing to die on." He picked his sandwich back up. "You know, Popp, from what I can tell, this stuff has always been running under the surface in this town. Does all this really surprise you?"

"Well, no. But that makes it even worse."

"How so?"

"It's like it's expected of us to act like this."

Duncan nodded. "Well, we don't have to feed into the stereotype, do we?"

"With Miss Poole around, you just might not have a choice."

Angus sat up straight. "We always have a choice, don't we, Mama?"

I shook my head. "Sometimes we think we do, but that's pretty much all you can really say for sure." I turned toward my husband who was shaking his head at my fatalism. "Go over to Mount Zion."

"All hades will break loose," he said.

I dug my spoon into the chili. "Or all heaven will. Maybe God's going to surprise us."

Duncan laughed. "He's good at that."

"Oh yeah," I said with a nod. "Much too good for the likes of a girl like me."

Duncan shook his head. "You say the weirdest things sometimes, Poppy."

I make it a rule never to interfere in my husband's business. But how could a quick visit to Poole Point hurt? I'd go as "one of the girls" with a "Well, *you* know" attitude. Conspiratorial. A "Duncan would kill me if he found out I was here" thing.

Which was actually quite true.

Bringing Angus should provide some sort of buffer, I reasoned after lunch. So after calling Miss Poole, I told him to grab one of his little history biographies, *Molly Pitcher* or something, and wash his face and hands. A smidge of guilt crept over me, but I figured that a bit of payback was fine once in a while. After all the diapers I'd changed, the baths I'd given, the meals I'd fixed him, the social events I'd missed because everyone else was busy and I couldn't find a sitter, after all of that, he could be a warm body, reading in a chair, oblivious to the fact that he was being used as a human shield, warding off the fiery darts of Miss Magda Poole.

"Cool," Angus said from the back seat. "Her name wasn't really Molly Pitcher at all." We drove down the wooded, private lane to the end of Poole Point. The house had been sitting there for one hundred and fifty years, a quarter mile from Tweed Creek.

Magda Poole's father, a real jokester according to the townspeople, had renamed it Poole Hall when he'd bought it. Before that it had been something like Haddonhurst or Thistlethwaite or something old English, dreary, and likely to be found in a Victoria Holt or Frances Hodgeson Burnett story.

Obviously, Miss Poole had been desperately in favor of the man-made Lake Coventry idea, for the old mansion now hovered on blue waters. I heard tell that time period had been the most vulnerable in the old woman's life. She made so much money just on the real estate deals alone.

"I always thought that Molly Pitcher was her real name, Gus."

"Nope, that was her nickname from giving the soldiers water and all."

A loosely buckled lane flowed newly tarred beneath the wheels of my car. Black walnut trees on either side held hands overhead like a long square dance line of dryads. Do-si-do and a hey nonny no.

Or something like that.

Poole Point reminded me of a shrunk Tower of London, as though someone had transported it across the pond and dropped it onto the mossy lawns. Miss Poole deserved a lot of credit. The woman knew how to make the most of her heavy stone house. Trumpet vines in a broad range of animated hues clung to the stones, hiding much of the drear and attracting hummingbirds. Fruit trees placed near the corners of the building shed their final petals in perfumed flurries. It must have had a wonderful display just a couple of days ago when the grasses looked as if the tender greens of spring had suddenly been overtaken by a snowy quilt of pink and white.

And then an idea arose.

"That's it!" I snapped my fingers as the car came to a stop.

"What, Mama?"

"I'll offer to do a watercolor of Poole Point."

"Oh. Okay." Angus couldn't hide the disappointment in his voice. I wasn't about to ask what he thought I was going to say.

The door opened before we'd climbed the hewn stone steps. Miss Poole herself greeted us. "Penny! Come in! Angus, sweet pea! I was hoping you'd come, too. Ira's got Nintendo set up for you in the library."

Ira, her large, dependable servant, was actually her "gentleman's gentleman." "I know I'm a woman," Miss Poole explained the first time we'd gone to Poole Point for dinner. "But Ira served Daddy, and I can't imagine calling him anything else."

I love Ira. There he stood in his crisp suit at the back of the foyer with a huge, swirly lollipop in one hand. To my surprise he handed it to me.

"Ira! You old sweetie."

"Hey, what about me?" Angus cried.

Ira picked him up and set him on his shoulders. "Just wait until you get into the library. I've got an entire tray of goodies set up for you."

"Stellar!" the boy cried, and I felt my skin redden. We'd been studying about outer space lately. Unfortunately, Angus didn't really understand what rang truly cool and what didn't. "Stellar" sounded nerdlike, plain and simple, but I couldn't bear to tell him otherwise.

Miss Poole led me back into the conservatory that overlooked the lake. What a shame she felt obliged to run things at Highland Kirk, because other than that, I admired this old soul. She never married, and how incredibly wise was that? She lived her life completely on her own terms. And those outfits! Well, today she wore one of those long, full denim skirts, espadrilles that tied around the ankle, and an oversized, white linen shirt that came from the men's department or more probably, some tailor's shop up in New York or down in Atlanta.

The earrings, some kind of Indian head nickels hanging low down from her lobes, strung onto a silver nail with lapis lazuli and rudely carved amethysts, brushed the soft folds of her neck.

"I had Ira fix us some coffee. I'm normally a tea drinker, love that extra bit of civilization; however, when someone's a coffee drinker, well, that's that, isn't it?"

"Oh, I like tea, too."

"But you prefer coffee."

"Yes, I do."

"Well, then."

The afternoon sun warmed the conservatory, a glass room with an India-style dome. Massive planters bubbled over with ferns and fronds and palms and plants I'd never seen but looked as if one touch would draw blood. Just by walking in the room I experienced what I supposed a hot flash might feel like.

And there rested two cups of steaming hot coffee!

Concentrate on the view, Popp. That cool lake, the pines, the blue sky, how much cooler life will be once the Boston cream pies are back where they belong.

I plucked a handkerchief out of my purse and wiped my forehead. "Thanks for agreeing to see me right away, Miss Poole. And you really didn't have to go to all of this trouble."

"Oh, it's no trouble." She indicated a heavy, forged iron table and chairs in the corner that looked like they belonged in an Italian garden.

We sat down.

"Now, what's this about? Or are you here to apologize for being late to the meeting the other night?"

"Well, no. I—"

"You know, it makes our church look bad when someone is late like that. Especially to a community function."

"Actually—"

"Naturally, I made apologies to the food committee the next day. I told them you'd been a bit frazzled lately, what with having to deal with that husband of yours and all, day after day."

"Miss Poole, please." I felt heat not only from the outside in now, but from the inside out. Sweat shellacked my back, slicking up the smooth surface beneath my shirt. "I've come to talk about the Boston cream pies."

"Oh, that!" The maven waved a hand. "It's all been taken care of."

"You mean with the ladies of Mount Zion?"

"Who cares what they think? They're not even a mainline denomination."

"Well, they are sisters in Christ."

"Oh, pah! The truth is, Highland Kirk had Boston cream pies years ago when we called the festival May Days in Mount Oak. They were the ones that stole it in the first place."

"But that was twenty-five years ago, wasn't it?"

"Which makes it high time we get it back!"

"But Miss Poole—"

"No, Penny. It's time to have it back! Besides you were the one who started this whole thing anyway."

Whoa.… I decided to try a different tack. "Well, what about our Christian testimony with the townspeople?"

"Oh, come on, Penny."

"I don't know. Maybe it's time we started treating each other with a little more respect."

"That's all well and good, my dear. But you're new to this town. You have no idea how far this all goes back."

I took a sip of my coffee. "Which just goes to show that maybe it's time for it to stop."

"I don't think that's possible."

"It is if you want it to be."

"Well, maybe I enjoy a bit of controversy."

I sighed, trying to find a new angle. Not that it would matter. So be it then. Duncan could just go on over to the Mount Zioners, give them back the Boston cream pies and live to rue the day. So be it. He was on his own. "All right then. Just trying to keep the peace."

"That's not your job, Penny."

I didn't like Miss Poole at all right now.

"Shall we talk about something else?" the elderly lady asked.

"I just have one question. What started all of this dissention, or doesn't anybody know?"

"Oh, that's easy to answer! It was the annual all-church Christmas concert back in 1968."

"What all-church Christmas concert?"

"Precisely. It doesn't exist anymore because no one could agree on what to sing. Some people thought anything written after 1950 was sinful; others wanted to sing Gaither music; and one man had written a song that was to be accompanied by electric guitars of all things. Well, you can just imagine."

"Unfortunately, I can. When it comes to Christians and their music…"

"Indeed. And then church splits always fuel the fire, troublemakers leaving and disbursing into existing churches or starting their own, which immediately puts them at odds with the original congregation. It's quite complicated, Penny."

"There's something to be said for the parish system, I guess."

"It's certainly easier that way," Miss Poole agreed.

I sipped my coffee. "No wonder the town doesn't want us involved."

Miss Poole smirked. "Oh, please! They fight, too. They just expect better of us."

"And so they should. Don't you think?"

"Maybe, but we are, after all, only human."

Christians aren't perfect, just forgiven. Like that holds any water with the nonbeliever. Like that's a viable "out," a worthy excuse for sin.

Magda Poole reached over and patted my hand. "I thought you might be proud of me, for giving in about the window and all."

"I hate to admit it, but it's nice to see the lake."

Miss Poole sniffed in through her nose. "You know, I was very instrumental in the lake being there in the first place."

"So I've heard. We sure do enjoy it."

"Good. And the tourist business has been wonderful for the town."

"Yes, it has."

I had a million questions I wanted to ask this woman. Where did she go to school? Why had she never married? What did she do out here all day, just her and Ira? Did she have any other family? Was she ever lonely?

"Penny?"

"Yes?"

"I gave in on the window and the songbooks, too. It was a good start. Please, I need to have those Boston cream pies."

"But why?"

Magda Poole's shuttered face told me I'd never know the answer to that one.

Later that day, I found that Duncan had failed to make it over to the Mount Zion church. What a relief!

Dinner conversation was interesting. Robbie actually graced the table with his jovial presence. A good thing because Angus was now steeped in *Benjamin Franklin, Man of Science, Man of Letters* and wouldn't be much good for this meal's discourse.

He talked about his newest girlfriend, a freshman at the community college named Ashley. I didn't feel a speck of worry. Robbie had yet to truly fall in love.

And then the Boston cream pie topic rolled around.

"I agree with Mom." Robbie forked pork barbecue into his mouth. "Besides, Miss Poole is one of your members, Dad. Don't you have more of a responsibility to minister to her, rather than to the town?"

"But she gives Highland a bad name, Rob," Duncan said.

I piped in. "I think she's really lonely. How long has her father been dead?"

"Twenty-five years or so," Duncan answered.

Robbie snickered. "We'll probably find out that Boston cream pie was his favorite dessert, and in his memory she wants to finally get it back to Highland."

I threw a roll at him. "Or, we'll find out she's just a controlling biddy who wants to stir up trouble!"

Even Duncan chuckled. "Maybe you're right. I've been fighting with this woman for three years, and it hasn't done a thing. Maybe I need to actually be her pastor."

"It's what you're best at, Dad." Robbie devoured the coleslaw.

I wasn't about to argue with his comment about his father. "Just turn on that Fraser charm." I ran a finger down the back of his hand.

Duncan blushed.

"Just like that," I said, thinking him more attractive just then than he'd been in weeks. Man. It wasn't even Monday. I loved it when he blushed.

Jody called me in Outer Banks.

"What did I do?" he asked.

"You breathed," I said. "That's all it took."

"I don't believe that, Poppy. You care about me; you know you do." His voice held a youthful nervousness, but more virile. "It wasn't about the sex for me."

"Well, it was for me."

"You're lying."

Oh, I could picture him there on the other end of the line. "Where are you?" I said to change the subject for just a minute.

"I'm in your driveway."

I groaned. *"You've got to get out of there, Jody."*

"Don't worry. I just came to adjust the panels on the refrigerator. Mr. Fraser called and said they'd come loose."

Mr. Fraser.

I breathed in deeply. *"Okay. Look, I'm sorry I left without talking to you. I should have called."*

"I can't stop thinking about you."

I wanted to laugh. So people really said that? I'd thought it was only in movies. *"I could say the same thing, but it's probably not like you're doing."*

He coughed. *"You're feeling guilty. Well, so am I."*

"You should."

"Maybe you were right to go away."

"You're a beautiful young man, Jody. You could have any young woman you want."

"But you're the one I love."

Help me, Lord. I'm trying to do the right thing here. *"You don't love me."*

"I do. You're so pretty. And you do such beautiful artwork. And you're nice, Poppy. How many twenty-two-year-old girls are nice?"

"I'm not nice. I had an affair."

He stayed silent.

"I'll be gone all summer," I said.

He sucked in his breath loudly. *"So that's just it?"*

"Yes."

Silence.

"What will you do?" I asked, expecting some pat *"Oh, don't act like you care what happens to me,"* response, but instead...

"I'll keep working." Yes, he was still a young man of Irish-Catholic descent. And I was the mother figure. He wouldn't sass me back.

"So this is it then?" he asked. *"Forever?"*

"Oh, Jody. Don't you get it? I've got children, a husband—"

"Who's never home. If I was your husband, I'd never let you out of my sight!"

"With good reason," I snapped back. "If I cheated on Duncan, I'd cheat on you, too."

"No!" he wailed like a wounded animal. "You wouldn't. It was different with us."

"How do I know that?"

"Did you ever love me, Poppy. At all? Even just a little."

I remained silent.

He cleared his throat, unable to hide his pain. "Answer the question, and I'll stay away from you."

My gosh, how could I have used this poor young man like I did? How could I cast him aside so easily as if he had been nothing more than an amusing game?

"Yes."

I was lying, but sometimes a woman forces herself to lie. For the good of all concerned.

So Duncan agreed to let the Boston cream pies rest where they were. "I really liked doing steak-on-a-stick," he said, as he climbed into bed that night. "I really miss our big charcoal pit in Maryland."

"Me, too." I remembered all the parties we'd thrown when we first moved in, all the kids splashing in the pool, music playing on the unbelievably boss sound system. Underwater speakers even.

"Now who in the world needs underwater speakers?" I said out loud.

Our eyes met, and we laughed like fools.

Duncan took me into his arms, even though it was Thursday.

Twenty

he 2 P.M. sunshine warmed our conversation spot in the front bow window. Chris chose this exact place for her first official coming out. Breakfast at Bill D's and coffee at Java Jane's at 6 A.M. was one thing, but an afternoon outing deserved a different tactic.

"I really want to go up to Hopkins soon, Poppy. According to the police report, there was another boy who climbed the tower, too. I want to talk to him. The fraternity denies having anything to do with it. But I just can't believe that."

"Still want me to go with you?"

Chris nodded, tucking some hair behind her ear. The same ear hadn't been impaled by an earring in months.

"I'm sure Daddy and Mother would be glad to watch Angus for a couple of days."

"That'd be good."

"After Crazy Days, though, okay?" I asked, then downed the last sip of my Guatemalan, wincing.

"That's fine."

I stood to my feet. "I'll be right back."

I walked up to the counter for a refill. Ellen sure was dressed up today. I heard she and the town's only divorce lawyer had been spending time together. Just above a pair of ivory and linen spectator pumps swirled a full skirt of fine linen, the good stuff, and those drop earrings looked like real aquamarines.

I handed over my cup. "You guys still going to do the coffee and tea stand at the festival?"

Ellen nodded, but she rolled her hazel eyes dramatically. "We're pretty much stuck. We've decided that this is going to be the last year we involve ourselves in such a circus, though."

"Why?" I felt obligated to feign oblivion. *The Proper Christian Ladies' Handbook,* chapter 6, "Dealing with Other Women Not of the Faith."

Ellen flung an errant, coiled auburn lock back over her shoulder. "I'm afraid the answer might be offensive to you, so I'll decline if you don't mind." Her tone, chilled around the edges like Lake Coventry on a mid-January day, caused me to realize that both Ellen and Margaret had been a bit standoffish lately. Ever since that horrible meeting Duncan and I had dubbed, "The Boston Cream Pie Massacre."

"It's the Boston cream pie thing, isn't it?"

"That's just part of it."

I felt myself blush, and my mouth tightened in the same way it did when I posed for a picture. My nostrils went horsy as well. "I'll have to admit, it's all gotten a little out of hand."

Margaret walked out from the back of the store. "You talking about Crazy Days?"

"Yeah," I said. "Just for the record, I thought I was doing the Mount Zion ladies a favor by taking on the Boston cream pies."

Ellen snorted. "Oh, please, Poppy. That's just the tip of the iceberg, and you know it. Do you think we really care who it was that did what?"

I felt stupid and petty. Maybe that *Proper Christian Ladies' Handbook* was right about the oblivion thing. I should have taken it further obviously. "I guess not."

Margaret opened the small fridge beneath the counter and leaned down on her haunches. "I think the churches should just take it over completely if you ask me. We could have our own thing in June."

"I agree," Ellen said. "If the churches in this community got along even half as well as the business community, we'd be having a lovely time of it."

I took the coffee from off of the counter and walked away. Ellen was wrong. The businesses made an art of stealing customers from one another. But why argue? People saw things as they saw things, and you could do nothing to make them look at life through your own glasses.

And there sat Chris, alone in the window. A real live person with real live pain, bigger than a May festival and Boston cream pies. They were all over town, too, people just like her. And here we all were, worried about some stupid, stupid booth. What are we doing here on this earth? People are hurting, dying inside and out, and we are worried about desserts, hymnbooks, windows, service times, drums, dramas, and drachmas. Shame on us. Shame on me. Visit the widows and the fatherless in their afflictions. Love your neighbor as yourself. Do good unto those that hate you. To him who knows to do good and doeth it not, to him it is sin. In as much as you've done it to the least of these, you've done it unto Me. Pray without ceasing. Give thanks in all things for this is the will of God in Christ Jesus concerning you. Concerning me.

The old hymn writer knew the truth about trusting and obeying.

There's no other way.

The plate glass window was egged again, and this time the vandals added flour to the recipe. I had no idea how they managed such a feat, especially at the upper portions of the window, but they'd done a great job. You had to admire their thoroughness, if nothing else. We hurried to get it down before it became a soufflé worthy of the *Guinness Book of World Records*.

"We used a hose with the nozzle turned onto the thinnest stream. Just shot that stuff right off of there," I told the church ladies that Monday night.

All of them had come. India and Joanna arrived first via ladybug. Charmaine picked up Sunny on the way, and Chris rode with me in the Subaru. After fried chicken with rice and gravy, Sunny's squash casserole, and my cucumber salad, Mildred sat us all down at the dining room table for shortcake with blueberries and real whipped cream. Sweet tea, too.

"I wonder who's doing it?" Joanna asked, already on her second round of dessert. India volunteered the fact that the woman ran five to seven miles a day. *Oh, brother,* I thought. *Women like this make me sick. And pass that whipped cream while you're at it.*

"I'm not sure, but if they squeeze chocolate glaze up there next time, I'll know for sure it has something to do with those Boston cream pies."

We yakked the whole time we ate. Well, everyone ate but Charmaine who sat there with a Java Jane's triple Red-Eye, clicking her retainer, talking about vices. "You know caffeine is a wonderful thing! I just been drinking these Red-Eyes like crazy lately, and boy, do I get stuff done now. I'm not in bed until three, and since Harlan gets the kids off to school, I'll tell you, it's just been a lifesaver! I've lost two pounds, too."

I wanted to tell her I found them and stuck them on my tummy in case she decided she wanted them back, but stayed quiet.

Joanna crossed her legs and said in an innocent voice, "Must be tough having to parade yourself before the masses each week like you do."

Charmaine pasted her TV smile on. "Oh, you'd be surprised, Joanna. It's not all about the singing and the clothes."

"I don't know. I've watched your show. It's *very* entertaining."

Chris rolled her eyes at me in disgust just as carnal me thought the conversation was getting interesting. Chris was miles closer to God than I would ever be until I got to heaven and had, say, about two whole crowns to cast at His feet because my attitude has always been so horrible.

Charmaine kept her cool. "You should read some of the letters I get. Some from the dearest people all over the country. Down-home types mostly."

"But you're so smooth on camera. And your production level is so high, not 'down-home' at all really."

Charmaine sat up straight, her green eyes deepening. "Well, no matter where they live, people expect a certain level of professionalism on TV. Cable TV made everybody more sophisticated along those lines."

"Didn't you all just move to town, Joanna?" I interrupted, trying to save the gathering according to chapter 21 of the *Handbook,* "Rules of Conversation at All Female Gatherings," the part that says insinuations should be frowned upon.

"Don't change the subject, Poppy, please." Charmaine wiped her mouth and set down her napkin. Her tone sounded weary, soft, and hurt.

"I'm so tired of all the veiled accusations I've been buried with ever since the mideighties, but I guess I can only set my own record straight. Joanna, honey, my life is an open book. Come take a look at our financial records any time you'd like. Right now, if you want."

I couldn't blame Charmaine for being defensive.

"That won't be necessary. So why do you do it then? The fame?"

Give it up, lady! For pity's sake!

But Charmaine said, "I sing to folks who need a song, who might have lost their own somewheres along the way. I encourage people who need a little hand to help them get back on their feet, and I try my hardest to show them Jesus. Oh, I know I get in the way sometimes, like we all do, but I love the people I minister to. And I'll tell you another thing. They don't have to invite me into their home every week, but when they do, I just count it an honor to be there."

I waited a few seconds for Joanna to respond, but nothing came from between her earth-colored lips.

Mildred said, "Do you sing, Joanna?"

"Not really. I wasn't raised in the church."

"Music is God's gift to His people. It touches a spot that nothing else can reach, brightens corners so dark the person hearing might not have even known they existed within her own heart until a song comes in."

Sunny nodded. "His throne room is filled with singing. I think that's what I'm looking forward to about heaven the most. Hearing the angels sing."

Chrissy reached for my hand, and we squeezed.

"Well, ladies, let's petition that throne." Mildred wiped her mouth. "Prayer is another divine gift. And this whole town needs a good praying over if you ask me."

"Can we start to add other prayer requests then?" Sunny asked.

"Fine by me." Chris gathered up plates. "In fact, it would be good not to have to concentrate on my own troubles every once in a while."

"Well, amen to that, Christine. 'Bear one another's burdens and so fulfill the law of Christ,'" Mildred quoted, breaking into the song "'Be not dismayed whate'er betide.'"

The covering of prayer that was about to descend was something we all needed desperately.

Duncan came home early the next night with a pound of backfin and a pint of coleslaw.

He busied himself crumbling the heel of a loaf of bread into one of the pottery bowls I had made during my master's work. "Well, I smoothed things over at Mount Zion," he said.

"You didn't give them the Boston cream pies back, did you?"

"No. But I met with the woman in charge of Mount Zion's booth. I think she was at the meeting."

"The don?"

"Popp!"

"Sorry." I was still angry about the way I'd been singled out at the meeting by that lady.

"Yes. Her name's Betty."

"I know. So what happened?"

"I told her we were sorry about the misunderstanding. That we were just trying to be nice."

"Good. What did she say?"

"Oh, she went on and on about 'that Miss Poole who thinks she can just run roughshod over the entire town' and all. Would you get me a couple of eggs and the mayonnaise?"

"Sure. Well, it sounds as if there's history between the two."

Finished crumbling the bread, Duncan dumped the crabmeat into the bowl. "Could be. Magda's never cared about having friends, though. It might just be animosity from afar on the part of Betty."

I handed him the eggs and the mayo. "I guess. Jealousy maybe, too. Miss Poole is so stinkin' rich. So, do you think the mess has blown over?"

"No, the businesses are just downright sick of us."

"You should have heard the conversation I had with Ellen and Margaret over at Java Jane's. They wanted to divide the festival next year in two. I don't blame them. Sunny's church and the stricter Bible churches have decided to have their own little festival, right across the street from the town square in the municipal parking lot." I poured myself a cup of coffee and sat down at the table to watch Duncan cook. The strains of "If I Only Had a Brain" filtered in from the living room.

"'Please be patient, God is not finished with me yet,'" I quoted the familiar saying, the words less tasty than a dried out turkey sandwich with no butter or mayonnaise.

"Bumper stickers create more problems than they solve."

"Well, you'll never see one on my car. Not with the way I drive."

Duncan shook a little Old Bay Seasoning into the bowl. "It's more than that, though, don't you think? I mean, the other day I saw a T-shirt that said, 'This Blood's for You.'"

"That's awful."

"I know, taking a beer slogan and inserting the precious blood of the spotless Lamb of God. No wonder nonbelievers don't take us seriously. If we don't take something so beautiful seriously, if we hold no respect for it, no awe, why should they?" He chopped up fresh parsley and chives.

I took a sip of my drink. "Yeah, I know."

Duncan started to gently blend the delicate crab mixture with a wooden spoon. I watched his hands.

"I really am glad God isn't finished with me yet, though."

"What do you mean, babe? Other than the obvious."

"I'm not one of those naturally spiritual people, Duncan." I set down my cup and reached across the hoosier for the mail. I needed something to hide behind. "I just don't like to do the things Christians are supposed to do. I hardly ever pick up my Bible. I only think about praying when I climb into bed at night, and by then I'm so tired. And even when there's something big I need to pray about, I can't get out of bed and get onto my knees."

No bills today. Just a couple of circulars and a card from Mother. I'd better go to the store tonight and buy a Mother's Day card. "It shouldn't be like this, should it? What's wrong with me?"

"What about the stuff you do at church?"

"It feels like a chore."

"I thought so. I'm glad you felt you could tell the truth." He smiled, set the bowl down on the table, and sat down next to me. His hands worked quickly as he formed the crab cakes. "It's a battle, Popp. It really is. It's why they're called disciplines."

"But it's pretty basic, isn't it? Shouldn't a Christian really love to be in the Bible and be praying and everything? Should it be this much of a struggle if God really lives inside of you?"

"Everybody struggles, Popp. God didn't fool us in telling us what we were getting ourselves into. Denying yourself and taking up your cross was never meant to be an easy task."

"I know. But shouldn't there be some satisfaction in the doing?"

He wiped his hands on a tea towel and reached for my hand. "Poppy, all our works are as filthy rags."

"I know that. My head knows that. But I look at myself and see someone falling down day after day after day. I don't have the strength to get up anymore, Duncan."

"Not on your own, babe."

"But do you know how many times I've prayed that God would give me a thirst for Him?"

"I know how that is. I was that way for years."

"Really?"

"Yeah. And I'll tell you another thing. I've already seen a change in you since you've been praying with those ladies. God reveals Himself in a lot of ways, Poppy. He's not limited to the Bible in drawing us closer to Him."

"Mildred and Charmaine have taught me a lot. Chris, too."

"Then rest in that now."

"I was hoping it would get easier as I got older. Isn't it supposed to?"

Duncan resumed forming the cakes, his hands slimy with the concoction. "Maybe. If there's something that's come between you and God, it can make it more difficult."

But I had to wonder if Jesus really lived inside of me at all. "Would it be that hard for God to send me even a teaspoon of desire?"

The next morning, Duncan turned on the lamp at five o'clock, half an hour before I left for my walk.

I blinked against the thick, intrusive light. "What are you doing, Duncan?"

"Come on. I timed the coffeepot last night. It should be ready."

"But it's only five o'clock."

"It's French Roast," he said proudly.

I said nothing. French Roast. He must have bought it at the IGA when he went out to buy the Mother's Day cards last night. Angus and I had fallen asleep in front of the TV. We had been watching a show about a bear family with a kindhearted yet bumbling father, an overbearing mother, a bratty daughter, and a normal son.

Well.

Duncan was already sliding into his running shorts and an old T-shirt. "Just come into the kitchen, all right?"

I threw back my sheet and yanked on my walking clothes. Why this togetherness thing this morning? Maybe he worried I was going off the deep end. And just how did one go off the deep end anyway? Didn't one go into the deep end? Wouldn't that be a better way to say it? Water covering the head and all. No air. Trying to swim farther than one could actually swim. Now that made much more sense.

As I expected, he had already poured my coffee, leaving it black while he lightened and sweetened his own. His Bible lay open on the hoosier table.

I sat down and sipped my coffee. "So we're going to try and study together again?" We'd been down this path at least ten times in the past six years.

"I'm hoping if we keep trying one day we'll get it." He flipped the fragile pages. "Where do you want to read?"

"The book of Acts."

"Okay."

I reached out and touched his gray hair, just above the nape of his neck. "What if we don't ever get it?"

He took off his glasses and leaned in close to me. "Poppy, to be honest, sometimes I wonder if we ever will. But we can't stop trying."

I nodded. "Yeah."

If we stopped trying on everything, we could just kiss Paisley goodbye.

Twenty-one

M iss Mildred and I spent the morning over at the square setting up for the Crazy Days of May. It wasn't the happy-go-lucky experience it used to be. Tension ran between the participants like airborne rivers of black molasses, sticky and bitter. Smiles remained few. However, the ladies of Mount Zion made sure they came over to Highland Kirk's booth. We all hugged and, according to chapter 8 of *The Handbook,* "Reconciliation," subheading "Reconciliation with a Sister in Christ," did lots of nodding and hand waving, as if the vibrations that dented the air from such activity helped to nudge away all the hard feelings.

And actually it did.

Christianity really worked if one followed it like it was meant to be followed. And that had nothing to do with *The Ladies' Handbook.*

We decided to put our booths side by side because, as one Mount Zion lady put it, "We know how to sell a cream pie or two."

Miss Poole didn't show up. An odd occurrence because normally she stood out there directing Ira, Duncan, and the elders like an Egyptian overseer. Tow that line. Crack that whip. Hear and obey. So let it be written, so let it be done.

The Impala was in for an oil change, so I had picked up Miss Mildred who had agreed to help Hallelujah! Baptist set up their fried chicken operation. "I also need to make sure those workmen drape the bandstand just right," she said. Poor fellows. They won't know what hit them.

An attitude of disdain pulsated over from the business owners' camp. The proprietors had truly had enough. I figured it would be years before we could completely repair the damage. The pastors looked sheepish, and the business owners looked miffed, for even though the rift between Mount Zion and Highland seemed to be filling up with goodwill, plenty of PCA Presbyterians walked by Methodists with their noses in the air.

Charmaine ran around in a pair of walking shorts and saddle shoes like some frantic angel of goodwill. Hey, hey, hey. Y'all this, y'all that. And won't everybody just try to be nice? India arranged duckies in a square pond at the Episcopal's booth, a headset on her ears and her hands doing music director type dips and swirls. Especially endearing with a duckie in hand.

Joanna, the traitor, acted like Miss Businesswoman instead of Mrs. Minister's Wife, and gave me a tight little smile. Maybe I really *wasn't* saved the way I judged her for being just like I was back in Baltimore. But I felt in my heart that my faith was real. Would I be so worried about it if it wasn't?

I couldn't figure out why I felt so threatened by Joanna anyway. Why did she even bother coming to the prayer meetings if all she wanted to do was prick at us? It felt like having a well-dressed Paisley there, doing her best to make things uncomfortable for everybody. What was her gig? And poor Charmaine!

Sunny had to work, so I watched her husband, Marc Tipton, set up a table across the street. Oak Grove Baptist Bible, fundamental, Bible-believing, King James Version only, went about their business quietly. "And it's for the best," Sunny had told me on the phone the day before. "After all, they sell beer there. And Madame Poliarza sets up a palm reading booth, so, that being witchcraft and all, well, thus and so."

But they set up their table with fresh flowers and gave away ice cold Coca-Colas and salvation tracts to all the workers from the festival. It was hard to fault for long anyone who gave away ice cold Coca-Colas. Although I have to agree with Duncan. How respectful is it to print up "Things Go Better with Christ"? There's that verse in the Bible that says at the name of Jesus every knee will bow and every tongue will confess.

Diminishing the name above all names to a soda pop slogan doesn't sit well with my soul.

I had just finished lettering the pricing signs when Mildred ran up, her high heels sinking into the sod. "Can you give me a ride over to church, Penelope."

"Is something wrong?"

"Oh yeah. It's the pastor's wife. She's in the church basement, and she can't stop crying."

"Hold on. Let me get my purse. Where's her husband?"

"He's there. He's the one who called the booth. He doesn't know what to do which is probably the root of the problem."

We hurried to the car, past face painting, helium balloons, silversmiths, weavers, pipe makers, and funnel cakes.

I yanked open my door. "I always thought working in a Fotomat wouldn't be a bad gig. No pressure."

She looked at me over the roof of the car. "As if you'd ever be satisfied with that, Penelope Huebner."

"Oh, I would. Or at least I'd like to give it a try sometime. But we'd still have church," I said, getting in.

Mildred nodded as I turned the key and threw the car into reverse. "You got that right."

"What's your pastor's wife's name, Miss Mildred?"

"Saundra Phelps."

It's so easy to think of pastors' wives as just the pastor's wife. No real identity of her own. In my few short years as one, I couldn't begin to figure how many times I've heard, "Oh, you must be the pastor's wife!"

"She can't handle the position," Mildred said. "Poor baby. Hiding behind those big hats and fancy Sunday dresses."

"You seemed pretty harsh on her before."

We drove in silence. Guess I'd said too much. But when we pulled into the lot, Mildred said, "Let's pray, Penelope."

"Lord Jesus, forgive me. Forgive me for doing to Saundra what I thought I'd never do. I forgot how hard it is. Help me to help her. In Jesus' name, amen."

"Amen," I whispered as I pulled into the parking lot surrounding the small, green, framed church building.

"Miss Mildred?" I got out of the car.

"Yes, Penelope?" She did the same.

"It's hard to play the role when you can't begin to picture yourself in the role."

She nodded. "I've got to remember that. Jesse David was my life, Penelope. Serving the Lord with him, well, I always felt I'd been created to do just that." She smiled sadly. "We'd better get in there."

She walked me across the brown-carpeted lobby to the staircase leading to the basement. "Is Herman still digging up your lawn?"

"He is. I'm about ready to kill him."

"Why don't you put a stop to it?"

"Keeps him out of my hair. He's bugging me to marry him now." Mildred laid a hand on the railing. "As if I'm going to give up my freedom to a man who digs holes in my lawn looking for gold."

"A true gold digger!"

"He plays the lottery, too. But what I want to know is why anybody would hand over his hard-earned money to the government when he knows he's not going to win big?"

We walked through the recreation hall back to one of the two Sunday school classrooms, where the sobs of Saundra Phelps awaited. My heart broke.

"How old is she?" I asked.

"Twenty-two."

"Oh, wow."

"I know. Poor baby."

We entered the small, particleboard-paneled room, and Pastor Phelps stood to his feet. "Thank the Lord you're here." Heavyset and dressed in a neatly pressed suit, the man wore a mixed expression of sadness and panic. Beside his wife sat two hard-sided suitcases. He cast a suspicious eye on me.

"This is Mrs. Fraser." Mildred introduced me. "Her husband is the pastor over at the little Presbyterian church down Tweed Road."

His eyes cleared immediately, and Saundra looked up from where she sat at a small, yellow, toddler table. She swallowed her tears.

Mildred sat down next to her. "Now what's this all about, baby?"

"I can't take the pressure any more, Mother LaRue." And she began to whimper now. My heart broke for her.

"What happened?" Mildred asked the pastor.

He shook his head and shrugged. "We were sitting at lunch going over this week's schedule, and all of a sudden she burst into tears and ran into the bedroom, pulling out suitcases and throwing her clothes inside."

"I can't do this anymore!" Saundra cried out. "I'm not perfect. I'm scared at the way they watch everything I do. I want to go back home to Pennsylvania!"

Mildred stood to her feet. "Pastor Phelps, I'd like Saundra to come to the farm with me for a few days. Just for some refreshment."

"What will the church people say?" Saundra sniffed.

"It doesn't matter, punkin," Pastor Phelps said. "You go on home with Mother LaRue. I'll take care of everything."

Now that was definitely a step in the right direction. I carried Saundra's suitcases to my trunk and got her situated comfortably in the backseat. "You're a beautiful woman," I told her with a smile. "They're lucky to have you here."

I didn't really know if that was the truth or not, but I figured it couldn't hurt. People tend to rise to loving expectations that are placed on them, or they freak-out. Hopefully, Saundra wouldn't continue to freak-out. Her perfect toffee complexion shone through the cried-off makeup, and though her eyes crackled with bloodshot lines, I could see their loveliness.

"Miss Mildred will take good care of you, Saundra," I reassured her. "She takes good care of me. So you said you were from Pennsylvania? Where in Pennsylvania?"

"Oxford."

"That's a wonderful little town! A friend of mine from college lives there."

And then I started asking all sorts of questions, surprised at how interested I was in Saundra Phelps's life. She had given up a lot to marry her husband. Miss Mildred would make sure she didn't throw it all away.

❦

I clicked off the light in the church kitchen at 3 A.M. Five hundred minia-
ture Boston cream pies nestled in appropriately sized, baby blue boxes tied
with white satin ribbon. I had to admit it, Miss Poole knew what she was
doing. These little treasures would be snatched up quickly, and we kept
the price the same as the Mount Zioners had charged the year before
though they'd used clear plastic, salad bar style containers.

I told Miss Mildred that when the Mount Zion ladies had realized for
the first time in twenty-five years that the May festival didn't have to mean
an all-nighter the night before the festival, they actually thanked us. I'd figured they were all at home sleeping like kittens. They'd be chipper in the
morning while we Highland Kirk women dragged ourselves over in the
blue smocks with white trim that Miss Poole had ordered for us.

"We'll use them year after year!" she proclaimed as she handed them
out around midnight. And then Ira came in with a silver urn of hot chocolate.

See, there you go. It was things like this that made Magda Poole
impossible to understand.

Well, the booth had been readied as much as possible, and the festival didn't begin until 10 A.M., so I could sleep until eight.

Bercie Barnhouse threw on her sweater and gave me a little kiss on the
cheek. "I thank God for you every night, Poppy. You've been so good for
this church."

While I stood there in shock, Bercie sped her little BMW out of the
parking lot.

I made sure the basement door was locked tight, then walked home.

Preacher's wife.

Always the last to leave.

When the Mount Zion Ladies saw us unloading the classy little boxes of
cake, they just threw *The Proper Christian Ladies' Handbook* right out the
window! I watched the skin of their faces creep from white to pink.

Betty cast a tight smile in my direction and continued threading pounded, marinated flank steak on a stick. The charcoal grills clouded the air, and the smell almost made me forget I'd eaten three Pop Tarts for breakfast.

Well, Highland had never marinated our flank steak so thoroughly, I wanted to yell over, to make them feel better. But as tired as I felt, I could only think about the merits of bringing a cot to the booth. Maybe next year.

If I even stayed around Mount Oak next year. After all, this was Robbie's last summer home, and half the stash belonged to me if I wanted to force the issue. I'd decided against going out West. With Robbie seriously considering St. Andrews in Scotland, it would be best to stay on the East Coast. New York City still placed number one in the running. And with Paisley in Boston...

I didn't even want to think about what Christmas would be like if I left.

My mind felt the battle raging more and more these days. Things were going so well with Duncan, growing my shame larger and deeper. I tried to remind myself it hadn't been *this* Duncan I had cheated on. It was another Duncan. And I had been another Poppy. Right?

At eleven-thirty the Star Spangled Jammers began a slow sizzle. I waved to Miss Mildred who'd just begun a slow, sultry version of "Orange-Colored Sky," singing about "walking along" and "minding my business." Ha! Miss Mildred drove everywhere and knew nothing about minding her own business, thank God, and I literally meant that.

Earlier that day when she arrived via a newly tuned Iguanamobile, I asked, "How's Saundra today?"

"Got a good night's sleep last night, but to be honest, Penelope, I think she's depressed. Honest to goodness depressed. Do you know her father is a judge? Can you imagine leaving that for Mount Oak?"

The mere thought of it depressed me, too.

"She's a sweetie pie, though. We ate a nice breakfast together this morning, and she insisted on doing the dishes while I got ready to sing. I think there's hope for her."

"Good."

And the crowds began to descend, pouring through the makeshift byways like corpuscles through a vein. One guy tried to haggle me down on the price of our pies. "I'll buy in bulk," he said.

I smiled. "Five dollars is a bargain no matter how many you buy."

The Mount Zioners had a line ten yards long. Maybe that would succor their anguish over our boxes. I hoped so. But tension seemed to string from booth to booth, and when the Star Spangled Jammers began tuning, I think we all breathed a sigh of relief. I hoped they would play loud, loud, loud.

At 12:30 a thick storm front cartwheeled across the sky. Ebony clouds bubbled and churned, covering the sun. Everyone took cover from the deluge. Hailstones shredded signs, while an almost horizontal rain soaked the booths and what wares couldn't be taken under cover soon enough. We ran to our cars, to stores in the town square, to any place with a roof. Many of the visitors just got into their cars and drove off.

At 4:30 the town square lay still and deserted.

At 5:45 the sun came back out and so did the booth workers, tending to the needs of the few die-hard customers that remained. Mostly other festival workers.

By 8:00 disassembled booths lay in stacks, and people gathered in clumps drinking cold cans of Coke from Sunny's church.

Duncan came up behind me, then put an arm around me. "Look at the groups. Dollars and Collars."

"And ne'er the twain shall meet. Why is it that way, Duncan?"

He shook his head sadly and kissed me atop my head. "I guess it's always been like this."

But I had to wonder why. It wasn't like the days of early Christianity where you either were a Christian or you sat in the coliseum and laughed and pointed while lions devoured those of the new faith.

What had gone wrong? Whatever happened to doing justice, loving mercy, and walking humbly with your God?

I kissed Duncan back, and he walked me to my car.

I drove toward the church, the back of my car filled with blue boxes tied up with pretty white satin ribbon. There had been time to sell only a hundred of them. Too bad I hadn't taken "bulk man" up on his offer.

The next day, Sunday, all churches reported their lowest attendance in the past ten years. The slick advertising banners came down on Monday, damaged from the storm and all.

Monday afternoon I wept deeply in my studio. I didn't know why. It was shameful, the way we'd carried on, I guessed. But I felt as though I could never again converse with Ellen and Margaret the way I'd done before.

All in the name of Jesus.

I ran into Charmaine at Java Jane's on Monday. It seems we both needed a caffeine bolster for our afternoon errands.

"I hate Mondays," she said. "There's so much running around to do after the weekend."

"I know what you mean."

I ordered a triple Red-Eye right along with her. "You got time to sit for a couple of minutes?"

"Sure."

"Angus!" I called, and he looked up from one of the comfy chairs where he sat reading *Harriet Tubman and the Underground Railroad*. "You want a drink? One of those blender things?"

"Okay."

I ordered one and turned to Charmaine. "So what do you think about Crazy Days?"

"I'd say God sure had something to say with the way He closed it down."

"What?"

Charmaine's mouth dropped open. "Oh, Poppy. You didn't see that?"

"Well, I just thought it was a storm coming through."

"And I thought you were a Presbyterian."

"Well, I am, but I don't see what that has to do with it." Actually, I did. But I really didn't want to admit that just then. I'm not a real doctrinal powerhouse.

She smiled. "I thought it was His way of saying He's sick of all this, too."

"Wow. You *really* think so?"

"How could I not?"

I shrugged, and we took our drinks from Ellen who didn't say anything but a quick, "Thanks." We sat in the conversational grouping Angus had chosen.

"I'll have to ask Duncan what he thinks. Does Harlan think that, too?"

"Don't know. Didn't ask." She took a sip. "Ahh. These are just so good."

I stabbed a straw through the lid of Angus's drink and handed it to him.

"And you know, Poppy, God used weather all the time in the Bible."

"At least He didn't send a cataclysmic flood."

"See? I think He's giving us a chance to make things right."

"If that's possible." Charmaine opened her mouth, and I quickly said, "I know, I know. All things are possible with God."

She patted my thigh. "You might try believing that. It may even help you accept Duncan's vocation."

"Oh, believe me, Duncan even being in the ministry proves that verse."

"You left a lot behind, didn't you?"

I nodded.

"Oh, honey. Maybe it's time to get rid of them for good."

Twenty-two

The drive to Baltimore proved colorful and peaceful. Chris fell asleep, and I listened to a CD I borrowed from Duncan. I decided to give Christian music an honest to goodness try. He suggested Michael Card. "You'll like the depth, Popp."

Har! Duncan definitely gave me more credit than I deserved with that one!

Beside me, Chris's face glowed pink and gold in the sunlight, her hair almost white it shone so blond. Even in sleep, a sadness lay over her features like sweat on a toddler. Surely not unnatural, but provided by an unusually exerting circumstance.

Poor Chris.

I stole glance after glance as we traveled Interstate 95. I wouldn't trade places with her for anything. Not anymore. Not with Josh gone and all. I had always said that, though, in my mind. Chris couldn't even draw a flower that didn't have one stem, loopy petals, and two spiky leaves coming out from the bottom. But now, it all seemed to materialize with a startling clarity like a March sun on a sixty-two degree day. High winds of reality scoured away any jealous humidity, whipping away the delusion.

Chris's son had died. And she could possess a fortune, a fabulous wardrobe, a house on a golf course, a Range Rover, and artistic ability, and I wouldn't trade places.

Oh, Chrissy. So beautiful.

So vulnerable now.

Forgive me. Forgive my pettiness, my jealousy, my unthankfulness.

It finally didn't matter to me that I was the ugly one, the fat one, the struggler.

Angus slept or read almost the entire time, commenting on various historical figures, making childish assumptions which warmed my heart. But for the most part, I listened to CDs and sipped coffee straight from the old Aladdin.

The downtown spires of the city materialized around three in the afternoon, majestic mountains of commerce rising out of the scrub of the shipyard industry and the monstrous cranes that lined the dockyards. So many people complained about the ugly warehouses and factories that greeted the travelers up I-95, but even my father once told me that the only reason the beautiful houses out in the valleys surrounding the northern parts of the city could be there was because of the money generated down there by the water.

I turned off the expressway and skirted the Ravens stadium with its purple seats and purple signs. We passed Camden Yards and eventually turned onto Charles Street.

I always had a secret desire to eat my way up Charles Street. Thai, Afghani, Japanese, Irish, French-Japanese, and Italian restaurants served their cuisines in the shadow of the large Roman Catholic Basilica. A cool little bead shop sat on one corner, giving me a strong desire to try my hand at macramé.

Oh, brother!

Finally, we passed Johns Hopkins University, Chris still asleep, thank God, and I literally meant that, and turned into one of the large, upscale condo buildings in Roland Park. Daddy and Mother's place. Lots of picture windows and sliding glass doors.

My dad waited for me on one of the little geriatric cement benches outside. He looked up as I pulled in, failed to recognize the car, and went back to the magazine he held.

I pulled into one of the nearby visitor spaces and jumped out, hurrying over to him in that college girl way. "Daddy!" I cried, surprised at how glad I was to see him.

"Poppers!" he yelled back and opened his arms.

The embrace didn't last long, but the warmth of him through his plaid cotton shirt felt comforting and nice.

"Nice car! I didn't know you got a new car."

Dad has always loved cars. The love of cars somehow passes down genetically from Heubner to Heubner.

"Duncan surprised me with it a while ago."

"Guess you're glad to be out of that van!"

"Oh, man. Am I!"

He hugged me again. And he smelled nice, still the same. No colognes. Just Safe Guard, Right Guard, and Binaca Blast. "I'm glad you're here, Popp."

I pulled back. "The others are still asleep."

"In that case," he said, reaching into his shirt pocket, "you can have the last peppermint."

I unwrapped the cellophane and placed it on my tongue. "Wanna see the car?"

"Of course. Lead the way. How do you like it?" he asked as we walked across the lot.

"It's nice. Easy to get out of first gear, good pickup, and more than enough space in the back for groceries."

He ran a knobby old hand over the front fender. "I've always liked green the best."

"Me, too."

It wasn't long before Chris and Angus came back to consciousness and realized the trip had ended. Chris climbed out, and Angus grabbed all of his books. After some more hugging, we levitated up to the eighth floor in the small, wood paneled elevator. I said a silent prayer. Mother awaited.

"Is Mother up there?"

"Sure is. And she's making your favorite meal. Stuffed cabbage rolls."

Our eyes locked. And then Chris's gaze joined in.

I hated cabbage.

"Just kidding!" Mother yelled as Dad heave-hoed a large Belleek tureen onto the table. "Irish Stew!"

"Now this really is my favorite," I said. What a delightful little joke. Miracles still happened apparently.

Homemade cloverleaf rolls arrived in a wicker basket with hand-embroidered Irish linen swaddling their warmth.

"Oh, man." I nudged Angus. "This is good eating."

"Do I have to have the stew?"

"Of course you do."

Mother waved a bony hand. "Oh, don't make him, Poppy. At least not for my sake. He's a grandson after all."

"Okay." I shrugged, determined not to start trouble right away. "What's for dessert?"

"Strawberries and raspberries with French vanilla ice cream."

After a quick "Bless us, O Lord," I scooped up a spoonful of stew. The salty brown gravy coated my tongue. The meat fell apart between my teeth, and the potatoes were halfway to disintegration before they had even left the bowl.

No one talked for the first five minutes. Mother had done such a wonderful job. And finally, when we had second helpings, Mother told me that Paisley had come to live with them.

Twenty-three

*D*addy and I strolled down Charles Street and onto the campus of Johns Hopkins. Homewood, the regal Carroll mansion, held court over the academic buildings, thoroughly attesting to the old saying, "They don't build them like they used to." Or that's at least what I thought.

Dad squeezed my hand as we walked along. "I'm glad you came up."

"You said Paisley would be home later on this evening?"

"Yes. Should get off work around eight."

Mother already informed me that Paisley had obtained a decent job as a tutor for Sylvan Learning.

"Does she know I'm coming?"

"No."

"Oh, Dad! Come on! Why didn't you tell her?"

"Because she'd come up with some excuse to stay out late or even go down the ocean or something."

That sure was the truth. "I wish you two would tell me why she left Boston."

"It's got to be up to her, Popp."

I laid my head against my daddy's arm, and we said nothing else as we walked around the campus. Until much later.

"I can't walk around here anymore without thinking about Josh," Dad said.

"Do you still walk here everyday?"

"Yes. We had him over a few times for supper. Thoroughly enjoyed his company. I still can't believe he's gone."

"I'm taking Chrissy to talk with the other guy who climbed the tower. I'm not sure where she's going with all of this, Daddy."

The breeze lifted his white hair off of his forehead. "I doubt if she knows herself, sweets."

We walked some more. "I'm glad Paisley won't recognize the new car. If we had brought the van…"

"Yep. She'd be going down the ocean."

The moment I saw Paisley, sitting on the white couch in my parents' living room, a great truth came upon me. *It really is all my fault.*

It had been easy to blame Paisley all of these years. She had been so contrary, so disobedient, so wont to do whatever the heck she wanted to do. She'd pushed me away, ridiculed me, ignored me, and thought me a fool. She'd had premarital sex, smoked Marlborough Reds or Camels without the filter, and though she didn't drink, she went to all of those filthy places with moldering chewing gum plastered beneath every surface and neon signs that advertised cheap domestic beer.

I was the mother.

It was up to me. It had always been up to me.

"Hi, Paise."

"Hi, Mom."

"I'm surprised to see you here."

"Yeah, well."

"What happened?"

"Didn't Grammie tell you?"

"No."

"I flunked out."

"What? Oh, Paise!" I ran over and put my arms around her. Paisley stiffened as she always did, but this time, I refused to let go.

"No!" I cried as my daughter wriggled. "No!"

Paisley continued to struggle, but I held on tight, my tears spilling onto the top of my daughter's hair. Still dyed black. She worked so hard at her grades.

Mother entered the room. "Let her go, Poppy."

"No, Mother. She doesn't want that."

Paisley shoved her way free and ran into her grandparents' bedroom.

I stood to my feet, shaking at each joint. Why did I always do the wrong thing? Why didn't I have a clue as to what this child needed?

"Well, way to go," Mother said.

I wiped sudden, hot tears away with my forearm, wiped my nose with my sleeve. "What would you know, Mother?"

"And what is that supposed to mean?"

"'Let her go, Poppy,'" I mimicked.

"And I was right! You saw the way she ran out of here." Mother sighed and sat down on the couch with a shake of her head. "Sit down, Penelope."

"What is there to say?"

"I didn't say I wanted to talk, did I?"

"Well, no."

"All right then."

I sat back down, thankful Angus and Chris were still in the kitchen helping Daddy with the supper dishes.

"We're some sick women," Mother said.

I nodded. "Poor Paisley. She must feel awful."

"I know." Mother took my hand and interlaced my fingers with her own. I stared down at the twin bone structure.

The tears gathered in my eyes again, but this time I blinked them back. We sat that way for several minutes, stiff and unable to move.

"I'd better go see to Paisley," I said. "Did she tell you why she flunked out?"

"Yes. I'll go help with the kitchen."

We stood to our feet simultaneously.

But Paisley had locked the door. I called, "I'm here. I'm not leaving tonight."

And the child didn't answer.

The phone rang.

I shuffled back into the kitchen to find Mother talking to my Aunt Lucy about *General Hospital* while the others still worked. The hall bathroom stood vacant, so I slipped inside, shut the door, bit down on a hand towel, and wept. Sinking to the floor, I wondered how I had lost my daughter so thoroughly.

When the chips came falling down on Paisley's head, she hadn't turned to me.

I had a lot to answer for and realized there, so close to Hopkins and TV hill, that losing a child comes in many forms.

Twenty-four

hat will this kid be like?" Chris asked as she emptied out the silverware. She hadn't seen Paisley, and though I'd gathered my wits and headed back to the kitchen, I couldn't bring myself to say anything yet.

I knew fraternity boys didn't corner any kind of market on mystique. Unless the ability to belch out the opening strains of "Smoke on the Water" fell into that niche. But obviously, Chris felt otherwise. Most outsiders felt otherwise.

I searched for the coffee filters, ready for some after supper java. Shoot, I held no hope for sleep anyway tonight. I had to approach my daughter sometime before the eleven o'clock news to demand an audience. Mothers couldn't let something like this go. And I refused to abnegate my position any longer. Besides, I know what failure is like. If anyone could comfort her it was me. As long as I went about it the right way. And fat chance of that, right?

Best to get on with the conversation at hand. "What do *you* think they'll be like, Chrissy?"

"Rich boys, I guess. Estates and trust funds and snazzy red imports."

"Racing green," I said. "Or black."

"See, Poppy?" Chris turned to face me. "You accuse me of being a reverse snob, and then when I don't get the right 'classiness'"—she bent her first two fingers on each hand for the quotation marks—"you always have to correct it. Good grief!"

She turned back to the silverware drawer, whipping around, her slumped shoulders a bony wall.

I decided the best course of action was to just go right on with the topic at hand. The last thing Chris needed to know was that she'd hurt my feelings even though I deserved it. "There are some nice boys in fraternities. Josh wasn't from that kind of background. And you know his friend Jason really well, right? He's a good kid."

"That's true."

"And they probably belch some other kind of music these days on boring weeknights. Like that group Mush Mouth or something."

Chris turned to me. "So it's not a party every night?"

"It didn't used to be. And Josh went with Zeta Chi. They're known to be a bit more serious about their education."

"Really?"

"Yeah. A lot of those boys are sponsored by older, more distinguished fraternity alumni." Of course, Chris knew that. But we seemed to be having a lot of the same conversations over and over since Josh died.

"What happened then, Popp? Why would those kind of boys get Josh to climb TV hill?"

"I don't know, Chrissy."

And it really was a mystery to me. The father of one of the other climbing boys was a Zeta Chi alumnus. He had agreed to talk with us tomorrow morning. I made the call back in Mount Oak, and I had to admire the man because if the situation were reversed, I don't know if I'd agree to the proposition.

Paisley walked into the kitchen.

Talk about a surprise!

Angus clung to his sister's back like a bony chimpanzee in denim overalls. Happiness spread itself on his pinched little face like butter on an English muffin. "Paisley's going to take me to Starbuck's for a kid's hot chocolate!"

Never mind it was seventy-five degrees outside.

Chris turned around from her place at the sink and cried, "Paisley!"

They hugged with sincere warmth, a natural embrace, organic and comfortable.

"Your grandparents told me you were here in Baltimore. Shouldn't you be in Boston?"

"I flunked out, Aunt Chris."

"Oh, Paise. I'm so sorry! Are you okay?"

"Yeah, I'll be okay."

Chris looked at me. "Why didn't you tell me?"

"You've got enough to think about, Chrissy."

"I know, but good grief, Poppy." She turned back to face Paisley. "What can I do, Paise?"

Paisley set her mouth in a thin line, then shook her head. "I'd like it if you could just not bring it up. I've got a lot of thinking to do about what comes next." Paisley's tone sounded deflated somehow.

Chris reached out a hand and rubbed Paisley's arm. "You got it."

"Would you pick me up something while you're there?" Why endure Fidge's Maxwell House when I could get a venti anything?

Paisley refused to meet my eyes, but she said, "Sure," in a regular, clear tone of voice. The most clear tone of voice I'd heard her use in four years.

I trailed my eyes over my daughter's slender frame, now covered by cutoff Levi's and a plain white T-shirt. A new tattoo glimmered atop Paisley's bicep. Lily of the Valley.

"Let me get you some money." I grabbed my purse off of the counter. Mother hung up the phone.

"I'm taking Gus to Starbuck's, Grammie," Paisley said.

"Oh, get me a venti decaf mocha latte with an extra shot, would you?"

My hands opened in shock, and I watched as my bag fell out of my grasp. I dropped to my knees immediately to pick up the spilled contents. "Well, I guess I'll take that, too, only not decaf."

So. Well, huh.

Go Fidge lady.

I hurried over to the Maxwell House, peeled open the lid and sniffed. Stale.

Mother crossed her arms. "You don't think I sent you all that coffee for Christmas without getting some for myself, do you?"

"You want anything, Aunt Chris?" Paisley asked.

Chris examined the three Heubner women. I felt what she saw before her. Three dark-haired women with the same brown eyes and a love affair with the coffee bean. I saw three women who had been given every advantage and still fussed about life though we had no right. I saw three women who were bratty enough to want their way and strong enough to fight for it, even if the fight was sometimes a losing battle. I saw three ridiculous people who had all the love in the world to give but were waiting to get it first.

"Just a plain old decaf for me, Paise," Chris said. "Small."

And that said it all, didn't it? Just a plain old decaf for Chrissy, while the Huebner women had to have mocha and special coffee. And the biggest size, too.

Man.

"Just black, too," Chris said.

"I remember," Paisley said. "Let's go, Gus."

He squeezed his arms tightly around her neck, and she pretended to choke. "You're funny, Paisley."

Paisley rolled her eyes and backed out of the kitchen. I heard keys clinking as she grabbed them off the console near the front door.

Why is it we'd give anything for upstarts to be subdued, and then when they become subdued we feel so sad? Failure isn't a bad thing, really, I reminded myself, remembering that verse in the Bible about gaining the whole world but losing your own soul.

"Do you know how long she was struggling with her classes?" I asked my mother.

"Pretty much from the start," she said, and both of us Heubner women sat down at the kitchen table. "But she's a strong one, Penelope. You've got to at least give her credit for that."

I chose to ignore that "at least" and said, "I've never accused her of being weak, that's for sure."

"She tried her hardest, probably all the more difficult to take."

Chris sat down at the table with us.

"I've got to talk with her about it, but I'm not sure what to say," I said.

"We never are sure," Mother said.

"I can't believe she never called. Does Duncan know?"

Mother nodded. "She made him promise not to tell you."

"Oh, man."

Chris shook her head. "I'll be praying for you, Poppy."

And Mother grew just a tad uncomfortable, but she hid it well, like she usually did by getting up and plucking a Kleenex from the phone table. She blew her nose, which was perfectly dry, as she sat back down.

"So did you get season tickets to Center Stage this year?" I asked, taking the cue.

"No. Last season they put on such an offensive play, and we had guests with us. It was embarrassing to say the least. This man grilling burgers, worried about all his possessions while his family was falling apart around him. And the language! Not just colorful, but tasteless. And you should see the painting exhibition we saw last month! It's dreadfully sad, in my opinion, what the arts have come to."

I bristled.

And then Chris said, "I agree. You can get offended for free just by turning on the TV." And then I sincerely agreed with Chris right away. When did shock replace beauty?

A self-epiphanous moment had erupted which meant I couldn't ignore it, couldn't walk away, not if I wasn't completely a lost cause, and I didn't think of myself as hopeless yet.

No matter what Mother says I assume she's wrong. I'm no different than my daughter.

Oh, this was just great. Not only was I responsible for my horrible relationship with my daughter, I was also responsible for my horrible relationship with my mother. Fabulous. What a revelatory day this was turning out to be. Poppy Fraser is the tick of the itch, the fly in the ointment, the ant at the picnic, the cricket in the corner, the bee on the clover patch.

I am the bug.

"Maybe I should go in for some kind of counseling," I muttered out loud, for my own benefit, really, because if you actually said the words, blew them out of your mouth however quietly, they counted more. The others weren't meant to hear. But they did, of course.

Both my mother and my closest friend in the world heard me. The one who bore me to the world and the one who bore me through the world. And they said absolutely nothing. Just looked at me with round eyes.

I stood to my feet.

Then I realized I had no planned course of action. So I sat back down.

"Have I ever been an easy person to get along with?"

"When you let yourself be," Mother said.

I turned and looked at Chris. "Well?"

"You really want the truth?"

"No. But I'm thinking this kind of opportunity only comes up once in a while."

"I've gotten used to you, Popp. As far as your mom goes, though, you can be a little defensive. With Duncan, too."

"And Paisley?" I asked.

The other two nodded.

"Oh, man."

Mother patted my hand. "Let's talk about something else."

Everyone else had gone to bed. Chris snored loudly on the sleep sofa in the living room. And Angus had snuggled up in-between Mother and Daddy.

I stood at my parents' bedroom door and watched them. Old people sleeping possess a certain poignancy, especially since my father only slept in pajama bottoms, and my mother still wore sleeveless, youthful, two-piece numbers. All that skin, sagging and soft, made them vulnerable in a way as they lay there, the light down comforter tucked around their waists. And there lolled Angus, a pale little peanut with speckled, papery arms draped all over him.

They'd left the light on in the bathroom and cracked the door.

Mother moved suddenly, opened her eyes and turned them toward me. "Everything okay?"

"Yeah."

"Good. Goodnight, Penelope, dear. Have a nice sleep."

"'Night, Mother."

I turned around. Incandescent light still splayed across the hallway floor from underneath the door of Paisley's room. I tapped on the smooth surface.

Paisley said, "Come in, Mother."

Well, at least she'd known I would show up.

So I opened the door and went into the guest room. Some boxes filled with Paisley's stuff towered in the corner. But the room still possessed that guest room ambiance with its dark plaid bedspread, tan walls, and duck pictures.

Paisley reclined on the bed with a pair of my old slippers on her feet. Remembering the Christmas my mother had given me those fuzzy, purple life rafts, I chuckled, grabbed a slipper, and shook my daughter's foot slightly. "I haven't thought about those things in ages. They're back **in now**, aren't they?"

Paisley smiled just a little. "You know what they say."

"Yeah. Were those in the closet?"

"Uh-huh. Grammie said she put them in there so she could think of this as your room."

Wow.

"Can I sit with you for a while?" I asked.

"Sure."

Paisley had been flipping through one of my old *Artists* magazines.

"Paise, do you want to talk about it to me?"

Paisley shook her head. "I can't, Mom. I don't know if I'll ever even want to."

"Can I just say one thing?"

Paisley's eyes hardened, just briefly, but she nodded. "I can't stop you."

"You can."

"Really?" She flipped a page of the magazine.

"Yeah."

"Okay, then. I don't want to hear it."

I bit my lip. "How's Sylvan?"

"I've only been there a few days. It's temporary."

"Do you want to go back to grad school? Try again down here maybe?"

"Not yet. I may take a teaching job or something. I really like Angus's age, you know?"

"Yeah. So, teach first grade or something?"

"Uh-huh."

"Well, the school year is almost over. Maybe you can get in someplace for the fall."

"That's what I'm hoping." She flipped another page.

"You'd be a good teacher."

Paisley looked up. "You think so?"

"I do. You'd want them to do well."

I wanted to tell her that someday she would look back on all this and it wouldn't seem so bad. She'd see it for the intersection it was. She'd see how she'd been given the chance to take a different road, one that had turned out to be rewarding and fruitful. But to trivialize this now, well, I had enough foresight to know it would be just what Paisley expected of me.

Paisley looked at the clock. "I'm going to turn in, Mom. I've got to be at work by eight tomorrow morning."

"You need a ride? I'll take you in the new car."

"No, thanks. I'll just take the bus down there."

I touched the slipper again. "I'll see you in the morning."

"Okay."

I stood to my feet. It wasn't an earth shattering conversation at all. But no one had become angry.

"Mom?"

"Yeah, Paise."

"I give you permission."

"What?"

"Tell me what you were going to say a minute ago."

Oh, my gosh.

"I just was going to say that I'm proud of you."

"I tried so hard, Mom. I always thought I was so smart."

"You are, sweetie."

Paisley looked at me, almost said something else, then scratched her cheek. "See you in the morning."

"Okay." I started to shut the door, then I popped my head back into Paisley's room. "Where does Grammie keep the Starbuck's?"

"In the freezer."

"Wow."

"I know."

Twenty-five

George Parkes was a wealthy man. I figured he sponsored one of the poorer, more promising lads of Zeta Chi. Of course, he might have *been* a sponsored boy "back in the day," as Miss Mildred would have said. Yeah, back in the day. Back in *my* day. I still didn't feel old enough to have grown kids.

The Parkes lived on a farm in Harford County. Nothing ostentatious about Harford County, for pity's sake.

"I'm glad they live out here," Chris said.

I just said, "Me, too," to be agreeable.

"It's friendlier out here."

"Uh-huh."

The driveway led us way off the road. I couldn't see the house for about half a mile, and then there it stood, in a copse of oak trees with some Dutch elms to the east and west of the sheltering grove.

In pristine condition, the original turn of the century farmhouse had clearly grown over the years. Large, quirky, and solid, it didn't appear to be some grand monument to success. Just a nice old house that someone cared about.

We pulled up, and immediately the front door opened. George Parkes dashed off the porch.

"Hello," I said right away, because I was the only one here who didn't have to be unsure. "Mr. Parkes?"

"Yes."

We shook hands, and Chris climbed out.

"I'm Poppy Fraser," I said so there'd be no confusion. "I called you back in Mount Oak and again this morning to get directions."

He hurried over to Chris. "You must be Josh's mom." His slender face deepened to a dark red, contrasting with his hay-colored hair. "I'm so sorry."

Chris looked first at me, and I nodded to encourage her.

"Thanks for agreeing to meet with me."

"Of course. Would you like to come inside?"

"All right," Chris said. "Is Ron home?"

"Yes."

"And your wife?"

"She died when Ron was five."

Well, that changed things a bit.

He showed us into the entry hall and led us back to the family room. Furnished comfortably, yet with masculine overtones, the space spoke sports with a wide screen TV, a bucket of golf balls, and some clubs leaning in the corner near the patio door. "You'll have to excuse this place. We moved here a couple of years ago, and, well, we saw no reason to decorate frillylike for Ron and me."

Chris looked down. "May I use your powder room?"

"Of course. It's down the hall on your right."

Chris grabbed my hand and pulled me with her.

"I can't do this," she whispered passionately once we stood in the large bathroom/laundry room near the kitchen. She leaned against the folding table that supported several stacks of neatly folded whites.

"You can't do what?"

"Make a big stink. I came up to Baltimore to make a big stink."

"I thought you just came up to find out more."

"No. I came up to make a stink, Poppy!"

"What kind of a stink?"

"A lawyer stink, maybe. I don't know. At least throw a bomb at the fraternity."

A stink bomb apparently. Oh, Chrissy. "But you've never made a stink in your life."

"I thought maybe Ron was protecting the fraternity. But the boy lost his mother, Poppy."

I purposely failed to bring up the painful irony of the situation. "Poor guy."

Chris focused on the large bottle of bleach. "So what do I do now? I can't just do *nothing*. That's not fair to Josh."

"You've got to talk to them now that you're here. He seems like a nice enough guy."

When we walked back into the parlor a sun-burned Ron had joined his father. Not really good looking, featurewise, he possessed light brown hair in abundance and wore his clothing well. Probably an Abercrombie and Fitch junkie. Not the preppie-at-all-costs type, though, judging by his Doc Martin sandals.

He stood to his feet immediately, displaying a great length of leg. "Mrs. Knight."

Chris's maternal instincts must have automatically kicked in. "Hello, Ron."

He shook our hands as his dad made introductions then seated us, Chrissy next to Ron on the couch and me in a plaid chair opposite his own.

Ron sat back down, low into the moss-colored sofa, knees sticking way up.

"I'm not sure where to begin," George Parkes said. "Maybe you could tell us the reason you wanted us to get together."

"I wanted to find out what really happened," Chris said. "I've only read police reports, but they couldn't possibly say everything, right?"

"Do you want Ron to tell you what happened that night?" George asked.

Chris nodded.

George nodded at his son. "It's okay, bud. Go ahead."

Ron sat up some and focused on his left hand, the one resting on the knee nearest the arm of the couch. "Well, we had gone through hell night.

It wasn't really too bad. A little embarrassing, but nothing major. But we drank a lot. Some of us did, anyway. But not Josh!" he hastened to say. "He only drank a little."

And he went on from there, telling about how three of them had sat around in the basement of the frat house, how a lot of the others were "pretty much passed out" all around them.

"So Ed—he grew up near TV Hill—says we had to go climb the tower. Like it was the final phase of hell night. He said it was punishment for not getting as drunk as the rest."

Mr. Parkes cleared his throat. "Eddie? He was there?"

"He was, Dad."

"Why didn't you tell me?"

"You know how Ed is. But I can't keep this inside any longer. I don't care what he does."

"Was he the other climber?" I asked.

"No, that was Dell Markham," Ron said.

"I never heard about another guy being there," Chris said.

"It's the first I've heard." George threw a perplexed look at his son.

My skin began to tingle.

"I didn't want to tell anyone," Ron said.

"Well, what did Josh say about Ed's suggestion?" Chris asked.

"He acted like he was all for it. He already had a reputation for being a brave kind of guy. Like, don't dare Josh on a bet or you'll lose, especially on physical stuff."

"What do you mean?" George asked.

"I don't know. When we'd play Frisbee and stuff, he always made these flying leaps and could fall, dropping his shoulder and rolling. And he was a great lacrosse player. He didn't flinch or balk at stuff, you know?"

Chris folded her hands in her lap. "Yeah, he was like that, even though he wasn't a big guy."

"We all went down to the Inner Harbor last fall. We parked in the garage by the Hyatt, and Josh walked on top of the wall around the top level."

Chris sucked in her breath. I took her hand.

"So you all climbed the tower?" George asked. "Ed, too?"

"The three of us freshmen did, just Josh and Dell and me."

Just Josh.

"Ed stayed put on the ground." Ron looked down at his hands.

"So this *was* an official fraternity activity then?" Chris asked. "Were you covering up for them by not telling about Ed?"

"No. The fraternity had nothing to do with it. That much is true. But we all thought it was real!" Ron said. "When we were starting up, Josh whispered that he was scared, and I said I was, too, and then he said something about not wanting to look like a chicken and really wanting to go far in Zeta Chi and all so he could get a sponsor, and he started up ahead of me."

"Were you scared, too?" I asked.

"Oh, man! If he'd have backed out, I'd have backed him up. Ed or not!" His words were passionately spoken, as if they were seeking some time machine to take them back to the moment when they would have meant something. "Dell would have, too!"

Ron looked right at Chris, his face stained a deep red like his dad's, his eyes like glass. "He just slipped, Mrs. Knight. It was cold, and he didn't wear gloves. I am so sorry."

No legal stink to make now. Not against Zeta Chi, anyway. Poor Chrissy.

"I climbed down as fast as I could," Ron continued, his voice vibrating with emotion. "But he was dead when I got to him." He leaned forward and dropped his head, inhaling deeply. "I go to bed each night thinking, 'If only I had said something!' And each morning I get up, and the first thing I think about is that I didn't."

"It's a heavy load he carries now," George said.

Chris reached out and placed a hand on Ron's knee.

"Where was this Ed guy?" I asked.

Ron sat up straight, and so did Chris. "He'd already left. He was gone by the time I got down. But he must have called 911 because the ambulance came not long after."

So it really was an accident. Just like they'd said. A big, cruel accident.

"I'm sorry, Mrs. Knight. I'm sorry I didn't say anything to the police about Ed. But I just couldn't. I know it was stupid. And I know what a big jerk Ed is."

"Josh must have known that, too," Chris said. "He made the decision on his own. And he had taken a drink of his own choosing. The coroner said so." Chris opened up her purse and pulled out the report. "See? Look at the blood alcohol level."

George took it, looked at it, then shook his head. We passed it all around, like some wretched shower gift, each looking at the line she had pointed out.

And we nodded simultaneously.

"He wasn't normally the type to drink, Mrs. Knight. I don't know why he had a beer that night."

"It's not your fault, Ron," Chris said.

"But maybe I could have prevented it."

"You couldn't have known, bud," George said.

"I don't know what to do," Chris said. "The police report said it wasn't the fraternity's fault, but I was hoping to find out otherwise."

George reached out and took her hand. "It clearly isn't anything the fraternity can take legal responsibility for."

"What's happened to Ed?" I asked.

George cleared his throat. "Nothing that I know of. Nobody even knew he had anything to do with it!"

Chris started digging in her purse for something.

I took the lead again. "How influential are you in Zeta Chi?" I asked him.

"I sponsor one boy every four years. Complete scholarship."

"At JHU?"

"Of course."

Go Blue Jays. My mouth went dry.

Chris pulled out a Kleenex and blew her nose.

"What about nationally?" I asked. Josh deserved more from me, his blood cousin, than a polite nod at Zeta Chi or an angry feeling at Ed.

"I'm quite active."

"How hard would it be to get rid of this Ed from Zeta Chi?"

"It wouldn't be impossible." But he sounded reticent.

I asked why.

"Ed's mother is my sister. I'm also his sponsor."

Chris broke down. It had to have come sooner or later, but what timing! I took her into my arms and looked harshly at George Parkes as Chris wept. "Get rid of him. I don't care if he's your nephew."

"I think we could come to some other arrangement," George said. "He's going to graduate next year."

"So he can lead some other freshman up there?"

"He's done it before this, Dad," Ron said, still not looking up. "Not always on hell night either. At least that's what the guys say."

George turned to his son. "Have you climbed up there before?"

"No. But he did it last year, too. Everyone's just turned a blind eye because he's your nephew. He's just been lucky up 'til now."

George Parkes blew out a sigh. "My sister will never forgive me for doing this to her son. I can't believe Ed would do that kind of thing."

"Oh, come on, Dad! He's a jerk!"

"If you don't do something, I'm taking Chris right back down to my father who's an attorney, I might add. Believe me, we'll press charges. Ed would get manslaughter or at least reckless endangerment."

Right? I hoped George Parkes wasn't a lawyer!

I hated to play hardball like this, but I couldn't bear for this Ed guy, who led people up TV towers and was a bully and a threat, simply to walk away with nothing to face. Ed deserved to pay some sort of consequence. The stiffer the better.

George shook his head wearily. "I'm sorry," he said again to Chris. "I'll take care of it. I'll do something."

"Mr. Parkes, I didn't mean to stir up this kind of trouble," Chris said.

Oh, come *on,* Chris! Don't play nice!

"It's okay." He stood to his feet. "You know, you try to be a good parent. But you can't see it all, can you?"

Chris wiped away her own tears. "No, you can't."

Ron stood up. "I'm sorry, Mrs. Knight."

Chris leaned forward and pulled him close to her. "You take good care of yourself, Ron. Please."

"We'd better go," I said. If there was one thing I'd learned as a woman interacting with men, it was knowing when to leave them in order that their dignity might be preserved.

And I didn't want to explode, either.

"Well, that whole thing could be classified as a stink," I said to Chris as I pulled out of the Parkes's driveway and onto Route 152. "And rightly so."

"I know! And I feel worse. How was I supposed to know they were related?"

"You didn't even know there was an Ed to worry about!"

"Oh, man. What's that boy's mother going to think?"

"Well, I'm the one who called for Ed's head anyway!"

"Yeah. But I didn't tell you to stop."

"Well, I wasn't about to back down!" I said.

"Do you think we did the right thing in sticking to our guns about Ed?"

"Yeah. He should really be kicked out of Hopkins, if you want my opinion. And Hopkins is a good school, Chrissy. They don't want their students in danger."

"I feel so nauseous." Chris opened the glove box. "You got any crackers in here?"

"They're in there somewhere. Look under the manual."

"That Ron was a nice boy, Poppy."

"Yeah. Poor guy."

"I know. Do you think they'll kick Ed out?"

"I don't know," I said, but I knew I was going to give the school a big tip-off. "He would deserve it."

We traveled west planning to have lunch at the Manor Tavern. I pulled into the Wawa convenience store. "Are you thirsty?"

"Yeah."

Two minutes later I was back with a couple of Cokes. I loosened both caps and placed them in the drink holders. "You okay, Chrissy?"

"Not really, Popp. I keep asking myself how he could do something so stupid? So utterly stupid?"

"He was only eighteen years old."

"I don't care! It was TV Hill, Popp. TV Hill! We've all heard about the bodies in pieces. We grew up with that. Josh did, too. He was old enough to know better."

"But he was drinking, Chrissy, and I know it's hard to understand."

"What's hard to understand, what is shaking my faith to the core, Poppy, is that I prayed for his safety his entire life! There wasn't a day that went by that I didn't pray for God to protect him. What's hard to understand is that the prayers in heaven for the safety of my child are countless. I know, I know, we pray for safety, still knowing that life is dangerous, still knowing that there are creeps like Ed out there lying in wait, but I expected God would come through in a situation like this. Why would prayers like that go unanswered? If a child asks for a piece of bread, is he handed a rock? I feel like I've been given rocks and scorpions."

She twisted her wedding rings on her finger as I tried to grasp for something right to say, something that would mean anything.

Chrissy grabbed my hand. "I wish that God would have left all my other prayers unanswered and given me just this one. It was the most important to me, Poppy. Didn't He see that?"

Chris turned to look back out of her window and I waited. But nothing more came, so I started up the car and pulled onto the road.

I had no answers just then.

"Really, Mrs. Knight, hazing is pretty much out of the picture now. At least hazing like you've probably heard about."

I grabbed Chris's hand as we sat in plain, wooden chairs before the vice president of student affairs. "So, what you're saying is that we're a little late in the game?"

Richard Fellows nodded his very shiny baldhead that reflected the square of the fluorescent light above him perfectly, sharp edges and all. "Of course, there are colleges that allow initiations that put the pledge in an embarrassing position. But it should never be painful. But that isn't the case here, I assure you."

"What went wrong that night?" Chris asked. "What could have been done to prevent it?"

He shook his head, his very round, deep brown eyes compassionate. "Nothing. And that, I'm afraid, is the truth."

"What about the drinking?"

"Well, clearly the boys who climbed the tower were underage."

I sat up. "But to try and stop that—"

"Exactly," he said. "It's impossible." He turned to Chris. "Mrs. Knight, you must know how horrible we feel about what happened to Josh. He was a promising young man."

Chris took a fresh Kleenex out of her purse, and Richard Fellows opened a desk drawer.

"I had our campus newspaper look through the lacrosse archives, and they gave me this shot from spring training. I hope you don't mind, but I took the liberty of framing it for you yesterday after you made the appointment."

In a very smooth, desk-job hand, he held out an eight-by-ten, black-and-white picture, matted in Blue Jay blue with a tubular white frame.

Chris gulped back a sob.

There was Josh. Just Josh.

His stick was high, the hard white ball snuggled in the netting. The ground had released his feet by a good three feet, and he was flying sideways through the air, stick back, ready to throw.

Forever and ever.

It was difficult to see his face behind the face mask, but my brain filled in the details. The expression spread across his features was happy, yet aggressive. And clearly he was yelling, "Ball!"

"Josh could be tough when he wanted to be," I said.

"Yeah, he could." Chris ran two light, shaking fingers over the image of her son. "Thank you, Mr. Fellows."

He smiled, and I wondered if he knew God. He seemed like someone who knew God. "I wish I could do more for you, Mrs. Knight."

Chris stood to her feet and put out her hand. They shook. "Me, too."

Out in the parking lot, I took Chris's hand, and we walked to the car, neither of us caring who saw or what they thought.

Twenty-six

*P*aisley actually looked nice. She came home from her tutor-
ing job that afternoon with four cups of Starbuck's. "Aperitifs
for the fashionably insane woman," she said cheerfully.

I definitely approved of the slim, yet long linen jumper, beige colored
with tiny embroidered green leaves trailing diagonally from Paisley's right
shoulder to her left hip. And the way my daughter had pulled her long
black hair back into a simple ponytail at the nape of her neck looked elegant. The hippie sandals and at least eight pounds of silver jewelry kept it
from being old school. Not to mention that fresh tattoo.

I was wise enough to know that the last thing I should do was send
out a compliment on the getup. It would smack too much of an "I told you
so." Unless, of course, one said it just right. And always on the backstage
crew of the school plays, I knew I didn't possess that kind of acting skill.

Instead, I took the coffee with, "You're just what the doctor ordered,"
and we sat at the kitchen table and heard about Paisley's day.

"I think I enjoy the middle schoolers the most," she said, taking off all
of her silver rings, sliding five different hoops out of her earlobes, removing any bracelet that wasn't tied on, and stretching her fingers.

"It's a good age." Chris took the top off of her plain-Jane decaf to let
the coffee cool. "They're old enough to sit still, but young enough not to
think they know everything."

"Exactly," Paisley said. "You know, it's so spooky how life can change
on you so fast."

I just nodded. Chris said she knew that first hand now, and Paisley rubbed her arm.

Mother stood to her feet and said, "I made some sausage Bisquick cheese balls for your father, but it's six o'clock, and he's not back from golf, so I say they're ours."

I couldn't agree more.

Coffee and cheese balls in the Heubner kitchen at six in the evening. Now how weird could life be? Mother had become spontaneous, and Paisley wore a darling linen sheath. Hopefully, I could keep my mouth shut and not say the wrong thing to set my daughter off, and well, that might make it a day to mark on the calendar each year. A day to celebrate. I could call it Zip It Up Day or Mum's the Word Day or something.

And, really, Mother was getting more groovy by the minute now that I had decided to take off my "Castle Glasses," those big defensive stone things I'd been wearing for decades. She actually wore jeans on her slender hips and had one of those new, feathery razor cuts she tucked behind her ears. And she even belonged to a reading group for mystery lovers. They called themselves *Aggie's Gals*. Was that cute or what?

Mother set five or so sausage balls aside. "Just so John won't feel completely forsaken."

Of course, Angus would have nothing to do with them, and Paisley sliced up a cucumber for herself. But there were no snide remarks about devouring someone else's flesh.

That night we three Heubner women sat outside on the small porch. Angus and Chris had fallen asleep in front of a DVD of *The Prince of Egypt*.

Mother and Daddy owned a DVD player. Had they always been this cool and I didn't realize it? If so, that was a classified bummer because they could have been taking us all on great family vacations, renting cabins and beach condos, eating at fancy restaurants, and going to the movies together. The term "extended family" might have applied.

The stars shone dimly through the lights of the city, and we watched the stripes of car lights, one red and one white, make their way up or down Charles Street.

"I love springtime," Mother said. "Even in the city."

"What really made you sell your house in the country and move down here, Grammie?" Paisley had changed into boys' athletic shorts from some all male, New England prep school and a large T-shirt from another prep school. This one had its own saint.

I willed myself not to ask how my daughter had come by them.

"The quiet was why I left." Mother polished her toenails a light frosty golden color. "Couldn't stand it any longer."

"What about all of your friends?" I asked.

"We still get together. But the group's slowly dwindling from cancer and heart attacks, which is hard. We probably still see each other just as much, but now I don't have to go rambling around in that house that I never liked much anyway."

"You didn't?" Paisley and I said it together, then looked at each other with our mouths open.

"I loved that house growing up!" I said.

"Me, too!" Paisley nodded.

"Well, I never did. Don't ask me why. I was perfectly content with our big rancher in Hampton."

I had always been under the impression that it was Mother who'd engineered the move out to Worthington Valley.

Mother sighed. "I thought Hampton was the be-all and end-all when we moved out there. I thought we had arrived, and I didn't ever want to move."

I remembered the stone rancher. I could see the roof of The Hampton Mansion if I swung high enough on my swing set, the glass panes of the cupola windows flashing sun-filled flares upon my eyes. But we'd moved when I was twelve, before I'd lost my identity as a seventh grade prep school girl. I often wonder how I would have turned out had I been born and raised in Dundalk or Essex. Probably a lot healthier emotionally.

So Mother hadn't been the social climber. It was Daddy. "Wow," I said.

"So it was your idea to move down here into town?" Paisley asked.

"Yes, Paise. We've got a nice life down here. We walk a lot. And there are lots of good coffee places around. The students are fun to watch, too. We spend hours down at the campus sitting on the bench and watching them."

I sat back and watched as my mother chatted with Paisley. I watched my daughter as I did when she had been a child, enjoying the sight of her, the different angles, the expressions. And I felt proud. Mother should be proud, too.

I heard the small, mahogany wall clock by the entryway chime once. Daddy must have set it on the lower chimes for the night.

Mother had long since gone to bed, but I sat with Paisley, drinking coffee and watching the almost deserted street. The girl could make a decent pot of coffee.

"You know you're welcome to come back with us, Paisley." It had been risky to say it, but I didn't know how else to word it.

"I know."

"But you don't want to right now?"

"No, Mom."

"I understand."

"Grammie and Gramp said I can stay here as long as I need to."

"Good."

"I'm just going to do what we had talked about before, apply for a teaching position for the fall, and then keep on at Sylvan this summer."

"I think that's wise. You know there's always a place for you with us, though. I could even have the studio made over into a little one-room apartment if you'd like."

Paisley smiled, turned to me, and took my hand. "Thanks, but—"

"And it's not like I'm even painting that much anymore."

"I know. Dad's told me that much."

"Really?"

"Yeah. He likes it when you paint. Did you know that?"

I felt more breeze on my eyes. "No. I always thought it was a pain to him."

Paisley shook her head. "No way. He thinks it's quite sexy, actually."

I let out a weak chuckle. "He told you that?"

"Oh yeah. Daddy and I have very candid conversations."

Obviously.

Keep it zipped, Poppy. Don't be the bug. Paisley's finally saying a few things "the way it is." Don't spoil it. But what would *The Proper Christian Ladies' Handbook* say about such a situation in chapter 14, "Motherhood"? Probably something about propriety and using every opportunity to get a lesson across.

Well, forget *The Handbook* tonight.

"You've always been close, you two," I said. "We never really clicked, did we?" I winced against the response.

Paisley cleared her throat. "No. I guess not."

"I'm sorry. I know it's my fault."

"No, Mom. It's not all—"

"Yes, it is, Paise. I'm the mother."

"Yeah, well, I didn't respond well. I know I wasn't an easy kid to raise. I've met some real corkers the past few days at work."

"Was it about Robbie, at all?"

"Sometimes. But not always. Not at first. And let's face it, Mother, Rob's a really easy guy to love."

"Yeah. Oh, Paisley, I wish you'd come back home."

"Mother, I can't. I've got to figure things out for myself now."

"But you've always been so independent."

"Not really. I spent the first half of my life trying to be just like you. I asked for art classes, had my hair cut short and permed when I was twelve. And then, I spent the next half trying to be the exact opposite."

What could I say?

Paisley squeezed my hand. "My whole life has revolved around you in one way or the other, Mother. Now I have to find out what's good for me, just me."

I put my arms around my daughter. "I'm proud of you."

Paisley only endured the embrace for a few seconds, then pulled back. She rose to her feet, kissed me goodnight, and went to her room.

Just after lunch a few days later we packed up the car to head back to Mount Oak. A motorcycle pulled up next to the Subaru and a young man dismounted.

Muscled arms pulled off the helmet to reveal the face of Jason Harkens.

Chris, thankfully, still lingered inside.

"I came to apologize to you, Mrs. Fraser."

"What for, Jason?"

"For breaking our trust. I promised you I'd take care of him, and I failed." He held his helmet in his hand and looked into its dark foam recess.

"It was *not* your fault, Jason."

"I wasn't there on hell night. There was an emergency at work, and I had to go in. I would've never let him go off with that idiot Ed."

"Well, he's getting his."

"I heard. He was taking his belongings out of the house this morning."

"Was he mad?"

"Oh yeah. Threatening a lawsuit and everything."

I exhaled forcefully. "I'd like to see him try."

"Yeah, me, too."

"Listen, Jason. Are you coming back to Mount Oak at all this summer?"

"Just for a week."

"Come over and see us, okay?"

He nodded.

"You should stick around for a minute. Mrs. Knight will be right out."

So he did. And Chris hugged him tightly and told him she knew that he had done all that he could because, well, Chrissy was like that.

Twenty-seven

uncan had sharpened all of my Prismacolor pencils and had cleaned out my brushes so that they appeared practically new. Paint spots had been wiped clean from the handles, and he'd even refinished some of my older ones.

"I know I could have bought new ones, but you've been using some of those since before the kids were born," he said when he showed me into the studio and displayed his handiwork.

Gone only a week, I could hardly believe my eyes when I saw everything beautifully organized on new shelving. The walls had been given a fresh coat of paint, and he'd installed bigger windows to the north and the south.

"And"—he opened a new door—"Ira and I were working long into the night to get this done."

I looked through the door as Duncan turned on the light. There on a blue-tiled floor sat a toilet. Bright white with a gold, old-fashioned looking handle.

"I got white because I though you might want to decorate it yourself with porcelain paints."

I shook my head in disbelief. Then I put my arms around him. Paisley was right. He did like the fact that I was an artist. "Thank you."

I kissed his lips.

"I never know what to do for you, Poppy. But when this idea came to mind, I knew it was a good one."

"So Ira helped you with the addition?"

"Yes. And Miss Poole even went with us down to the hardware store to pick out the commode."

"You're kidding me!"

"No. The funny thing is, she knew her way around that store like she worked there."

"Maybe she owns it."

Duncan raised his eyebrows. "Now there's a thought."

"Any more Boston cream pie ingredients on the big window?" I asked.

"Nope. Betty the don confessed to her pastor that her grandson did it, and he told me."

"No way!"

"Hard to believe, isn't it? People getting that mad over a Boston cream pie sale?"

I flipped off the light. "Where's Robbie?"

"Studying at the library. He's got an algebra test on Monday. We day tripped to Williamsburg yesterday and bought him a kilt at The Scottish Store."

"You didn't!"

"Yep. St. Andrews is definite now, Popp."

It came as no surprise. He'd been whistling "Scotland Forever" for the past month.

"He's leaving at the beginning of September. He decided for sure while you were gone." He put his arm around me. "Just you and me and Angus after Labor Day."

He sounded so sure, I thought. But with Robbie gone...well, I had one less excuse to stick around Mount Oak. All my excuses were drifting away, one by one by one.

Thing was, I wouldn't have this kind of studio if I went out on my own. Especially not in New York City, for pity's sake. I couldn't get an *apartment* the size of my studio shed for under fifteen hundred a month. And Duncan had been so wonderful to do this, had been thinking of me, Poppy, the inside-my-brain-Poppy that Mother birthed all those years ago.

We walked into the kitchen, a very clean and tidy kitchen, where a fresh pot of coffee awaited. Duncan took down two mugs.

"I did a wedding last night. A quickie."

"Anybody I know?"

"No. Just two locals who wanted something private. They had decided to get married the day before."

"Wow. You mean you didn't make them do any counseling?"

Duncan shrugged. "You know, Popp, the way I saw it with these two was this. They weren't parishioners, and they would have just gone down to the courthouse. At least this way, they're doing it in a church, and there's something noble in and of itself in that."

"Especially these days." I opened the refrigerator door and got out the half and half for Duncan.

"But you'll never guess what the bride did." He took the container and poured a healthy amount into his cup.

I took a sip of my coffee, longing for a cup made from the coffee Paisley had tucked in my suitcase. "First of all, you've got to tell me what the dress looked like."

"Ivory, babe." He shook his head. "It was ivory and very plain. Just above the ankles. All that netting stuff poofing out."

"Ballerina length. Love that. Did it have any decoration on it? Like just a little lace or some seed pearls?"

"No. But it did have one of those little jackets. The short kind with the long sleeves. I can't remember what they're called."

"A bolero jacket?"

"I guess that's it. Can I finish the story?"

"Almost. Pumps or sandals?"

"Pumps."

"High heeled or low?"

"Poppy!"

"Well? Come on, Duncan. A woman has got to be able to picture the bride to get the full impact of the story."

"Okay. Her heels looked to be about the same height as your navy blue church pumps."

I nodded. "Okay, you can go on then."

"Well, I got to the part where I say, 'Do you promise—'"

"Wait! What about the headpiece?"

"Just a sprig of those lacy little flowers at the back. Her hair was pulled back into a bun, just in case you were wondering."

"Of course I was."

"So anyway, I said, 'Do you promise to love, honor, and obey him?' And right away she said, 'I will not obey him.'"

"No way! What did you do?"

He laughed. "I've never had that happen to me before."

"Well, what did you do?"

"I just looked at the groom and said, 'Is that all right with you?' And he nodded and said, 'I guess so.' So I turned to the congregation and said something like 'Let the record show, the bride will not obey her husband.'"

"As if there's some wedding court reporter there or something!"

"I know. Honestly, Popp, I don't know if I did the right thing or not, but I just freaked."

"I give that one two years. Tops."

"Although I hate to say it…me, too."

I took out my wedding album that night. It had been years since I'd flipped those heavy pages lined in gold tone strips.

I had longer hair then. It looked nice curled like that. Seventies-ish. But that was okay. It wasn't overly dated. A decade earlier it might have been a beehive, so it could have been a lot worse.

Angus bounded up onto the couch, blankie at the ready. "What are these?"

"It's Daddy's and my wedding album."

"Stellar. Can I see?"

"Uh-huh. And don't even ask if you were around then because you know you weren't."

"Okay." Silky edge of blankie under his nose, he snuggled in close.

I flipped through the album four times that night. Once with myself. Once with Angus. Then Robbie came in and wanted to look.

Chris looked great in the yellow bridesmaid dress. But, if I were truthful, I looked every bit as good. There Gary stood, stiffer than a coat of mail and smiling like crazy from the line of groomsmen. And Duncan. He had this smug grin on his face. Yeah, I got her for good.

For keeps.

And finally, I took the volume into the bedroom, propped it up on my lap as I sat back against some pillows and looked at it with Duncan.

"Would you do it all over again?" he asked.

At that moment in time, I would. "Yes," I said in all honesty.

"Me, too. There's not a thing I would change about the past twenty-four years."

I wished I could say the same, but I wasn't about to spoil the moment. "We were a nice looking bride and groom."

"You're still pretty, Poppy. Just as pretty now."

I laid the book on my lap and looked at him. "Really? You still think I'm pretty?"

He smiled and took off his glasses. "I do."

When I knocked on the door of the farmhouse the next morning, Mildred LaRue, swallowed almost whole in the tentlike recesses of a rajah looking nightgown and robe, tied her eyebrows in a knot. "A little warning by way of the telephone might have been nice, Penelope."

"I've never really thought of myself as an overly nice person, Miss Mildred."

Mildred pushed open the screen door. "Come on in. I'd offer you fresh coffee, but I see you've brought your own."

"I was out on my walk and decided to make it a nice long one and come see you. Wow, Miss Mildred, look at your hair!"

The darkened hair buzzed about her head like a million bees. Every small movement of her head shook the frizzy strands.

"Now *that* is going too far. You can barge in here at six-thirty in the morning, but that automatically means you leave any comments about my person right at the door. You understanding me?"

I nodded. "Sit down, Miss Mildred. I'll fix you some breakfast."

"I'm not sure whether that would be a favor or not."

"It's just eggs. If you've got some."

"Well, all right then." Mildred pulled out a kitchen chair and groaned as she sat down. A steaming cup of coffee sat on the green-and-white checked tablecloth. "Saundra will be over in a bit. We got a doctor's appointment this morning. Eight o'clock."

"Really? Who you taking her to?"

"Dr. Wheelock."

"He goes to our church."

"I know. I hear he's a good man."

"So Saundra is pregnant?" I pulled a frying pan out of the cabinet beneath the cooktop.

"Yes. Explains a lot, doesn't it?"

"No kidding! No wonder she was so emotional."

"You got that right."

I turned the stove dial to number nine and placed the heavy frying pan onto the burner. This was going to be fun. Har. Why on earth did I think cooking for a cook like Miss Mildred was a good idea? "You got any cayenne?"

"Baby, now what do you think?"

"Where is it?"

"Spice cabinet's right over your head."

"So how's Saundra feeling?"

"Good. No nausea yet."

"That's good." I slid a dim yellow cardboard carton of eggs out of Miss Mildred's Stone Age Frigidaire. "So when's she due?"

"January."

"Has she been over here much then?"

Mildred reached behind her and began pulling out silverware from the drawer. "Yes. I'll tell you what, Penelope, Saundra's a wonderful girl. She really was just hiding behind all that finery. She's asked me to help her with the women's Sunday school class. Said she really didn't know what in the world she was doing teaching it in the first place other than that her husband kept saying, 'But the last pastor's wife taught it!'"

"She should be coming to our prayer meetings, don't you think?"

"I'll ask her. It sure would do her a world of good to know she's not alone in her trials."

I cracked four eggs into the hot pan. "How do you like your eggs?"

"Scrambled."

"Me, too. Mind if I make myself some?"

"Go ahead. But Herman's going to be over soon, and with the way that man eats, you might want to make the entire dozen."

I cracked the rest of the eggs. Great. The pan was way too small. Maybe Miss Mildred wouldn't notice.

"We got together for prayer while you were in Baltimore," Mildred said. "Would you bring me that coffeepot, Penelope?"

I did. "How did it go?"

"Good. I just can't get a read on that Joanna woman."

"Me, either."

"I'm not feeling the spiritual connection."

"I don't feel it either." I stirred so carefully my throat constricted. But I refused to spill egg onto the burner because I'd never hear the end of it. A healthy dose of cayenne dove straight down from the half-moon slot in the spice can right into the middle of the eggs. Hmm, looked pretty. Sunrise in a pan. "I wonder why she comes?"

Mildred shrugged. "I think she wants to be a good preacher's wife. Like it's a job or something. She's coming for pointers."

"You really think so?"

"I do. I'm surprised she doesn't take notes!"

"Want some toast?"

"That'll do."

I turned the broil knob above the oven to high.

"You pretty much do everything on high heat, don't you, Penelope?"

"Unfortunately, yes." I stirred the eggs. "So what did I miss at the last church ladies' prayer meeting?"

"Well, we talked a lot about Crazy Days." Mildred shook her head, her large brown eyes heavy with regret. "We been fighting in this town for decades, Penelope. The Mount Zions stealing people from the Pentecostals, Presbyterians taking on disenchanted Episcopals, Episcopals taking on Catholics. I've never liked it, but it seems there's nothing anyone can do about it."

"It finally went too far." I scraped a cookie sheet from a stack of like pans on top of the refrigerator.

"Do you remember Jesus praying, 'Father I pray that they would be one even as We are one?'"

"Yeah, I do."

"It was important to Him, Penelope. Unity is found all through the Bible, but we've divided ourselves, dissected every moving part, separating ourselves to the point of exclusiveness not only with the world but with each other. Pastors refusing to sit next to Christians who don't believe like they do. People fighting over minute doctrinal points. It's heartbreaking."

"We forget we're just branches, Miss Mildred. We forget about the Vine we're attached to, focusing all our vision on the other branches and not the Source of life. I wish I knew what the answer was."

"Well, I can tell you, not that I'm always good at following it myself. But I always think of Jesus, and I think of Him washing the disciples' feet and cooking them fish, and I remember that He showed us that above all we are servants."

Servants.

I felt tears begin. "Miss Mildred, I've got a confession to make. I'm not a worthy servant at all. I'm just as guilty as anybody. I accuse people at Highland of having agendas but never once have I opened myself up and said, 'Here I am, Lord, send me.'"

"It's a big step, Penelope. One that needs the Holy Spirit right there beside you, guiding you and comforting you."

"I've always told myself it's just my husband's job."

"It may be his job, but you have a choice whether or not to deny yourself and take up the cross, Penelope."

"But aren't there lots of pastors' wives who just sit in the pew on Sunday, and have other jobs and do their own thing?"

"There are."

"Are they wrong?"

"The comparison game is one you'll always lose, Penelope. The fact is, you're miserable doing things the way you've been doing. Trust and obey, baby."

I turned my back, opened the bread box, and laid several slices on the pan.

Mildred took a gentle slurp of her hot coffee. "So Miss Joanna says she recommended the churches have their own function next year."

"That's right. Put all the bad kids in the corner together."

"Mmn, hmn."

"Then we'll do nothing. Ever again."

"I know, baby."

"We deserve it."

"I know that, too."

I opened the oven door. Figures. I forgot to move the oven rack up to the highest slot! "Where are your oven mitts?"

"Hanging on a hook on the back of the pantry door."

"Do you think we'll ever get these churches back on speaking terms?" I asked.

"*We* won't. But I wouldn't call it a lost cause just yet."

"Why not?"

"Because sometimes God's just got plans."

"Well, that's true."

"'Course it is, Penelope. Mildred LaRue doesn't lie."

"Never?"

"Not about the Lord."

That, heaven only help us all, was the truth.

Twenty-eight

After refusing a ride home from Miss Mildred's, I walked down Highland Lane, slowly negotiating the two miles that separated the bungalow from the farmhouse. Saundra had shown up in a maternity dress.

I suppressed a grin. She won't start showing until at least the sixth month. I guessed Saundra truly expressed herself through her clothing. Miss Mildred talks about her hiding behind her fashion, but if anyone knows how to speak using colors, textures, and all manner of trim, it's Mildred LaRue. Maybe that's why Miss Mildred and Saundra understand each other so well now.

Pastor Phelps smiled like someone coming out of the theater after a good movie. "Thank you for taking her to the doctor's, Mother LaRue. I get a little leary around female doctors."

"You're not the first man to feel that way, Pastor," I said.

"You just leave everything to me," Mildred assured him.

The way he kissed his wife then, so tenderly and kind, hit me with a force I'm glad I didn't foresee. Because just then, I realized that lately I've been on the receiving end of kisses just like that. Duncan's kisses were so tender now, so purposeful yet sweet. They held within them enough power to make me stay and enough pain to make me leave. When he kissed me with such trust and intimacy, I felt The Masquerade grow larger. I saw myself for the shadow I was, and as hard as I had tried to forget, the truth within our marriage was gone. I could not get around it. I could not break through it. I could not get under it. I could not get over it.

I just couldn't get over it.

One thing remained certain; I couldn't live like this anymore. He'd been trying so hard lately. The studio. The car. And, if I were honest, he did all sorts of little, nice things for me. Everyday things. So what if he forgot Valentine's Day? That happened months ago. Didn't I need to be understanding? Didn't I need to count my blessings?

What a sinner you are, Poppy.

The apostle Paul said, "If we confess our sins, He is faithful and just to forgive us our sins and to cleanse us from all unrighteousness."

Oh, Jesus, I've been so involved in all the tasks, all the chores, all the duties, I've forgotten You. I've been looking at the other branches forgetting You are the vine. I am a woman of unclean lips in a nation of unclean lips. I've taken in Your Word Sunday after Sunday, have led studies and prayed out loud, and yet my heart has grown fat and dull, sluggish and tired. I've forgotten how to abide in You, and it isn't working anymore. It just isn't working.

I would never be restored without that confession of which the verse spoke. I'd given it enough time. But how could I tell him? *Oh, Jesus. How can I tell him?*

After walking for thirty minutes or so, I turned down the driveway that led into the church. The narthex doors yawned wide, breathing in fresh air to sweeten the sanctuary.

The Saturday morning buzz of deacons and devoted ones filtered into the sanctuary. Someone was vacuuming the Sunday school rooms in the basement. Elder Barnhouse sat in the pews straightening the hymnbooks and pew Bibles with a ruler, while Bercie, in a pink tennis skirt scattered with green frogs, dusted the communion table and the pulpit.

"Do you know where Pastor's water glass is?" she called to her husband.

"It's not there?"

"Nope."

"Must already be down in the kitchen. I'll go down and make sure there's a clean one ready for the morning."

She looked up at me standing in the doorway. "Well, hey, Mrs. Fraser!"

I have told the woman at least a hundred times to call me Poppy. Clearly a lost cause.

"Hi, Miss Bercie! How're things coming?"

"Oh, fine. It's gonna be a nice service tomorrow. Pastor's talking about grace."

"My personal favorite," said Mr. Barnhouse. "Without it, the rest means nothing. Hear you had a good trip. We were praying."

"Thanks. It was nice."

"And your folks were well?" asked Bercie.

"They were fine."

It amazed me how some of the parishioners remembered every little detail. If I prayed like they did…well, maybe I wouldn't be such a mess!

"Is Duncan here?"

"Back in the office."

"Okay, I'll go find him. You all take care!" I said with a wave.

And they waved back and told me they'd see me bright and early in the morning.

Down the hall toward the offices, my sneakers squeaked on the white speckled squares of taupe linoleum. A regular, metallic thump echoed from the secretary's desk. I poked my head inside to find Miss Poole officiously stapling the new announcement sheet she decided to spearhead, "To keep the bulletin from being such a bulky mess, Penny, dear."

When I read the last typo regarding the Low Self-Esteem Support Group that meets over at India's church, I knew it had been the straw that had broken the maven's back, so to speak. *The Low Self-Esteem Support Group meets at St. Edmund's Episcopal this Tuesday at 6:30 P.M. Please use the back door.* Not the front door as it should have read. But I had to give her credit for sailing the winds of diplomacy this time. Maybe Ira suggested it. So now, all I had to do was the drawing on the front each week. Duncan's been talking a lot about gift-based ministries these days. And honestly, I was suspicious about it until someone gave me a job I loved.

Which reminded me. I'd better get home and do that drawing. Duncan would have to give out more details about the sermon than just "grace." I mean, it surely reigned as the most beautiful characteristic of

God's plan for His people, but some more information would be helpful.

"Hi, Miss Poole."

Magda Poole looked up, her long earrings with the silver Indian coins on the bottom swaying front to back. "Hey, Penny. Have a nice trip?"

"Yeah. It was fine. Sad in a lot of ways, but…" I shrugged. "How's the announcement sheet coming?"

"Wonderfully. It's going to be much better now."

I took no offense. The woman spoke the truth.

Duncan came in with Angus at that moment.

"So can you give me more info on your sermon?" I asked my husband. "What aspect of grace are you talking about?"

"Grace greater than all our sins," he said. "Like the old song."

Miss Mildred's message to me, too. Hmm. Okay, Lord.

Five minutes later I settled myself in my studio, ink bottle open, and a freshly cleaned silver-nibbed pen in my hand.

Grace.

How does one draw a picture of grace?

I set pen to paper, and the ink flowed in a turgid, glistening line. My wrist moved slowly as I outlined a rude cross and upon its surface inscribed many words. Painful words so familiar to humanity itself.

Selfishness.

Pride.

Thoughtlessness.

Hatred.

Bitterness.

Anger.

Materialism.

Jealousy.

Adultery.

And at the bottom of the page sat one word, heavily inked on the outline of an eraser. It said GRACE.

Grace that pardons and cleanses within.

Glory to His Name.

"You just have to take it, Penelope. God has already forgiven you.

Jesus has already died for whatever you did." Miss Mildred's words filled my brain. "Trust and Obey."

In thin, light pencil, I drew the suffering Christ, muscles straining, head bowed beneath the heavy, thorny crown.

Oh, Jesus, I prayed. Oh, Jesus, Jesus, Jesus. I'm asking You one last time to forgive me.

I climbed in bed that night. Duncan slept soundly beside me, having turned in early. And for the first time in many years, I was actually looking forward to Sunday.

He took it all to the cross with Him, and He said, "It is finished."

I hummed "A Mighty Fortress Is Our God" on the way to Bill D's after Sunday service. The choir had sounded as horrible as ever. Duncan's sermon had basically been boring, but I found myself reading forward from his text in Ephesians and enjoying it immensely. After all, if I couldn't keep my mind on my husband, St. Paul wasn't a bad alternative.

All of us also lived among them at one time, gratifying the cravings of our sinful nature and following its desires and thoughts. Like the rest, we were by nature objects of wrath. But because of his great love for us, God, who is rich in mercy, made us alive with Christ even when we were dead in transgressions—it is by grace you have been saved.

Rich in mercy. Rich in mercy. My God is rich in mercy. Indeed that mercy, that grace didn't diminish my sin, it merely rose larger, richer, and more beautiful so that it might cover it completely. The same grace that covered my sins saved me. If I couldn't trust myself, I could certainly trust my God, my God so rich in mercy, so filled with love that He gave His precious Son for me.

After the service I made rounds with the church members, gladly, for the first time since arriving at Highland, and I prayed that God would extend a portion of His mercy into my hands, so that I might help distribute His love.

Once the church parking lot had emptied and we'd piled in the car, Duncan announced we'd have brunch out. Fine by me. Bill D's makes biscuits fluffier than Gabriel's wings. Once in town, Angus and I hopped out of the Subaru, and Duncan drove off to park somewhere along the square. Taking his little hand in mine, I walked inside the cool of the restaurant and said hello to Bill. He found us a good seat near the air conditioner.

Duncan laughed when he came in and saw I'd already loaded up my plate with biscuits and gravy. "Looks good. Maybe I'll live a little this morning and get the same."

"It can't hurt you, Mr. No Flab."

By the time Duncan returned with an identical plate to mine, India Clemmings had joined us. "I just finished up, but I thought I'd bring my tea over and visit."

I introduced her to Duncan as "The Ladybug Girl."

"So that's your car out there by Java Jane's?"

"Yes, it is."

"So," I said. "What's been happening over at the Episcopals since the Crazy Days thing?"

India curled her lip. "Nothing! Bunch of stick-in-the-muds. They're blaming it on everybody else. Especially *you* guys with those Boston cream pies and all."

A scapegoat.

An Old Testament institution made into a Christian tradition. According to *The Proper Christian Ladies' Handbook,* a scapegoat could be found most anywhere. But the quicker the better. Of course, if one took the blame and *acted* humble, that was even better!

"Miss Poole really stirred something up that time," I said.

"I know. I think the churches have finally done it for good."

"There's got to be some way we can make amends." I swirled an extra biscuit around in some gravy.

India started picking apart a paper napkin. "I don't know how. How can we get along with Mount Oak when we can't even get along with each other?"

Duncan planted his fork in a small wedge of potato. "You know, this is the hardest part about being a Christian in my estimation."

"What?" I asked.

"It's knowing deep down that it should be better, that it could be better if we all learned to control ourselves. It's knowing that we've got the greatest power source available to help us, and all we do is get in our own way."

I could say, "Amen to that," and I did.

"All one has to do is read the epistles. Paul begs for unity. So there was a problem with this from the very start."

"So what's the answer?" India asked.

"Humility. He didn't consider equality with God something to be grasped. But He humbled Himself and took upon Himself the form of a servant."

I thought about Jesus washing the disciples' feet, like Miss Mildred said. Dusty, dirty feet, washed by the spotless Lamb of God.

Fifteen minutes late for the Monday prayer meeting, Chris rapped on Mildred's kitchen screen door.

"Come in!" everybody yelled.

I stood to my feet and pulled out the chair next to me. The flesh on Chris's face emitted a glowing blush, and her eyes radiated excitement. "I've got the best news!" she said in contained jubilance, circling around the table on the rattiest pair of flip-flops I had seen in years. Must have dug them out of some storage box in the attic.

Miss Mildred asked what it was and got up to pour Chris a long glass of iced tea to go with the barge-sized platter of fried chicken sitting in the middle of the table. Sitting next to a quiet yet pleasant Saundra Phelps, I had already done the disappearing act on three thighs.

"Jason Harkens lost his fraternity sponsor! There's no way he'll be able to return to Hopkins to finish up this year!"

I dipped my head, shook it, and said, "What?"

Mildred patted Chris's hand. "Sit down, honey. The heat must be getting to you."

"No! It's really great news!" Nevertheless, she did sit down, and grabbed a drumstick off the platter.

Joanna Jones-Fletcher said, "Well, first tell me who this Jason Harkens is."

In between bites of chicken, Chris told us the whole story. "And so this is the idea I got when I talked to him on the phone tonight. What if we got a scholarship fund together for a worthy Zeta Chi member? What if we got the town to help with a bang-out fundraiser to establish the Joshua R. Knight Scholarship fund?"

India nodded. "It's a good cause. Education and all."

"Just to a member of Zeta Chi?" Joanna asked.

"Yes. That would be the point," Chris said. "It would make the fraternity never forget what happened, but it would be redemptive."

I looked at the others. "I like it. What do you think, Miss Mildred?"

"I'm all for it. I'll sing at the fundraiser. For free."

I stood to my feet and got the small pad Miss Mildred had sitting by the phone on the counter. Pen, too. "Okay, music's taken care of."

I sat back down and started to write. "Oh, Miss Mildred! Green ink, too?"

Joanna lit up. "I loved the GLOs in college. I'm all for this idea. And maybe it should be a lacrosse player. Your son played lacrosse, right?"

Chris nodded. "A Zeta Chi member of the lacrosse team."

"Sounds good to me," I said, writing it down on the pad. "I'll get my dad to do the legal work for free."

"You can count on me for the public relations and the advertising," said Joanna.

Sunny blushed some more. "I don't really know what I could do."

My sorority instincts kicked back in with a vengeance. "You'll do the name tags and table arrangements, Sunny."

"Okay. I think I can handle that."

"Of course you can!" Charmaine piped up for the first time. "What about me? If Miss Mildred is going to do the music, well, I'm fresh out of talent then."

Chris said, "We'll count on you to emcee. And maybe I could be a guest on the *Port of Peace Hour*. We can get donations from across the country that way."

"I'll have to convince Harlan," Chamaine said. "But I've got a lot of leverage on that show that I never use. I say the time has come."

Saundra Phelps just smiled and ate saltines. So much for no nausea, poor thing. She didn't pray out loud later on, but her heartfelt amens, her soft "Yes, Father Gods" gilded the feathers on our wings of prayer.

I told Duncan all about it that night as we climbed into bed.

"Wow," he said. "Think you've bitten off more than you can chew with this one, Popp?"

"Absolutely."

"And you wouldn't want it any other way, is that right?"

"You got it, Right Reverend Fraser."

He took my hand and caressed my face.

Monday night. All right.

Twenty-nine

*I*ndia had the right idea with the ladybug angle. And I told her so as we breakfasted together early one morning before she had to be at church for work. We sat in Java Jane's, engulfed by the velvet chairs. Eating strawberry cream cheese scones, we drank coffee and got to know each other some more. My perception that India could probably be categorized as the classic loner seemed to be accurate. The oldest of two girls, musically inclined since the age of five, she'd never really cared much about socializing with friends. Didn't need it. Not when a girl had Bach and Beethoven for her best friends.

"I think ladybugs are kind of a universal symbol for happiness," India said. "They make me feel so tender inside."

"It's that rhyme." I bit off a corner of scone.

"Ladybug, ladybug"?

"Yeah. Think about it. Every time one lands on your arm, don't you feel sorry for it?"

"I guess so."

"Exactly. I mean, the poor dear has lost all of her children. And in a fire."

India shook her head. "Oh, no, no, no. I always assumed she'd made it home in time!"

"Not me. Worst case scenario every time."

"Really? You don't think she made it home?"

I laughed. "It's just a nursery rhyme, India."

"Well, I know, but still."

"I think most people take your view of it. They're not lost causes like me."

India wrinkled her nose pleasantly, but I couldn't help but notice she offered no argument about the "lost causes" statement.

I pulled a list out of my purse. "Okay, so the pastor of your church is all for helping us with this?"

"Yes. He said the gardens in back would be in full summer bloom by then, and he'll make sure the courtyard bricks are blasted clean with the hose."

"Can you believe he agreed to do this?"

India leaned forward. "He's not as wishy-washy as he seems. Although I'm not what you'd call a real cream puff, so I didn't know if he'd listen to me."

I examined her. Despite her forty extra pounds and dark, spiky hair-cut, she had quite the darling face. "I don't think you give yourself enough credit."

She shook her head. "When there are women like Joanna Jones-Fletcher around…"

I waved a dismissive hand. "Contrived. It's all contrived."

"Okay, like Chris then."

"Now *that's* a different story. Just take comfort in the fact that truly beautiful women like Chris…the ones who are pretty inside as well…don't have a clue as to their outward beauty."

"Yeah, maybe."

"I mean, wouldn't you rather beauty be bestowed on someone who deserves it?" Now *that* sounded like a good outlook.

"I guess so. So what's happening with the gala?"

"Well, we've got the place. Now we need to go around to the busi-nesses and beg for food and paper products."

India held out her hand for her portion of the list. She looked down. "Oh, good, The Sweet Stop. I love that place."

I did, too. "See about some chocolate covered strawberries. Maybe a truffle for the goodie bags we're giving out as they leave."

"Will do. Gotta go or I'll be late."

"See ya."

I checked my wristwatch. Onto the next church lady. I had to be finished with my rounds before Robbie went to class and had to drag Angus with him. I know the educational system has tumbled downhill, but I hope British Lit is still beyond my lastborn.

I gulped down the rest of my coffee and made for the IGA.

Sunny waved from her position at the cash register. "I've got good news!" she cried. "I can't even believe it myself."

"What is it?" I eyed the display on the end of the cereal aisle: $1.99 for a box of granola. Wow, that was a good price. And with the way cereal prices had gone through the roof, pound for pound, steak was cheaper these days!

"Marc said we could use the sound system from Baptist Bible. In fact, he said he'd be glad to come over and set it up."

"Wow!"

"Yes, ma'am. I have to tell you, I was scared to even ask, but nobody had talked about needing it, and I knew we would, and so I did. I just did. At supper last night I said, 'Marc, remember that boy who died?' and then I told him the whole thing. I can't believe I had the nerve."

"That's great!"

"Yes, ma'am. And did you know that Marc is really a good technical sort? He told me we don't have to even think another thought about it. He's even going to set up the tables for us."

"I can't believe he's come around like that. I mean, after Crazy Days and all."

"Yes, ma'am. But we did give out Cokes and all." A customer came up, and she began to scan the items. "But I can believe it when I really think about it."

I nodded. "Well, you would know your own husband better than I would."

"Oh, it's not that. It's just that we've been praying for months now. Who knows how much power God's been storing up for us on our behalf? I mean, stuff He knew we'd be needing now."

"You're right, of course."

"I just never knew to look at God like that before. But you ladies have taught me so much these past months. Sometimes I feel like God is right beside me."

"You doubted that?"

"Well, sometimes. It's hard at our church sometimes. Wearing the right clothes and saying the right things, and I'm so quiet. I thought of Him as so unapproachable and well, like some king or something. Not to sound disrespectful," she hastened to add.

The customer, an elderly man, listened with interest and a smile, but didn't say anything. He just handed Sunny the eggs and then the bread as she bagged his groceries.

"That's not disrespectful at all," I said. I pulled my list out of my purse. "Here are some businesses I need you to ask for donated items we'll need for the gala."

The customer paid for his food, picked up the bag, and turned to me. "What's this all about?"

I briefly explained what happened to Josh, talked about Jason Hearkens's lack of a sponsor, and the planned scholarship fund.

He scratched his baldhead. "That so? Well, I'm with the Lions Club. Maybe I can convince the members to set up tables at the grocery stores. To sell tickets. Maybe you can come to our meeting tomorrow night and explain it all." He shrugged. "We really didn't have much on the agenda, so you'd be doing us a favor."

I handed him my card and took his name and number. "Okay, Mr. Webb. Thanks. I'll be there tomorrow night. What time?"

"Seven o'clock. We meet down at the elementary school."

"I'll be there."

"Good." The man grinned. "I'll be waiting out front."

He left with his bag of groceries. Must have a bum knee, I thought, watching him limp slightly as he made his way through the automatic door. Poor man.

Sunny shook her head, her long blond hair flailing out like the swings on an amusement park ride. "I can't believe the way this is falling together."

"I've planned lots of charity stuff in my time, Sunny. It always does."

"But this seems to be kind of supernatural."

I thought about it a second or two, then nodded. "Yeah, maybe you're right."

I grabbed a few boxes of cereal, paid for them, and was speeding over to Joanna's a couple of minutes later. Through the center of town and onto Coventry Circle, I negotiated my Subaru.

Coventry Circle was a parade ground for pristine old homes. Mostly Victorian, not my favorite period of architecture to be sure, the houses still emanated a majestic aura with their thick lawns and colorful border gardens.

Joanna lived at number 2109: completely white, rounded porches anchored either side of the three-storied house, and a cupola served as a sunlit crow's nest complete with a cock-a-doodle-doo weathervane. Stained glass windows at interesting locations provided colorful relief to the pale, lacy facade. And all this for just the two of them.

As if that seemed fair! Well, Joanna used to be a stockbroker. And actually, she'd signed on a couple of clients here in Mount Oak. She probably wasn't hurting at all.

Reverend Quentin Fletcher whirled out the side door and cycloned an officious path toward his car as I pulled up, announcing my arrival with the sudden scream of a very surprised set of brakes.

Wow, was he good-looking or what? Movie star good-looking. Not model good-looking. Say what you want about Hollywood, but their men have more character to their looks than the fashion world does. His hair, thick and black, stayed put in the breeze, however. Hairspray?

Oh, well. Nobody's perfect.

He waved and called, "You must be Poppy Fraser!" as I climbed out of the car.

"And you must be Reverend Fletcher."

"Forget the Reverend stuff. Call me Quentin."

We met in the middle, just by the front walk lined with fuchsia petunias and white alyssum. Hanging baskets of bleeding hearts between each porch pillar swayed slightly in the summer zephyr.

"You heading off to church?"

"Yes. Joanna's roped me into printing off the handouts for the gala." He fished a hand into his pants pocket and came up with a set of keys with various colored plastic rounds around each one. So this guy took that verse about redeeming the time quite seriously. No trying three keys in one lock for him.

"You don't sound too thrilled."

He combed through his hair with well-manicured fingers. Guess I was wrong about the hair spray. "I'm not. I'm a busy man."

Oh, brother.

I smiled. "Then don't let me keep you. Nice to meet you. Bye." Bigger smile, and down the walk I sashayed without a backward glance.

I'm a busy man.

Well, lah-dee-dah.

I pushed the doorbell, and Joanna appeared half a minute later looking perfect as usual.

Admittedly, I've got a problem with these people. More than jealousy. I felt complete, un-Christianlike disdain and unadulterated superiority.

Oh, man! Will I ever be able to control my old man? A one-second prayer for a quick change of heart accompanied my "Hi, Joanna."

"Hello, Poppy. Thanks for coming over here. I've got some coffee on. Would you like a cup?"

"I never turn down a cup of coffee."

Joanna led me back to the old kitchen. That was a surprise. And the kitchen was surprisingly messy. Not a Chris kitchen, but not a Fraser kitchen either.

"I hope you don't mind us sitting back here. I like the sunshine in the morning. It helps me get through the rest of the day."

Well, huh. That sounded different from anything she'd ever said before.

So we sat together, sipping weak coffee out of surprisingly ordinary mugs and going over the public relations for the gala.

"Quentin's printing off the handouts for the churches today. Under threat of life and limb, I might add."

"So I gathered."

Joanna set her forearms at the edge of the table. "He's driving me crazy."

"I know that feeling."

"No, really. You seem like a very well-adjusted woman...."

What a crock!

"And your husband seemed so nice at Crazy Days."

Well, that much was true. They didn't come any nicer than Duncan.

"That's all I want from Quentin. Just to be a nice guy."

"Was he a nice guy when you met him?"

"Not at all. Arrogant and confident. You couldn't tell him anything, Poppy."

"And you thought that was terribly sexy because he had the looks to go along with it, right?"

"Exactly." Joanna shook her head and picked up her coffee mug.

"I wish I knew what to tell you."

"Yeah, well, waking up one day and realizing you married someone for all the wrong reasons is not something anyone foresees when she's standing at the altar looking like Grace Kelly." Joanna waved a hand. "I don't know why I even said anything. I figured if I got involved in your little group, maybe I'd get some insight into handling marriage with a pastor. But, really, I think I'm just not cut out for this sort of life."

"Give it a chance, Joanna. To be honest, I'm new at this pastor's wife stuff myself."

"Really?"

"Yeah. Duncan just became a pastor four years ago. I still don't really like it. But it's his thing, and I've got to be supportive."

That sure sounded good.

Joanna got up to get the coffeepot. "There's a big difference between Duncan and Quentin, though. Duncan really lives his calling. With Quentin it's just a job. He doesn't really even believe the Bible."

I couldn't understand that. "I've always wondered how men who don't really believe in the faith go to theological seminaries and become pastors."

"I don't know because it sure isn't about the money!"

I breathed in deeply. "What about you? Is faith hard for you."

"Extremely. And that's probably the bulk of my problem." She topped off my coffee. "I'm a lot of things, Poppy. I'm superficial, proud, and greedy, but I'm not going to pretend I'm something I'm not. Not like Quentin does."

I sighed. "You're sure in a pickle."

"I know." She sat back down. "And if I leave him, well, I'll ruin his ministry."

"Such that it is."

"Such that it is." Joanna suddenly smiled and slid behind her usual veil of professionalism. "Well, that's enough of my woes, let's get on with business."

And I knew just then that Joanna Jones-Fletcher's stay in Mount Oak was limited.

"Well, then. I've got a list of the businesses you can visit for freebies." I ripped a sheet of paper off my pad, Joanna's name on the top.

Joanna took the list and nodded. "Okay. The Patio for pastries, good choice. And what's the Photo Stop for?"

"Disposable cameras."

"Sounds good. You want me to follow the gala up with a mailing, snapshots and all?"

"Yeah, that'd be great."

"I'll get a photographer, too. We'll want this to be covered in the *Sentinel.*"

"Good."

"It's coming together," Joanna said.

"Well, it's a good cause."

"Chris's life makes mine seem like a dream."

"I guess so. But you don't have to live her life, you have to live yours. And if you're miserable…"

"You're miserable."

I wanted to tell her to turn to the Lord. That if He could keep me married and somewhat sane as a pastor's wife, He could do the same thing for her.

Maybe next time.

After all, didn't these things take time? I hadn't exactly been Miss Caring until a couple of minutes ago. I hadn't even tried to act the part.

But something inside me told me to take a chance. People expect pastor's wives to talk like this. I'd only be rising to expectations, not pouncing down and thumping a Bible. "Joanna? I notice you never pray at the meetings. I mean...has anyone ever told you who Jesus *really* is? What He really did?"

"Not really. To be honest, I was raised by just my dad. And he was an atheist. He hit the roof the first time I brought Quentin home."

"Would you mind if I told you about Him? I promise I won't preach a sermon or anything like that."

"No, Poppy. Actually, I think I'd like it."

And so I did. I told her about the Creator God who sent His Son, His beloved, beautiful Son into a dark, sinful world full of hate and wars and death and abuse. I painted a portrait of words, a stunning portrait of a love so dazzling, so wonderful, it was the only perfection we would ever know until we saw that Son, Jesus Christ, face-to-face.

I dug down into my purse and pulled out a tiny green New Testament. "I know you've probably got a lot of Bibles here and at church, but read this, Joanna. It's a modern translation, so it's easy to understand, and you can take it with you wherever you go and read it when you can. But please, read it with an open heart. I promise you, if you believe, it will change you forever."

"I'll read it." She took the book. "And may I ask you any questions I have as they come up?"

"You've got my number."

"Yes. Okay, then."

The portal closed, and we sat quietly, in discomfort for several seconds. "I hope you'll still keep coming to the prayer meetings, Joanna."

She gave a weak laugh. "Maybe someday I'll even say a prayer."

Next stop, the Charmaine Hopewell abode.

The Hopewell's inhabited a large, sixties Volvo of a brick rancher on the east edge of town. Must have been Harlan's doing because Charmaine definitely seemed the type to build a brick-front colonial in the new development north of the mall chocked full of extras. Corian counters, crown molding, garden tubs, and a gas fireplace with a remote in the master bedroom. Charmaine seemed to be a woman of creature comfort and overstuffed couches.

I knocked on the door and was greeted by an eight-year-old, plump girl, who, unfortunately, looked nothing like Charmaine. "Is your mom home?"

The girl rolled her eyes, heavy, round, green eyes with pale lashes. "Mama!" she hollered, but it really came out Maw-Maaah. And that was a first class whine if I had ever heard one. This little miss could put Paisley to shame! "You wanna come in or what?"

I smiled a scrunched-up grin that refused to creep up to my eyes no matter how hard I tried. "I'll wait here."

"Whatever." She disappeared.

Oh, brother.

"Poppy!"

I heard Charmaine before I saw her veer around the wall that separated the small slate foyer from the living room. "Hi, Charmaine!"

"Well, come on in. I can't believe Victoria didn't show you in. Sometimes I just wonder where her manners are! Victoria!" she bellowed.

"What?" the child answered from somewhere else in the house.

"You just wait until after Mrs. Fraser leaves. You're in big trouble!"

No answer.

I knew what Victoria knew. Charmaine would either forget all about it or let Victoria think she forgot. The really, really good thing about it was—Victoria wasn't my child! And I had no delusions that I "could straighten her out in a week" if I were suddenly given custody of the surly munchkin.

"Come on into the kitchen. Mama's in there making a dump cake." She leaned forward. "That's about all she can do these days."

"Why?" I didn't even know that Charmaine's mother lived with them.

"Arthritis. And she won't take anything." She rolled her eyes, apparently a common occurrence at the Hopewell house. "'If the good Lord wants me in pain, I'll be in pain!'" she mimicked.

I dropped my mouth open and shook my head. "That's got to be the strangest thing I've ever heard!"

"Don't I know it! But anyway, that's the way it is. I've got some coffee on for you."

Feeling as if my caffeine addiction had reached a level of fame I'd never foreseen, I followed her through the living room. That distinct "Plug-Ins" smell infiltrated the air all around me, and surprisingly the house shone, a spectacular example of cleanliness being next to godliness. One could never tell about these things. I'd pegged Charmaine as a "messy" for sure!

I peeked into the family room to the left of the living room. There it was, the overstuffed couch with big, soft pillows. And man, was that one of the biggest TV screens I'd ever seen outside of a movie theater! Actually it might have been bigger than some of those cheesy multiplex cinemas I'd gone to in Baltimore.

The furniture couldn't be described as anything I would pick out. The end tables matched the coffee table perfectly, and the knickknacks and wall arrangements looked like she'd bought them at one of those "girl parties" church ladies found themselves invited to all too often. Brass things that would vibrate little leaves and such if one slammed the front door too hard.

The other two Hopewell children, boys younger than Victoria, pounded Nintendo handsets wired to an older TV across the room.

"We just had the kitchen redone last year."

White Eurocabinets.

"Nice and bright," I said, thinking that didn't sound complimentary enough.

"Mama." Charmaine laid a hand on her mother's back. "This here is Poppy Fraser. Remember me talking about her?"

"Mama" nodded and smiled and looked back into her pan. Obviously more than the cartilage at the end of her bones had deteriorated. Poor dear. "Hi, there, Mrs…what's your maiden name, Charmaine?"

"Whitehead. And don't you say nothing about it, Poppy. I got rid of it the day I married Harlan, and I've never been regretful."

"Hi, Mrs. Whitehead."

Charmaine poured me a cup of coffee. "Have a seat at the table."

I sat down in the upholstered, swivel chair and set my bag on the white, melamine table. "Any news from Josef's yet?"

Charmaine handed me a cup. "I don't usually make my own coffee, so I hope it's all right."

Words a coffee drinker hates to hear.

I took a sip, grimaced automatically...then, hey, "This is good, Charmaine!"

"Then I'm as surprised as you are! I just guessed on the proportions."

Mama continued to spread the cherries on top of the pineapple.

Charmaine yanked open the refrigerator door and pulled out a Diet Coke. She sat down in the chair catty-corner from me. "I talked to Josef yesterday. Practically needed an interpreter, though!"

"So what did he say? Yes? No?"

"He said he might could do the appetizers, but no main course. And, to be honest, Poppy, he's not the kind of guy to provide sliced prime rib and ham."

"I can't picture him under those red lights myself."

Charmaine sighed. "Well, maybe we can get Jeanelle to do it."

I winced. "Oh, man, Charmaine. After the way we all acted at Crazy Days about the food and all? I don't know."

"Well, your son works there, doesn't he?"

"Yeah, but, that doesn't make it any easier to ask."

Charmaine waved a hand. "Oh, shoot, Poppy, they can get a tax deduction, can't they?"

"I have no idea."

She patted my arm. "Well, I'll go and ask her. You know me, I'm not the type to take no for an answer."

Well, that sure enough was true. Seemed like golden pipes went hand in hand with lead heads if Charmaine and Miss Mildred were any indication.

We went over a few more details, and I readied myself to go when Harlan Hopewell himself walked into the room.

Bald as a watermelon!

I really thought I had succeeded in not reacting. I didn't move a muscle, didn't gasp, didn't even change expression, or so I thought.

"I know, it's some wig, isn't it?" he boomed.

"You'd never know you were bald!" I blurted.

Oh, man! I shook my head. "Oh, my gosh, I'm so sorry. It's just such a shock!"

Charmaine was sucking in air so hard, she couldn't get out any laughter. She looked like a child who had just stubbed her toe and was winding up for the big cry.

Finally, it spilled.

And Harlan Hopewell joined right in, his forehead wrinkling up, his face deepening to maroon. "It's amazing how they even did that preacher flip at the front of it, isn't it?"

He held out his hand, and I was glad to shake it.

Victoria ran in to see what was so funny, but nobody noticed. She went back to the overstuffed couch in the family room and hollered. "Shut up! I'm trying to watch *Saved by the Bell*!"

Are all TV people different than they seem? I wondered. What was it like to see a different face in your own morning mirror than what the world saw every day?

Hmm.

I stopped in at the church to pick up Angus. I fully admitted my surprise to Duncan. "Harlan Hopewell was a really nice guy."

"He's so scary on that show."

"I know! But he's so funny. He just sat right down with us and gave us some really good ideas."

"I thought you said Charmaine said he wouldn't want to help out."

I shrugged. "Well, she was wrong, I guess. He said he'd be glad to talk about it on the *Port of Peace Hour*."

"Well, just goes to show you. You never know."

That was sure the truth.

Thirty

*T*ra!"

There he stood on the other side of my kitchen screen door. Just standing there in the July heat. Come Monday, the fourth would rain down upon the vacation industry of Mount Oak. No holiday for the locals. But they faced the fact that the Fourth of July financed the whole month of December later on in the year.

"Hey, Mrs. Fraser. Sorry to be disrupting your Saturday."

"Why are you just standing there?"

"I didn't want to disturb you. Just thought I'd wait by the kitchen until you came to refill your coffee."

Oh, not the coffee thing again!

A lot of people took this kind of thing as a sign from above. Heavenly behavior modification. But I was waiting for something more physical, like fibroid cysts in my breasts or a rapid heartbeat.

"Well, come on in. We've got the air conditioner going in the living room."

I pushed open the screen door and ushered him into the sweltering kitchen.

He looked around him appreciatively. "I love this room. Was telling Mag—Miss Poole—that we should do something like this to one of our rooms at Poole Point."

"I'd even do it for you!"

"No kidding?"

"Nope. I love painting murals."

I pushed through the swinging door and into the family room where Angus watched *The Wizard of Oz*. Still. A year from point of purchase. This had to be some kind of record. He saw Ira.

"Mr. Ira!" He jumped to his feet and leapt into Ira's robust arms.

"Gus!"

Nothing prettier than an old person and a young person smack dab together and happy to be there.

"Sit down, Ira, and I'll get you some sweet tea."

"I sure wouldn't refuse a glass of tea, Mrs. Fraser."

As I turned to go into the kitchen, I saw Magda Poole's gentleman's gentleman pull a long register tape of candy dots out of his suit coat pocket.

I smiled and thought how terrible it was that he'd never had kids of his own. Well, he had Miss Poole, and surely that was even more of a challenge!

Wonder what *she* wants?

And to send Ira over for her. Must be big.

I poured the tea and added a slice of lemon for old Ira. If anyone deserved a fresh slice of lemon, Ira did.

Already plugged back into the movie, Angus had comfortably settled himself on Ira's lap. I handed him the tea, then sat down in the nearby Stickley armchair I refused to let Duncan sell. "So what does Miss Poole want you to tell me, Ira?" I made my voice sound light and airy, friendly.

He shook his head. "I came on my own, Mrs. Fraser. She'd never have asked you this herself." He took a large sip of the tea. "That's just what a hot day like today is asking for."

"What's your dilemma, Ira?"

Did Miss Poole actually need a favor? That would be the day!

"It's about the Zeta Chi gala. She really wants to be involved."

Man.

"Oh, Ira. Things are going so *well* with this. We haven't had any major glitches so far. Of course, there have been some minor trip-ups," I heard myself beginning to bleat, "but nothing out of the ordinary. And the community is agreeing to help, too. And after Crazy Days I thought for sure we'd totally severed ties with everyone. It was all so un-Christian and all. Well, to be honest"—I stood up and leaned over to cover Angus's ears—"you know she always stirs up trouble."

"Hey!" Angus cried.

I sat back down. "Sorry, bud."

"Nobody knows that better than me. But I don't think she wants to do too much. I know she won't take over the gala, if that's what you're afraid of."

"How can you be sure of something like that?"

"I just can. Now, you know I know Miss Poole better than anyone."

"Well, yes."

"If I promise, on my own word of honor, that she won't cause trouble, will you let her help?"

I shrugged. "What is it she wants to do so badly?"

"She wants to manage the fund."

"What?"

This was too much.

"Think about it, Mrs. Fraser. Look what she's done with her daddy's money! She's more than quadrupled the estate since he died, and it was something *then*, let me tell you."

"She'd have nothing to do with the actual gala?"

"Nope. And let's be realistic, Mrs. Fraser. How much money is this little thing really going to raise? Maybe enough to put this Jason fellow through for his senior year, but then what happens next year? Another gala? One more year of money and then back to the drawing board?"

He did have a point.

"Did Miss Poole say all of this?"

"Yep. I'm telling you, she's a whiz."

"Let me talk it over with Chris."

He set Angus gently beside him on the couch and stood to his feet. "That's all I ask."

He stuck out his hand and we shook.

Miss Poole really did have a point, I had to admit. I couldn't imagine having to put together one of these fundraisers every year.

"Also, Mrs. Fraser, she's got quite a few cronies with lots of money. I'd be willing to bet they'd put a good amount into the fund as well."

We walked into the kitchen, and Ira rinsed out his tea glass and set it on the drain board. "So, once you know, will you come out and officially ask her to do this?"

"Ira!"

"I know it's asking a lot—"

"You're doggone right!"

"But I can't tell her! Then she'd know I'd been meddling on her behalf."

"Okay. I'll ask her. But you owe me one big time on this, Ira."

He waved a hand. "Oh, I owe everybody big time, Mrs. Fraser. I've been running interference for Miss Poole for years!"

Thirty-one

When I awoke at five-thirty the next morning, the heat had already begun to constrict the area. July could be oppressive here, even worse than Baltimore in August. The air conditioner Duncan had propped up in our window spoiled the look of the bedroom I'd lovingly whitewashed when we first moved in. It didn't match the white iron bedstead or the secondhand furniture I stained white, then antiqued with a wire brush and a speck of sadism.

However, on days like this, who cared what the Sears special looked like? Sometimes form really did mean nothing when function at a low price was necessity.

No sense in trying to go back to sleep. I put on my walking shoes and decided to take a leisurely stroll by the lake this morning. Java Jane's didn't open until seven-thirty anyway on Sundays.

By the time I went to the bathroom then examined my tired, middle-aged, looking-more-like-Mother-everyday face and my oh no—more-gray-hair-by-my-left-ear mop, it was almost six o'clock. Flipping off the light seemed to be the best idea.

Duncan sat on the bed in his running clothes. "G'morning, Popp."

"You're going running in this heat?" I pulled my walking shoes out of my closet.

"Better do it now. It's not getting any cooler. You going out walking?"

"Yeah, just by the lake today."

He stood to his feet and shook them a little. "I'll get the coffee going while you head out. Then we can have breakfast together before the kids get up."

"Really? On a Sunday?"

"Maybe it would be a better start than our usual routine."

"Well, that's the truth." I peeled off my nightshirt while he walked out of the room. His progress was easily heard by the progression of squeaks in the old hardwood floor.

Two minutes later I crunched a path toward the lake. Duncan whizzed by me with a wave and a wink. What a good man. I wasn't sure what else I could expect of him. Why didn't I think I had a good marriage? He was nice, courteous, did the chores, took care of the kids when he was home, and provided for us in a way that provided for his own well-being.

I looked back on the day I succumbed to temptation, and for the first time in seven years, found no rationalization, found no excitement, and found nothing to which I could cling.

Grace! Grace! My head screamed down the long, dark empty tunnel to my heart. But just then, I found no comfort.

Elder Barnhouse handed me the communion plate and smiled his wonderful grin. "Jesus died for you," he whispered, as he always did. I love that so much.

I took a cracker from what looked like an offering plate.

A cracker? What happened to the big loaf of brown bread? I'd always loved the way Highland Kirk just passed around the loaf and each participant pinched off pieces. I liked the intimacy of our shared time as the body. All eating the same loaf, all touching it, unconcerned about cold germs and the like.

My gaze circled the congregation. Where did Bercie go? I had seen her sneak in the side door with the plate during the prayer Duncan always offered up at the end of the sermon. But she didn't tiptoe back to her seat as usual.

I lifted the cracker to my nose.

The smell was familiar, something from my childhood. But I couldn't place it.

Duncan stood at the front, no big loaf of bread—the kind he used for the "breaking of the bread"—sat on the table. I made eye contact with him and discreetly held up the cracker. Barely shaking my head, I raised my eyebrows in a big question.

He responded in kind. Unnoticed by anyone else.

He took a cracker when the four elders returned to the table. Then he turned his back on the congregation. I knew he must be tasting it.

People threw questioning glances at each other. Why the change? Of course, other churches used wafers, they knew. Some used grape juice; some used real wine. There was no set way to hold communion. But this seemed wrong, or at the very least a strange departure.

Duncan began. "On the night He was betrayed, He took the bread and broke it." He lifted a cracker and broke it. Face unsmiling, solemn. And he said the familiar words, "Take, eat, this is My body, which is given up for you."

We all seemed to be waiting for the "Do this in remembrance of Me."

But Duncan hesitated. He came around to the front of the table and leaned casually against it, his robe billowing with air. "You've noticed by now that this isn't our normal fare for the Lord's table."

A hum of agreement, relief as well, buzzed around the nodding heads of the congregation.

"When Jesus conducted supper on that final night, I imagine it was the bread of the day. The Passover supper. We know that it was unleavened, like this cracker. We know it was simple fare."

He held out the cracker.

"It's not about the cracker, is it?"

No, I said within.

"Or what kind of cracker, is it?"

No again.

"I'm not sure what happened downstairs this morning, but we've got a savory cracker for our communion."

I sniffed it again and figured it out. Chicken-in-a-Biscuit.

Oh, dear.

Oh, Lord Jesus.

Poor Bercie.

"But this is the *Lord's* table. He was a common man who ate common food and wore common clothing. If His ministry were mirrored here on earth in our time, He probably wouldn't be eating free range chicken with truffles, now would He?"

A couple of people chuckled.

He shook his head and smiled. "He'd be eating food like this. Simple food like Chicken-in-a-Biscuit crackers."

Duncan turned back around and resumed his place behind the communion table. "It's the Lord's table, beloveds. And He invites us to eat. Remember now why we do so. To remember Him, to show Him our devotion. It's not about the food itself, and it never has been."

He bowed his head, his thinning hair on top exposed to the entire congregation. He looked up, raised the cracker, and said, "Do this in remembrance of Me." He snapped it in two.

After the service, I found Bercie Barnhouse crying in the basement. "Who's ever heard of the like?" she wailed. "Chicken-in-a-Biscuit! It was all that was in the cupboard down here. I thought I could do it at the last minute. We were running late this morning, and all I could get done was the juice, but that's another story. But when I went to get the loaves a few minutes before communion, they were gone! I had taken them out of the freezer and set them on the counter after Sunday school. I have no idea what could've happened to them!"

In utter truth I replied, "It was the most meaningful communion of my life." I put an arm around the older woman and let her cry.

And I cried with her.

Duncan came down about ten minutes later. "You weren't upstairs, Miss Bercie." He handed her his handkerchief.

"I just couldn't. I'm so embarrassed!"

Duncan said, "I'll be right back."

Two minutes later he returned with a cracker and a small plastic cup of grape juice. And he gave Bercie Barnhouse communion right there in the basement. My Duncan. The loving shepherd of this flock.

I wept some more knowing now that I would never leave this man, and that fact left me with only one alternative.

Duncan took Angus and Robbie home after the service, and I walked my navy blue pumps right up to Mildred LaRue's house.

Those shoes definitely weren't made for walking, I realized as a blister began to form on my heel. And, shoot, I couldn't help but pop it, then peel the loose skin. How painful was that? Talk about going from bad to worse.

The Masquerade had been just the same. My whole life was like that. I took minor pains and pricked and prodded and pulled them until they reached the supreme amount of pain per square centimeter, inch, foot, or yard they could possibly reach.

Things seemed to be going so well now. Paisley had e-mailed me almost every week since the trip to Baltimore. Mother and Daddy had been helping out with the scholarship fund and were calling every other day. Robbie's grades came in above average, and he was still a virgin. Or at least I thought that since his latest girlfriend had broken up with him because, as she put it, "You're such a square, Rob."

Angus seemed to be settling into his brain a bit more. Honestly, he didn't seem quite so far ahead as he had as a three-year-old. Maybe I'd succeeded in stifling him back into some normal mode of human development. Duncan still worked a lot, but he was trying. Chris, while not going so far as a latte, still seemed to be budding under the sunshine of purpose.

"Hi, Mr. Winfred!" I hollered as I walked up Miss Mildred's driveway.

"Hello, Penelope."

Now I hadn't had a whole lot of contact with Herman Winfred. But, I reasoned, he must have been something in his day. His face must have undergone some type of permanent smile wave, and if he was a little odd with his hole digging and whatnot, well, he more than made up for it with his tall good looks and perfectly starched, blue button-downs. Hard to believe someone could be that wrinkled and still be handsome.

"How's it coming?"

He leaned an elbow on the top of his shovel, his light brown eyes skewering my dark brown ones. "I'm not as crazy as I seem, you know."

"I never said you were crazy."

He wagged a long, jointy finger. "You'd be lying if you said you didn't think it."

"Okay. You're right."

He leaned forward, looked back at the house to see if Miss Mildred was about, then said in a whisper, "It's not unfounded."

"I'm not following you."

"These holes. I got a really good reason for digging them."

This should be good.

He jerked his head toward the house. "I was cleaning out the attic for Mildred when I found a journal written by her ancestor."

"Really?"

"Sure did. He really did bury gold out here, Penelope."

"Why didn't you tell Miss Mildred that then? You know she thinks you're a nut, Herman."

"I'd rather have her think I've got a screw loose than to get her hopes up and then disappoint her. It's terrible when Mildred gets disappointed."

"I've never seen her disappointed."

"She hides it pretty good. But I remember ten years ago, when we thought we might be getting a recording contract, and then we didn't. She didn't sing for a month."

I couldn't imagine Miss Mildred not singing.

Herman lifted up his felt fedora and scratched his white hair. "And she never tried for another contract either."

"That's a shame, Mr. Winfred."

"Yep, it is. Seems to me a woman her age with that much talent should have made it bigger somewhere along the line."

"Seems to me you're right. But who knows about these things. You hear some of the awfulest voices these days."

"Mmm, hmm."

"Well, I won't tell her what you're really up to."

"I'd be glad if you didn't."

I said a few more words, wished him well, and walked up onto the porch. The stroll from town left me deflated and sweaty. My hair had constricted into tighter curls that lined my skull like some black, sheepskin helmet.

I rapped on the screen door, and Miss Mildred answered a few seconds later looking cool and more relaxed than I had ever seen her with a green caftan on her body and a glass of iced tea in her hand.

Maybe relaxed wasn't accurate. Maybe subdued fit her mood.

She handed the tea to me. "Saw you from the kitchen window."

"Thanks."

"You walked all the way over here?"

Boy, she looked tired, too.

"Just from town."

"Still."

"I know. I had to talk to you." I thought maybe if I confessed first to Miss Mildred, she'd help me with what I should say to Duncan.

Mildred led me back to a part of the first floor I had never seen. It was a small room, paneled in pine and furnished with just two peach-colored la-z-boys and a two-tiered lamp table between them. The light from a TV vibrated from the corner, but the sound was low and overpowered by the air conditioning unit in the window. Childish drawings papered the walls.

"Have a seat."

"This is a nice, comfy room."

"I call it my 'boudoir.'"

I pointed to the pictures. "Sunday school students?"

"Uh-huh. Taught for thirty years. Vacation Bible School, too. But you didn't come here to hear about these children, Penelope. Is it about the gala?"

"No. I need some good advice."

"Well, sometimes I'm not in the mood for giving advice."

I raised my brows. "Did I actually hear those words come out of your mouth?"

"You did."

"Why?"

She looked away. "It's Saundra. She miscarried early this morning."

"Oh no. Oh, Miss Mildred. Poor baby. How's she doing?"

"Not good. She started bleeding last night. Went to the hospital for an ultrasound early this morning, followed by a D & C around eight."

"Were you there with her?"

Mildred nodded slowly. "I thought sure the Lord was giving her that baby. That He was giving her someone down here to call her own."

"I'll take a meal over this afternoon."

"Don't bother, baby. We got plenty of our own resources for that." Mildred's eyes teared over. "I don't know why this has got me so upset, Penelope. But it does."

"Well, you've been taking her to the doctor, haven't you? You've been with her every step of the way for the last few weeks."

She sniffed. "Even went out and bought a few little sleepers."

"How's Pastor Phelps taking it?"

"Hard."

"I guess so."

"You ever have a miscarriage, Penelope?"

"No. Chris did, though. She had two before finally conceiving Josh. And then only the medical establishment kept him in there for the next seven months."

Mildred plucked a Kleenex from a box on the end table. "You think she'd talk to Saundra?"

"I think it would do them both some good."

A while later, after Mildred's tears vaporized, I said, "Did you tell Herman? He didn't say anything about it when I pulled up."

"Nope." Mildred shook her head and blew her nose. "Sure hope he doesn't find Grandpop's gold right now, though. It wouldn't even be fun."

I arose and fixed Miss Mildred her own glass of iced tea.

Mildred took it with a "Thank you" and said, "I'm sorry I don't have any advice for you today, Penelope."

I put my hand on Miss Mildred's knee. "Can I just ask you to pray for me then? I'm going home to take care of all that business with Duncan." How I could speak so calmly, I didn't know.

"God will give you strength. I've been praying for you for a long time."

"Then pray just one more time, Miss Mildred. Pray as hard as you've ever prayed."

Mildred's eyes filled with tears again. "I will, baby."

I kissed Miss Mildred's cheek, turned up the sound on the Lawrence Welk Show, and turned to go.

"Penelope?"

"Yes, Miss Mildred?"

"You know I love you, don't you?"

"I do. Do you know how much I love you?"

"Yes, I do. Life's too short not to say the important things that a woman feels."

"Oh, Miss Mildred." I felt myself beginning to tear up, too.

"Now you get on, Penelope. Go do what you got to do."

I returned outside to the stifling heat and the long road home that seemed shorter than it ever had before.

By the time I finished my walk to the bungalow, the temperature had reached 102 degrees, and I was soggy with sweat, lightheaded, and exhausted. Everyone was sleeping in the living room. Duncan's body, stretched out on the couch, supported Angus. Robbie lay on his back on the floor, his breathing steady and deep.

See?

They did perfectly fine without me.

Feeling more alone than I could remember feeling before, I finally knew it didn't really matter if they *could* survive without me, they would simply never have the chance to find out.

The moisture in my clothing began to cool. Going into the bedroom to change, I wondered how to broach the topic with Duncan. Maybe Robbie would watch Angus while Duncan and I took the boat out on the lake.

How does one start such a confession, Lord?

My foot brushed my suitcase beneath the bed. So I laid it on the bed and sat down beside it breathing in the smell of leather and lining. I began to weep soundless sobs as I said good-bye to the thoughts of escape, the musings of flight from a guilt that would never die in any place but the arms of Christ and the forgiveness of my husband. I said good-bye to New

York City, the Colorado Rockies, and any other place to which I may have gone. I said good-bye to anyplace but home with Duncan, Paisley, Robbie, and Angus.

"I know about it, babe."

I jerked my head back at Duncan's words.

"I know about the affair."

He stood there, still in his church clothes, tie now rumpled, a large streak of sweat down his front where Angus had lain. His hands hung at his side as his eyes filled with tears. I didn't know what to do, what to say, what to even think because standing before me now was the way out of this. One way or another. After all of these years.

"What do you want me to do?" I asked.

He shook his head. "I can't bear to see you torture yourself any longer."

"How long have you known?"

"I've always known."

"How?"

"It doesn't matter, Popp. I'd really rather not say."

"I need to know."

"Paisley."

Oh, God. Oh, GOD!

"I'm sorry!" I screamed the words. "I'm so sorry, Duncan."

My heart shattered—an explosive pain so deep, so widespread, like an eight-foot-by-eight-foot square of glass dropped from a twelfth story window and landing flat, shards and splinters sliding and tumbling across the asphalt in an outward wave. I stood to my feet, swayed, then fell forward into my husband's arms. And he caught me in a tight grip saying, "I've got you, Poppy. I've got you."

Seven years.

"Don't leave me, babe," he whispered as I sobbed. "Please, Poppy."

"How can you say that?" I wailed.

"Because I forgive you."

With a strong hand he lifted up my chin, a prying motion against my will. "Do you hear me?" His eyes, red and weeping, drilled into mine. "I forgive you."

"I'm sorry."

"I forgive you."

"I know, but—"

"I forgive you. Listen to me, Poppy. I forgive you. I forgave you years ago."

"I'm sorry," I rasped once more, the sobs returning.

Duncan led me to the bed, threw the suitcase to clatter loudly upon the wooden floor, and sat me down. "Look at me, Poppy." He reached down and took both of my hands in his. "Please."

I looked up into a face so devastated my breath caught, imprisoned within my lungs. Duncan slipped to his knees in front of the bed. "Poppy, do you honestly believe the fault is all yours?"

Words wouldn't come. All I could see was his face, the eyes so brown and familiar I knew each speck of gold, each glimmer of bronze, eyes broken with grief.

"Poppy, the blame is mine."

"But I own the shame, Duncan. I do."

"Not any longer. Oh, Popp, if I had been the husband you needed, you *deserved,* Joe Callahan would have meant nothing to you."

That he was so sure of that stirred something inside of me. I saw his strength as though for the first time, and I can only describe it as a filling of love, a new river of emotion surging and rising and flooding over the bulwarks built up over the years.

"Do you forgive me, Poppy?"

This was grace.

"I need to hear you say the words. I promised to protect you when you pledged to keep yourself only unto me. I failed. I left you wide open and alone."

Only God's Spirit gave me the strength to say what came next. "I forgive you, Duncan."

He pulled me into his arms, and we cried together. Man and wife. Our hearts once more placed firmly in each other's hand.

Thirty-two

I woke up early the next morning, tied up my shoes, and made for Java Jane's. The world felt new again. I felt reborn. Healed. Ellen had just unlocked the door as I walked up. "Come on in, Poppy."

Margaret waved from behind the counter. "Hey!" She started to make my Red-Eye. "So, is there anything you want to ask us about?"

I picked up the *Washington Post*. "About what?"

"That gala."

I raised my eyebrows. "I thought you didn't want anything to do with the churches anymore."

Best to play this one cool.

Ellen crossed her arms. "Well, from what I hear, you all sound like you're starting to get your act together on this one."

I laughed and forgot about my cool. "I'm as surprised as you are!"

Margaret smiled. "It sounds like a good cause. For that boy and all."

"Yeah."

"So, do you need coffee and tea?" Ellen asked.

"We sure do. Can you set up an espresso bar right there during dessert?" I sat down in my purple chair.

"Absolutely!"

"Stuff like this is tax deductible," Margaret said. "So we'll do the good stuff: cappuccinos, mocha lattes, the whole bit like that."

"How much are the tickets per head?" Ellen asked.

"Five hundred bucks for the diamond patrons going on down to thirty."

"Ooh, yeah, we should do the fancy stuff then." Margaret turned to Ellen. "Maybe we should bring all kinds of syrup."

"Absolutely, and we could…"

I tuned them out, picked up the paper and turned straight to the comics.

The church ladies gathered for their weekly Monday meeting. I looked around at my friends. I used to feel so alone in my role. Not any more. And really, I never was. It seems stupid that churches isolate themselves from each other like we do. We need each other so desperately.

Miss Mildred went all out with the food. I'm talking layered salad. I'm talking real creamed corn. I'm talking fried tomatoes and chicken fried steak with brown gravy. "We have a lot to celebrate tonight!"

"Such as?" Chris asked.

"All the bases are covered for the gala now. Right, Penelope? Here, pass the bread."

I took the narrow basket. "Yeah. And we still have three weeks left."

"And Saundra and the pastor are trying again to have a baby. She says she'll be back in a few weeks and would appreciate your prayers until then." Obviously about to pontificate, Mildred sat in her chair at the head of the table. "So we've got something else to pray about now."

Chris bowed her head. "Josh will take care of that little lost baby."

India nodded, and so did Sunny, who also added a "Yes, ma'am, he sure will."

But Joanna stood to her feet. "I don't understand you people. One boy dies in his prime, and a perfectly healthy woman miscarries, and you can thank God for that?" She leaned down and grabbed her purse. "This is too weird for me."

Before anyone could say much of anything, the screen door banged behind her.

India said quietly, "I wonder the same thing at times. How can we thank the Lord for these things? The world is so bad, and if God is so personal and so perfect and all…"

Mildred nodded. "Yes, it is bad, India. But sometimes the perfection of God isn't seen in what happens, baby, but in how we as His children respond."

"That's hard to live up to then," India said, doubt heavy in her voice.

I laid a hand on her arm. "But that is what grace is all about. And that's what living by grace, by faith, means."

"We're not in this alone," Sunny said.

"'We have a Friend who sticketh closer than a brother,'" Charmaine said.

Mildred took her hand. "And we have each other."

Maybe Robbie was right in a way. To question the inevitable always leads to anger and disillusion. But to trust, to be used to right the wrongs, to deliver God's deliverance, well, that was a blessing indeed.

Later than night I had a long talk with India on the front porch of Mildred LaRue's. And some good praying went on afterwards. Really good praying.

Mildred LaRue style.

Thirty-three

God blessed; that was certain. No other explanation remained for the fact that a thousand people bought tickets to the gala, a gala that cost the Joshua Reynolds Knight Scholarship foundation absolutely nothing. What a great town.

We had to move the affair from the courtyard of the Episcopal church to the grand ballroom at the old Mount Oak Hotel. Harlan Hopewell himself convinced the owner. We'd thrown open the French doors that surrounded three sides of the room, and the party became an indoor/outdoor gathering. And not one major dispute erupted other than the fact that a few people thought Miss Poole shouldn't control the purse strings, until someone pointed out that she didn't need any more money herself and was quite adept at managing what she had.

God blessed in the sunset that night. The sky threw on a peach gown with a pink shawl for the gala and did it so easily as if to say, "Beautiful? This silly old thing?" And the breeze was enough to dry our sweat but not mess up our hair. Well, God made women, after all, so it isn't surprising to realize He understands our wrinkles and our ways.

I planted myself by the espresso bar after dinner had ended and the dessert table had been picked clean, except for one oddly shaped piece of French silk pie that no one wanted. I took the piece over to my father who sat in deep conversation with Harlan Hopewell. Mother and Paisley did the jitterbug together right underneath Miss Mildred's nose as she sang "In the Mood," and Robbie and Angus clapped in time from their seats near the back.

Charmaine emceed beautifully, of course. Sunny's table arrangements of larkspur and tiger lilies brightened up each table. And India had composed a song just for the occasion and played it at the close of the program on the piano, accompanied by cello and flute. She titled it simply, *Joshua*.

But when Colonel Bougie handed Betty from Mount Zion a cup of punch and asked if he might sit beside her for a spell, I knew that something wonderful was happening in old Mount Oak.

When the cleanup crew had almost finished, Marc Tipton efficiently organizing guys from churches all over town, Chris put an arm through mine.

"You done good, Popp."

"You too, Chrissy."

"Jason really seemed to appreciate it. Although he was a bit embarrassed at having to talk about what the scholarship meant to him."

"I never knew anybody could blush to that deep a shade of red."

"I know. And it was nice what he said about Josh."

"Yeah. He was a good kid, Chrissy. I miss him."

Chris nodded. "We always will. The pain hasn't gone away, though, Popp. You know that, don't you?"

"Yeah. I do."

Ellen hollered, "Last call to all you worker bees!"

Chris turned to me. "What'll you have?"

"I don't know. Whatever you're having."

Chris put up two fingers and said to the Java Jane's girls, "Two lattes, ladies. The largest you've got."

I put my arms around her, hoping that when people we love go to heaven they're allowed a peek at divine moments such as these.

Multnomah Publishers®

The publisher and author would love to hear your comments about this book. *Please contact us at:* www.multnomah.net/thechurchladies

About the Author

Lisa E. Samson lives in Maryland with her husband and three children, ages eleven, six, and four. She was christened Catholic, attended mass with her father on Saturday nights, and attended a Bible Presbyterian church with her mother on Sundays A.M. and P.M. and on Wednesday nights. Lisa attended a Methodist school from second through twelfth grade and went on to do undergraduate work at a strict Baptist university. Upon graduation from a more liberal Baptist university in 1987, she spent the summer at Oxford studying at Wycliffe Hall, an Anglican seminary. Because she and Will moved frequently during their early years of marriage, Lisa attended four PCA Presbyterian churches and one Presbyterian Church USA. She now attends a nondenominational Bible church with her family, where you'll also find her leading worship with her guitar on Sunday nights and trying to figure out just how to lead a choir. Maybe one day she'll figure out those tricky hand motions directors do! These days, however, she finds that when she lays her head down on the pillow at night and offers her prayers to God, she comes simply as His child and a woman who wants to love Jesus more than she does.